"[Greenberg] delves with authenticity and compassion into the lives and minds of three female characters. . . . This well-written page-turner by a surprising author . . . features true-to-life characters who are entertaining and compelling. A must read for fans of smart women's fiction."
—*Library Journal*

"The shared adversity these women face is portrayed realistically and tenderly. . . . The three women are well drawn, and Greenberg displays an admirable ear for realistic dialogue. Fans of Deborah Copaken Konan, Sarah Pekkanen and contemporary ensemble fiction will enjoy this debut novel."
—*Booklist*

"Upbeat and snappy."
—*Publishers Weekly*

"Funny and moving."
—*Connecticut Post*

"Mike is as clever, astute, and perceptive as he is brilliant. He has beautifully pulled off the three female voices in this novel—a rare feat for a man—with tremendous wisdom and insight. I can't wait to see what he does next."
—Jane Green, *New York Times* bestselling author

"Who would have guessed that a guy who works for ESPN could write such a terrific novel for women? *All You Could Ask For* is smart, sensitive, very funny—and reminds us that our closest friendships constitute a second family. This book, and these women, surprised me all the way through, and moved me to tears and laughter both."
                              —Dorothea Benton Frank,
        New York Times bestselling author of *The Last Original Wife*

"Mike has taken something almost impossible to do—write about the opposite sex facing a heart-wrenching challenge you haven't faced—and done it with breathtaking grace and wit. I read *All You Could Ask For* with slack-jawed admiration. Hands-down rookie of the year!"
                              —Bruce Feiler,
                     New York Times bestselling author of
                The Council of Dads and *The Secrets of Happy Families*

All You Could Ask For

ALSO BY MIKE GREENBERG

Why My Wife Thinks I'm an Idiot:
The Life and Times of a Sportscaster Dad

Mike and Mike's Rules for Sports and Life

All You Could Ask For

MIKE GREENBERG

WILLIAM MORROW
An Imprint of HarperCollins*Publishers*

HarperCollins books may be purchased for educational, business, or sales promotional use. For information please e-mail the Special Markets Department at SPsales@harpercollins.com.

A hardcover edition of this book was published in 2013 by William Morrow, an imprint of HarperCollins Publishers.

FIRST WILLIAM MORROW PAPERBACK EDITION PUBLISHED 2013.

Designed by Lisa Stokes

The Library of Congress has cataloged the hardcover edition as follows:

Greenberg, Mike, 1967–
  All you could ask for : a novel / Mike Greenberg.—1st ed.
    p. cm.
ISBN 978-0-06-222075-2 (hardcover)—ISBN 978-0-06-222076-9 (pbk.)—ISBN 978-0-06-222077-6 (ebook)—ISBN 978-0-06-223981-5 (audio) 1. Women—Fiction. 2. Female friendship—Fiction. I. Title.
PS3607.R4496A79 2013
813'.6—dc23
2012027371

ISBN 978-0-06-222076-9 (pbk.)

13 14 15 16 17 OV/RRD 10 9 8 7 6 5 4 3

This book was written in memory of Heidi Armitage
And it is dedicated to the best friends anyone could ever ask for:
Stacy Steponate Greenberg, Jane Green, and Wendy Gardiner
Now, and forevermore, Heidi's Angels

The thing is, to have a life before we die.
It can be a real adventure having a life.

John Irving, *The World According To Garp*

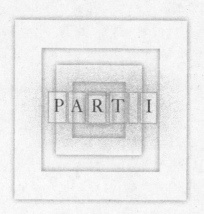

PART I

BROOKE

WHOSE ASS IS THIS?

It certainly isn't mine.

That's what I was thinking as I looked. I mean *really* looked.

I have a great ass. I've always had a great ass. I've known that since my freshman year at Colgate, when I pledged Tri-Delt and my first night I drank two plastic cupfuls of cherry punch with grain alcohol and allowed a cute Sigma Chi to kiss me while we danced. His name was Paul Didier and he had close-cropped auburn hair and blue eyes, and a general goofiness about him that didn't seem quite as annoying drunk as it did sober the next day when he showed up at my dorm with a dozen roses. That was the end of him. Cute and goofy is fine for dancing and slightly sloppy kisses but no more, and certainly not for roses.

When he saw the lack of excitement on my face for the flowers, I actually felt sorry for him. He looked like a puppy who'd peed in the house and wanted—*really* wanted—to go back in time and undo it. But, you know, dogs can't clean up pee, just like goofy boys can't pretend not to have bought you roses after one night of drunken smooching.

"You know, I'm a freshman too," he stumbled, looking more like the puppy every second, "and I don't know anyone here. I'm from the Midwest, and you seemed like the coolest girl ever."

"Thank you," I said, in the same tone you might use to chasten the puppy. "It just seems a little soon."

"I know," he said, and started for the door, still holding the roses as he stepped outside. Then he turned back to me, squinting in the bright sunshine of a clear September morning. "You've got a great ass, Brooke. I really wanted to tell you that. I'm glad I did."

That appealed to me, as corny as it was. I waited an appropriate amount of time before I chased him into the courtyard and ripped the flowers away from behind him.

"Where do you think you're going with those?" I asked.

The goofy grin reappeared, and he moved toward me tentatively. "Can I call you later?" he asked.

"Yes, you may," I said, and spun on my heel and marched away, knowing full well he was staring. I didn't turn to see him though, no way. My mother raised me better than that.

Back in my room, with the flowers tossed thoughtlessly on the bed, I lifted my Benetton sweater and stared behind me into the full-length mirror my druggy roommate had glued to the back of our door.

He was right. I had a great ass.

That was twenty years ago, and I'm not sure how closely I've checked out my ass since. I think through the rest of college I always thought of that cute puppy dog of a boy (whom I let kiss me two more times before I sent him on his way) and just *knew* my ass looked great. And then I met Scott, and from the first night we were together he has made me feel beautiful. He still does, too, even after the twins and the C-section, and all the dog poop and cat litter and stomach viruses and coffee breath and eye gunk and accidental farts that threaten to drain the romance from a marriage. He still *always* manages to wink at me at just the right moments.

I love when he winks at me. When he winks, I'm his girlfriend again, the supercute debutante he fell so hard for that after our first date he, too, bought me a gift. Not a dozen roses but even cheesier: a calendar with photos of exotic locations on it, on which he had used a pale blue marker to write suggested plans for us on randomly selected dates.

"Well, I guess this boy is finished," my friend Charlotte said when I showed her the calendar.

"I don't know," I said, and I guess I smiled more than I realized, because Charlotte smiled back and just like that, we both knew I was going to marry this one. And I did. And it was the best decision I ever made. And now he is turning forty years old and I've made another decision, only this one may be the worst of my life.

I got the idea from my girlfriend Ingrid, who is Swedish and beautiful and used to model. We were having coffee after tennis about a month ago when she slapped herself on the forehead.

"Oh shits!" she said, in the Swedish accent that takes her from simply beautiful to out-of-control, even-I-can't-stand-it-and-I'm-a-woman gorgeous. (Hers is the *only* house at which every dad in Greenwich insists on picking up his children after playdates. But she's also very sweet and real, and less judgmental than any of the city-girls-turned-wealthy-housewives who mostly populate this town.)

"What's the matter?" I asked.

"I told Stefan I would leave a check for him in the mailbox this morning," she said. "I am completely forgot!" She started rustling through her bag. "I'm sorry, Brooke, I have to go right now."

"I'll go with you," I said, and I did, in part because I had no choice—she had driven me and needed to take me home—and also because Stefan is *my* contractor, too, and I notice he spends a lot more time at Ingrid's house than he does at mine. I have generally found that the best place to find a man who works with his hands is at the house of the prettiest blonde in the neighborhood.

So we raced back to Ingrid's, and she was adorably frazzled as she rushed to her sunny office over the garage and ransacked two drawers in search of her checkbook. That's one of the reasons I like Ingrid: that builder would have waited patiently in her driveway until a week from Thursday if it meant he'd get one more smile from her in that perfect little tennis dress, but she was rushing about because she's the only one who doesn't realize that.

"I'm be right back," she said, and rushed past me out of the office and out the front door. I turned to follow, but something caught my eye before I did, a blur that raced past on the screen of Ingrid's desktop. At first I wasn't even sure what it was. Then I took a step closer and saw my dear friend fully naked. Just a flash, and then she was gone. And then she was back, and then gone again. It was a series of photos—nudes, tasteful and beautiful—running as a slideshow on the desktop. It was breathtaking, really, and only *she* could pull it off. No other woman I know could have a series of naked pictures of herself as her screen saver without coming off as pathetic, or at least narcissistic and sad. But with Ingrid, it just seemed beautiful, perhaps because she looked so beautiful. And, sitting there, I made the decision I am seriously questioning right now. For my beloved, romantic, successful husband's fortieth birthday, I am giving him what every man wants. Naked pictures of his wife.

SAMANTHA

WHAT THE HELL IS this naked woman doing there?

That was the first thought that went through my mind. But the strange part is how long it took any emotion to hit me. At first I was just puzzled, innocently so, as though finding nude photos in my husband's e-mail was no different from finding a pair of socks in the refrigerator: *What on earth could THOSE be doing there?* It was several minutes before the significance struck me. This wasn't like socks in the fridge. This was like lipstick on a collar, or an unrecognizable bra beneath the comforter. This was serious trouble.

Maybe it didn't dawn on me quite so fast because I hadn't had my coffee yet. Or because I was so surprised that I'd found my way into his mailbox at all. Or maybe it was simply because I was still very much in the warmth and glow that new brides feel; I had only been married for two days.

When the urgency of the matter began to sink in, it settled slowly, the way you feel a fever coming on: first as just a dizzy spell, then gradually spreading as a tiny tingle beginning in my stomach, and then my legs, and ultimately all the way to my fingers and toes. And then I was freezing, which really sucked because I didn't have anything at all warm to put on.

I didn't think I'd need it in Kauai.

I went to the gorgeous master bath in our suite, this luxurious paradise we had checked into just the night before. The carpet was soft beneath my toes. It had felt so good when I kicked off my shoes after dinner, after the champagne, after the swans that swam past our perfect, candlelit table, and after the perfect little toast Robert had made: *It's finally just us.*

Ours was the textbook disaster wedding, for two reasons. One was my father's money. The other was the election. Taken in order: (1) My dad didn't approve of Robert because he's fourteen years older than me, and (2) Robert's career required that, at the time of our whirlwind courtship and wedding, we spend every waking moment talking to people we have never met and feigning interest in every word they said. That seemed all right to me, even if it wasn't so exciting, because at least it suggested Robert believed in something. My father didn't believe in anything aside from money, and thus he wasn't going to allow me to marry an older man, whom I'd met on an elevator three months before, without a prenuptial agreement. And the thing about that was Robert had no problem with it at all; he was understanding and mature. "If I were your father I would feel exactly the same way," he told me.

That's why I married him. Because he says things that grown men say.

It was *me* that got angry with my father, who has never approved of my lifestyle, my love of sports, of being outside, camping, hiking. He's never understood why I don't care about the only thing that matters to him in the world, which is his money.

"One time, when I was eleven years old," he told me, "I lost my baseball glove. I left it in the park and when I went back to look for it, it was gone. I was afraid to go home, I was afraid to tell my father I lost my glove. Because I had an appreciation for the value of the glove, but my actions seemed to demonstrate that I did not, and I knew how disappointed my father would be in me."

I couldn't resist. "It's hard going through life with your father disappointed in you, isn't it?" I said.

"Don't be fresh."

"So what happened?" I asked.

"What happened with what?"

"With the baseball glove," I said. "What happened when you eventually told your father?"

My dad waved his hand in the dismissive way that only he can. "Nothing, really."

"Nothing happened?" I asked.

"Not really, no."

I shook my head. "Then what is the point of the story?"

"Every story does not have to have a point, young lady," my father said. "I only want for you to be happy. But as your father it's my job to keep you from making the biggest mistake of your life."

Just what every girl dreams of hearing on her wedding day.

The thing is, it wasn't a mistake. Robert is different from any boy I've ever known, beginning with the fact that he isn't a boy. He's a man. He's the district attorney of Los Angeles County, California. He puts bad guys in jail; how could you have more of a man's job than that?

We met in Sacramento, when I was in town for a friend's wedding. I was stepping toward the elevator in my hotel when I noticed an attractive older man staring at me. He was wearing a blue, pinstriped suit and a navy tie, something a leading man would have worn in a movie in the forties. But there was something soft about his eyes, no matter how hard his clothes were. I let the elevator go and just stood there, without pressing the button for another.

It didn't take him long. "I'm sorry," he said. "I didn't mean to stare."

I waited. I think I smiled.

"Listen," he said, moving slowly toward me, "I don't mean to bother you, but I have had a great day. I mean a *really* great day. And I just can't fathom going up to my room right now by myself and sitting there and watching television. I know you don't know me, but I'm a nice person and you look like a nice person too. I would love to buy you a drink and just sit and talk. We can talk about anything you want, anything in the world you're interested in. You have my word of honor as a gentleman, which I am, and a Boy Scout, which I never was but that's only because I couldn't rub two sticks together and make a fire, that I won't try anything. We can go anywhere you want and talk about anything you want."

He paused a moment to catch his breath, then finished: "I suppose this is a very long way of saying: Hello, my name is Robert, can I buy you a drink?"

Three months later I had left my job, given up my apartment in New York, moved into his house in the Valley, and we were engaged. *And* we were preparing for an election.

The reason he had had a *really* great day that night by the elevator was that the state leaders of his party wanted him to run for lieutenant governor. (I have to admit, I didn't even know that was something you ran for, I just thought the governor chose a running mate, like a vice president. You learn something new every day.) The next two months were a blur, an endless whirl of cocktail parties and handshakes and conversations behind closed doors. When it was over and we'd won, neither of us had the energy to plan a wedding.

"Let's just do it this weekend," Robert said, in a giant, empty hotel ballroom, hours after the cheering and the music had faded and the only sound was the industrial brooms sweeping away the confetti. "We'll do it quietly, at the house. We'll throw a party in a few weeks if you want but let's just do it now. I want so badly to be married to you."

He has an amazing ability to be sensible and romantic in the same conversation. I'd never met a man who could be either one of those, much less both. How could I not marry him?

So I did.

My father insisted on flying out, so he did.

And his girlfriend insisted on serving lunch, so a caterer did.

And Robert's office sent flowers and the governor sent champagne and two local television stations sent reporters and cameras. I guess it was not the way most girls envision their wedding day, but to tell the truth I never really envisioned mine at all. In fact, this was probably the best way for me to get married. I think if there were three hundred people in a church and I was wearing a colossal white dress with a veil and a train and flowers and attendants and trumpets and all the other things, I would just burst out hysterically laughing. It's just *so* not me.

Anyway, *that* is what Robert meant when he said, "It's finally just us," over dinner last night. Then he carried me over the threshold into this sumptuous suite, and he took my clothes off slowly in the pitch blackness with the sound of waves breaking on the beach just outside, and we made love standing up and then again lying down, and when it was done we snuggled in the soft carpeting and I could feel his heart beating against my chest, and as it slowed and his breathing steadied I thought to myself: *For the first time in my life, everything seems as though it is the way it is supposed to be.*

Then it was eight o'clock this morning and Robert was wide-awake. He wakes up filled with energy; this morning I felt his energy pressing against my thigh, so we made love again, quickly this time, and then he was off to a massage while I lounged for a while before calling room service and asking for coffee and granola and yogurt. I had my own spa appointment to look forward to, and then we were taking our first scuba lesson in the afternoon. I wasn't even thinking about my little game when I sat down at the desk and opened Robert's laptop; it was just by force of habit that I typed those three words.

You see, Robert's laptop has two separate means of entry. The first offers access to only the standard functions: Internet Explorer, Microsoft Outlook, a variety of games. Then there is a portal that requires special clearance, and Robert has told me for as long as I've known him that among the documents he signed upon being appointed to his office was one affirming that he will never, under any circumstances, allow unauthorized access to persons without clearance, regardless of his relationship to them. I laughed when he first told me about it, and said, "Reminds me of Al Pacino telling Diane Keaton not to ask about his business." But Robert didn't laugh. I left it alone.

So, every morning since I moved to L.A., the first thing I do is take one shot at accessing the portal. I've seen him do it, from across a room, and I'm almost certain I've counted thirteen keystrokes. It's hard to be certain because he flies through so quickly, but I'm pretty sure it's thirteen. So, every morning, before breakfast, I take that one try at cracking the code. (I need to explain that I really, truly was not suspicious, nor did I doubt Robert's character in any way. This was just a game I began as a lark and then became accustomed to playing every morning. Once I typed in the wrong password, the computer blocked access to the portal for thirty minutes and automatically opened the screen saver, which was a picture of Magic Johnson shooting a hook shot against the Celtics. Robert loves the Lakers. He was born and raised in Los Angeles and doesn't care much about football or baseball or any sport except basketball and, specifically, the subset of basketball that is the Lakers. So, every morning I pour myself coffee and toss a handful of granola into a bowl, cover it with yogurt and some berries, and then I sit at the desk and say good morning to Magic. It's fun. And it's harmless. Or it was, until this morning in Hawaii.)

I long ago decided his password *had* to be related to the Lakers, so every morning I try some combination of Lakers names that require thirteen letters: *KobeMagicWest; MagicJohnson1; Worthy&Jabaar; PhilIsA-Genius; LakersForever*. None of them worked and I never expected them to. That's the thing: I really never cared what might be behind that locked door. Until this morning in my bridal suite in Kauai, with the palm trees swaying and the parrots chatting, and the surf and sea and a masseuse awaiting, when in the midst of all my bliss a funny thought entered my mind. I counted the letters in my head; four, then five, then four. It added up to thirteen, and it was just too funny not to try. So, with the innocence only possible in the soul of a newlywed, I took a sip of my coffee and entered the password that unlocked my husband's secrets.

FuckLarryBird.

And there I was, behind the locked electronic door, inside a passageway leading to god knows where. It was probably completely illegal, what I had done. Like *seriously* illegal. My husband might actually have to arrest me, prosecute me, and send me to jail. A little smile crossed my lips at that thought and I knew I had to figure out how best to leave no evidence I had been in the portal.

Then I started to laugh. Fuck Larry Bird? Seriously? I don't even know where I came up with that. Robert's stock joke is that he doesn't hate criminals; he merely seeks justice, so the only people he hates are the Boston Celtics. But I've never heard him specifically say, "Fuck Larry Bird." In fact, he rarely swears at all.

Then I noticed the Microsoft Outlook icon. It was blinking, in an unusual way. If such a thing is possible, the icon was blinking at me *suggestively*. I had to click on it. I *had* to. So I did. And that's where I found the photo that seemed so out of place. And that's when the thought went through my mind: *Who the hell is this naked woman? And what is she doing in my husband's inbox?*

 KATHERINE

FUCK HIM.

Those were the first words out of my mouth this morning. Which should come as no surprise since they're the first words out of my mouth every morning. They have been for nineteen years, since the last time I saw Phillip alive.

I love saying it that way. Phillip is still very much alive, and he's better-looking than ever and insanely wealthy, too. Not that I'm bitter, much. But when I say "the last time I saw Phillip alive," what I mean is the last time I saw him before he became dead to me.

Anyway, still in bed, and after I say "fuck him"—with the emphasis on *him*—I think of Dr. Gray and Thic Naht Hahn, and I take three long, deep, cleansing breaths. I count to five on the first inhale, and curl my lips into a half-smile. Then I count to five on the exhale. Then I inhale for six, and exhale for six. Then in for seven, out for seven. And the half-smile on my lips puts my head in a peaceful place. Then I sit up tall and let my feet slide off the bed and rest firmly on the hardwood floor, and I place my palms together firmly in front of my chest. Then I take four more deep breaths, and on each exhalation I repeat The Meditation.

> *May I be filled with loving-kindness*
> *May I be well*
> *May I be peaceful and at ease*
> *May I be happy*

Only then do I open my eyes. My breathing is long and deliberate as I cross my bedroom and sit gently before the mirror in my vanity. The breathing is my connection to the now, to the present. Dr. Gray says I worry too much about my past. Thic Naht Hahn says I shouldn't worry so much about my future. The one thing they seem to agree upon is that I need to spend more time in the moment, and it seems to me that since one of them is an Upper East Side shrink and the other is a Buddhist monk, if there is anything about my life that they fully agree upon it is probably worthy of consideration.

I force myself to move slowly through the apartment. Moving slowly does not come naturally for me, neither does the meditation or the breathing or the yoga, but it helps.

In the refrigerator, I find the plastic bag marked TUESDAY. I empty its contents into the blender, add a half-cup of almond milk, and flick the switch. Thirty seconds later I am drinking a shake as I flip on CNBC. It is five minutes past six.

Ten minutes later I am on the treadmill with buds in my ears, squinting as the sun rises above the towering skyscrapers. The stock ticker is scrolling beneath the silent faces on my television. Nothing exciting there, nothing I didn't know last night. Up and down the channels I ride, never once raising the volume. There isn't any reason to listen to the television in the morning. All you need to do is read. On the business channels they scroll the S&P futures and results from the trading in the Asian markets, on the news channels they scroll the headlines of the day, on the sports channels they scroll the scores, on the network channels they scroll the weather. I am fully informed by merely reading the bottom three inches of my television. The people talking are a complete waste of time.

I strap my heart-rate monitor in place beneath my sports bra and start to walk. After a five-minute warm-up it is time to get serious. I crank the treadmill to seven miles per hour and the incline to three degrees. It is totally silent in my apartment; the only sounds in any of the fourteen rooms come from my running shoes squeaking on the band. I don't have the music on yet. I save that for about twenty minutes in, when I need a little encouragement. Today I feel great, and I crank up the treadmill early in my run. Eight miles per hour. Four degrees of incline. That's a lot. But I can handle it. I click on my iPod and scroll through the list of artists. Who should we listen to today? Dr. Dre? Snoop Dogg? Eminem? It feels like a day to go new-school. I click on Jay-Z.

After a shower I am in the dressing room, where I have laid out my wardrobe the night before. A double stretch wool anatomical jacket and matching skirt by Brioni, covered by a waterproof silk parka trimmed with Mongolian fur—it's supposed to rain—and Prada ankle boots. Then back to my vanity, where I breathe a deep sigh at the sight of my reflection; not such a pretty picture at this hour of the morning, especially not with the bright sunlight streaming through the windows directly behind me. Still, it's nothing that can't be salvaged. A few strokes and pats and brushes and dabs and I am as good as new, or as new as I can be.

Then I bow my head slowly and close my eyes. I know the car is waiting downstairs. I know the day is waiting outside the window. I know the vultures are waiting around every turn, but now is not the time for those. I reconnect with my breathing. Inhale deeply, exhale deeply. In, out. In. Out.

> *May I be filled with loving-kindness*
> *May I be well*
> *May I be peaceful and at ease*
> *May I be happy*

I raise my chin and allow my eyelids to peel gently apart. "Fuck him," I say, looking myself square in the eyes, "and all the others out there like him."

In the lobby I find Maurice waiting. He tips his cap as I approach and hands me a grande skim latte with no foam. "Good morning, Katherine," he says in his usual familiar tone.

"Back at ya," I say, my customary response.

"Cold out there today," he says, and hands me my *Wall Street Journal.* "You'd best bundle that thing up." He motions disapprovingly at my parka. "We need to get you some warmer clothes."

I smile. "Maurice, my friend, you do not want to know how much this parka cost. It damn well better keep me warm."

As though on cue, a gust of wind rises as we exit the revolving door, making it quite hard to revolve, even with both of us pushing. Maurice is wearing an "I told you so" expression as he opens the rear door for me. He is too adorable. I wouldn't put up with such bullshit if he were not.

The true bustle of a New York morning has not yet begun: the only signs of life on Park Avenue are a few hearty joggers making their way toward Central Park and an old man sweeping away debris in front of the

French bakery across the street. This is my favorite time of day in the city. Sometimes I ask Maurice to drive down Fifth Avenue, just so I can look out the car windows and see the peacefulness. There is nothing in the world more serene than an empty thoroughfare.

"Any stops before the office?" Maurice asks as he slides into the driver's seat.

"Not today, thanks."

The television in the rear console of the limousine is tuned to CNN and I am staring at the crawl when my bag begins to vibrate. I realize I am receiving a call, which is strange, because no one *ever* calls before eight in the morning. I dig out my BlackBerry and the moment I see the number I know immediately who it is and why she is calling. I do not answer the phone.

"Anything special going on?" Maurice asks from the front.

"Nothing at all," I reply.

Only now I am not telling the truth. That phone call was from my mother, with whom I have not spoken in over a month. But I know why she is calling. I glance at the date in the banner across the top of the *Wall Street Journal* and realize I am right. I hadn't even thought of it all morning long.

"Hey, Maurice, you'd better be nice to me today," I say.

"Why would I start that now?" he asks.

"Because today is my birthday," I tell him. "And it's a big one. Believe it or not, today I am forty years old."

BROOKE

SO, SCOTT IS TURNING forty next month.

It's hard for me to believe.

He is still so much the boy who took me to Van Halen concerts, and did Jell-O shots at McSorley's, and knew where to get excellent cocaine at a time when that was useful information. He is still very much that boy, only now that boy is a man. A man who held our babies so delicately in his strong hands. A man who rises before five every morning and travels all over the country and often sleeps in airport lounges but never misses a recital or a baseball game and, best of all, never behaves as though he is a hero for any of it. He is a man who can discipline his children without yelling, run a marathon to commemorate a birthday, and still seduce his wife with a well-timed wink.

Don't get me wrong; he isn't perfect. I don't mean to suggest he is. Like all men he is still a boy and boys are always trouble—especially the dreamy ones. The first time he met Mother, she pulled me aside and said: "I'd be worried about this one." And I asked why, and she said: "The *really* handsome ones are always dangerous." And he is. He makes me swoon. He still has those dancing blue eyes and wavy hair; his face looks hardly at all different from the way it did fifteen years ago. Maybe younger, in fact, since having his eyes fixed—sometimes it takes me a moment to recognize him in old photos with those Coke-bottle lenses he used to wear. So he isn't perfect, but he still makes me laugh and he still makes me quiver after seventeen years together; I think that's pretty good.

And if he, in fact, does look younger than he did when we were in our twenties, I haven't done so badly either. I may not look just as I did—mostly I see it in the lines in my face, especially around the mouth—but the way I look at those crevices is they were dug slowly and surely from all the smiles I have smiled in my life, and so I wouldn't give any of them back for anything. Not a chance.

However, there is now the issue of my ass, which I suddenly find myself staring at in a way I haven't ever before. It is still shapely, plump perhaps but not in a bad way, more round than large. Sort of like Beyoncé. I have always been curvy, which is fine so long as you are not lumpy, which I have certainly never been, nor am I now, but as I look closely at my ass, it seems to be headed if not for lumpiness then at least toward bumpiness, and I'm not sure I would be any happier to be bumpy than lumpy in these photos I am taking.

My husband travels all over the world nearly every week, and if I don't want him to look at pornography, or younger, pretty girls, it only seems fair that I hold up my end of the bargain. Ours is *that* sort of a marriage, has been since our first Valentine's Day, when he bought me the slinkiest negligee ever from Victoria's Secret. It was two sizes (at least) too small, so I sneakily exchanged it before I wore it for him and when I did, it drove him absolutely mad with desire, and I loved that. Scott is a brilliant man, and powerful, but I can turn him into a trembling boy, the one he was in business school, before the bonuses and stock options and Range Rovers and speedboats. In short, we both know who wears the pants in our house: My husband does. But there is equally little doubt which of us really has the power.

So he will love this gift and he will love that I thought to give it to him. Now I just need the courage to go through with it. Which brings us back, once again, to my ass, which I am staring at now in the cramped little room off to the side of the nail salon where they do my waxing. The salon is owned by Sarah, a lovely Korean woman who almost met my twins before I did; she was giving me a pedicure when my water broke. That sort of experience creates a bond, and on top of that I occasionally bring Megan in for manicures—I started when she was only three—so Sarah has watched my family grow and I, too, have watched hers; her grown children are always in and out of the salon, and I adore how proudly she speaks of the daughter who is a nurse and the son studying to be a lawyer. I feel Sarah and I have shared quite a lot over the years, and yet I cannot imagine exactly how I am going to tell her why I am here today.

Because if I'm going to do this, I'm going to do it right. The photos will be tasteful and, hopefully, beautiful. But let's face it—they are going to be more about sex than art, and if I want my husband to choose them over smut then we need to smut them up, at least a little. There will be nothing splayed, nothing gaping, nothing vulgar, nothing of that sort, but there will be full frontal nudity and with that NC-17 rating comes an obligation.

Bring on the wax.

I've never done this before, but I have friends who have, and they have told me to just remove my pants and underwear, that no one bats an eye at the nudity. So I did, and then I sat on the cushioned table that was covered with a long sheet of paper, and I waited.

Sarah entered the room with a huge smile on her face and a thirteen-year-old girl by her side.

"Hello, Brooke!" she exclaimed, apparently oblivious to my state of undress. "This is my niece! She wrote a paper on the origin of the steak knife and I knew you'd love to read it!"

There is obviously no chance that is what she actually said, but sometimes her English is a bit of an adventure.

"How lovely," I said, nodding and frantically tugging down my tank top. I didn't offer a hand because I didn't have one to spare. "Do you live around here?"

The girl nodded. She did not speak at all. Neither did Sarah—*she* just stood beaming at her niece. But the trouble was that pretty soon it had been too long since anyone had spoken, so I did again.

"Well, Sarah, we're going to try something a little different today," I said.

"Oh yeah? What?" Sarah asked.

I was staring right at the girl. I couldn't see myself explaining what I was here to do—much less actually doing it—with a tween standing close enough to me that I could brush her hair if I wanted to. The girl was just standing silently and politely, as though she were awaiting instructions from me, but those were clearly not forthcoming as I was so uncomfortable in my state of undress I could hardly speak.

And then finally, thankfully, Sarah clued in, picking up either on my nerves or my balled-up thong on the table, or perhaps the three-quarters of my butt sticking out beneath my top.

"Ooooohhhhh," she said, and leaned toward me. "You having an affair?"

That made me laugh hard enough that I forgot for a moment about my circumstances and put both hands over my mouth, and just like that I was all out there. I covered up quickly and glanced right at the girl, who did not bat an eye.

"Come on, lie down," Sarah said, and then she turned and said something to the girl, who turned to me and nodded politely and then she was gone, and I was on the table, flat on my back, as Sarah began to heat the wax.

"You know," she said ominously, "this is going to hurt."

SAMANTHA □ □ □

ALL OF A SUDDEN I felt pain unlike any I can ever remember.

The numbness that at first spread about my body like gushing water was replaced by a searing agony. Suddenly I couldn't keep up with the number of emotional hammers pounding away at me: stunned disbelief, murderous rage, agonized sadness. And, worst of all: pity. I have never before felt as sorry for anyone as I suddenly felt for myself.

I dove into the bed and buried my head beneath as many pillows as I could stack. I wanted total pitch-black darkness. I wanted never to see again. The pity threatened to consume me completely, and it occurred to me that self-pity is the most devastating of all emotions. Anger can be motivational, sadness can be galvanizing, but pity is crippling. I couldn't even cry, because I didn't have the strength. I could hardly take a breath, my chest felt heavy and constricted. I tried to breathe deeply, to gather my thoughts. How had I gotten here? I was twenty-eight years old. I had joined the Peace Corps out of college. Then I was a television producer in New York. Now I was a cheated-on newlywed.

That was when I smelled him. One of the pillows piled atop my head must have been his, and all at once he was all over me. I tried to get away but accidentally I rolled to his side of the bed and found myself in the slight indentation he'd made when he slept, and then my hip touched a wet spot and I shot out of the bed as though it was a cannon. That was *his* wetness on the mattress—we'd made that wetness together—how long ago? It felt like days had passed, but how long had it been really? An hour? Less? I could feel him on me, on my flesh, inside me, and without thinking I stripped off everything and dashed to the shower. I turned the water as hot as I could stand and scrubbed. Once my skin was as pink and clean as I could get it I turned off the water, put on a sports bra and running shorts and sneakers, and then I was outside, steps from the beach. And then I started to run.

I didn't know where I was going. I didn't even really know where I was, I just knew I needed to run, to recapture myself. The self-pity threatened to stop me, threatened to knock me to the ground, but I pushed on. *I am not someone who feels sorry for herself,* I told myself. *I am not.*

I really am not. I feel sorry for so many people but never for myself. I feel sorry for all the same people you do: orphans, circus freaks, single mothers, homeless children, widower fathers, crack babies, drug addicts, blind peddlers, deaf beggars, and anyone missing an arm, a leg, or any other valuable appendage. But for you it likely ends there, while for me it is just the beginning.

I feel terribly sorry for the woman who worked at the drive-thru window at the Dunkin' Donuts near my father's house in Connecticut. It could be twenty below zero and there she would be, leaning out that window with no coat, no gloves, making change, handing out coffee, always with a smile on her face. I would marvel at her contentedness, even envy it at times. Once I asked her why she always seemed so happy, and she launched into a life story too horrendous to be believed. It was the story of a husband who beat her and a daughter who died in a car crash and a month of sleeping in the mudroom of her church, and she concluded by saying: "This is the happiest time of my day, being around all these nice people." I looked around and saw the typical groups of folks you'd expect in a Dunkin' Donuts; they didn't all seem so nice to me. But this was the best part of her day, serving inexpensive snacks to ungrateful masses of people. This was her life. And then one day she was gone. I don't know what happened, she just disappeared. I tried asking everyone I could in the store, but no one knew what happened to her. She just stopped showing up. The manager told me: "Often our people find better jobs and they don't bother coming back to quit." But I knew that wasn't the case; she would never have left that job unless something awful happened to her. And I'll never know what it was. When I went home that night I realized I didn't even know her name. And that made me so sad I cried myself to sleep.

I also often feel sorry for people I've never met.

For instance, just the other day there was this woman who wept uncontrollably when she was called to "Come on down!" on *The Price Is Right*. It was clearly the most exciting thing that had ever happened to her, and it was completely ruined by some jerk who bid one dollar more than she did on the cost of a lawn mower, and he wound up on stage playing a game with dice while she stood there hoping for another chance. But I could see on my watch it was going to be time for the showcase showdown next, so there would be no more chances for her. And that hopeful look on her face made me cry. That poor woman had waited her whole life to come on down, and that was all she got.

There was another woman on that same episode I also felt sorry for. She *did* make it up on stage and played a game where she would win a car if she could guess how much it cost. The car was a little Mazda. I don't know that you could have fit two people and two bags of groceries in it, but this woman guessed the price was $78,000. Drew Carey was so taken aback by her guess I thought he was going to have to be carried away. But, bless her heart, this woman felt really good about her answer, and for that one minute she was just as sure as she could be that she was going to win a brand-new car. Of course, everyone in the studio and everyone watching on television knew before she did that she had absolutely no chance, and for those few seconds when she was the only one in the world who still believed, my heart ached for her.

So, there are those moments in my life practically every day. And when you combine them with all the regular ones that get to you as well, like the starving children with distended stomachs, it is basically a full-time job. I think the only person I've never felt sorry for in my whole life is me.

Why would I? I was born with every advantage imaginable. My family is wealthy, I am healthy, I've always been able to choose whatever path I like. Yes, my father can be petulant and insensitive, and yes, he is now dating a woman only four years older than I am, but that isn't really *my* issue. I feel sorry for my mother, who died so young, and my younger brother, who always idolized our father and has felt personally betrayed and disillusioned by Dad's failings, but none of that has kept me from pursuing my interests or living my life. I have never imagined *anyone* would feel sorry for me, much less me feel it myself, until I typed "Fuck-LarryBird" into my husband's laptop on the first morning of our honeymoon and found myself staring at a nude photo of a woman it took me a moment to recognize.

The woman was attractive but by no means perfect, nothing you would ever see in *Playboy*, or whatever online site men use for their porn these days. She wasn't airbrushed or artificially tanned, she wasn't waxed and enhanced in all the most important places, but she was pretty, and about twenty years older than me. Or nineteen years, actually, to the day, now that I think of it. When I first met her on the campaign, I recalled, we laughed when we figured out we shared a birthday. I remember she said: "Funny, I could have been your babysitter." It didn't seem so funny at the time, and even less funny now was the note she'd attached to the photo.

Something to remember me by while you're in Hawaii with your daughter.

So now I was just running, as hard and as fast as I could. I didn't know where I was going, but that really didn't matter. Because when you're running away from something rather than running toward it, it doesn't make much difference which way you go.

 KATHERINE

THEY SAY IT'S BETTER to have loved and lost than never to have loved at all.

Well, how fucking stupid are *they*?

That expression, or the sentiment behind it, is one of those things we've made up to make ourselves feel better. Like when we say it's good luck if it rains on your wedding day. Of course that isn't good luck; it is, in fact, the very definition of *bad* luck. But we announce that it is good luck so we don't have to feel bad about being wet at our own wedding. I remember when my friend Heidi was married, right here in Manhattan, she and her fiancé arranged for a double-decker bus with an open top to transport the guests from the church on the Upper West Side to a social club by Gramercy Park. The trouble was that it poured. I mean, *poured*. My lasting recollections are of Heidi with a garbage bag over her dress and a shower cap over her hair to keep the rain from spoiling all her photos, and all the guests crammed into the lower level of the double-decker bus. I ask you, was that good luck?

Of course it doesn't mean the marriage is doomed. In fact, Heidi remains happily married and has three little boys whose names currently escape me, but the point remains there was nothing lucky about the rain on her wedding day, and neither is there anything better about loving and losing than never loving at all.

"Oh, fuck him," I said.

"What's that, Katherine?"

I had forgotten about Maurice. "Nothing."

"You keep talking to yourself, I'm gonna need to take you somewhere other than that office," he said cheerily. "You may need to see a doctor."

I do love Maurice. He is a genuinely nice man, and in my experience those are not so easy to find. I think if there is such a thing as reincarnation—*and* if there is any justice in the universe—Maurice should come back as a supermodel, or a basketball star, or George Clooney. If Maurice were to be reincarnated as Heidi Klum, I would not for one second begrudge him the legs that never end or the perfect skin or the hair that always returns to the right place in the wind. It would make me happy, in fact, to know that the winners of the genetic lottery actually earned their good fortune through good deeds. Otherwise it's all just random, luck of the draw, and some people get to be gorgeous and thin and the rest of us don't, with no rhyme or reason.

If Phillip gets reincarnated, on the other hand, I want justice. And I have found just the perfect sentence, an appropriate comeuppance for a lifetime spent with looks and wealth and no appreciation whatsoever for his good fortune. I came across it just the other night, watching *Dirty Jobs*. (I love that show.) The episode began with scenic shots of what appeared to be a ranch, the sun rising on a picture-perfect morning, and then Mike Rowe came on and said something like "What a perfect day to collect some horse semen!" And that's what he spent an hour doing. When the episode was over, I went online and read all about the collection of stallion semen, and it was fascinating. Turns out the most common method for collection is with an artificial vagina, but in some cases that doesn't work, so someone needs to manually extract the specimen from the stallion. That's right, *manually*. And as I was reading all about it, one thought kept ringing in my mind: If there is such a thing as reincarnation, I hope Phillip comes back as the guy who jerks off the horses.

Does that sound bitchy? I don't mean it to. It's just that he was the second man in my life to let me down so dramatically that I was unable to cope. The first was my father and let's face it, no matter how bitterly disappointed you may be in your father you still never wish upon him a lifetime of giving hand jobs to horses.

But the days when Phillip and I were together do not seem real to me anymore, which is to say I recall a lot of events but I have no recollection of how they felt or tasted or smelled. I remember meeting a shy, brilliant boy in the registration office on our first day at the Harvard Business School. He was older than I, by seven years. He'd been on Wall Street and his firm was paying his tuition in Cambridge. He was a genius, and they all saw it even then, as anybody would have. I remember his bushy black hair, unkempt and curly in the back, which did not suit his face at all. I remember we were both outcasts, to a degree; me because of my father, Phillip because he came from the wrong side of the tracks. Phillip was from Brooklyn, the very definition of self-made. His father, a sweet and charming man, delivered milk. Phillip, on his way to graduating first in our class at HBS, always told me, "They don't teach us anything in these schools more valuable than what I learned on the streets in Brooklyn." Phillip was a fighter, and he fought dirty when he had to.

I also saw a different side of him, though. I was the only one around with whom he would occasionally let his guard down. He could be very funny. His humor was caustic and sarcastic, which I thought betrayed his insecurity at being the only Brooklyn boy in the most prestigious class in American education. And he loved old movies, as I do. That was where we really bonded. He especially loved Humphrey Bogart; in fact, the only time he was ever goofy was when boarding an airplane. No matter where we were, he would always break into the famous lines from *Casablanca*.

"You're getting on that plane," he would say, baring his teeth like Bogart, in a vocal impression that was dead-on. "If you don't you'll regret it. Maybe not today, maybe not tomorrow, but soon and for the rest of your life."

I have always loved that movie, and I loved Phillip madly. It was an

Ingrid Bergman kind of love, only I was much too selfish to ever consider sending him away for the good of the Resistance. Let Paris fall and the Germans come marching up Fifth Avenue, I wasn't letting that man get away. Which is why the way it ended hurt me so, and why to this day I hope to someday see him whacking off a stallion.

They say the best revenge is living well, and I'm not buying that, either. Nobody is living better than I am; I have a duplex on Park Avenue, a driver, a chef, an assistant, and a killer house in South Hampton, and I did it all on my own. But I still haven't gotten past what happened with Phillip and I doubt I ever will, and I wish to god he was ten times more miserable than I am.

If that sounds bitchy, I guess I don't really care.

SAMANTHA

FUCK HIM.

With every step I ran, those words were in my head. And they were liberating; those two words freed me from my self-pity. Anger is inspirational. Anger has launched wars, cured diseases, conquered civilizations; it's not always the most beneficent of emotions but damned if it doesn't help get things done. And now it was helping me. The anger surged through me and propelled me with each step I took. It helped. And as I ran, I started to remember who I am.

Fuck him.

I'm not a politician's wife. I'm a jock. I was the captain of the soccer *and* lacrosse teams in high school. I ran three marathons my senior year of college. When I lived in New York I played ultimate frisbee in Central Park every day. I climb rocks and mountains, I ski, I surf. I don't stand on a makeshift stage in hotel ballrooms, smile blankly, and wave.

Fuck him.

I got a job at MTV Sports after I got out of the Peace Corps and I loved it. I produced shows about extreme athletes, shows that took me all over the country, all over the world. I filmed motocross racers and skydivers and cliff divers and skateboarders. I trekked across an Arizona desert for three weeks, shooting a guy who runs forty miles a day barefoot for fun. I filmed guys climbing mountains on bicycles and fighting crocodiles with their bare hands. And along the way I participated in most of it. I jumped out of an airplane with a parachute, off a mountaintop with a bungee cord, and over a Volkswagen on a motorcycle. I walked on hot coals, collected honey from a swarming hive of bees, and swam with a great white shark. It all seems like it was so long ago, a different lifetime, but it wasn't. Come to think of it, the swim with the shark was *this* year on *this* island. I'm *still* that girl, I just took a little break from myself.

Fuck him.

The sky was impossibly blue and there was no sign of a cloud anywhere. It was one of those perfect days you only get in Hawaii, that wonderful kind of hot only the islands can provide. As I broke a sweat, my legs settled into a very comfortable gait. I don't remember ever feeling so loose or so strong. Every step was freeing, every breath invigorating. There was no strain, no fatigue, no pain, just the rhythmic beating of my heart accompanied by the crashing waves on the beach. Overhead, gulls were singing and in the distance a Polynesian song was playing. It was the most peaceful, perfect, beautiful, Zen experience I have ever had. I was fully one with the sky and the sea and the earth. And with every step I took and every beat of my heart, I heard the same words in my head, again and again.

Fuck him.

I haven't any idea how much time passed as I ran; I would have run forever, but eventually my body needed fuel. I could feel it begin to cry out for water, for food, and I remembered I hadn't eaten any breakfast at all. The timing was perfect, as I was approaching what appeared to be a gorgeous hotel, so I just ran straight in through the front doors, through the lobby, and found a restaurant out by the swimming pool. I wasn't even breathing heavily as I asked for a menu. I wanted the healthiest food they had, the healthiest food imaginable. I felt as though I wanted to eat the earth.

"May I have fresh fruit, please," I asked a very pleasant waiter who came to take my order, "and nuts if you have them, and granola, and lots of cold water."

"Will this be a room charge?" he asked.

"No, I'm not staying in this hotel."

He asked where I was staying and I told him, and then I asked how far apart the hotels were.

"I'm not sure exactly, miss," he said. "I can get the exact distance if you'd like."

"If it isn't too much trouble."

A moment later he was back with the most beautiful plate I've ever seen, a huge platter piled high with ripe grapefruit, pineapple, berries, and assorted other explosively colorful treats.

"I asked at the desk," he told me as I sank my teeth into a mango. "They say it is about eighteen miles from your hotel."

I finished chewing and looked up at him.

"Excuse me?" I said.

"Eighteen miles," he repeated, "that's what they said. How long did it take you to drive here?"

"I didn't drive," I said, "I ran."

"Wow, pretty long run," he said, "nice way to start the day. Enjoy your lunch."

Lunch? I thought.

"What time is it?" I asked.

"Almost noon, miss."

I had been running for three hours.

"Thank you very much," I said.

I devoured everything on that platter and loved every bite of it. I ate berries and figs and raisins, almonds and walnuts and macadamia nuts, mango and pineapple and coconut, and I drank a pitcher of ice water, then asked for another and finished that one as well. When I was done, I leaned back in my chair and let the sun bathe my face. I wanted to run some more, or maybe swim. I just needed to digest for a few minutes first. Then the pleasant waiter was back, humming amiably as he cleared the table.

"Would you care for anything else?" he asked.

The sun felt so good on my cheeks.

"Yes," I said, without opening my eyes. "Are there any rooms available in this hotel?"

BROOKE

I GUESS I DON'T say a lot of things that surprise people.

I'm a mom, and as a mom I guess I mostly say things that people are expecting to hear.

No, Megan, you may not sleep over at Parker's on a school night.

Yes, Jared, you must finish the asparagus if you want to have a fudgesicle.

I'm also a wife, and I don't suppose Scott is very often surprised with most of what he hears me say.

Sweetheart, we are having dinner with the Ronsons on Friday. Don't forget she's pregnant but you're not supposed to know.

If we're going to do it, lock the door, the kids are probably awake.

I also play tennis with a group of girls three times a week, and our conversations aren't that shocking either, I would say.

I'm seconds away from getting my period.

I swear if she makes one more comment about my colorist I am going to serve the ball directly into the back of her head.

So, I almost never get to see a look of complete surprise on anyone's face. And, really, there's something a bit awful about that. I don't suppose anyone wants to be known as "predictable." I pride myself on being dependable, but I never want to be predictable, because that feels about a half step away from boring.

Thus, I can honestly say there was something thrilling about the look on Pamela's face when I said to her: "Next week, I want you to photograph me naked."

At first she didn't speak. Then she blushed, and shook her head a bit as if to clear her ears.

"I'm sorry," she said. "What?"

"I want you to shoot me naked."

She paused again. "Wait a minute, darling," she said, "which of us do you mean would be naked?"

And then we were both giggling, in a way I don't get to giggle very often anymore. We giggled the way Megan and her girlfriends do when I accuse them of having crushes on one of the Jonas Brothers, or on the supercute boy a grade ahead of them, with the curly hair. We giggled like lifelong girlfriends, which actually we are not: I have only known Pamela for four years, since the night I had to keep Scott from punching a woman in the face.

Pamela is a generation older than I, and one of the core friends every woman needs to have. You know what I mean. First, every woman needs a sister, and if she does not have one then she needs a friend who is like a sister: one who cares for your children as though they are her own, and will tell you in the car if you have too much blush on. Then there is the friend who knows everything that is going on, who keeps you up on all the gossip, whether it's by telling you *Brad and Angelina are really split up this time and she's engaged to her astrologist,* or *Susan came home and found Richard in the hot tub with Anna Demetrio; apparently, they had bathing suits on but, please, that is beyond inappropriate.* Every woman needs that friend, too. And then, most important, every woman also needs a friend who is like a mother, but one she'll actually listen to. When my mother tries to tell me I am making a mistake, half the time I go ahead *because* she has questioned me. But every woman needs a friend who will tell you when you are about to go wrong: *Don't feed your children tilapia, it has too much of the bad Omega-6s and not enough of the good Omega-3s. Don't stay in that hotel: there is nothing for the kids to do and it's a twenty-minute walk to the nearest decent restaurant. Don't try the Metamucil wafers, they don't make you regular, they make you stuffed and bloated.* That's a core friend every woman needs.

Pamela is that friend to me. She is older and worldly and provides the perfect sounding-board; I can't recall ever needing advice and failing to get it from her. She's also the best photographer in Greenwich, which doesn't hurt, either. That's how we came to meet her. We bought her, or we tried to. And then she felt bad that we didn't and let us have her anyway. I should explain.

It was a fund-raiser at the school, and I told Scott we had to pick one silent-auction item and make sure we won it. He selected a session with Pamela, a renowned photographer, so we'd finally have professional photos of the kids and, as he put it, "a decent-looking holiday card." All evening long he was staked out at the auction table, quickly raising any bid that topped ours. When there were about thirty minutes remaining, it became clear it was down to Scott and one other man, a pleasant-looking fellow with older kids. I watched Scott and this man go back and forth, raising each other and staring each other down as though they were playing high-stakes poker. (Men can be so funny; they were only raising it $20 each time, but the drama was such that I thought one might eventually slap the other across the face with a white glove.) The final blow was delivered by my husband when it was announced that there was one minute remaining. With a flourish, he took the pen and raised the total by $200. The other fellow looked at the bid, looked at my husband, and nodded his head in a respectful concession. It was over. Scott had won.

Then the announcer began the countdown. "Ladies and gentlemen, the auction will be closed in ten seconds. Nine, eight, seven, six, five . . ."

To my horror, a garish-looking bottle blonde with enormous boobs sauntered up to the bid sheet. She scooped up the pen and wrote something down, just as the announcer reached "one." Then she walked quickly away, her ass swaying tauntingly in too-tight white jeans.

I looked at Scott and saw he was stunned. He literally couldn't move. So I went to the sheet and saw she had raised him by $5. No previous bid had been raised by any less than twenty, but here she had sloppily written "$605" and her name and that was it. When I went back to Scott's side, he was shaking.

"Did she top it?" he asked.

I nodded. I really hoped he wouldn't ask the next question.

"By how much?"

I told him, because I couldn't get around it, and he turned beet red. "Brooke," he said, "you're the debutante, so you know about these things. What's the etiquette here? Because if that was a guy I would punch him in the face."

"I think that would be a bit much," I said.

"Do you mean in this case? Or with a guy? Because if it was a guy I *would* punch him in the face."

"Sweetheart," I said, "you do realize we can hire this photographer for three hundred dollars less than this, don't you?"

"That isn't the point," he said, and he was right. It wasn't the point.

In the end, it turned out Pamela was at the party and saw what happened and she agreed to accept our bid as well and couldn't have been sweeter about it. We had a drink with her that night and began a friendship that has meant everything to me. And now here I am, giggling with my friend as I explain to her that because she has shot my children and my husband and me so wonderfully, and produced four sensational holiday cards for us, now I want her to come to my house and take pictures of me naked.

We planned it for a Tuesday—as it turned out, we had to wait a few days after my waxing to allow the redness to fade. (Nothing has ever hurt like that did, by the way. I would rather deliver triplets drug-free in the back of a taxi than go through that again.) Once the children were on the bus, I set about trying to create the proper atmosphere in the house. The first decision to be made was selecting a room. The bedroom seemed the obvious choice, but ours is not the sexiest bedroom. Our bedroom is comfy and very cozy, and I love lying in bed talking with Scott with a fire going, but the bedroom is the place where we have most of our sex, and most of it isn't fabulously romantic. Mostly it consists of quickies on weekend mornings before the children wake up, and it can never be especially spontaneous, as I have become obsessed with locking the door first because I simply cannot handle the idea of being caught in the act.

"Sweetheart," he breathed heavily into my ear one time, "the kids aren't at home."

"What if Lucy comes in?" I said.

"Lucy is a golden retriever."

"I am aware of that but she does barge in here all the time."

"But she's a dog."

"I cannot have sex with the dog watching," I said, sitting up, "it's inappropriate."

Since then he's never balked when I demand the door be locked. Pamela laughed hysterically when I explained all this, by the way, and suggested the sexiest photo of all might just be me, nude, beside an unlocked door.

But so much for the bedroom. I next considered the kitchen, which is where we spend most of our time as a family, usually me cooking or puttering around and the kids eating or doing their homework at the table or curled up watching television on the sofa in the family room, which adjoins it. Scott has repeatedly told me he never finds me sexier than when I am cooking, but frankly I think that is just an effort to get me into the right frame of mind for a quickie after dinner. It often works, by the way—I'm not complaining—but I'm still not sure it's the right room for the photos.

Neither, then, is Scott's office. Aside from the desk and chair, the only things in there are a computer, a fax machine, a copier, a printer, two telephones, a small television monitor, and a Bose radio. There is nothing in the room that is not connected to a power cord.

The kids' rooms are obviously out of the question, as are the bathrooms, even the master with the whirlpool tub, because if even a hint of a toilet is in the picture it ruins the effect completely. And I'm definitely not prepared to do this outside by the pool, because if my social-climbing, nosy, never-keeps-her-mouth-shut neighbor should get so much as a glimpse of my naked ass, it would be pretty much the equivalent of showing it on the evening news.

So, I am left with a really strange problem. It's like being all dressed up and having no place to go, except it's the opposite. I want to be completely *un*dressed. But, even in my own home, I feel as though I've got no place to go.

SAMANTHA

WHEN I OPENED MY eyes, the waiter with the pleasant smile was still standing before me, waiting for me—I guess—to laugh, or maybe to cry. But I wasn't going to do either. Suddenly I felt very serious, and very certain of what I needed.

"Can you please ask the hotel manager to come see me?" I asked.

"Of course, miss," he said. "But may I ask again, will your meal be charged to your room?"

"No, I'm not a guest in this hotel," I said, "but I'm going to be one very soon."

"Very well," he said amiably, "will you be paying with cash or a card?"

"Actually, I haven't got any money," I said, "but I know where to get some."

His pleasant smile was wavering. I think he thought I was crazy, and considering the conversation we were having I couldn't blame him.

"I will have no trouble paying for my lunch, don't worry," I said. "I just need three things, please. I need the hotel manager, I need a telephone, and I need a glass of champagne."

He brought me the drink first and it was fabulous, so different from the glass I'd had last night when I was drinking a toast to the rest of my life. Now, in the light of day, especially in the brilliant sunshine, it was clear how silly that had been. Not just because I had typed "FuckLarry-Bird" into a computer and found out my husband wasn't the man I thought he was, but for a million other reasons as well. In the sunshine, it was clear that the only plans worth making are ones for later in the day. There's no way to know what the next week or month or year are going to bring, much less the whole rest of your life. The only permanent thing is impermanence. This was what I came to understand right then, right there, with the sun on my cheeks and the champagne on my lips. The notion that you could actually know what you want for the rest of your life is illogical and unreasonable. The best you can do is figure out what you want for lunch.

"Hello, miss."

The voice came from behind me, a different voice this time. It wasn't the waiter; it was a handsome, older man in a white blazer. He had the same amiable smile as the waiter but a much deeper voice and an air that suggested he was very much in charge. He seemed European, perhaps Spanish.

"My name is Eduardo Marquez. I am the hotel manager. Is there anything I can do for you?"

I didn't say anything for a minute, largely because I loved the sound of his voice. He sounded exactly like that character in the movie *The Princess Bride*. I just wanted to sit silently in the warm glow of the sun and luxuriate in the sound of his baritone.

"Miss," he said again, and I could tell he was about to lose his European cool, "I was told you wanted to see me. Now, what can I do to be of service to you?"

I sighed deeply, gathered my resolve.

"Well, Mr. Marquez, it sort of goes like this: I'm supposed to be on my honeymoon at the Four Seasons, but it turns out my husband is fucking a woman who works for him, which is horrible in so many ways, not the least of which is that my father thought all along he was an asshole and now it turns out my father was right, which if you knew my father you'd know is almost as bad as finding out my marriage isn't going to last a week. But the good news is, I'm over it. Over it, and over *him*—it just took a little time and a little thought and I accomplished both of those on my way over here. So all I really need now is a phone so I can call my father and we'll have my marriage annulled, and then I'll enter the next available triathlon here on the island and stay in your hotel to train for that because you have the best fruit I have ever tasted. Then after I finish the triathlon I'll move back to New York and go back to my job in television, and if I never meet another man that will be just fine with me."

I wish you could have seen the look on Eduardo Marquez's face: it was the most delightful combination of skepticism and awe I can ever recall. I'm sure he thought I was either full of it or insane, or maybe he thought I was both, and either way it made no difference to me, because I was so wonderfully certain that I was neither.

"Well, miss," he finally said, adjusting his tie, "perhaps the first thing I could do is bring you the telephone you asked for."

"That would be great," I said, and I reached out to shake his hand. And when we shook, I put my other hand over his as tenderly as I could. "Thank you very much for your help."

He bowed a little, and backed away slowly. I took the opportunity to drink my champagne, which continued to feel great going down. But now I also wanted something healthy, a smoothie or protein shake or even some green tea; I had work to do. Training would have to begin immediately. I looked at the waves breaking on the beach and suddenly I yearned to be in the water. I would have dashed into the ocean right then if I wasn't so sure Eduardo Marquez would have a conniption if he came back to find me gone.

Then I started to think about Robert. What would he find when he got back to the suite? How exactly had I left it? I couldn't remember. I hadn't packed anything; my clothes, jewelry, makeup, toiletries, they were all still there. He would probably return to find me out of the room and think nothing of it, think I just went for a run or a swim or a stroll on the beach. He'd be a little surprised I hadn't left a note, or texted him with my plans, but he certainly wouldn't be anxious. Maybe he would get into bed and lounge, waiting for me to come back so he could pat me softly on the butt, which is his signal that he wants to have sex. I could picture him now, lying in the bed, stripped to the waist, reading a newspaper, waiting for me. How much time would pass before he became concerned? Maybe that time had already come. Maybe he was out looking for me right now. Maybe he was asking hotel staff if they'd seen the athletic-looking blonde he'd checked in with. The first thing he'd do was call my phone, and wait for the connection, which would take a little extra time on the island, and then he would hear "I Gotta Feeling" by the Black Eyed Peas somewhere in the room, and since he knows that's my ringtone he'd know I left my iPhone behind, and that's when he'd become concerned. Because *that* would be completely unlike me. He'd go through my things next, and find I'd also left behind my bag and my backpack, with my wallet and passport and driver's license, and I think what he'd think then is that I'd been kidnapped; taken, literally, from the hotel room, because I would never venture even outside the door without any of those. That thought brought another smile to my face. *Fuck him.* Let him be worried. Let him contact local authorities to report a missing person. Let him call my family and ask if they'd heard from me. In fact, let *me* have talked to my father first; let my father be the one to tell him the marriage is over. No one would enjoy that more than Dad would and he'd do a great job of it, he'd put all the "motherfuckers" and "cocksuckers" in the right places. He's very good with those.

"Miss, here is a telephone, property of the hotel. Any charges you incur can be added to your bill at the end of your stay."

It was Eduardo Marquez; he'd snuck up on me. And there was something different about him now, something softer—or at least less suspicious. His smile seemed less forced, less rehearsed. There was something very pleasant and charming about him.

"Thank you," I said, and took the mobile from him. "I'm very much looking forward to staying here."

Then I took several deep breaths, filling my lungs until they ached in a way they hadn't while I was running those eighteen miles. The salt in the air was invigorating, and made my mind feel crisp and sharp. I dialed without looking at the digits, and then I took one more deep breath before I hit *send*.

"Hi, Dad, it's me," I said when he answered. "I'm having sort of an unusual day."

 KATHERINE

"HELLO, MOM, THANKS FOR calling. Yes, it's sort of a big day."

There is nothing more challenging for me than being chipper with my mother. She has the amazing ability to take any topic—even a birthday greeting—and give it a funereal tone. I think it's something in the way she lowers her voice when it comes to certain words, and not the usual ones, like "cancer" or "tax evasion." Like in this conversation, for instance, I could easily see if she whispered either the "birthday" or the "fortieth," but she did not, she spoke both of those in a normal tone. But she lowered to where I could barely hear when she said: "I hope you know how *proud* of you I am." The whole sentence was muffled, as though she covered the receiver with a sweat sock, and the word "proud" was practically indiscernible. She speaks as though she is constantly apologizing for the interruption, and has all my life, or at least since Dad went away.

In her defense, I suppose there *is* something vaguely funereal about a fortieth birthday. It certainly signifies the end of something. Not of life, but of something. It signifies the end of my youth, for one thing. I am not, and never will be again, a young woman. No one will ever again call me a "girl," not that many ever did anyway, but it was comforting to at least know it was a realistic possibility. If I were picking words to whisper, I would say "getting older" and "starting to feel it in my back" so softly you'd need to read my lips.

Those were the thoughts rattling about in my head as I walked into my office. Leave it to my mother to have me thinking about the end of my youth and the increasing stiffness in my lower back first thing in the morning on my birthday.

I am the chief administrative officer of a large investment bank in Manhattan. The title was created for me. To my knowledge, there are very few—if any—other CAOs in major American companies. I began in the legal department, putting to use my dual Harvard degrees in law and business, and ultimately rose to the position of general counsel. Then they added human resources to my purview and named me executive vice president. A little more than two years ago I was recruited by another bank, a smaller one in California, with an offer of the very top position. But Phillip didn't want to lose me, motivated at least in part by our personal history, so he created the CAO title exclusively for me. (The running joke, of which I am well aware and not overly concerned, is that I am the Chief Asshole of the Organization.) I am also currently the highest-ranking female executive on Wall Street, with oversight of our legal, HR, and corporate outreach programs, and a personal staff of eleven.

My assistant is Marie, a stunningly pretty bimbo from Brooklyn, whose title is team manager, but who, for all intents and purposes, functions as my personal confidante. I admire Marie for the exact reason I initially disliked her: she looks like a slut. She showed up her first day with an attitude—and an outfit—that seemed to make no secret of her intentions: she was here to find a man. Some women get an MRS degree from a prestigious university, but Marie was nowhere near smart enough for anything like that; she matriculated into Wall Street instead, wearing too much blush and a skirt that barely concealed her pubic hair. Within three months she had been asked out by at least a half-dozen of our bankers and by the end of the year she was engaged to one of them. I assumed that would be the last I ever saw of Marie's stunning cleavage but, to my surprise, it was not. When she interviewed for her current position I asked her why she chose to continue working. The question clearly took her aback and hurt her feelings. "With all due respect, Ms. Emerson," she replied, her Brooklyn accent heavy, "the way you dress I don't figure you have to work either. So I guess I work for the same reason you do: I love my job." The position was hers right then, and it was the only time in all my years on Wall Street that I have ever apologized to anyone.

Now, on my birthday, Marie took one look at me and followed me into my suite.

"Whatsa matter, boss?" she asked, without saying hello.

I began pointlessly shifting papers about on my desk, trying to appear busy so as to avoid the conversation. "Who says anything is the matter?"

"Is it a man?" she asked.

"What's a man? I've never heard of one of those."

"You know: a despicable creature that smells bad most of the time."

"I thought that was a dog," I said.

"No, dogs smell bad *all* of the time but they aren't the least bit despicable."

I smiled at her. "Marie, I'm enjoying this Neil Simon conversation, I really am, but I have a crazy day so I'm afraid I'm going to need you to exit stage left."

She turned to her left, then back to me with a slightly confused expression. Her innocence always makes me smile. Marie is the perfect example of how life is all about your expectations. Her life is better than she had any right to imagine, thus she is the most honestly happy person I know. I, meanwhile, was raised with endless expectations, my life is a limitless menu of options, and thus I am the most honestly dissatisfied person I know. Sometimes dual master degrees from Harvard can bite you in the ass.

"All right," I said, softening my tone. "It's my birthday today."

Her eyes opened like full moons. "Wow! Happy birthd—"

"Please." I cut her off, reaching out my arm. "I don't feel like talking about it all day."

"I get it," she said, whispering. "Happy birthday, boss."

"Thank you."

"Any big plans? What are you doing to celebrate?"

"You're looking at it."

"No, no," she said, shaking her pretty head. "That's not good enough."

"I appreciate the thought."

"NO!"

That took me aback, I'll admit.

"You've been so nice to me," Marie continued, more calmly. "I am *not* letting you spend your birthday just working and going home. You and me are doing something tonight, anything you want, my treat."

This conversation was making me sad. And embarrassed. "That's very sweet of you to offer," I said, "but you really don't have to do that."

"I know I don't *have* to," she said. "I want to."

I'm not sure exactly why I was fighting this. There was part of me that definitely favored the idea; it seemed it would have to be more fun to go anywhere with anyone than to go home on my fortieth birthday and watch *American Idol*, which I would have to watch because there was nothing left on my TiVO. Perhaps the most pathetic thing I can think of to tell you about my life is that I have *nothing* left on my TiVO. Everyone I know is always talking about how far behind they are on all their shows. I, on the other hand, am fully caught up. I have watched everything on television that I ever wanted to.

"What would you have in mind?" I asked, trying not to betray my interest.

"You name it," she said. "You name the club, you name the restaurant, you name the bar, you name the Broadway show, you name the movie. Whatever it is you name, that's what we'll do."

"Well, I've seen everything decent on Broadway, and there are *no* good movies playing, and I'm not really the type to go to a bar or a *club*," I said, wrinkling my nose at the word as though I didn't like the taste of it. "I can't imagine going to a *club*."

"So it's dinner," she said. "Anywhere you want."

I thought about it for a minute until suddenly her eyes got huge and round again. If she were a cartoon, a lightbulb would have switched on over her head.

"I know what we need to do!" she said, with great enthusiasm.

"What?" I replied, in the same excited tone, mocking her for absolutely no reason. (Here is this sweet girl getting excited about making birthday plans for me, not even knowing which birthday it is, and I'm giving her a hard time for it. I swear, sometimes I understand why my reputation is what it is.)

"I have a terrific idea and I know you're going to turn it down," Marie said, undeterred by my bitchiness, "but I want you to think about it, okay? Really consider it, because I think it's a great idea."

I waited.

"There is a guy who lives in my building that I'm dying to fix you up with . . ."

Now this was humiliating. "Stop."

"No, wait," she protested. "He's very handsome and very nice. I've talked with him in the elevator, he's divorced with no kids, wears great-looking suits, looks to be about the right age—I think it's a winner."

I know Marie's building. She lives on Central Park West. Her fiancé is one of the more successful bankers in our real estate development business. But there was simply no way.

"I can't do that," I said.

"Why not?"

"Because," I said, "what could be more pathetic than going on a blind date on your birthday?"

She smiled. "Sitting at home on your birthday watching *American Idol*," she said. "Which, I might add, has sucked for the last three years anyway."

I've never in my life mentioned *American Idol* to Marie. She's more insightful than I give her credit for sometimes.

"What makes you think he's even available tonight?" I asked.

"I can find out," she said, bubbling. She could sense I was giving in. "I have his mobile."

I shrugged. Then I sighed. Then I rolled my eyes. And then, finally, I ran out of gestures that indicate exasperation.

"All right, *call* him," I said, as though I was agreeing to a highly skeptical business deal, which, in a sense, I was.

"I will," she said, all excited. "I'll be right back."

Five minutes later she was back, and beaming.

"Eight o'clock," she said. "Gramercy Tavern, just the two of you. He says he'll be the one in the blue suit. I think he was trying to be funny."

I tried to muster a laugh, but couldn't.

"The way you dress," she continued, "I told him he'd know you the minute you walk in the door."

"Well, thanks for the added pressure."

"Boss, don't be ridiculous, your clothes are *too* fabulous," she said. "I may sneak by and peek in the window just to see what you're wearing."

BROOKE

SO, WHAT ARE YOU wearing?

It's funny, but I could never count how many times my husband has asked me that. Sometimes jokingly, sometimes not. From wherever he is on the globe, Scott knows that he is not allowed to go to bed without calling me first to say good-night. I want mine to be the last voice he hears before he goes to sleep, and whatever he wants that voice to be I am willing to give him. He will invariably begin the conversation by asking what I'm wearing, and I can usually tell from his tone whether he wants to know that I am in flannel pajamas or if he wants the Jenna Jameson voice and the fantasy wardrobe. I will talk him through any outfit he wants—he's fully aware I don't own any of it, of course—and I will talk as long as it takes until he is ready for sleep. (The hilarious times come when he is in Europe or Asia; there have been occasions when I've had these conversations in hushed tones at soccer practice or in the parking lot at school.) As I've told you, I expect my husband to be completely faithful to me, and I accept that with that demand comes some obligation on my part. When he needs it I give it to him, and in return he never seeks it anywhere else. Seems fair to me.

Anyway, the point is he always asks: "So, what are you wearing?"

And I can't count the number of times I have told him I was wearing absolutely nothing.

"Just six-inch heels and a smile, sweetie," I've said breathily, time and time again.

So, it struck me as more than a little ironic that this was the first time, the very first time, that I was genuinely wearing nothing at all, but it wasn't Scott who called me.

It was my babysitter, and that turned out to be an emergency.

Long story.

Or maybe it isn't that long. It starts in my house, where Pamela and I could not find a single suitable place to take these pictures. Thankfully, Pamela knows me well enough to know when I am becoming discouraged. She could see the moment was going to be lost if we did not act quickly and so she did; we packed up and went to *her* house. It was fabulous at her house, even if her house isn't so fabulous. Pamela is an older divorcée with exquisite taste but not a whole lot of money. The best way to describe her style would be "hippie chic"; she is, after all, a child of the sixties and still flashes peace signs every now and again. So her house is about the way you might expect an aging hippie artist's house to look: lots of psychedelic colors, groovy lighting, tapestries on the walls, a collection of framed rock 'n' roll album covers in the living room. It was awesome for me, because it was so not me. There was something very appropriate about doing something as unusual as taking nude photos in a place as unusual as Pamela's house. I even asked her to fire up some tunes for us. I wanted some rock 'n' roll, and I wanted it loud.

"I think I know just the thing," Pamela said with a mischievous twinkle in her eye.

She practically bounced out of the room to hit the music. I started to think this must be what it is like when a model says she clicks with a particular photographer. I always assumed that was just phony Hollywood-speak, but now I could see it is very real. I just *knew* that Pamela understood exactly what I wanted. I trusted her enough in that moment to put my life in her hands.

Then the music started. Led Zeppelin.

Oh yeah.

I'll tell you a little secret: I'm sort of a rocker chick. I know I don't look it. And I know I don't behave like it anymore. I'm a mother now, a tennis gal, a classroom mom and—hopefully—a hot suburban wife, but inside I'm also still a rocker chick. Aerosmith, Van Halen, Led Zeppelin, Cheap Trick, Pink Floyd, I love it all. And in that instant, when Robert Plant's voice flooded my ears, the only way I can think of to describe the feeling is *orgasmic*.

I was rocking out and playing air guitar, and god bless Pamela, who came in banging her head around like we were at Woodstock, and I just don't know that I've had that much fun in years.

"How about a drink?" I asked her loudly, above the music.

"What do you have in mind?"

"I don't know," I said. "White wine?"

"Hell no!" Pamela shouted. Her eyes were twinkling again. "I think I know just the thing."

Then she was off to the kitchen and I was left to shred it in the living room. As Led Zeppelin rocked out I went right along with them, singing as loudly as I could, on my knees like Tom Cruise in *Risky Business*.

"Try this on for size!"

Pamela was carrying a silver tray, upon which there was a sliced lime, a shaker of salt, a shot glass, and a bottle of Patrón tequila.

"Are you serious?" I asked.

"You better believe it!"

"At ten o'clock in the morning?"

"Listen to me, sweetheart," she said, placing the tray down on the coffee table. "I assume you don't want these pictures to look like ten o'clock in the morning. Am I right?"

"You are *so* right," I said.

"Okay then," Pamela said, and poured a shot of tequila into the glass. Then she took my right hand and licked the inside of my wrist. She poured some salt over the spot and raised the glass to me. "Here you go, babe. Let's do this right!" Without hesitating, I licked the salt, took the glass, and shot the tequila, then took a slice of lime and sunk my teeth into it. The whole thing was fabulous, absolutely *fabulous*. I haven't done tequila shots in years. The drink was tangy on my lips and warm in my chest. It tasted good and felt even better.

"Let me do one more," I said, and I did, and it was even better the second time.

Then Pamela was holding her camera and staring me right in the eye.

"All right, sweetheart," she said, more gently now, reassuringly, "are you ready to do this?"

"One more thing," I said.

"Anything."

"Do you have *Cheap Trick at Budokan*?"

She smiled and left the room again. I began to unbutton my coat. Underneath was a teddy I had picked up after I saw Scott not-so-subtly admire a similar one on Jessica Biel in a movie. Seemed like a good way to ease into this. I let the coat drop to the floor and stared at myself in a mirror decorated with Grateful Dead skulls.

"Not quite Jessica Biel," I said aloud, "but not half-bad."

Then I heard the screaming from the Japanese audience as the drums began to play the introduction to "I Want You to Want Me."

And then Pamela was behind me in the mirror. "No time like the present," she said.

I've never been so ready to do anything in my entire life.

SAMANTHA ▣ ▣ ▣

"SO," MY FATHER SAID, "are you ready to admit I was right?"

"What's that?" I asked.

"I was just wondering if you had come to any conclusions about my views on this fellow you met and decided to marry fifteen minutes later."

My first thought was that this couldn't be happening. I don't mean my father browbeating me, that has been happening all my life. But how could he know? I had yet to tell him anything.

"Dad, what's going on?" I asked.

"I have a better idea," he said. "Why don't you tell *me* what's going on."

Every once in a while I get a glimpse of how my father came to be such a successful businessman. It is not just that he is ruthless (which I suspect he is) and brilliant (to which I can attest firsthand) but he is also very cunning, and this was the perfect illustration. Obviously he knew something, but I didn't know what, nor did I know how he knew it.

"Listen, Dad," I said, fighting desperately to keep all the positive energy from being sucked out of me, "as I said I'm having sort of a strange day. It's pretty clear we both have something we want to say, and I can't tell you how much it would help my state of mind if you would just go first."

He chuckled on the other end of the line. There was something not so malicious in his chuckle, which is unusual for him. Normally, when you're arguing with my father and he laughs, it sounds like Vincent Price in "Thriller." But this was different. He was going to give me a break. I could tell.

"Sweetheart," he said, "Robert called me."

I have no idea why that should have come as a shock to me. There were only two people on the planet who were aware anything was going on. I was one and Robert was the other, so it only stood to reason that if my father was aware of a problem it was Robert who alerted him to it. But why? I'd only been gone a few hours.

"He told me what happened," my father said.

That's when it hit me. I never shut the laptop off, never logged out, never yanked the power cord out of the wall, nothing. I just left it on and open for him to find the nude photo of his campaign manager splashed across the screen. I felt a little smile cross my lips. *Good. No better way for him to find out.*

"What did he say?" I asked. To my surprise, my voice cracked a bit. It sounded as though I might cry, which seemed odd at first but then suddenly I realized tears were streaming down my cheeks.

"To be honest, he was very forthright," my father said. "I give him credit for that. For a lying sack of shit, he's a pretty straightforward guy."

I laughed a little.

"He said he had something he needed to tell me," my father continued, "and that he wanted me to hear it from him first. He said he's been carrying on with a woman from the campaign, I think it was that brunette with the huge tits that lectured me about smoking."

"It was," I said.

"He said that he had taken up with her months before he even met you and that he was confused, and he didn't know what to do, but that he loves you and wants to make the marriage work. And that he planned to tell you about it at the appropriate time, but somehow you obviously discovered something today that sped up that process. Am I reading that correctly?"

"Yes, you are," I said.

"He asked me to be open-minded about the situation and to please help him try to find you, as you'd disappeared without a trace. That was pretty much all he had to say."

I took a deep breath. The air still smelled fresh and salty.

"What did you say to him?" I asked.

"Darling," he said, "when I was in college there was a huge fellow who lived in the same house as I did. His name was Alvin. He was a mountain of a man, must have been six foot eight, and very muscular. He was a cretin, and also a thief. One day I discovered that a few hundred dollars—which was all the money I had at the time—was missing from my room. I was sure Alvin had stolen it. So do you know what I did?"

"You left it alone and let him keep the money?"

"No."

"You confronted him?"

"No," my father said. "Not exactly."

"Dad, what did you do?"

"I put a note in his room that said I knew he took the money and that if he simply returned it I would leave it alone and never speak of it again."

"And?" I asked.

"And what?"

"And so what happened with the money?"

"To be honest, darling, I don't really remember."

"Dad," I said, "you are developing an alarming habit of telling stories that don't apply in any way to the circumstances."

He chuckled gently again.

"Maybe you're right," he said. "Maybe I'm getting old. But now I'll tell you what I said to Robert when he called me earlier today."

I wasn't sure I wanted to hear it, whatever it was. I closed my eyes.

"I told your husband that in my life I have been lucky in many things, but that the luckiest I have been is that I never ran up against you, Samantha, in a board room. You would have scared me to death, because you, darling, are the only person in my life tougher than I am."

I couldn't stop the tears now, and I didn't bother to try.

"Why did you say that?" I asked.

"For the best reason anyone ever says anything," my father said. "Because it's the truth."

"I want to get my marriage annulled, Dad," I said. "Will you help me?"

"I think that is the best idea you've had in a very long time. Robert is an ambitious man, Samantha. I recognize that quality in him because I used to be an ambitious man myself. Maybe I still am one, to some degree. What he saw in you was the right wife for whatever it is he thinks he's going to be someday, governor or president or wherever he hopes his ambition will lead him. You have the right background, the right family, the right looks. I don't blame him for wanting to marry you."

He paused for a moment.

"The problem, darling, is that Robert is an asshole. And that is an issue that was eventually going to be insurmountable. Your figuring it out quickly is probably the best thing that could have happened."

I laughed a little. "Thanks, Dad," I said. "I think I'm going to stay in Hawaii for a while."

"Sounds nice," he said. "It's nighttime here, darling. First thing in the morning I'll have lawyers on a plane, they'll be there tomorrow to handle everything. They'll make sure to get everything you left behind, and replace anything that may be missing."

"I'm going to be fine, Dad," I said. I meant it.

"I know that," he said. "Call me tomorrow. And if Robert shows up looking for you, my advice is to kick him in the nuts as hard as you possibly can."

"I love you, Dad," I said.

"I love you, too."

I'm twenty-eight years old, and I've never really felt close to my father. He is such a powerful man, and rather than admire that, as many little girls do, I resented it. My father never made me feel like I was the most important person in his life. He was always at a meeting or on the phone or coming home just before my bedtime, in time for me to put my arms around his enormous shoulders and give him a kiss and then scoot off to bed before I could bother him at the end of a long day. Maybe that's what appealed to me about Robert. He's another one who is always on the phone or at a meeting, and maybe he spent more time with me than my father did because I was of greater use to him than I was to my dad. Maybe I married him because he reminded me of my father.

None of that is too much fun to think about.

But here's the good news. As of this moment, I am free. I am in paradise, and all I want to do is exercise and soak in the sun and the salt in the air. I don't need a husband to do any of that, and I don't need to be the little girl whose father didn't want her either. Today, when I *really* needed him, my father was there. That counts. It doesn't make up for everything, but it makes a difference.

And so, I waved to the manager to ask for a room and another plate of fruit. I felt wonderful. And I hadn't stopped crying yet, but I was really sure that once I did everything was going to be all right.

KATHERINE

I WOULDN'T SAY I'M looking for a man.

I wouldn't let *you* say I am, either. It aggravates me to no end to answer questions about the lack of men—or a man—in my life. It isn't as though my world is incomplete because I do not share it with a man, nor do I feel a husband would validate anything about me. I am a smart, successful, single woman and I am wholly unapologetic about that. I don't need to explain myself to the men I compete with professionally, nor to the happy wives I encounter regularly—those bejeweled and be-Birkined grown-up sorority girls who compete with each other over matters like which summer camps their children attend. And I *certainly* don't need to explain myself to my mother, who is in no position to lecture anyone on the subject of marriage. The truth is, I have everything I need in life and what I do not have I am more than capable of supplying myself.

Which is not to suggest it wouldn't be nice to have someone to share it with. Of course it would. It would be lovely to be checking my watch late in the business day, smiling wickedly because tonight is my birthday and I know *he* has something devilish cooked up for me. It would be heavenly to come home to a dimly lit room, an open bottle and two glasses sparkling on the table, Billie Holiday singing in the background. Those would be delightful. Frankly, it would just be nice to have someone ask me how my day was and actually care about the answer. The only people who ever ask me about my day work for me.

But that's it.

What I do not accept is the antiquated notion that somehow I am less of a woman—or less of a person—because I do not have a man in my life. It is not as though I have never been with a man. I have been with more than my share, both before and after Phillip, and aside from the time I Maced one who wanted to marry me there have been very few catastrophes.

That came during the era I refer to as BP (Before Phillip). I was quite a different girl then, not only because I was so young but because I had the common girlish belief that men came in an endless supply. I may not have been the prettiest girl but I did all right—I always have; I've always known just the ways to hide the worst and accentuate the best, just where to wrap a sweater, or drape a scarf, or toss a ponytail. I knew how to be coy, how to be flirtatious without betraying the air of standoffishness any girl worth her salt can carry. I could carry that air with the very best of them, even the very prettiest, and I was always very bright, which in the time of BP was generally received by boys as an attractive quality. (I have found that the older men get the less interested they are in your intellect, which years ago I assumed would be the reverse. It seems to me the more confident a man becomes in himself the more he should welcome the challenge of an intelligent woman. Some part of that assumption is obviously flawed. Maybe it's the part about men becoming more confident as they grow older. I'm not sure.)

Anyway, I had my share of boys tell me they liked me in high school, and then in college I had one tell me he loved me. That was Christian, the boy I Maced. I do regret that; not that I wish I'd married him, but the poor guy didn't deserve to be temporarily blinded. All he ever did was love and deflower me and I was a willing participant in both of those, even if I didn't ever really consider marrying him. I told him I did, though, perhaps because I was eighteen, and when you're eighteen and someone is talking about forever, you naturally assume they don't really mean it, because next Thursday feels like an eternity from now.

I met Christian at a fraternity party, wearing a baseball cap backward and holding a plastic cup spilling over with stale beer. (I should be clear: *he* was wearing the ball cap and holding the beer. I was wearing a pale blue sweater set and holding a Coach bag.) He was handsome and huge, a lovable lug in a football player's body, only he didn't play football; he didn't play much of anything when he didn't have to. He was raised by an alpha-male father, who only wanted his boy to be a jock and never appreciated his genius. Christian hid his intelligence the way you might cover a scar on your face; he caked makeup over it in the form of drunken tomfoolery, varsity wrestling, and overall goofiness. But every now and again, the makeup would smudge and the scar would show beneath it. Truthfully, he had a head for numbers unlike any I have encountered even to this day on Wall Street. He was also the top wrestler of his year in the Ivy League despite the fact he never trained and rarely practiced. He had such natural ability he coasted on it; I will always believe he could have been an Olympian had he set his mind to it.

He was attracted to me immediately, I think because I was precisely the sort of girl of whom his father and meathead friends would disapprove. I didn't drink to excess, I didn't use the word "party" as a verb, and I didn't wear jeans so tight I had to lie down to zip them up. We dated casually for a time, beginning in my freshman year (he was two years ahead of me), and then became more serious. He was my first lover and he knew that, and he was very tender and kind the first time, grinning clumsily through the whole thing and constantly asking if I was all right. I cared deeply for him but was certainly not in love with him, though I told him I was when he professed his love to me, mostly because he took to saying it all the time and it would have been rude and uncomfortable not to respond in kind. I never imagined I would break his heart. I always envisioned us parting tearfully after his graduation and then remembering each other fondly, perhaps meeting by chance ten years later and shacking up for a weekend if neither of us was married.

The day before he graduated, I had final exams to finish and was thinking of him already in the past tense. I lived in an apartment off-campus by myself, and unbeknown to me, Christian befriended my superintendent and persuaded him to unlock my apartment while I was out taking my last exam (Twentieth-century American Literature; we read *The Great Gatsby*). I came home relieved and ready to spend one final night with my boyfriend. The last thing I was expecting was to find anyone in the apartment, even if that someone was kneeling just inside the door, holding a ring in one hand and a bouquet of roses in the other. All I recognized when I pushed open the door was a person where a person ought not to be, and instinctively I reached for my bottle of Mace. I think Christian was either professing his eternal love or he was on the verge of doing so; either way, he wasn't focused enough on what I was doing to avoid the spray aimed directly into his eyes. It was around the moment he hit the ground, his howl of pain still echoing, that I realized who he was and what he was trying to do. Needless to say, it wasn't the neatest of breakups. His eyes were bright red from the Mace *before* I turned down his proposal of marriage, but to this day I've never been quite certain where in his eyes the crying ended and the Mace began.

So that was the boy who wanted to marry me. There have been any number of others who came later, after Phillip, when I was no longer quite so certain of my footing, and I suppose I'd have to admit I've occasionally allowed myself to occupy a place in relationships that I'm not so proud of. Let me give you a few examples and you tell me if these sound like a woman whose self-esteem is in the right place.

There was Alan, who dumped me in couples therapy. Somehow, it hadn't occurred to me that being in couples therapy before we were even engaged should have been a sign.

Henry was adorable. I once cooked dinner for him and he arrived, broke up with me, and then asked if he could still stay for dinner and perhaps watch a bit of television until the traffic died away, and I let him.

Jack was even worse. I tried to end it with him one evening while we were out for dinner. Tearfully, he talked me out of it. Then we went home and had sex, and then he told me I was probably right and we should break up.

But none of them hurt the way Phillip hurt. Hell, all of them put together didn't hurt the way he did. And to have to see him now, as I do every day, is sometimes more than I think I can bear. I suppose that's why I start every morning with the words "fuck him." I assume healthy, well-adjusted people have a more optimistic way of greeting the new day.

Perhaps tonight will be different. Perhaps this will be better. Perhaps this fellow Marie has arranged for me to meet will be unlike the others. Perhaps we'll have great chemistry and he'll be funny and smart and handsome, though that's the least of it for me so long as he's not repugnant. If I can tolerate the sight and scent of him (if he smells, it's over) he doesn't have to look like Pierce Brosnan. In fact, I think I'd prefer he did not. If he looked like Pierce Brosnan, I would spend every moment we were in public acutely aware of everyone wondering why this guy who looks like Pierce Brosnan isn't with a woman who looks like Sandra Bullock. I would be wondering myself. There *is* such a thing as being too good-looking, as far as I'm concerned. You can't be too rich but you can be too handsome.

Maybe this one will look more like Matthew Broderick (so funny) or Denis Leary (so manly) or Stephen Colbert (I know I am not the only one who is attracted to him). And he'll be sweet and smart, and appreciate how hard I work, and maybe he'll love old movies and Italian food, and he'll drink dry vodka martinis and wear elegant suits and just a hint of facial hair, not a beard or anything, maybe just long sideburns or a neatly trimmed goatee. Maybe he'll be hugely successful and we'll be a power couple, and he'll send me naughty texts during a break between meetings in Hong Kong, telling me all the fun things he's going to do with me when he comes home.

Maybe the start of a new decade will really be a new beginning for me. Maybe forty will be my new thirty, or better yet the thirty I missed out on because I was moping over Phillip. Maybe this night will be one I always remember, a night that changes my life. Those were the thoughts going through my mind, and really those are the worst possible thoughts to have, headed into a blind date. How much more pressure could you possibly place on someone you have never met than to expect him to change your entire life? Unrealistic, unproductive, unreasonable, and yet that's where my head was all the while that José was blowing out my hair, and then while Anastasia was making me up, and then still as I selected from my wardrobe (Chanel lambskin blouse and fantasy fur pants, Christian Louboutin Madame Butterfly booties, Christian Dior Chantilly Lace coat). There was a tremble in my stomach when Maurice shut the door to the car, and as we began downtown, I poured myself a short glass of Chardonnay from a bottle I'd grabbed from the fridge upstairs. I caught a glimpse of myself in the rearview mirror and raised the glass in a toast.

"Get a hold of yourself," I said to my reflection. "He's only a man and it's only your birthday. There'll be plenty more of both to come."

I was finishing my second glass when we pulled up to the restaurant. My watch said it was four minutes past eight, which meant I had two minutes to kill. I have always believed in arriving six minutes early for a business meeting and six minutes late for a date. In both cases, I like the message it sends.

"You ready to go?" Maurice asked.

"Of course," I said. "Why wouldn't I be ready?"

"I dunno," he said. "I just haven't seen you like this in a while."

"You mean *this* glamorous?" I asked grandly.

"I mean *this* nervous."

I had hoped it wasn't that obvious. "Don't be ridiculous, I am *not* nervous."

He didn't say anything.

"Maurice," I whined, "I'm serious. I am *not.*"

"Whatever you say, boss," he said with a disapproving sniff. "You ready to get out?"

"Yes, I am," I said, and downed the rest of the wine.

He came around quickly and opened my door. The air rushed in. It was a windy night, and I instinctively raised my hand to protect my hair. There was something exciting about the briskness of the air, the darkness of the evening falling across Manhattan.

"I'll be here," Maurice said as I stepped past.

I tapped him on the cheek. "Take the rest of the night off," I said. "I'll see you in the morning."

"What are you talking about? How will you get home?"

"There *are* taxis, you know," I said. "Perhaps you haven't heard, Maurice, but not every person in New York has a driver."

"Don't do it, Katherine," he said. "Don't get cute on me."

"What are you talking about?" I glanced at my watch. It was six minutes past eight o'clock, time to go in. "How am I getting cute?"

"You know what I'm talking about," he said. "When I pick you up tomorrow morning you better not still be wearing this same outfit, if you know what I mean."

I laughed. "Maurice, as of today I am officially an old lady. If I want to have tawdry, meaningless sex with a stranger, that's exactly what I'm going to do." I winked and gave him a quick peck on the cheek. "Keep your fingers crossed. I'll see you in the morning."

"Go get him," Maurice said, and then he was back in the car, out of the wind.

I paused in front of the restaurant and took a deep, cleansing breath.

May I be filled with loving-kindness
May I be well
May I be peaceful and at ease
May I be happy

Then I pushed through the revolving door and before my eyes had even adjusted to the light I saw the blue suit making a beeline for me. My date smiled warmly as he approached, striding confidently through the crowd, extending his hand to shake mine.

"Oh my god," I said softly. "You have *got* to be kidding me."

BROOKE

"YOU HAVE *GOT* TO be kidding me!" I said, when Pamela said the telephone was for me.

I had left very specific instructions only to call in case of an emergency. Apparently, whatever I was about to be told rose to that level, at least in Pamela's mind, and in that of Lourdes, my babysitter. I was *so* not ready to take that phone call. Not because I was afraid of what she might say. I was just so *into* what Pamela and I were doing.

All my life, I have associated sex with romance, with art, with gentleness and quiet. The musical accompaniment, in my mind, has always been classical: Mozart is sexy, Tchaikovsky is sexy. Beethoven is not. Beethoven wrote music to march to. Mozart wrote music to make love to. I even use those words all the time; Scott and I could sneak downstairs while the kids are watching television and do it with me bent over the washing machine and I would still describe it as making love. And that is all well and good, making love always has and always will have its place. But as of today, I realize it is not the only option. There is a rock-'n'-roll way of going about this as well. There is a Rolling Stones, AC/DC, Quiet Riot way of going about it. I didn't actually have sex with anyone today, but while I was rocking out—fully naked—with Pamela snapping photos and shouting encouragement and offering the occasional shot of tequila, there is no doubt in my mind I had an orgasm. It was in my mind and in my spirit, but let me tell you, it was every bit as good as having one anywhere else.

Pamela felt it too. "I feel like we're fucking!" she shouted to me, over the whir of a blowing fan and Janis Joplin's scratchy vocals.

The truth is, I never use that word. Not in that context, anyway. I use the F-word, occasionally, as an expletive. *What the fuck happened to my car keys? What a fucking mess Megan's room is. I really don't give a fuck how big her earrings are.* Those are all perfectly acceptable usages. But just to say *We're fucking?* I would never, not in a million years. How graphic, vulgar. How *ugly* that sounds to me.

Or it did until today. Today was different. Today, when Pamela said it, and as I let it rattle around in my mind, it didn't sound dirty anymore. It sounded sexy.

So that's what I learned today, about sex and about myself. I learned that sex doesn't have to be sweet and romantic. It doesn't have to be about love, at least not all the time. Sex can be about power, and rock 'n' roll. It can be about fucking. Sometimes that's okay.

Then my phone rang.

Again, I had given strict instructions to Lourdes not to call unless there was an emergency. Had the phone rung and her number appeared after three o'clock, I would have been concerned, but it was only noon when she called. The kids were still in school. Had anything happened to them, the school would be calling, not Lourdes.

"Answer this, please," I said to Pamela, tossing her the phone. "Unless it's a true emergency I don't even want to know why she's calling."

Pamela answered the phone and I started to dance. I did not want to let the moment get away. I liked it here, in this sexy, boozy, rockin' reality.

"Sweetie, I think you need to take this," Pamela said, a funny look on her face.

I flopped down on the couch and crossed my arms over my chest. "You have *got* to be kidding me," I said, pouting. Pamela tossed the phone over and it landed on my bare thigh. I picked it up.

"Hello?"

"Mrs. Brooke!" It was Lourdes and she was shouting. "I am in the emergency room!"

I sat up, suddenly sober despite a bellyful of Patrón.

"What happened?" I asked.

"I was cleaning and a Wiggles bobblehead fell off a shelf and I think it broke my toe!"

"Oh my gosh, which one?"

"I think it was Jeff!"

"No, I mean which toe?"

She was distracted then. I heard voices. Someone else was speaking to her.

"What's that, Mrs. Brooke?" she asked.

"I said I want to know which toe is broken, not which Wiggle fell on it."

Lourdes didn't answer. She was distracted again. I heard the voices in the background.

"Lourdes," I said, more loudly. "Are you all right?"

"Mrs. Brooke, they are calling me in to see the doctor," she said. "I'm sorry but I won't be able to pick the kids up at school!"

And then the line went dead. I could feel tears welling in my eyes as I looked up and found, to my surprise, that Pamela was crying too.

"You have to go, don't you," she said. She pulled a woolen blanket off an armchair and spread it over me, then plopped down beside me on the couch. "Damn, that was fun."

I laughed a little. "Thank you," I said, and kissed her on the cheek.

"Thank *you*," she replied.

I sat up and shook my head. I needed to drive, to get my kids, to be myself again.

"Let me get your clothes," Pamela said, and ran her fingers through my hair.

"Hey," I said, "I just need one other thing."

"What's that, darling?"

I looked directly into her smiling eyes. "Do you have a cigarette for me?" I asked. "I quit years ago, but after this I definitely think I need one."

SAMANTHA ▣ ▣ ▣

"NO, THANK YOU," I said, as Eduardo Marquez offered me a cigarette. "I don't smoke." We had just ordered dinner, and I couldn't figure out if I was on a date here. Or if I wanted to be.

"Will it disturb you if I do?" he asked.

"Not at all," I said, though it wasn't really true. I never could stand the smell of smoke, not even from a fireplace. Some people find a roaring fire cozy in the wintertime, not me. I can't stand the smell of the smoke in my clothes, in my hair. And as for cigarettes or cigars—nothing could be more repulsive. (Robert insisted I take a puff of his victory cigar the night of the election and it almost ruined my evening.) However, there was something debonair in the way Eduardo drew a cigarette from the case in his jacket pocket, and something of a flourish in the way he brandished his lighter. It was a cool lighter, stainless steel or perhaps silver, thick and solid-looking with a Spanish word I didn't recognize engraved in the handle, perhaps a name. Whose name would he have engraved in his lighter? A wife? A girlfriend? Did he have either of those? Was I on a date?

"It is a habit I solemnly regret," he said, "but one I will never leave behind."

"How old were you when you started?"

"Nine years old," he said, and laughed gently at the look of horror I'm sure was on my face. "Yes, it is horrible. But there wasn't a boy who didn't smoke when I was in school."

"I grew up in Connecticut," I said. "I remember some kids started smoking when we were about twelve or thirteen. Nine years old, that's just crazy."

"I never thought a thing of it until I came to live in the States. Last year I was in Madrid and I lit a cigarette for a pregnant woman in a restaurant. She was quite far along. After living in America for so long, I hesitated to do it."

"I would hope so."

"But I thought to myself that if I did not, surely she would find someone else who would. The cigarette was dangling from her lips. It would have been rude of me to pull it out, so I decided to light it for her instead."

He dragged gently on the cigarette. His fingers were long and slender.

"It seems to me a shame that you have spent four weeks on the island now and seen nothing of it," he said. "It is admirable to see how dedicated you have been in your training, and I have no doubt this has been fine therapy for the personal difficulties of which you informed me on the day you arrived, but I cannot imagine you don't have some time to experience the sights and culture of the island."

"Have I really been here four weeks?" It felt as though I had arrived yesterday, and perhaps dreamt the rest of it.

"As of tomorrow, yes."

"It has flown by, really flown," I said. "Our breakfasts have been a lovely part of that."

Every morning since that first one, without fail, I have begun my day with a swim in the ocean. I am in the water by six o'clock and usually for more than an hour. Then I trudge up the beach and fall into a comfortable chair by the pool, where I inform a waiter (most days the same one with the pleasant smile from my first day) that I am ready for my tea and granola and ask him to please alert *Señor* Marquez that I am safe. This began my second morning on the property, when Eduardo told me it was strictly prohibited for me to be in the ocean so early, because there was no lifeguard on duty.

"Let me ask you this," I said to him that day. "If you catch me doing it, what is the punishment?"

"I beg your pardon?"

"I mean, I'm sure I can't go to jail for swimming alone when no lifeguard is on duty. I couldn't be arrested or anything. Could I be thrown out of the hotel?"

"That would be at the discretion of the general manager," he said.

"Aren't *you* the general manager?"

"*Sí, señora.*"

"So, Mr. Marquez, are you going to throw me out of the hotel if I go swimming by myself every morning?"

He hesitated. "Certainly not," he said. "I do not condone it but I will allow it, on one strict condition."

"What is that?"

"Every morning when you are finished, your first obligation is to see that I am informed immediately of your safe return."

I stuck out my hand, and he shook it gently. "We have a deal," I said.

And so, every morning I order my breakfast and I make sure Eduardo Marquez is aware of my return. And every morning, without fail, he has appeared a few minutes later and joined me, uninvited, for breakfast.

"It has been my pleasure every morning," he said tonight, puffing contentedly on his cigarette, politely holding it as far from me as he could. "I look forward to it every day."

"I do too," I said.

And I realized, to my surprise, that I was thinking about what it would be like to be in bed with him. I wondered if he was thinking about it too. I couldn't tell, which was strange. Was I just out of practice? It's not as though I was married for thirty years, I was barely married for thirty hours. And I was only *with* Robert for a few months before that. It seems hard to believe, but a year ago at this time I was completely single, wholly unattached, being actively pursued by two or three men of varying significance. Surely a year ago I had no trouble detecting any man's intentions, or his level of interest, or determining whether or not I was on a date.

"On second thought, I think I *will* have a glass of wine," I said, having declined at the start of the evening. I've not had a sip of alcohol this whole month. My every second has been consumed with preparation, training, but all of a sudden a glass of wine sounded really good. "Something dry and crisp."

"I know just the glass," he said, raising his hand for the waiter.

Of course he did. He is one of *those* men. If you think about it, you can pretty much divide men into categories based upon what they drink and how much they know about it. There are beer guys, and we all know who they are: fun, fraternity guys with baseball caps on backward, meeting you for dinner after a softball game. There are whiskey guys, who take themselves very seriously and—whether they acknowledge it or not—are the most misogynistic of all the drinkers. Men who drink gin are very straitlaced, men who drink vodka are very deep, and men who drink champagne are usually very gay. And then there are men like Eduardo Marquez, who drink wine and know a great deal about it. I've never been with one of those before. I was raised by a scotch-drinker, married a beer-drinker, dated all of the others, including the champagne-drinker (*yes*, he was gay), but I've never spent any real time with a wine man.

Until tonight.

"Marco," Eduardo said, "bring a bottle of the '88 from the cellar beneath my office."

"Oh," I said, holding out my hand to stop him, "just a glass for me, please."

"If that is all you want that is no problem," he said, and sent the waiter off with a wave, "but if you are only going to try one bottle from our list, this is the choice."

"I assume you don't usually sell it by the glass," I said.

"You assume correctly."

I batted my eyes at him and smiled. My goodness, look at me, making eyes at a man ten years older than the man I married, who himself was too old for me. Strange, too, because there isn't anything about Eduardo that would normally appeal to me. He isn't athletic or headstrong, or arrogant. Maybe this was just about the moment, the island and the breeze and the sound of the ocean, or maybe my hormones were in overdrive from all the training, or maybe I was just a mess from all that has happened. Or maybe, just maybe, I was finally getting smarter. I have to believe that's a possibility, too.

KATHERINE

I GUESS IT ISN'T true that we get smarter as we get older.

At least, it isn't in my case.

After all, here I am, forty years old, and I am still stupid enough to imagine I can be fixed up by a little hottie in my office and have it turn out as anything other than horrific. And embarrassing. And insulting. And just plain sad.

I felt all of those emotions as I entered the restaurant and greeted, with my firmest handshake, the man I had been arranged to meet. His name was Ken Walker. He was tall, which was nice, and his suit was exquisite, power blue with a faint verdant pinstripe, and a silver tie and unmatched pocket square. His hair was silver, too, full and thick and neatly parted, as though he had just run a comb through it while waiting for me to arrive. His hands were strong and his palms callused but his nails clean—regular manicures probably—but the rough hands signaled golf or weightlifting. He seemed terrific, actually, in so many ways, there was really only one obvious problem, but it was a big one, especially on this of all nights.

Ken Walker *had* to be sixty years old.

At minimum.

With a little Botox, self-tanner, and the right trainer, he might actually be closer to seventy.

You've got to be kidding me.

The small-talk portion of the evening was a total blur. I couldn't tell you now where he works, though I know he's a lawyer, or where he grew up, though I know he moved to New York after college, or, for that matter, which college he attended. He told me he was divorced, which I already knew, and that he lived near the park, which I knew as well. He told me how fond he is of my assistant, Marie, and I noticed a paternal manner when he spoke of her, which infuriated me. For crying out loud, Marie is smoking hot with tits out-to-*here*, but this old bastard acts as though she is the daughter he never had.

I wasn't really listening to Ken, in part because I was replaying in my mind the conversation I'd had with Marie that morning in my office. The one in which I allowed myself to be talked into this calamity, this date with Kirk Douglas. When she had described him to me, hadn't she said: "He is about the right age"? I think she did. And that begs two questions. How old does she think this guy is? And, more disturbing, how old does she think I am?

What thoughts, I ask you, could possibly be more depressing than those?

BROOKE

WHAT, I ASK, COULD be more depressing than racing home from a nude rock 'n' roll photo shoot to sober up in time for your kids to come home?

I have to admit I was feeling a little sorry for myself when I pulled my car out of Pamela's driveway, with a raincoat draped over my shoulders and the seat belt strapped between my boobs. I don't get too many chances to let loose, and when I do it's usually *so* choreographed. For example, I might get invited to a particular event and think: "That's a night when I'll really party hard." Or Scott might make arrangements for us to have a suite in a fancy hotel, and he'll say: "That night, we're going to act like we're back in college." And all that is well and good, and it's fun, but the truth is that if we *were* in college we would do a lot less talking about it. I remember so many nights that began innocently at the library and ended with a cute boy I hardly knew feeling me up.

The point of it all is that I had no intention or expectation that this photo shoot would turn out to be such a tequila-drenched, rocking good time, and *that* contributed greatly to how much fun it was. And now, I thought, as I inched home slowly, because the idea of being pulled over drunk and practically nude scared me to death, it was over because of a Wiggles bobblehead doll.

The irony of *that* is, my husband and my kids make fun of me for keeping those around. We still have dozens of them, even though my children lost interest in the Wiggles years ago. But I keep toys from every stage of their lives. Every Christmas, the kids go through their old toys and pick out some to bring to the church, because it is important for them to understand how lucky they are, that not all kids have toys to play with at Christmas, much less *too many* toys. And then, whatever does not go to the church, I save.

I still have all the puzzles we used to sit on the floor and put together. I still have the stuffed animals Megan couldn't dream of going to sleep without. I still have all the books I used to read to them in bed (*Goodnight Moon*, *The Very Hungry Caterpillar*, *The Going to Bed Book*). I would no sooner throw those away than I would old photos. They aren't simple playthings, they are snapshots of moments in my life I will never have again, moments I never want to forget: my babies being babies, needing me for everything, wanting nothing more than to spend endless time with their mother.

So, just before I got underneath a long, hot shower to complete the task of sobering up so I could pick up the kids and take them to visit Lourdes and her toe in the hospital, I stopped to look at some of those books and toys. And, as I always do, I got a little teary. And then, as the shower spray brought me fully back to life, I started to laugh. And I stopped being sad about having to leave the photo shoot. Some things just matter more than others.

SAMANTHA ▣ ▣ ▣

WHAT IN THE WORLD is wrong with me?

That's what I was thinking as I allowed Eduardo to pour my third glass of wine.

Here I had been training nonstop, filling my body only with the purest fuel, the most natural and delicious and healthful foods in this tropical paradise: fresh fruits, vegetables, lean meats, gallons of water, steaming cups of organic green tea. But now this wine tasted so good, and felt so good going down, so warm in my chest and throat. And it mixed beautifully with the breeze and the saltwater smell of the ocean, and with the man who had known enough to select it and poured it for me so gracefully. There was something athletic in the deftness of Eduardo's fingers, something very sensual in the care he took with the smallest of tasks. It reminded me of a cat, while Robert—and every other man I've been with—is so much more a dog, panting, eager, dopey, clumsy. I've always preferred dogs to cats, but now as I savored the wine on my tongue and felt the breeze in my hair, I found myself intrigued by the cat.

"It seems to me that women in this country apply so much pressure to themselves," Eduardo was saying. He was sitting with his back straight and his tie perfectly knotted. "It is unfortunate. This country gives women freedoms they do not possess anywhere else in the world, at least nowhere that my travels have taken me, and yet instead of rejoicing in those freedoms it seems sometimes American women are strangling themselves with them."

"In what way?" I asked, interested.

"In every way," Eduardo said. "I see them here every single day. Beautiful American women on their honeymoons, on holidays, on family vacations. The women invariably seem to be enjoying themselves less than the men. The women are so concerned with their appearance, so concerned with their image, so competitive among themselves, at times I worry they are not enjoying themselves at all."

"But you're wrong," I said. "I have been here for a month and all I have done is train, and I am having the *most* wonderful time."

There was a mischievous twinkle in his eye. "Yes, but it seems to me your situation is a little bit different, is it not?"

"In what way?" I asked, even though I knew the answer. I was curious to hear how he would phrase it.

"Well, you are seeking to accomplish a very specific goal. In your triathlon, someone will be a winner, and all who finish will have achieved something special. The way I see these American women competing with each other and with themselves, there are no winners, there are only varying degrees of defeat. The expectations they place on themselves are unrealistic and, I believe, harmful. American women are more successful, accomplished, intelligent, and beautiful than the women of any other country, if only they themselves could figure that out."

"Come on," I said, "I've been to Spain, to Italy, to France, there is no way you can say that American women are more stylish and beautiful than European women."

"I can say it, yes I can," he replied, nodding slowly. "And I suppose I could also say that you just made my point for me."

For the life of me I could not remember how we got onto the subject in the first place. What I found myself thinking was that underneath his suit Eduardo might not be so muscly, which might be a nice change of pace. Robert was so firm, his arms, his chest, his legs, and I have always thought I liked that; I'm an athletic woman, why wouldn't I be attracted to athletic men? But something about this man seemed like it might be pleasing in a different way. Maybe he wouldn't be quite so hard in all the places Robert was, maybe he wouldn't be so hairy, either. Maybe he'd have smooth skin, like that of a woman, and it would be soft against mine. Maybe, too, he would make love the way he speaks, gently and elegantly, unlike Robert, whose lovemaking was volatile and loud. Robert made love like it was a competition, which for him I think it was. One time I thought I heard him counting, as though he was trying to kill two birds with one stone and combine our sex with a workout for his abs. Having sex with Robert was all about him; he initiated it, he dictated how we would do it, and when he finished, it was over. Maybe with Eduardo it would be, at least partly, about me.

To my surprise, I had butterflies as I watched him sign our bill with an elegant pen he took from his breast pocket. Then he sent the waiter away with a wave of his hand. Our dinner was finished, the bottle of wine empty in the center of the table.

"This was a pleasure," he said, with a smile that seemed to glow in the light of the candle. "Thank you for spending such a lovely evening with me."

"The pleasure was mine," I said noncommittally. That was my plan, to be noncommittal. Whatever was going to happen was going to be instigated by him.

"May I assume you will be training in the early morning hours, as usual?" he asked.

"You may."

He nodded and then glanced at his watch. "Then we should be getting you back to your room," he said. "May I escort you?"

"You may," I said.

And escort me he did, that was the perfect word. He stood and buttoned his sport coat, then extended his elbow and I took it, and he led me through the hotel like a bride down the aisle. Neither of us spoke as we waited for the elevator, or as the doors closed and then opened on my floor, nor on the entire walk down the long hallway to my room. Once there, he gently lowered his elbow and spun formally on his heel to face me.

"Once again, this evening has been my great pleasure," he said. "I hope that we will have the chance to do it again before you leave the island."

And he took my hand and squeezed it, firmly, between his two, and then he slowly raised it to his lips and kissed me ever-so-gently on the palm.

"Good night," he said, with a shallow bow, and then he turned and made his way slowly back toward the elevator.

My breath caught in the back of my throat as I watched him the whole way. I did not move until I heard the bell ring, signifying the arrival of the elevator. And I listened as the doors opened and then shut again, and I stood in silence a long moment after that, waiting for footsteps that never came.

"My lord," I said and sighed. "That was by far *the* best handshake I ever had."

I fished my room key from my bag and pushed open the door. Once inside, I stopped in front of the full mirror. I looked terrific. My hair was windblown but it looked nice that way, especially with the dark tan I had developed. My arms looked especially good, thinner than at any time I could remember, and tight. I don't think I ever looked better, or at least I don't recall ever feeling better about the way I looked.

And then there was a gentle knock at the door and my heart jumped.

There isn't any question why he'd have returned. Nor was there any question that I wanted him to. It felt right. I turned very slowly and crossed the room, hesitated as I put my hand on the knob, but only for a moment, and then took a deep breath and pulled it open.

And just as quickly as it had settled, my breath froze in my chest. And my smile disappeared, and all of the warmth and softness and vibrancy and light drained from my body. I felt my eyes well up and I had to tighten my throat to keep the tears from overflowing, and I had no idea what I should do or what I should say or how I should feel. For the man I found in the hallway was the last man in the world I had expected. It wasn't Eduardo Marquez at all.

It was Robert.

 KATHERINE

"I MUST SAY, I have never been quite so surprised in my life."

About half of my blind date with the senior citizen had passed before I began to pay any real attention to what he was saying. I was so taken aback by his age, and so devastated by what it implied, that appetizers and cocktails were merely a blur. Ken Walker was having a conversation with me, and at the same time I was having a conversation with me, and if at any time two people are talking to you and one of them is yourself, then that discussion is always going to win out. As a consequence, I couldn't tell you nearly anything about the man or about what he had been telling me until around the time my second martini began to soak in.

I love martinis. I take vodka, always, extra dry, straight up with olives. I love olives. Hell, I love *everything* about a martini. I love the feel of the glass. I love when the icy coating on the stem begins to melt and leaves condensation on your fingers. A martini is like a naughty girl, all dressed up and clean but filled with secrets to tell when the moment is right.

For me, a martini can solve almost any problem, and whatever problem one cannot overcome can always be slain by a second one. The second martini of the night usually comes near the end for me, as I can hardly handle a third. But on this night, with Ken Walker blathering on about god knows what across the table, I was finishing my second drink before the entrées had been served.

" . . . And I've never been so surprised," he was saying as I tuned back in, and I realized this was probably as interesting a moment to jump back in as I was going to get.

"I'm sorry, you've never been so surprised by what?" I asked.

"By his gayness, I suppose," he said.

Well, that was quite a surprise. That's also a tough one to dance around. I couldn't think of any way to avoid asking whom he was talking about, so I did the next best thing.

"I'm sorry," I said, folding my napkin, "would you excuse me a moment? I'm just going to run to the ladies' room."

He stood up as I did, which I must confess I liked. Those sorts of manners appeal to me, especially because I am usually so vigilant in guarding against them. Ninety percent of my interaction with men is professional, and like all professional women I am always protective of my equal footing. I don't *want* a man to hold the door for me walking into a conference room, I don't *want* him standing up if I do during a meeting, or greeting me with a kiss on the cheek if he's going to shake hands with everybody else. I don't want to be different when I'm working.

But out to dinner, I don't mind if I am.

Anyway, I didn't really have any need to be in the ladies' room but I needed to kill a minute or two, so I checked my face, and as I did only one thought was in my head.

What the *fuck* is it Marie sees that makes her think I'm so much older?

My skin looks fabulous, even around my eyes. I don't see wrinkles, bags, crow's-feet, dark circles, lines, frames, spots, or blemishes, and I haven't even had anything done yet. I haven't had my eyes done, lips done, nose done, ears pinned, or jowls pulled back. I haven't used Restylane, Botox, Juvederm, Latisse, or even a chemical peel. I'm sure someday I'll start getting all that help, and that will be fabulous. But for now I'm looking damn good, no matter what Marie seems to think.

So I was feeling better about myself when I returned to the table, and when Ken again rose from his seat I found myself in a much better mood.

"I'm sorry about that," I said. "Now, let's start that story over again. I don't want to miss any of it."

He smiled. "I hadn't seen Chet in twenty years. We grew up together, went to law school together, lived across the street from each other in Scarsdale when I was first married. He moved to Colorado for a professional opportunity in the early nineties, I got divorced shortly after that, and we just sort of lost touch. So, about a month ago, he calls me at the office out of the blue, tells me he's in town, wants to catch up, talk about old times, let's get together for a drink. Sounds like a great idea to me, so we meet at a place down in the Village about two weeks ago. I could tell he looked a little different the moment he walked in. My first impression was that he was wearing makeup, but I put that aside and we started to chat, talking about law school and all that. So then I asked how Barbara was doing, and he gave me this funny look and said, 'You know we haven't been married for fifteen years, don't you?' So I said I didn't know that, and then he got the strangest look in his eye, this glimmer, like a mischievous smile, and he said: 'Also I finally came out of the closet and am currently living with a twenty-nine-year-old man named Evan.'"

Ken paused a moment, took a sip of his martini, and then went on.

"Well, I didn't know what to say. I've never been quite so surprised in my life."

"What part of it surprised you?" I asked.

"Well, first, just that he was gay, I never suspected that at all. Not that it makes any difference to me."

"Yeah, not that there's anything wrong with that," I said, and laughed.

He didn't seem to get it.

"You know," I said, "from *Seinfeld*."

"Oh," he said. "I've never seen a single episode of that show."

Wait a minute. Who the hell has never seen a single episode of *Seinfeld*? Was Ken Walker too old to have watched *Seinfeld*? Should I be making Dick Van Dyke references?

"At any rate," he went on, "I couldn't just sit there speechless so I asked him what his boyfriend was like. And he said: 'Well, the sex is fantastic but the age difference can be quite challenging.'"

What I wanted to say was "I know exactly what he means." But I did not. Instead, I said, "So, what did you say to that?"

"I said, 'I understand. It must be difficult to spend time with someone who doesn't remember when Kennedy was shot.'"

That was the last straw. Was Ken Walker now suggesting that I remember Kennedy being shot? I don't remember *either* Kennedy being shot. To me JFK has always been just an airport and a set of initials.

"You know," I said, containing myself, "I don't remember when Kennedy was shot either."

He laughed. "Of course you don't," he said.

Then the food came and we ate, and I ordered a third martini the moment my entrée arrived and finished it before I finished the filet mignon.

In the taxi headed home, after coffee and crème brûlée and his asking for my phone number and me offering a quick kiss on the cheek instead, I called Marie. She answered on the first ring.

"So," she said, "how did it go?"

"Went great," I said, "I may marry him."

"Oh no." She sighed. "What went wrong?"

"Nothing," I said. "I just can't imagine being with someone who has never seen an episode of *Seinfeld*."

"What?"

"Forget it," I said. I had to move past this. "Pack a suitcase, we're going away. I'm taking a vacation and you're coming with me."

"Katherine," Marie said, "you've never taken a vacation in all the time I've worked for you."

"I haven't taken a vacation in a lot longer than that. Pack a bag, sweetheart, we're leaving tomorrow."

"Where are we going?"

"I don't know yet," I said. "We'll figure out the details later."

BROOKE

I LOVE PHOTOGRAPHS.

I always have, from the time I was a little girl. I remember my father taking me one time to the Museum of Modern Art to a photography exhibit. I don't recall the artist—I was only six years old—but I do remember the photos were black-and-white, shot in New Mexico or Arizona, of Native Americans in their daily lives working on farms, pumping water, tending to animals, driving tractors, and I still remember how vivid the faces were. That's what I love about photography, as obvious as it sounds: it's *real*. My mother loves surreal painting, impressionism, Salvador Dalí and René Magritte, all the "out there" artists. That stuff mostly just makes me nervous. A nose is meant to be on a face, not disconnected and hovering overhead, adjoined to a bird's wings. I prefer photos because they tell a story.

That's why I love to look at the pictures I have on the wall that separates my children's bedrooms. They are all black-and-white, and when viewed in sequence they tell the story of my life. Of *our* lives, really, Scott's and the kids' and mine. They begin with Scott and me in college, him with his hair so long and wavy. He loved wearing his hair that way, and he tells me all the time that the day he leaves Wall Street will be the last time he visits a barber for the rest of his life. He's kept his hair so neatly parted and short for so long almost no one we know remembers that flowing mane he used to have, but I do. And I can still see it, on my walls, any time I want. When I do, I can go back to those days when he was wooing me, and he was so sweet and uncertain, wearing thick glasses and denim jackets and black boots. That's the way I remember him.

If you follow the wall, left to right, top to bottom, you follow our journey. Scott and me in Hawaii, when he was afraid to go scuba diving for fear of being eaten by a shark. He kept saying, over and over, before we went down, "All I can hear in my head is the theme from *Jaws*." Then we went down and it wasn't at all scary, at least I didn't think so, even after a tiny fish the size of my thumb took a nibble out of my leg, but Scott saw the blood and was convinced every Great White in the Pacific Ocean was going to smell it and he panicked and almost went too fast back to the surface. The photo I have on the wall is of the two of us after that dive, our hair dripping, wearing wetsuits, Scott drinking his third beer, trying to relax. You can still see the fear in his face. I love that picture.

Then there is the picture of me and a very old man atop the Arc de Triomphe, with the Eiffel Tower in the background. That was our first trip together, Paris in the spring, the year we got married. And Scott asked this old fellow to take our picture but his elementary-school French was so rusty that the old man thought Scott wanted a picture of *him* with me, and it was so funny, the man was really serious about it as he posed with his arm around my waist and his hand directly on my butt. I've never seen a picture where I am laughing as hard as I am in that one.

Then there are the standard photos: the wedding, the baby shower, me holding the twins when they were an hour old, and Scott holding them both over his head, one in each hand, when they were two. There is Scott the day his team rang the opening bell on the floor of the New York Stock Exchange, the four of us fishing on our boat, the two kids simultaneously falling off water skis, and every Halloween costume the kids have ever worn, including the one great year when I talked Scott into dressing up and we went as Batman and Cat Woman and Robin and Bat Girl. We all look awesome in that one.

And so, tonight, I have new photos to show my husband. But they are certainly not going to be displayed where anyone, least of all our children, will ever see them.

The pictures are spectacular. When Pamela brought the contact sheets to my house the day after we took them, I was more nervous than on the day of my wedding. She had the most mischievous look on her face when she came around the side of the house, as though she'd been hiding in the bushes, waiting for the school bus to pull away so she could sneak inside.

"You are going to loooooove these," she said, and pulled a manila envelope out of her ridiculously large handbag. "Are you ready?"

I nodded, and she dropped them on the table. At first I was confused. Pamela has taken pictures for me on at least a half-dozen occasions, and usually she brings over a hundred images to choose from. Here there were only eight. I looked at her and frowned.

"Were the rest so awful you couldn't bear to show me?"

Her smile was filled with reassurance. "Quite the opposite. These, my dear, are perfect. I don't want you going through shot after shot comparing how your naked ass looks in this one versus that. You are so beautiful in these eight pictures it makes me cry."

I picked up the one on top, handling it gingerly, as though it might tear into pieces if it grazed my fingernail. I was in front of a giant window, facing out, and the sun was streaming over me. My face was turned upward into the light. The arch of my back looked sexy and sleek and my breasts were like shadows. It was stunning. My eyes filled with tears as I gently placed the sheet back on the table and lifted the next, in which I was turned away from the camera, standing amid the overflowing collection of potted plants in Pamela's den. My butt looked full and round but not soft. My right hand was reaching out, my fingers caressing the leaves of an orchid, something very sensual in the touching.

"That one is my favorite," Pamela said.

I smiled. "I've always had a great ass," I said.

The rest of the pictures were just as perfect as the first two. Pamela had chosen exactly right. She had known exactly what I wanted them to be and she had nailed it. The photos were sexy, sophisticated, daring, tasteful. They were beautiful.

When I was finished looking at them, I leaned back on the couch. "Pamela, these are precisely as I imagined them. How did you capture exactly what was in my mind?"

"That's what art is, my dear," she said. "It is your imagination come to life."

"But this was *my* imagination," I said. "It's *your* work."

"Is it, Brooke?" she asked. "Look at them again. Who do you see in these images?"

I picked one up, held it close to my face.

"This is your work," she said to me. "It's *your* art. I just pressed the buttons."

KATHERINE

ANOTHER DAY, ANOTHER YEAR older, same greeting for the break of dawn.

Fuck him.

Today, the words have a particularly pungent taste in my mouth, because today I need to talk to Phil. I am always especially aggravated when my day begins in his office, which usually happens two or three times a month and never of my own choosing. In all the years I have been working beneath him, which is well more than ten, today is the first time I've ever called *him* for a meeting.

May I be filled with loving-kindness
May I be well

May I be peaceful and at ease
May I be happy

After the breathing and the protein shake and the heavy sweating on the treadmill, I am at my mirror, contemplating Buddhism and my blind hatred for Phillip. They do not really go together, and yet I believe in them both to the deepest place in my soul. Thic Naht Hahn writes that one of our biggest faults is to fail to celebrate not having a toothache. The idea goes something like this: We all know how painful and irritating it can be to have a toothache, and we all suffer when we do, but why is it we never take time to think how nice it is not to have a toothache?

That's brilliant, I think, and insightful, and it applies to absolutely everything, but it does not answer one fundamental question: What do you do when your toothache never goes away?

I know what you're thinking, and you're right. Phillip isn't a toothache. He may have begun that way, but when we have a toothache we visit the dentist and alleviate the pain. For nearly twenty years now I have been putting off that visit. I could go any time I choose, I could forget about our time together, move past it, work anywhere else for anyone else and never see Phillip again, and yet I do not, and that is no one's fault but my own. In that way, I guess it is less like having a toothache than it is like driving a sharp stick into your own mouth and leaving it there for twenty years, which is a pretty stupid thing to do and I know that, and still I hold on to my stick. And every time I feel the pain, I repeat the same words.

Fuck him.

In the car, Maurice is his usual jovial self. "Come on, boss, you have to tell me what happened last night."

"Didn't you see how I was limping on the way to the car? Shouldn't that be some indication? I doubt I'll walk normally again for a week."

"Boss, I'm not buying that and I don't like the way you joke about it."

"Well, I'm not faking the limp," I said. "My back is absolutely killing me." It really is. Has been for two months, and it's getting worse. Another reminder of my advancing age, as though being fixed up with some-body's grandfather isn't excruciating enough.

"Katherine, I know I have no right to demand anything, considering I work for you and not the other way around, but I have overstepped my bounds before and I'm going to do it again: I *demand* to know what hap-pened last night."

"Actually, Maurice, if you must know, it was very disappointing, and I went home feeling sad and alone."

That stopped him cold.

"Boss, I'm sorry."

"Forget it," I said, "that's over. I have big news."

"Good news, I hope?"

"I think so. I'm going on vacation."

I was still watching him in the rearview. A look of confusion replaced his embarrassment, which was a welcome change.

"Really?" he said. "I can't recall you ever going on vacation."

"Neither can I, and that seems like a bad thing," I said. "I'm leaving this afternoon."

"Where are you going, boss?"

"Out West, my friend," I said. "Colorado."

I HATE PHILLIP'S ASSISTANT. Her name is Danielle LaPierre, which, as I am fond of saying, is French for "the Peter." And, as I am also fond of saying, the name suits her, because if any woman can be referred to as a dick, it would be Danielle. Any time I am waiting to meet with Phillip, she inevitably buddies up to me and chats my ear off, always on the same topic.

Men.

Danielle is a forty-ish divorcée, attractive enough, no kids, and she is obsessed with finding a husband before, as she charmingly puts it, "it's too late." And the way she speaks with me always leaves the distinct impression that she views us as in the same boat. That is annoying, but it is not what *really* bothers me about her.

What really bothers me is I do not know if Danielle knows of my past with Phillip. I suspect she does, if only because Danielle is the sort of woman who knows everything you might hope she did not. And if she *does* know, then there is no doubt she subtly rubs it in my face all the time. She loves to tell me stories of the extravagant vacations Phillip takes with his family, or the sweet little gifts he surprises his wife with "just because." If she does know of our past, I hope you'd agree that Danielle is a cold-blooded bitch, but because I am not certain that she knows and probably never will be, I am always left to wonder, and that makes the time I have to spend with her almost too much to bear.

In recent months, I have taken to amusing myself when I talk to Danielle by inventing boyfriends, and then bringing each of them to a sudden and stunning demise. "Alex" was transferred to Juneau, Alaska. "Henry" was decapitated when his car was broadsided by a freight train. "Stanley" accidentally stumbled upon a mafia killing and was placed in the federal witness protection program.

On this day after my birthday, I was telling Danielle the stunning news about "Milton," who was found dead in his bathroom after accidentally allowing a shortwave radio to slip into the tub while he was taking a bath.

"He hated showers," I sniffled.

That was when Phillip arrived.

"Come on in, Kat," he said.

He never calls me Katherine anymore, and I never call him Phillip. I suppose those are our respective nods to our past together, we'll always have those names in the way Bogey and Bergman will always have Paris. Now we are "Kat and Phil," which sounds more like a pair of Army buddies than it does old sweethearts.

"What's shakin'?" he asked, sliding out of his suit jacket and hanging it over the back of his chair.

"Not much, I'm well," I said.

He stopped, looked at me, and turned his head sideways, the way a dog might if it hears a sound it doesn't trust.

"Somethin' up?" he asked. "You don't seem right."

"No, I'm good," I said. Phil looked at me for a minute without saying anything, and to fill the silence I said, "It was my birthday yesterday," and then wished I hadn't.

"That's right, of course. I'm sorry I didn't send anything, been so damn crazy with everything here." He came around the desk and gave me a quick hug. "Happy and healthy and many more."

"Thanks," I said. I knew damn well he didn't know it was my birthday. "I'm forty."

"How about that," he said, back on his side of the desk, his hands clasped behind his head. "We're getting up there, aren't we? I'll be forty-seven soon enough."

"Next Thursday."

"That's right. Listen, happy birthday. You do anything special for it?"

"I'm going to, that's what I'm here to tell you. I'm going to take a month off."

"Really," he said. The look on his face was priceless. "When are you thinking of going?"

"This afternoon. I'm taking my assistant for the whole time, at full pay. And I'd like to take the Gulfstream. You're not using it until Friday."

If there is any benefit to working for a man who once broke your heart and knows it, it is this. When it comes to anything personal, I tell him what I want and he never equivocates. I'm not exactly sure why; it is not as though if he told me I couldn't take the company jet I would cry and say: "It's bad enough you married that bitch you cheated on me with, now you're going to make me fly Delta?" But there is still a little bit of that in there, somewhere, and whenever I can use it to my advantage, I do.

"Where are you going?" he asked.

"Aspen," I said. "I haven't been there since I was a girl. I'm going to climb a few mountains, ride a few horses."

"I can't remember the last time you took any time off."

"It's been a while," I said, and stood up. "I'm going to get a few things in order and I'll be out of here around noon. Please have them ready for wheels-up at three. I'll be at Teterboro a little before that."

He gave me a nice smile, one I almost never see anymore. "Have a good time," he said. "Be safe."

Then I was back in the anteroom, nodding to Danielle.

"I'm taking some time off," I said to her as I passed. "Milton would have wanted me to."

WHEN I TOLD PHIL I needed a few hours before I could take off for Colorado, I was telling the truth, but not the whole truth. The implication was that I needed to tidy up a few affairs and pack, while the truth was I had been up most of the night doing both of those. But there was one important meeting I needed to attend before I could go to the airport, one I would never tell Phil about, even though he is my boss. In fact, I wouldn't tell anyone about it, not even Maurice.

Dr. Gray is my own little secret.

You don't have to say it, I already know: there is no reason to be ashamed of therapy. And, really, I am not ashamed. Maybe it's more "embarrassed." Or "protective." However you choose to characterize it, I do not acknowledge to anyone that I have been in intense psychoanalysis pretty much my entire adult life. You see, I exist in such a competitive world that to admit to needing help would be tantamount to admitting weakness. I know all the men I work with, and who work for me, are looking for my flaws, looking to find a soft spot, and so fuck them, I refuse to show one. And while I know there are no similarities between the two, the reason I keep my therapy secret is the same reason I don't walk into a board meeting and complain about menstrual cramps, because anything that puts me on even less of a level playing field than I already am seems like it is best left out of the discussion.

Dr. Gray is comparatively new, and I love her. I have seen a long list of New York's finest and most discreet shrinks. I've been at it so long one of them retired and another recently died. I have also read just about every significant book on self-help and mental health published in the last twenty years and some older than that, everything from *The Road Less Traveled* to *Don't Sweat the Small Stuff*, and I've learned bits and pieces from all of them. I have delved deeply into my past, time and again, always reaching the same obvious conclusion: I don't trust men because the two that really mattered to me both let me down, and so I battle them in my past and all the others in my present and the trouble with that is it doesn't bode well for my future. It's obviously a challenge to find a man to love and to trust when I greet each new day with the words "Fuck him and all the others like him."

The truth is, I haven't really needed a shrink to explain any of this to me. I don't think it takes a psychology major to figure out that a girl whose daddy disappointed her so terribly will have issues with men. And of the many ways a father can disappoint a daughter, mine, I think, was the worst, because he never got the chance to make it up to me, and worse yet he always said he did it *for* me, which seemed to make it better in his mind even though it was so obviously not, so I don't need a therapist or a book to understand that is part of my problem. And then there was my relationship with Phillip and the way that ended. I suppose I was pretty much doomed right then.

So, the question is: If I know my problems so well, why do I continue to go to therapy?

There are two reasons. The first is rather sad, I guess, but it is true, and that is that I don't really have any other woman I can talk to. The only women in my life either (a) work for me, (b) compete with me, or (c) are my mother, and there is just too much that you cannot say to women who fall into any of those categories. So there is that, and then there is the other reason, which is my deeply ingrained belief that eventually I am going to get better. It will just take the right doctor, or the right relationship, or an epiphany of some sort, any of those three might do it, and the way I see it, the doctor is the one most under my control, so I'm not going to give up on that. And if there was ever any chance I was going to give it up, that went away when I met Dr. Gray.

Dr. Gray's practice centers on the Buddhist principle of mindfulness, which is to say whatever you are doing, your mind must be fully committed to it. To always look to the future is as dangerous as always looking to the past, because we live only in the present. And, even though this sounds like a cliché, my relationship with her is probably the best in my life; it is that valuable, that wonderful. And so, on this day after I turned forty and was fixed up on a blind date with a man old enough to be my father, I wasn't going to take off on my first real vacation in a decade without conferring with her.

"I think this is absolutely perfect for you," she told me. "They don't put monasteries at the tops of mountains by accident. The tranquility will be wonderful. Go easy on the shopping and the restaurants, they have those here too. Climb mountains, ride horses, breathe deeply, and when you return I want you to answer one question, and if you need to spend hours each day thinking about the question, that's fine with me."

"I'm ready," I said.

"When you come home from this vacation, I want you to tell me what it is that makes life worth living."

"Oh good," I said, "I was afraid it was going to be something deep."

She shook her head at me. She isn't much for my sarcasm. So I tried again.

"You know," I said, "a lot of people would be happy with one of those T-shirts that says your friend went to Aspen and this is all you got."

She shook her head again.

"Okay," I said. "I'll make a note to spend some time thinking about it."

"Good," she said. "But, Katherine, try to do it without making a note."

And with that, I was on my way.

SAMANTHA ▣ ▣ ▣

FEELINGS ARE A FUNNY thing, because there isn't always an easy way to explain them.

I can't always account for why I react in a given situation as I do, and I have grown comfortable with that uncertainty. I guess that's why it didn't come as a total surprise when I opened the door, found my ex-husband standing before me, and burst into a hysterical fit of laughter.

I know what you are thinking: nervous laughter is very common. I'm aware of that, but this was not that. This was a belly laugh, as though finding Robert outside my door was a scene from a funny movie.

I could tell Robert was completely taken aback by my reaction, and I really can't blame him. He stood in the doorway waiting for me to calm down so he could say something, even "hello," but I just couldn't stop. It was a howling laugh, the sort that would drown out anything short of a scream on his part, and he didn't look like he wanted to scream. He looked earnest, as though whatever it was he'd come to say was very meaningful and serious, the kind of look you'd have when approaching the family at a funeral, which I guess was appropriate under the circumstances.

We stayed that way for a little while, me laughing and him looking sheepish and awkward in the hallway, and then I suppose I could have invited him in but I wasn't sure I wanted to. So he just waited patiently until I quieted down and then finally he spoke.

"Hello, Samantha," he said, "I'm glad to see you haven't lost your sense of humor."

That was a pretty good line. He delivered it well, too. He always was very comfortable with himself, I have to hand it to him.

I hesitated. "Hello, Robert. It's been a long time."

"Too long, and that's my fault," he said. "May I come in?"

I really didn't have an answer to that so fast.

"Believe me," he continued, without any hint of awkwardness, "I am under no misapprehension here. I have no expectation of forgiveness or anything like it. I certainly am not asking to come inside because I expect anything to happen between us. I just have some things I want to say to you and I think it would be best to say them in private."

That sounded about right. "Okay," I said, and stepped backward into the room. I pulled a chair out from behind the writing table and placed it in the center of the sitting area. Then I took a seat on the couch and motioned for him to take the chair. It was like a little courtroom: he was on trial and I was the jury.

"Make your case," I said. "You've got as much time as you need."

"If it please the court," he said, with a smile, "I'll begin at the beginning."

Always comfortable, always glib. I could see how a girl could fall for him.

"I make no excuses for what you found in my computer," he said. "That was the product of a relationship that began long before I met you and did not end, as it should have, the day after our first night in Sacramento. I've been thinking about how to say 'I'm sorry' to you for that. The words themselves don't seem to be nearly enough, and yet I can't think of anything better to say or to do. If there was some action I could take to better deliver my apology I would do it, but I can't come up with anything better than just the words themselves. So, I'm very, very sorry, Samantha, for my inexcusable behavior. You are a good person and you deserved far better than that."

I nodded. He was right.

"Also, I want to say something else, for the record, and that is that I do not love Stephanie and I never did, and I absolutely do love you. What we had was real for me in every way, even though my behavior would seem to contradict that, and I don't blame you a bit if you do not believe me but it is the truth. I have no idea if that makes any difference to you or not, but in case it did I wanted you to know it."

I nodded again. "It does, a little."

"Okay, well, I'm glad."

Then he cleared his throat, and his expression changed. I recognized that expression, remembered it from the campaign. It was his "time to get down to business" expression. I knew he was now ready to tell me what he had *really* come to say.

"There's one more thing, Samantha, and this is probably the most important part of all. I want to tell you why I didn't go after you that day, why I didn't try to find you, and why I haven't made any effort to talk with you since."

"I didn't know you knew where I was," I said.

"Initially I didn't, of course, but it wouldn't have been hard for me to find out. You're registered under your own name and the credit card on file is your father's."

"You're right," I said. "So why didn't you come after me?"

He sighed and leaned forward, closer to me than he had been before. "Well, I can either tell you the truth or I can tell you the lie I have been telling myself for the past month."

"This is getting interesting now," I said. "Let's hear them both, I'm not in any hurry."

"The day you left, the first thing I did after I collected myself was call your father. I knew you weren't coming back and I found your wallet and all your credit cards in the room so I knew you had no way of getting anywhere without him. So I called him and told him exactly what had happened. I apologized to him and told him I would do whatever he thought was in your best interest. He told me his first and only concern was for your safety, and he didn't like you being alone without a wallet or a phone. I told him I shared that concern, but also that I was fairly certain you were in very little danger and that my guess was that he would hear from you before I would. As it turned out, I was right about that. He called me after he spoke to you, to tell me that you were safe. He was very cordial through the whole thing. He told me very matter-of-factly that you wanted to annul the marriage. I asked if he thought I had any chance of changing your mind, and he said he was certain that I had none. As I recall, he said something about you never changing your mind, and how lucky he was he never had to try to negotiate against you in a boardroom."

I smiled. I couldn't help myself.

"I think I said I felt lucky never to have had to face you in a court-room, and he said I didn't have to worry about that. He told me his law-yers would be in touch within a day, which they were, and so long as I didn't want anything from you or from him there would be no trouble, which there was not. The next day I called him one more time and said I just wanted a chance to talk to you, to tell you I was sorry. He laughed and said that he was sure you knew I was sorry, and that the best thing I could do for you was just leave you alone. And so I did. He arranged to have your things picked up from our room, and I flew back to L.A. and told myself that I was doing what was best for you, leaving you alone and letting you get on with your life. That's the lie I've been telling myself since this happened."

That room was the quietest place I've ever been. For some reason I couldn't hear the ocean anymore, I couldn't hear the whir of the ceiling fan or the music from the buffet by the pool. All the sounds I had grown accustomed to faded away. There were just Robert and me.

"The truth, however," he said, "is a lot simpler than that. The truth is I did it for me. When your father told me it would be best for *you* if I stayed away, that gave me a very convenient escape. It made it very easy for me to justify never having to face you, never having to own up to what I had done. And I told it to myself enough times that I actually started to believe it. But then, just the other night, it hit me that I wasn't staying away because it was easier for you, I was staying away because it was easier for me. And the *real* truth is if there is anything I should really do for you it would be to have the courage to sit here and let you say what-ever it is you want to say to me. So that's what I'm here to do. You deserve to tell me what you think of me, and I deserve to hear it, and if you need some time to think first I will gladly wait downstairs for an hour or until morning if you'd prefer. You take your time and figure out what it is you want to say, and I will listen. I owe you that much. And I hope, in some real way, *that* will make it easier for you."

He sat back in his chair, and I leaned back, too.

"Another thing," he said, in a softer tone. "If I'm wrong, and the truth is you really *don't* have anything to say, and my being here really *is* making it worse and not better, just tell me so and I'll leave right now and you'll never have to deal with me again."

My father and my husband, they both *always* know what to say.

"Also," he said, "there is one other thing."

He looked a tad uncomfortable now. I leaned forward just the slightest bit.

"I don't know exactly the right way to say this, but if by some miracle you want to give us another try, if you feel in your heart that what we had was meaningful enough to overcome what I know was unforgivable behavior on my part, please know there is nothing on earth I would want more. We wouldn't have to make any promises, we could just try again. I would do it right this time. Not in the whirlwind of an election. A proper relationship, a courtship, with dinner dates and flowers that actually come from me, not a staffer. If you had any inclination to give that a chance, I would consider it a miracle and I would do anything to make you happy. If that means resigning my office, I will do it tomorrow. If you want to move back to New York, we could do that and I'll go into private practice. What I'm trying to say is that I realize now what I should have realized from the second I saw you outside that elevator, which is that you are the most important thing in my life and if there is any chance that I haven't destroyed this completely, please tell me. If there is any shred of hope, any at all, I will take that as a blessing and I will do everything I can for the rest of my life to prove to you I am worthy of it."

He pushed himself forward out of the chair so that he was on his knees before me.

"I love you with all my heart, Samantha. I know you have no reason to believe that, and I know there is almost no chance you would ever consider being with me again. I'd just ask you to think about it, even for a minute, and if it's out of the question I will understand. But please know that whatever you decide, I love you and I will spend the rest of my life regretting what I did."

Then he was on his feet.

"I'll be waiting downstairs," he said. "Take as much time as you need."

I looked down at the spot where he'd been on his knees. I'd never really noticed the carpeting before. It was orange with black zig-zagging lines and would have looked ridiculous anywhere else but somehow seemed perfectly in place here. And while my head was down, I heard the door shut softly and I looked up and he was gone. I closed my eyes and pictured him as he'd looked just before he walked out the door, with his hand on the knob. Was he wearing his wedding ring? I think he was. I had taken mine off down by the pool the day I arrived here, the day I met Eduardo, the day I ran away from my marriage. But Robert was wearing his today. Had he worn it all this time? Or had he just put it on to come see me? It would be interesting to know.

Then I sprang off the couch and ran to the door, raced down the hall. I caught up to Robert as he stood waiting for the elevator.

"Wait," I said, "come back. I don't need any time. I know what I want right now."

BROOKE

I LOVE DAYS WHEN everything feels different.

I guess I shouldn't say it that way. I don't love *all* the days when it feels different, like when someone dies and everything feels different. I don't love that. I recall the day Grammy died, my mom's mom, Brooke, for whom I was named and whom my mother and I look just like. Sometimes I'll see an old photo and it always takes a moment to say whether it's her or me, I usually have to look at the clothes. She had wonderful style, furs for every occasion, sensational hats, but *that's* how alike we look—I have to see what she is wearing before I know it's not me.

The day she died was unlike any other. She had cancer and no one told me. When she lost weight, they told me she was dieting. When she lost her hair and needed a wig, they told me she was just experimenting with a new look. I wanted to wear a wig, too, because she did. My mother bought me one, a long blonde one. I was thirteen. When she died, it was a complete shock. I hadn't seen her in over a month, she'd been in the hospital but I was told she was in Europe visiting friends. Then one night Mother pulled me away from the television.

"I have something important we need to discuss," she said.

And she told me, quite matter-of-factly, that Grammy was gone. And it was like I was standing between a wrecking ball and a decrepit building: first the ball hit me, which hurt, then it scooped me off the ground and crashed me into the building at full force. I was crushed. All the air went out of me.

"When?" I asked. "How?"

"She'd been ill for some time," Mother said stoically. "She died the day before yesterday. There is a new dress upstairs for you to wear to the funeral."

"What do you mean she'd been ill? I didn't know she'd been ill."

"Darling," my mother said, her voice going to that place it always does when she explains something she thinks I'm not capable of understanding, "I just couldn't bear to tell you."

The next day at the funeral, what I remember most was wondering how anyone else could be having a regular day. I remember seeing construction workers at a job site, lunchboxes at their sides, eating sandwiches and drinking from thermoses, and all I could think was: How in the world are they just going about their business as though everything is normal? Don't they know Grammy is dead? Don't they know I'll never feel those long nails scratching my back again? Don't they know how chewy her oatmeal cookies were? Don't they remember when she took me to see *Annie* on Broadway and then bought me the soundtrack and how we would sing the song "Maybe" together at the top of our lungs? How can they just be going about their business as though this is just any regular day? Don't they know everything is different?

That's the kind of different day I hate.

But today is the kind I love. Because tonight is the night. Today is Scott's birthday. Tonight he gets his gift. I felt the tingle in my stomach the moment I woke up. Driving the kids to school, stopping at Whole Foods, stopping at Soleil Toile for something special to wear under my robe, arranging the bedroom, readying the fireplace, placing the candles, choosing the music. Then placing the book of photos Pamela made into a velvet box, tying the ribbon, attaching the birthday card the kids designed. ("I signed it *for* you," Megan told her brother. Twins are so funny.) Then dropping off the two of them at Mother's for the night. When Scott comes home, it will be just the two of us. And it will be different from any other night. In the good way. I'm not even going to make him lock the door.

SAMANTHA

BACK IN THE HOTEL room, I reversed the seating arrangements.

This time I took the chair in the center of the room and put him on the couch. He looked a good deal less comfortable on the couch. Men like Robert know how to sit erect in hard-backed chairs, they know how to maintain the crease in their pants, how to keep their suit coat from rising up in the back. I guess that comes from years of experience in classrooms and boardrooms, or, in Robert's case, courtrooms. They're a lot less comfortable on couches. No matter how distinguished the man, no matter how well-dressed, if you look at him seated on a couch he still looks like he's asking your father for permission to take you to the prom.

Now Robert was on the couch in my hotel room, fidgeting with his clothes, trying to get his pants and shirt and sport jacket straight. His legs were crossed and he had a look of cautious optimism on his face. I remember that look. He would use it in debates when his opponent was attacking him. It was a look that indicated that no matter what was said, Robert was ready to respond. I could see it in his face; he *knew* I was going to take him back.

"Robert, I just want you to know that it did help a lot that you came here. More than I would have guessed. If you'd asked me yesterday if it would make any difference for you to come, I'd have said 'no,' but I'd have been wrong, for a couple of reasons. The first is that it makes me feel less stupid. All this time I've wondered how I could have fallen in love with such a complete asshole. And now I see that, at the very least, you aren't a *complete* asshole. There is *something* redeemable in your character, and that's good news for me. It means I can trust myself again. So that helps."

I don't know why, but I stood up and started pacing as I spoke. I wasn't looking at Robert. I was staring down at the floor, carefully considering every word.

"In fact, in some strange way I have more respect for you now than I did before everything happened. I don't know how many men would have done this the way you did. I think a lot of men would have stayed away because it was easier."

"Let's not make me out to be a hero," Robert said.

"Don't talk," I said. "You said everything just right. I want to remember it that way."

He smiled and did that thing where you twist your finger in front of your lips, like locking your mouth and throwing away the key.

"You are most certainly not a hero," I continued, "but you may actually be a decent human being, or at least one with a shred of decency. If you hadn't come here I would never have known that. So I'm happy for that as well."

A sense of calm was washing over me as I spoke, an unclenching. And I realized that, as focused as I have been this month on relaxing, in actual fact I haven't relaxed at all. But I was relaxing now.

"I'll also tell you that it really seems to me you came here with no ulterior motive, no self-serving motivation, for your career or otherwise. I didn't believe that when you started talking but I do now, and I am impressed by that as well. You really did do this for me, and that matters to me. And the things you said and the way you said them were perfect. You apologized for exactly the right things in exactly the right way, which leads me to believe you really understand what you did and you really are sorry. And *that's* the best part of it all. So, thank you, as strange as that seems. Because you made the effort and it helped, and it is going to keep helping. This makes everything that happened a whole lot less awful, and under the circumstances I really couldn't ask for more than that."

And with that I was finished. Those were all my thoughts. I was suddenly tired, maybe for the first time since the day I arrived at this hotel and started training.

Robert was off the couch and walking toward me. I recognized his expression again: he was in serious seduction mode now. He walked right up to me and looked soulfully into my eyes. He raised his hand and brushed it softly against my cheek as though he was wiping away tears. But I wasn't crying.

"So," he said, "I guess the question is, where does that leave *us?*"

I stared right into his eyes. "It leaves us in a much better place than we otherwise would have been," I said. "And that's all."

He flinched a little. Our eyes were locked, and I could tell he was trying to see if there was any crack, any room at all for negotiation. I stared at him for all I was worth. There was no room for anything.

"Can we at least be friends?" he asked.

"There really isn't any point in that," I said. "This is not a time in my life I'm going to want to remain in touch with. I will learn from it, I will always remember it, but I will not treasure it. And while I don't hate you or wish ill upon you, I don't have any real interest in talking to you ever again."

We were still staring, but now that was a formality. It was him who was obliged to look away first, and after a moment or two he did. He lowered his eyes and nodded, and then he turned slowly and started walking toward the door.

"What are your plans?" he asked over his shoulder.

"My triathlon is next week, then I'm going back to New York."

His hand was on the knob now. "Be well," he said.

"I wish you good luck," I said. "And, if you ever do run for president, I'll say nice things about you."

He turned to face me, his hand still on the door. His eyes looked cloudy, like maybe he would cry. Not here, in front of me, but later.

"Will you mean them?" he asked.

I just smiled. I didn't need to say it. We both knew the answer.

 KATHERINE

BEING ON A HORSE always reminds me of my father.

My mother is petrified of horses, always has been. She doesn't care for animals at all. As I recall, she once told me if a cat looked at her in a particular way she would need to be hospitalized.

But my father loved horses especially, loved everything about them. There were stables less than a mile from our house when I was a girl, and I cannot count how many Saturday afternoons we spent there together, Dad and me. My mother would make us pancakes for breakfast and then—if it was a nice day—the two of us would walk, hand in hand, to see the horses. When I was little, we would ride together, me snuggled into place in front of him on the saddle. I can still smell the oil embedded in the leather and the ever-present poop from the stables and the after-shave my father used, all mingled together. If you asked me to describe my childhood, at least the best parts of it, I would describe the way those Saturday afternoons smelled.

I began to ride competitively when I was nine and continued until Dad went away. He encouraged me to continue but my heart wasn't in it. Besides, even if I wanted to, Mother wouldn't have allowed it. There was no way she was going to traipse from one stable to another, one horse show to another; she wouldn't even allow my riding boots in the house. "They've been wading in the crap," she would say. They remained in a plastic bag in the garage when I wasn't wearing them.

When Marie and I got to Aspen, the first thing I wanted was to go riding. At Buttermilk Mountain, they offered horseback riding and private lessons. I suggested to Marie she try it.

"I don't know, boss," she said. "If it doesn't have a motor, I'm not sure I can drive it."

"Listen," I told her, "first of all, as long as we are here let's drop the title 'boss.' You're here to enjoy yourself just as I am. Secondly, if you have never used a mode of transportation that doesn't require a key to start, you are in for a day you will never forget."

"Katherine," Marie said, sounding frightened. "I barely know how to ride a bike. There's no way I can ride a horse."

I considered that for a minute. "All right, here's the deal. On this trip, I am going to help you and you are going to help me. Before we go home, you are going to learn to ride a horse, which I will help you with, and in turn you will help me figure out what makes life worth living. When we have both succeeded—when you can ride a horse and I can answer that question—we'll go back to New York."

Marie was just staring at me. Then she blinked, and then blinked again, and then a few more times without changing expression. Finally, she said, "So you're saying we might be here awhile."

"That's right."

She looked concerned.

"What's the matter?" I asked.

"What should I tell Adam?"

Her fiancé, who also worked under me at the bank. Sometimes you can take advantage of things like that. "Tell him I said I need you here," I said.

She thought a moment. "I didn't bring that much stuff," she said.

"Have you seen the stores in this town?"

"Katherine," she said, "I can't afford to shop in Aspen."

"Let me handle that part," I told her. "Your job is to figure out what makes life worth living. If you do, whatever it costs will be money extremely well spent."

"Are you serious?" she asked.

I took her hand. "Dead serious," I said.

Finally, Marie smiled. "Holy shit, Katherine," she said. "This is going to be fun."

THE HIKE TO CATHEDRAL Lake came highly recommended. Everyone in town suggested it for something scenic and challenging but reasonable for two in-shape women who aren't accustomed to hiking at an elevation of eleven thousand feet.

On the first day we tried something shorter, as a warm-up, climbing up a dusty mountain trail called "Smugglers," covered in rocks and patchy grass, with a view of the town that grew more spectacular as we ascended. From the peak we hiked across a pass and into a gorgeous meadow, bursting with sunflowers and grass as high as your waist, then down a challenging trail that crisscrossed over a roaring stream called "Hunter's Creek."

On the second day, we hit the mountain.

We had new boots, new backpacks, new water bottles, new sunglasses, and good attitudes as we drove the twelve miles up Castle Creek Road to the bumpy, rocky turnoff, right up to the trailhead. It was a few minutes after seven when we began, and we agreed to each go at our own pace and meet at the lake. The mountain air was cool and dry as sandpaper, but the sunshine on my face warmed me to my toes. When I reached the steep section of the climb, with eight switchbacks coming in rapid succession, I was in a full sweat. It felt good. Better than good, it felt wonderful. Even the ache in my back didn't bother me, at least not nearly as much as it had been. It is one thing to perspire alone in your apartment, or in a dingy, crowded gym. It is another entirely to be out in the fresh air *doing* something that makes you sweat.

An hour into the hike, I was in love. I loved the rich green of the pines, the powdery white on the trunks of the aspens, the pale blue of the cloudless sky. I loved the way the air smelled, like sugar, if such a thing is possible, or buttermilk, sweet and fresh and clean. At first I had my ear-buds in but I soon took them out and stashed my iPod in my backpack. The sounds of the rustling beneath my feet and the birds flying past and the chipmunks scurrying across the path were more than enough. It took a little less than two hours to reach the lake. It would take longer than that to fully describe it to you. The stillness of the water left my mouth agape. I suppose I have become accustomed to oceans and rivers, where there is a current and a rhythm, where the water has a sound. This water made no noise, it had no rhythm, it was stunningly, achingly still. I longed to throw a stone into it, so I did and then watched the ripples extend slowly as far as my eyes could see. And the color was unlike anything you could imagine. It was described to me as "emerald green," but that is underselling: it was far richer than that, more vivid, a color so intense I could almost taste it. I could certainly feel it. You know a color has moved you when to *see* it is only the beginning of the experience.

Then there was a rustle and I remembered Marie. She came over by me, dropped onto her butt, and took a long sip from her water bottle.

"So," I said, standing over her, "what do you think?"

"I'm spent," she said. "Give me a minute to recover."

That made me feel even better. Marie has got to be twelve or thirteen years younger than I, and in great shape, but there she was, on her ass, while I stood over her feeling strong.

"Let's eat," I said, and flopped down on a rock.

The serenity of the lake and the distant peaks, including Cathedral Peak at almost fourteen thousand feet of elevation, were blissful.

We had gorgeous lunches in our backpacks: gourmet sandwiches, vinaigrette potato salad, chocolate protein shakes, and oxygenated water. The food was like fuel, healthful and nourishing. When I was finished, I felt satisfied and strong, the way food is supposed to make you feel but almost never does. I need to spend more time at the tops of mountains, I thought. Food feels better up here. It tastes better, too.

When we had finished eating and were zipping the remains of our lunch into recyclable trash bags, Marie said, "Katherine, can I ask you something?"

"Of course," I said, though I didn't care for the tone of her voice. She sounded apprehensive, and I was in no mood to have my blissful state interrupted.

"Why don't you have a man in your life?"

My heartbeat, which had slowed in the serenity of the mountains, resumed its New York rate. Thump-thump. Thump-thump.

"Who's to say I don't?"

"I know you don't," she said. "And I always wonder why."

Absently, I started digging about for flat stones. I used to be pretty good at skipping stones on a lake when I was a camper, I was pretty sure I could still do it.

"You know, things just have a strange way of working out," I said slowly. And then I decided to be honest with her, because it felt wrong to be dishonest in the presence of the lake and the mountain, so I said, "I tell myself that my career makes it impossible for me to carry on a real relationship. But that isn't actually true. I could if the circumstances were right. I guess they just haven't been for a very long time."

"Were you ever married?" Marie asked.

"Nope."

"Ever close?"

I stood up, five or six smooth stones in my hand. "What's with the third degree?"

Marie held up her hands, as if to pacify me. "I'm sorry, Katherine. I don't mean to make you feel uncomfortable. It's just that you told me we're staying here until we figure out the meaning of life and that sounds pretty complicated. And while I know you really well, in some ways I don't know you at all. For example, I didn't know if you were divorced or anything."

I guess I asked for this. "No, not divorced. Never married. Proposed to, once. Wasn't the right man. Had the right man for a little while, then he decided I wasn't the right woman and that was pretty much it for me."

"You loved him?"

"Oh, god, yes."

She smiled. "Now this is interesting," she said. "He broke your heart?"

I tossed a stone. It skipped nicely across the top of the water. There was something very soothing about watching the ripples drift farther and farther away.

"Yes, he did," I said, watching the water, my back to Marie. "He broke my heart."

She paused. I could hear her breathing behind me.

"Go ahead and ask what happened," I said. "I don't mind telling you."

And so she did, and I did. For the first time in the nearly twenty years since Phillip became Phil, I told someone besides a psychiatrist what happened, the insecurities and the lies and finally the night it ended. I never looked at Marie, I just kept skipping stones into the lake. When I was finished, I turned around and saw she had tears in her eyes.

"I'm so sorry that happened to you," she said softly.

"Yes," I said. "It rather sucked." I took a few steps toward her and dropped down onto a rock. I put my arm around her shoulders. "But wait," I said, "I haven't told you the best part yet." Marie looked right into my eyes, and I said, "I haven't told you his name."

"He's someone I know?"

"Yes."

Now she sat straight up. "Do I know him well?"

"Not as well as I do."

She leaned in close and put her hands on my knees. "Oh my god, Katherine, who is it?"

I smiled. "Phillip Rogers."

It took a second. No one ever called him by his full name anymore, even me. Then she got it and her eyes bugged out so wide I thought they might pop out of her head. She was blinking crazily and nodding and shaking like I'd just told her she'd won the lottery.

"You're talking about Phil?"

"That's right."

"Our CEO?"

"That's right."

"Pardon my language," she said, "but are you shitting me?"

"I shit you not, my friend," I said, and stood up and brushed the dirt from my butt. "I shit you not."

Marie sat in silence for a while, and finally she said, "It must be so hard for you in the office every day."

"Sometimes I think it's too much," I said. "Sometimes I think I need to leave. I almost have, several times. He's moved mountains to keep me, I'm not exactly sure why. I'd like to think it's because he believes he can't afford to lose me, but sometimes I think what happened back then has something to do with it, like he can't let go, or he feels guilty. Or a little bit of both."

"I don't know how you do it."

I laughed. "Well, maybe one of these days I'll just up and get the hell out. Move back to Connecticut or maybe here."

"You can't do that," she said, in a serious tone. "It would kill us all."

"I'm sure the bank would survive."

"I don't mean the bank. I mean all of *us*. The women who work there. You're an inspiration to us all."

"Don't be ridiculous," I said. "Most of them hate me."

"No, they do not," she said, punctuating her words sharply. "They love you, because the men fear you. You're the only woman I've ever met that men are afraid of."

She meant it. I could tell. "Well, that isn't all it's cracked up to be."

"I'm sure it's tough," she said, "but we need you, boss."

I strolled around a bit, looking at the earth, at the blue-gray stones, at the soft grass, at the shadows cast by the giant pines, at anything other than Marie. Then I looked up into the sky, took off my sunglasses, and let the golden sunlight warm my face. "Well, that feels good," I said, my eyes closed. "I'm not sure it makes life worth living, but it feels good."

BROOKE

I DIDN'T GET TO show him the pictures.

Not right away, at least. He attacked me before I could show him, before I could even mention them, before I could say anything at all, and that was fine. We've been married a long time; at this point our best communication is nonverbal. Like if we're at a party and he glances at me and I give him that look that says: I'm done here, time to go home. Or if we're with the kids all day and they're bickering and Scott shoots me the glance that means: I need a half-hour of peace or I am going to have to sever one of my own toes. I know him, he knows me, our eyes can usually say every bit as much as our lips, sometimes more.

So tonight Scott came home to a surprise. I'm sure he expected the usual birthday treatment, which is a house decorated with homemade signs and a cake baked and frosted by the loving hands of his children. He has never complained about any of that; in fact, I recall last year after a lovely birthday dinner, just the four of us, he raised his glass of wine and said: "What more could a man possibly ask for?"

Even the kids, then seven years old, understood how nice that was.

To me it was like music, because I feel the same way. So many women I know want so many things, they spend more time and energy thinking of what they do not have than enjoying what they do. I try not to be that way. I have a good man who loves me, I have beautiful, healthy children, what more could a woman possibly ask for?

So I know that Scott would have been perfectly satisfied to come home to the usual warmth and clutter of his twins and their mom, but tonight was going to be different. Tonight he was coming home to his wife, not his kids' mother. On the table where he leaves his briefcase, I left a note, written in fiery red ink on white-and-pink stationery. It said to open the bottle of champagne he would find on ice in the dining room, then to take off his tie and his shoes and come upstairs. It said he did not need to lock the door.

I first heard him when he turned the knob and came in the bedroom. The bottle was under his arm, the glasses between his fingers, and the note between his teeth. He didn't see me. He could have, if he was looking the right way, but he was not, he was looking toward the bed. I was on the chaise. When the designer who helped me put together the bedroom described the chaise, she said it was meant for having sex on. I laughed when she said that but she was serious. That was seven years ago, and tonight I would find out if she was right.

Scott's eyes hadn't adjusted to the dim lighting yet. I could see him squinting, reaching out with his free hand to find the bureau, to keep from banging his knee.

"Brooke?" His voice was uncertain. I took a deep breath, let it out.

"Happy birthday, Mr. President," I said.

Scott spun sharply, the glass flutes clinking between his fingers. He still couldn't see so well. He stepped toward me carefully.

"Can't you see me?" I asked breathily.

"I can't."

I snapped on the lamp behind me.

"How's this?"

I was stretched out as long as I can go on the chaise, my right leg crossed over my left, my hair falling down my back, curled for him the way he likes. I was wearing a satin robe, cinched high enough that you couldn't see what was beneath it. I had one hand resting gently on my stomach and the other on top of the end table beside the chaise. Under my hand was the pink velvet box. Inside the box were the pictures.

"Would you like champagne?" he asked. His voice was deep but I could tell he had to work to get it that way.

"I'd love some," I said.

He poured two glasses and handed one to me, standing right over me. He put the bottle down on the table, right beside the velvet box. Then he knelt beside the chaise so his face was equal to mine. His eyes said everything. They said he loved me and wanted me. They said no man could ever want more than he had right now.

I smiled. "Happy fortieth birthday," I said, and clinked my glass against his.

We both drank a little. The champagne was light and sweet and fresh.

"I have a very special gift for you," I said.

I don't know if he heard me or not, I'm not even sure if I got all the words out, because then he was kissing me so hard I couldn't move. He pressed his lips against mine and my head went back into the soft chaise and I was pinned. I could feel him shaking, I could feel his heartbeat. He pulled away quickly and downed the rest of his champagne in one bubbly gulp, then he placed the glass on the floor.

"I need you . . . right . . . now," he said.

My hand was still on the velvet box. I had envisioned giving him the pictures first. But it didn't much matter if that waited until afterward. The pictures were meant to make him excited, and I'm not sure how much more excited he could possibly have been.

I lay back and felt him land on top of me. It felt good, even if some of it didn't. He was breathing hard, right into my ear, I could feel the heat of his breath, the wet of his tongue.

"Kiss me," I said.

And he did.

After, when I had caught my breath and he was still searching for his, I put my hand back on the velvet box.

"So, it's time for me to give you your present," I said.

"That was the best present I could ever have asked for," Scott said, still panting a little.

"But it isn't all you're getting."

He put his hand on my tummy, very tenderly, and looked right into my eyes.

"Actually, Brooke, I was thinking about that today. I think I know the one thing I really, *really* want for my fortieth birthday."

I smiled and waited for some extreme, perverted sexual suggestion; Scott likes to joke around that way. But then he told me what it was he wanted, and I saw in his eyes he wasn't kidding. And I put my hand on top of his and squeezed it hard as the tears started pouring down my face.

SAMANTHA ▣ ▣ ▣

I WONDER IF IT happens this way for everybody.

For me, it has always been like this: any time I am feeling my best, strongest, and healthiest, I am also at my most emotional. And maybe never more than right then, strolling that beach for the last time. I was so strong I was practically bursting with energy. For the past six weeks, I had eaten and drunk only the best fuel (except for three glasses of wine with Eduardo), slept nine hours a night, practiced yoga breathing during long walks on the pristine beach, listened to the waves crashing and the children laughing in the surf. Now, for two days, I had been at rest, conserving all my strength for tomorrow, permitting myself nothing more strenuous than this final walk on the sand. I would compete tomorrow and then go back to my life, the one I had before Robert. Back to New York, back to working, to traveling. Back to men, too, I suppose. I wasn't sure exactly how I wanted to handle that part of it. My guess was that it would handle itself. I didn't plan to be looking for anyone, but I did expect someone to find me. It might take months, or years, or less than a week. However that works out would be fine for me. I was a wiser, stronger woman than I'd been before. I was a different person. I looked forward to seeing how this person fared in the world, like a character in a movie that I'm rooting for. That is what I was, I figured. A character. And I was rooting for me.

So, if I was as strong as I had ever been, physically and mentally, why couldn't I seem to keep from crying? Every sound, every wave, every gull, every breath made me sentimental. I was nostalgic for this part of my life already, even though it wasn't over. But once you know how something is going to turn out, I suppose it *is* over, in a way, and I knew how this would turn out. I would compete tomorrow, and it would be wonderful; I hadn't any doubt of that. Then I would go back to the world and begin anew. And even if I did someday come back to this place, I would never come back to this time. This time rescued me. It nourished me, brought me back to myself and beyond, made me better than I have ever been, and once I leave, it will be gone forever. In a way, I wanted so badly to stay, to remain here for the rest of my life, but I knew I couldn't, because this wasn't my life. All of this had been preparation, though I didn't yet know for what. But I was sure it would be for something, and I was also sure that when it happened I would know what it was.

I walked to the end of the beach and back, more than three miles on the sand, and when I returned I found Eduardo waiting for me. He was wearing a white jacket and using his hand to shield his eyes from the sun. The breeze had picked up in the afternoon and it blew his hair away from his face. He was always so tidy it was jarring to see him in the wind.

"You look very casual," I said to him, "you ought to try it more often."

"I do not spend much time on the beach," he said. "But for your last day, I gladly make an exception." He sounded sad. You'd have to know him well to hear it in his voice, but I could hear it. "Have you got every-thing you need?"

"Anything with carbs, I'm eating it. I had pancakes this morning; I think my system almost went into shock. I have so much energy, if this race doesn't start soon I'm going to jump out of my skin."

"I asked Chef to prepare a special dinner for you tonight," he said. "Fresh pasta, he makes it himself, with a delightful sauce that is just a bit rich with cream and fresh vegetables. It is fabulous. He prepares it for me on my birthday."

I put my hand on Eduardo's cheek.

"What time would you like it delivered to your room?" he asked.

"About five," I said. "I want to try to be in bed at eight. I don't know if I'll sleep at all but I'll try. I'll be down for breakfast at five."

"I'll make certain the kitchen is ready for you."

My hand was still on his cheek. I took my other and wrapped it around his waist, thrust my face into his shoulder, and let it all go. I cried hard, really hard, and it felt wonderful. Eduardo said nothing at all, just held me gently at the waist.

He left it to me to decide when to stop, so I stayed buried in his jacket, his embrace, his smell, until the tears stopped and then longer than that. It felt so good to be held.

"Thank you so much for everything," I said, my face still embedded in him. "You have made this all so perfect for me."

He did not respond, which was unlike him, and so I peeked up into his face and found, to my surprise, that he was crying, too. Softly, not enough that you could hear it, but from as close as I was there wasn't any question his eyes were welling with tears. I had a feeling if I asked about it he'd have blamed it on the sun, but he'd have been lying. I put my face back into his shoulder and let him hold me. There wasn't any reason to say anything about it. There wasn't any reason to say anything at all.

KATHERINE

IF THERE'S ONE THING I pride myself on, it's my musical street cred.

And by that I mean that I am a straight-up gangsta. Yes, I'm a white girl from Greenwich, and I have no tattoos and I've never busted a cap anywhere, but I have gravitated toward hip-hop music since the first time I heard "The Message" by Grandmaster Flash. I know the entire genre well enough that I could host a hip-hop show on an urban radio station. From Grandmaster Flash to Sugarhill Gang to Run-D.M.C. to Public Enemy to N.W.A. to Tupac Shakur to Biggie Smalls to Snoop Dogg to Jay-Z, I have been there, faithfully, through it all. I belittle all other forms of musical expression and I belittle anyone who doesn't appreciate the beauty, simplicity, ferocity, and authenticity of hip-hop.

So this John Denver thing is really hard for me to explain.

Let me start when Marie and I made our way down the mountain from our hike to Cathedral Lake. Walking through the forests, along-side the streams, the rushing water echoing in my ears, I realized that all my life I have been yearning to be here and didn't know it. All this time I have known that something was missing and now I knew what it was.

It was this place. I felt as though I was finally home. I said as much to Marie when we reached the bottom. I was leaning against the hood of our car, and I pulled out my water bottle. My back was aching and tight-ening up and I rubbed it. "I need a massage," I said.

Marie walked up behind me and started to knead my shoulders, and I laughed.

"That wasn't a request," I said. "It was a suggestion. Let's go back to the hotel and book massages, my treat, one for you, one for me."

"I've never had a massage," she said. "Is it weird?"

"It is weird that you have never had a massage, yes. But having one is not weird at all. In fact it is rather wonderful, and the perfect way to complete an afternoon spent climbing up and down a mountain."

"Do I have to be naked?"

I took a long swig of water. "On this trip, darling, you don't *have* to be anything."

She seemed to like that.

I looked up into the sun, toward the distant peaks, watched an eagle sail lazily across the horizon. "My god, I love it here," I said. I feel like I've come home."

"Just like John Denver."

I almost did a spit take. "What's that?"

"From the song 'Rocky Mountain High.' He says he came home to a place he'd never been before. It was here he was singing about; he lived in Aspen." Marie smiled. "My mother *loved* John Denver. We listened to him all the time when I was growing up."

"Really?" I said, amused. "You grew up in Brooklyn listening to cheesy country music?"

"First of all," Marie replied, insulted, "John Denver was not a country singer, he was a folk singer, and he was a poet and he was brilliant. He wasn't cheesy. If you love hiking in the woods you would *love* John Denver, that's what all his songs are about."

"Okay, okay," I said, relenting. "I'm sorry I said that. Tell you what. Let's go take off all our clothes and hire two handsome men to rub us down, what do you say?"

She smiled. "I don't know if Adam would like the way you said that, but it sounds good to me. And I'm going to make you listen to John Denver while we're here, and I *promise* you're going to like him."

I stretched my aching back, got behind the wheel of the car, and gunned it back into town. I was looking forward to a massage, a steak, a bottle of wine. I didn't expect John Denver's name would come up again, not on this day, this trip, or ever again.

I was wrong about that one.

OUR FIRST WEEK IN Aspen was blissful, nothing short of that, and that's not a word I throw around. I rose with the sun every morning and did not, I repeat did *not,* say "fuck him." There seemed no reason to say it. Maybe it was the altitude, or the way the sun glowed as it rose above the mountain, or the way the food tasted, the air smelled, the wind sounded. I got into the car only to drive to the more distant hikes; everything else was within walking distance or easily reached on a bicycle. I even got Marie on horseback. She sat with her eyes glued shut as an aging mare named Tank moseyed around a field at the base of Buttermilk Mountain.

It was on our seventh day that word about Phillip reached us.

It reached Marie first; she had her BlackBerry on the table as we shared granola and yogurt and multigrain pancakes at an adorable breakfast spot called Peaches. The phone reverberated so fiercely it shook the silverware beside it, and Marie absently picked it up to look.

"That's a text," she said. "I'll just make sure it's not an emergency."

Then her already-wide eyes bugged out cartoonishly, and I became scared that it *was* an emergency, except she didn't look upset. She looked enthralled. She looked as though she had watched an entire suspense thriller in a quiet movie house and just now found out who the killer was.

Then she looked up at me and smiled. "What is it?" I asked.

She looked once more at the BlackBerry. "I have no idea how you're going to feel about this," she said. "I'm just going to show you."

She handed it to me, gingerly, as though I might drop it if she were not careful.

"What the hell is it?" I asked, before I looked. "You're making me nervous. Is this bad news? Am I going to be upset? You know I have no interest in being upset out here."

"Just read it," she said. "You won't be upset."

So I did. And I wasn't upset.

BROOKE

WHEN I WAS LITTLE, I wanted to be a clown.

Like in the circus. I always loved the clowns, because I loved the makeup. I have always loved makeup; sometimes I think I may have missed my calling, that I should have gone to Hollywood and been a makeup artist. I think I would have had the best time with that. I would have loved transforming a handsome actor into a werewolf or a zombie, or even the less dramatic stuff, just making the actresses look as pretty as they could. That sounds like fun.

As a girl, I thought makeup was so glamorous. Probably because Mother wouldn't allow me to wear any, none at all. Not to church, not to school, not to sleepovers, not even alone in the house.

"That's for women," she would say, when I fingered her brushes or lipstick. "You are not yet a woman. Be a girl. You'll have plenty of time to be a woman."

I haven't followed that path with my daughter, not at all. I had Megan playing with makeup when she was three years old. I bought her lip gloss and eye shadow and blush and let her play with them to her heart's content. So I take great pleasure in seeing my daughter in makeup. But never more than today.

As I lounge on my bed, curlers in my hair, champagne in an ice bucket on the end table, I'm watching as Edith does Megan's face. Edith is my stylist; she's been doing my roots and blowouts for five years, usually at the salon. This is the first time she's been in the house. But special occasions demand special accommodation, and it doesn't get much more special than this.

Megan's eyes are so bright, wide like mine, but the lucky girl got her father's turquoise sparkle. I watch Edith apply just the gentlest dash of mascara, a splash of color on the cheekbones, a hint of eye shadow. Nothing garish; there is an appropriate amount of makeup an eight-year-old girl can handle and Edith knows exactly what it is. She and I spent an hour on the phone making that clear so that today I wouldn't have to worry about it.

Today I don't have to worry about anything. I awoke alone in my bed. Scott had spent the night in a hotel. The groom isn't allowed to see the bride on the wedding day, even the second time.

I walked on my treadmill for forty minutes while Scott took the kids to the diner for breakfast. They had pancakes, I think, though he promises me he made them eat scrambled eggs as well. I'm not sure I believe him; Scott would eat a shoe if you put maple syrup on it, and that unfortunate appetite has been handed down, but today isn't the day for fighting over that. Let them eat chocolate bars if they want—I'm in too good a mood.

I worked out and then took Lucy for a long walk into the woods. That's heaven for a golden retriever. It was one of those spring mornings that promise to get hot in the afternoon but at nine A.M. you need a light sweater. Lucy and I tramped in the woods for about half an hour, then came back to the house where a massage table was waiting in my bedroom.

I had the massage and then Edith arrived and brought the champagne, and we drank it together and spent about an hour on my hair. And now I am lolling in bed, watching my angelic daughter being made up so she can be her mom's maid of honor. She looks as happy as I feel. And why not? Half her friends' parents are divorced, and two more separated within the last year. I was afraid the kids might be embarrassed by the idea of their parents renewing their vows, but to my delight I see they take it as what it is: a hell of a lot better than the alternative.

Jared is downstairs with his father. Proud, too, like his sister; eight years old and his father's best man. That was the first thought I had: this time the kids could be part of it. It's corny, I guess, but it's perfect.

It's not a wedding like our first one, more like a cocktail party with a minister on the guest list. Six couples, just our closest friends, and Mother. Fifteen in all if you count the kids. Seventeen if you include

Scott and me. And the pastor makes eighteen for dinner, if he stays. We told him he was welcome, he said he'd play it by ear.

Now Edith has finished with Megan and my daughter looks more beautiful than I have ever seen her. "Edith, it's perfect," I say, and get back in the chair myself so she can finish my hair. It's almost time. We will be married again at six, have cocktails for an hour and then enjoy a lovely dinner. Everyone is already here, hopefully enjoying the hors d'oeuvres. Who doesn't love shrimp wrapped in bacon? And smoked salmon over cucumber slices? And lots of champagne.

I will join them all in about twenty minutes. Megan will go down before me and announce that it is time. There will be no music or anything like that, no marching down the aisle. Everyone will just take a seat and I will meet Scott in the center of the room and he will take my hand, and the kids will be by our sides, and Reverend Walsh will say a few words about how refreshing it is in this day and age to perform a second marriage for people who aren't divorced. And everyone will have a nice laugh at that, because if you think about it it's rather a funny line. Then he'll say something about how special it is for the children to be present, special for them and special for us, and if I'm going to cry at all today, that is going to be the time. But that's all right, because Scott will probably tear up then too, and even if he doesn't, Pamela will be bawling on the sofa, so I won't be alone. And then the reverend will simply ask if Scott and I promise to spend the rest of our lives together, and we'll say we do, and then we'll all have steak and sea bass. And it will be perfect.

"This," I say to Edith, raising my glass as she puts the final touches on my hair, "is the very best day of my entire life."

SAMANTHA ▢ ▢ ▢

I HAVE NO IDEA why I decided to pack.

The race is tomorrow. I won't fly to New York until the day after that, or the next day. I haven't even looked into flights yet. For all I know I won't be able to get back to the mainland for a week. And yet, for some reason I felt the need to put my things together tonight.

Maybe it's just the nervous energy; I'm doing something for the simple reason that I *need* to do *something*. I remember this feeling well, because I used to be a jock. I guess I still am, but I used to be a jock with goals rather than just an outdoorsy chick, which is what you could call me now. I used to play matches, I used to train, practice, have teammates, count wins and losses. I loved that. I loved the feeling I used to get in my stomach before a big soccer game. I also played lacrosse, field hockey, a little basketball, but what I really loved was soccer, mostly because of the running. Basketball was about the dribbling, lacrosse was about the stick. Soccer was about the running, and I've always loved to run. When I was in high school, I was the best soccer player in Greenwich, and before our games I couldn't sit still, I had to fidget with something all the time, pace the floors, run in place, and that's how I feel now. I can't sit still, I can't keep my hands at my sides, so I'm packing my suitcases tonight even though I'm not ready to go anywhere.

It's funny to see some of the things I brought with me. This was, after all, my honeymoon, at least it was when I packed. Thus the lingerie. God, it all looks so uncomfortable. Lacy camisoles, frilly undies, sexy thongs, plus three pairs of heels and fancy jewelry to sparkle over candlelit dinners. I haven't worn any of it, not once. I've worn nothing but sports bras, tank tops, running shoes, and shorts. I wear jeans to dinner. Haven't worn a dash of makeup, absolutely nothing, not even the night I had dinner with Eduardo. All the clothes and the jewels and the makeup look old to me, like ancient artifacts from a life that existed long ago but is now extinct. Who was that girl? What did she think? What did she want? Where is she now?

And where is she going?

That's the question that really matters. I can remember who she was, and what I remember best is that she really didn't know what she wanted. She liked her work but that wasn't what her life was about. She wanted a man, and found one, and he turned out to be the wrong one, but even if he hadn't he still wasn't the answer. As I think hard about her now, I realize the girl who wore these clothes didn't know what she wanted, mostly she was going about her life hoping that what she wanted would find her, and I realize now that was a mistake. You can't just close your eyes and hope everything turns out all right. That's a fine strategy for jumping out of an airplane, but it's no way to conduct your life. In order to get anywhere you must first know where it is you want to go. Then you can figure out how to get there. So that's my next move. Finish the race, go back home, then figure out where I want to go and make a plan of how to get there.

I had finished packing and was pacing again when I heard the knock.

A little smile crossed my lips. Finally, he had come. And I knew what I wanted to do. I wanted to go to the door. I had wanted to all the time I had been here. There wasn't any question in my mind about it. I walked slowly across the room, took a deep breath, opened the door slowly. And, once again, the man I found on the other side took my breath away.

"Hello, sweetheart," he said.

"Hello, Daddy."

"You didn't think I was going to let you do this thing all by yourself, did you?"

I put my face directly in the center of his chest and let him hold me, which he did, tightly. So much it was a little hard to breathe, but not enough that I wanted him to let go. Very few things in life are perfect. This was close enough. In a way, this was the best moment of my entire life.

KATHERINE

HAVE YOU EVER HAD an epiphany?

Let me tell you, it's awesome.

I'm sure epiphanies come in all different shapes and sizes, like a religious statue producing tears or a painting seeming to breathe, and I'm sure there are horrible epiphanies as well, and I shudder to think what those must be like, because mine hit me like a ton of bricks and if it had been horrible I'm not sure I would have been able to handle it.

For me, it was a moment of clarity, a moment when I realized how much I have been my own enemy, and for how long. It was a moment when I finally understood what Dr. Gray has been telling me, and all the other therapists before her, about how it actually *is* me who is in control of my feelings, not others. It is actually *me* I have been hurting all these years, not others. It is, in fact, *me* I have been angry at, not anyone else.

It came to me not in a vision or a dream, not on a hike at the top of a peak looking down upon the world, but rather in the form of a text, looking down on a plate of pancakes. That text changed everything, because when I read the words I realized they meant nothing at all, even though they were the words I have been waiting half my life to hear.

Phil's marriage broke up, he moved out, rumor is SHE was cheating on HIM!

I didn't know who sent it. But even without knowing who it was from, I knew it was true. Phillip's marriage was over. *She* was cheating on *him*. And, obviously, everybody knew it. In its own way, that's every bit as bad as having to give a horse a hand job.

So, let's see: Phillip left me for Holly nineteen years ago and married her less than a year after that, so for eighteen years I have waited for these words. I have dreamt of them, fantasized about them, prayed for them, written them in ink, chanted them in meditation, spoken them aloud daily, and now they were staring me in the face on the blush-smeared screen of Marie's BlackBerry, and the way they made me feel was a revelation more powerful than any I have ever had in a church or a conference room or the front row of a concert.

They made me sad.

There was no joy, no euphoria, no *in your face*. I had not won anything. In fact, what I realized was that I'd lost more than anyone. Because this wasn't about me at all. It was about them. Only for me had it ever been about me, and every shrink I've ever had has tried to tell me that, but I guess in life you have to figure out the really important things for yourself. And when I read those words, I did.

"So, what do you think?"

It was Marie. I had almost forgotten she was there.

"I think I would like to try listening to John Denver on my hike today," I said. "Can I borrow your iPod?"

AFTER BREAKFAST I RODE my bike to the base of Smuggler Mountain. The hike had become my favorite way to start the day in Aspen, a twenty-five-minute jaunt, steep most of the way, rocky and raw underfoot, with sensational views of the town and the mountains in the distance. And the reward at the top is the best: an observation deck with the most sensational vista. You feel as though you can see forever. I hustled up every morning after breakfast, got my heart rate elevated, got a little sweat going, then I planted myself on my butt and began my deep breathing. If no one was around, I shut my eyes and did a quick meditation.

> *May I be filled with loving-kindness*
> *May I be well*
> *May I be peaceful and at ease*
> *May I be happy*

Normally, I had my earbuds in so I could listen to my hip-hop as I climbed, but today was different. Today I listened to John Denver.

Which, for me, would have been a giant step even if I hadn't liked it, which I did, in spite of myself.

First off, I *got* it, which I would never have imagined I would. And, in truth, I may not have if I'd been anywhere else. But where I was is exactly where *he* was when he wrote it all, at least that's what Marie tells me and she seems to know, and after listening to the first song I knew she was right because I could see it.

He sang about an eagle and a hawk, living in rocky cathedrals that reach to the sky, and I could see them, not in my mind but in front of my eyes, birds on the horizon.

Then he sang about poems and prayers and promises, and about the children and the flowers, and about a woman filling up his senses, and all of the imagery was right in front of me, all the lyrics about love and inner peace and the beauty of nature, and I loved it, every word. By the time I reached the top and dropped to my knees on the observation deck, I was a devotee.

I popped the buds out of my ears and was unscrewing the top of my water bottle when I heard footsteps rustling behind, which always disappoints me at the top of Smuggler's. There is nothing better than being alone on that platform. I just wanted to take a long drink and then sit and listen to more of the music, looking out over the universe below.

Then I got a look at him.

He was tall and thin and looked to be about my age. Not the age Marie thinks I am, more my actual age. He was also in serious shape. Before I even noticed his face, I noticed his crisp biceps and forearms, the arms of an athlete, sinewy and long, not overly muscular, not the sort of muscles you get from lifting weights, more the sort you get from doing things those of us from the city come here to do. He was dark-haired and angular in his face, with pronounced cheekbones and jaw, and he had just the right amount of stubble. Plus, he had the ultimate accessory on a leash behind him, a spectacular golden retriever ambling slowly, sniffing the ground. Both the man and the dog looked like they spent a lot of time on the mountain.

I did what I could with my hair.

"Spectacular day," I said, as casually as I could manage.

"Isn't it?" His voice was higher than I imagined, less rugged than his jaw and stubble suggested, but that was all right.

"What a gorgeous dog," I said. I needed to get him talking. I'm good at talking.

"Yes, she is," he said, and made a kissing sound—toward the dog—and the golden trotted toward us and nuzzled up against his hip. "Ten years old and she still climbs Smuggler's in twenty minutes." He knelt beside the dog and wrapped an arm around her. "What a good girl," he whispered to her. Then he looked up at me, squinting a bit in the sun. "She's Florence, I'm Stephen."

"Katherine," I said. "Pleased to meet you."

"You from New York?"

"Is it that obvious?"

"No, but everyone in this town knows each other and everyone else is visiting either from New York or Chicago. I took a guess. You look more like New York than Chicago."

"Is that a compliment?"

"No. 'Your beauty is creating a solar eclipse' is a compliment. That was just an observation."

Well. I had certainly not expected this rugged, good-looking, outdoorsy guy to also be quick on his feet. I would actually have preferred him to be well beneath me intellectually. Now I knew how all those men I'd dated had felt. "So, I suppose you're from here," I said finally, because I couldn't think of anything funny.

"Actually, I'm from Chicago but I've been here fifteen years. They say you come for the winters and stay for the summers. I'm living proof." He pulled a bottle of water and a small bowl from his backpack, poured some of the water, and put it down for the dog. "When I was growing up my family used to come here to ski," he continued. "I came out one time in my early twenties for the summer music festival and never left. Never will. There's no place like it in the world."

"I get that feeling," I said. "I feel like this air could add ten years to your life."

"The air, the altitude, the people, you'll love it," he said. "How long are you in town?"

"Actually, I don't know. It's sort of open-ended."

He got a funny look when I said that. If I wasn't mistaken, he looked interested. Maybe he was just being friendly, hospitable, proud to show off his adopted home, but I don't think so. He glanced down and, I thought, slid his eyes toward my left hand.

"Well, I would be happy to show you around a little," he said. "Have you been to Jimmy's?"

"I haven't."

"Do you like hamburgers? The best in the world."

"I love hamburgers," I said. I hadn't eaten a hamburger in ten years.

"Terrific. It's right in town. We'll be there around six for drinks if that works for you."

My heart sank. "We?" I said, trying to sound casual.

He patted the dog. "Florence and me. See you there?"

I tried really hard not to look as relieved as I felt. "See you there."

I turned my head as casually as I could manage as he walked away. I looked out over the valley as I listened to the crackling of twigs behind me. They were going off together, the man and the dog, maybe across the meadow and down Hunter's Creek. Maybe he was going somewhere I didn't know anything about. Either way, I needed to see what his butt looked like.

"Hey," I shouted, turning my head so I got a great look before he turned back. Fit but not flashy, in shape but not showing off. Spectacular. "Why did you name her Florence?"

He smiled. "That's my second favorite city."

"I like it," I said. Actually, I loved it. "See you tonight."

He nodded, and off they went. A man and his dog. A gorgeous man and his dog. Perhaps soon to be *my* man and his dog. It could happen. Stranger things have.

As I watched him walk away, something inside me changed. For the better, I thought, and forever. From this moment forward, I decided, I really am going to be filled with loving-kindness. I really am going to be peaceful and at ease. I really am going to be happy. Who knows what might happen. Maybe Stephen would make a move on me tonight. Maybe we'd have a one-night stand that would become a treasured memory, or maybe it would be more than that, much more. Maybe I'd wake up in his bed after a night of rapture and affection and look out his window and see the sun coming up over the mountain and decide I would do as he did, stay forever. And maybe we'd be together.

And maybe none of that would happen, but isn't it wonderful that it might?

I stood and brushed the dirt from my butt, went right to the edge of the platform, and beheld it all, the trees, the streams, the gondola at the base of Aspen Mountain. I watched an airplane cross the entire horizon and touch down at the airport a few miles away. The horizon was limitless, just like my life, filled with endless possibilities. And that, I realized, is the answer to the question, the one about what makes life worth living. It's about all the wonderful things that might happen, if only we'd let them. And I knew, right then and there, that someday I would look back and say that this was the best day of my entire life.

PART II

Samantha R.
BreastCancerForum.org
Greenwich, Conn
Date joined: 9/30/2011

Hello, my name is Samantha Royce, and I have breast cancer.

Is that how you're supposed to start?

I don't exactly know the etiquette here. I suppose my beginning sounds like something from Alcoholics Anonymous, where I have *also* never been, by the way, but I've seen it in movies and read it in books, you make your introduction to the group and then you tell them your problem. Perhaps it works the same way in a breast cancer support chat room. I really don't know. I guess, like a lot of other things right now, I'm going to have to figure it out as I go along.

I think I should tell you who I am, because it's important to me that you know that I'm not just a cancer patient. I hope no one takes that the wrong way. I know you're all cancer patients, too, and I don't want to minimize that, I really don't, but that's not who I am, just as I assume it's not who you are. I assume you're all somebody just like me, somebody's daughter, somebody's sister, maybe somebody's wife. Maybe somebody's boss. I'm some of those, not all of them. I'm not anybody's boss, or anybody's wife, and I'm not sure if I'll ever be either one. I mean, I wasn't sure last week, before this bomb was dropped on me, and I'm even less sure now.

So who am I? I'm 28 years old. I was raised in Greenwich, Connecticut. I love sports, not so much watching them as playing them. I love to be outdoors, hiking, biking, running. I'm a good athlete. Just three weeks ago I finished the Ironman Triathlon in Kona, Hawaii. It was a 2.4-mile swim, 112 miles on the bike, and then a full marathon; I completed the course in 10 hours, 23 minutes, and 17 seconds. I have never felt healthier, stronger, better in my life. The idea that I might be sick could not have been further from my mind.

I came back to New York with my father two days after the race and began to get my life back together. (It's a really long story how it had come apart. I won't get into all the details today, maybe another time. I'll just say that I married the wrong man. But there's no need to feel sorry for me. I'll bet marriage is a wonderful thing if you choose the right person, and maybe I'll find that out someday, but I'm all right with it if I don't, I really am. I felt that way before my diagnosis and I feel that way now.)

I was planning to go back to work as a television feature producer and I still am, but I couldn't get in to see my old boss for a few weeks, so I was just taking a little time off. I rather liked the idea of easing my way back in. I went to visit old friends, ate in some fabulous restaurants, joined a new gym, started looking for an apartment. Everything was really mellow and nice, and after two months in Hawaii it was mostly terrific to be back in the hustle and bustle.

One of the things I needed to do was go up to Greenwich to see my gynecologist. I hadn't been in over a year, between travel and my ill-fated marriage and a variety of other reasons too, among them being I had grown tired of the lecture the doctor is always giving me. You see, my mother died of ovarian cancer when I was just eleven years old, and my aunt Judith was diagnosed with breast cancer when she was thirty, so my doctor has been pounding into my head that I need to start having mammograms much younger than most women, and even advised I should see a genetics counselor, because my family history puts me in a high-risk category. And I appreciate her concern, I genuinely do, but when you're young and healthy you're just not thinking that way.

Except this time I listened.

Part of the reason, ironically, was that I'd been feeling so good. I'd been treating my body so well in every other way: nutrition, exercise, training; consultation with medical doctors just felt like it fit. Plus, as I mentioned, I had a bunch of free time on my hands.

So I went.

My gynecologist made the appointment for me at Manhattan Breast Radiology Center last Tuesday. I couldn't have been less agitated about any of it. In fact, I felt empowered; it was just one more piece of my over-all commitment to health. The entire time my boob was being squeezed flat in the machine I was contemplating becoming a vegan, and beating myself up for disliking the taste of carrot juice.

The exam wasn't as bad as I feared. The worst part was not being allowed to use lotion or deodorant; I was paranoid I would smell. But the machine itself was fine really; a little uncomfortable, but certainly I've been more uncomfortable before. It didn't feel like it took so long, either, and when it was done I got cleaned up and dressed and sat and waited, surreptitiously sniffing about my armpit the entire time. Then the radiologist came back in the room with a funny look on her face. It's not a look I've ever seen before, but I could read it immediately. She had news for me, and she didn't want her expression to give it away.

"Samantha," she began, "we did a mammogram, an ultrasound, and we did some additional views, and here is what we found. You have what are called abnormal calcifications in your left breast. Knowing that you have the family history we spoke of, I think we should do a biopsy."

"I'm sorry, what?" I said. I'd heard every word, I just didn't have any idea how to respond. All I could think of was to ask her to repeat herself.

"You have a cluster of abnormal calcifications in your left breast. I can explain to you in as much detail as you like what that means—"

"You don't have to do that," I said. "I know what it means." I didn't. I had no idea what it meant, I just really didn't want to have it explained to me. "Should I go get a second opinion?" I asked.

"Really, this isn't an opinion," she told me. "If you want someone else to look at your films before we do the biopsy, we can arrange that, but there isn't any question about what we are seeing. I don't want any of this to seem scary for you. It is likely that there is nothing at all to be concerned about, but considering your family history there is no doubt in my mind we should perform a biopsy."

"When do we do that?" I asked. I rubbed my hands together. My palms felt cold and clammy.

"Let me make a quick phone call," she said. "If I can get the insurance approval, we do it right now."

And she did. She numbed the upper area of my breast with a shot, then dug a needle in and removed some tissue. It hurt, a lot. Even with the Lidocaine. And she told me we would know the results in forty-eight hours. That was on Tuesday, in the afternoon. I don't think I slept at all Tuesday night, or Wednesday night either. I skipped the gym both days. I didn't answer my phone, or respond to a single text or e-mail. Time moved achingly slowly. Whereas before I had been energetic and hopeful, I was suddenly lethargic and sad. Then the phone rang, nearly six o'clock Thursday evening. I didn't recognize the number, so I answered it.

"Hello, Sammy."

It was my gynecologist. Only people who have known me since I was little, as she has—I grew up with her son—call me that. I haven't used the nickname in ten years. I don't mind the name but her tone bothered me. She sounded like she was trying really hard not to alarm me, which alarmed me a lot more than if she'd just come out and said it.

"What did the tests show?" I asked.

"I think you should come in tomorrow morning and we'll talk about it."

That was when I went from lethargic to frantic. My hands were shaking. I held the phone away from my head and watched it quiver in my fingers.

"You have to tell me now," I said, the phone still away from my mouth, "I can't wait until tomorrow morning."

I clicked the phone onto speaker and placed it on the floor, then I lay down flat on my tummy to hear what she had to say.

"Samantha, there are abnormal cells, they are cancer cells," she said, her voice tinny and hollow. "We should talk about it in person, but you're going to need to see a breast surgeon."

I could feel my heart beating against the wood floor.

"They are malignant cells, but they are noninvasive cells, which in regular English means they do not look like the kind of cells that will spread, but it needs to be taken care of. When we sit down to talk, I will give you the name of a breast surgeon."

I sat up, cross-legged, and shouted toward the phone.

"What do you mean a breast surgeon? Like a boob job?"

"Not at all," she said, and as I listened I started to breathe deeply, in and out, in and out, just like at the beginning of a yoga class. "In the old days there were surgeons who would do everything, one afternoon they might do two gall bladders, fix a hernia, and then do a breast surgery. But now they have people who do only breast surgery. I will send you to one."

I was starting to get it. I think I knew the answer before I asked the next question.

"Are you saying I am going to have to have my breast removed?"

There was a long silence in the space between my knees and the phone. I filled it as best I could with my breathing. I was in no hurry to hear the answer.

"That isn't going to be a decision I make," she eventually said. "That will be a decision you'll make in consultation with the surgeon. But, candidly, I would tell you I think that is going to be a possibility, yes."

I did not say anything. I did not think anything. I breathed in and I breathed out.

"As you know, Sammy, you have this family history," she continued, "and this history means you are at a disproportionately high risk for breast cancer. So, while you might consider just doing a lumpectomy, taking out only the affected area, I think it is certain the surgeon will talk to you about taking off your breast, and I would say that in my opinion that would be a very reasonable option."

I put my hands on my breasts, cupped them, squeezed them. They're small, always have been, but they're firm and proud. I haven't thought about them much, really, since I was a girl. I like them, I suppose, but I don't think I *love* them and I surely know I don't *need* them.

"Let me ask you," I said, still cross-legged, still shouting toward the phone, "if I have the surgery and they take off my breast, would that be the end of it? Would that mean it was gone and I'm totally out of the woods?"

"The answer is not as simple as yes or no. I don't want to make this complicated for you, but doctors can be like lawyers sometimes, we don't like to speak in absolutes . . ." Her voice trailed off.

I opened my eyes, picked up the phone, turned it off speaker, spoke directly to her. "Dr. Leslie, I have known you since I was a little kid. You knew my mom, you've known me my whole life. I played spin the bottle with your son Elliot when I was in sixth grade and he was chewing grape-flavored bubble gum when he kissed me. What I'm asking you to do, even if it's not what you're supposed to do, is tell me the real truth the way you would tell a friend, not a patient, because I am scared to death right now and the only thing that will make me feel better is knowing the whole story, whether it's good news or bad."

She paused a second. "You know, Elliot is a doctor now," she said. "He's a resident at New York Presbyterian on Broadway. I'm sure he'd love to catch up with you sometime. Hold on, let me close my door." It sounded like she set the phone down, then I heard some rustling, then she was back, breathing a little heavily, speaking a little more softly. "Okay, here's the deal. We are dealing with a couple of 'ifs' here, so I can't promise you anything. But if you do have only a noninvasive cancer, which means the kind that does not have a propensity to spread, and that's *all* they find when they do the mastectomy, then, in essence, you are cured. We never like to speak in absolutes, and that isn't just to cover our ass but it's because sometimes things happen that we don't expect to happen, things that shouldn't happen. But the answer you are looking for is YES, if all they find is what I think they are going to find, then YES, in any way that really matters you are cured after they remove the breast."

So that made my decision for me, right there, on the floor, the phone in my hand, her voice still registering in my ears but not in my brain. I had heard everything I needed to hear. There would be other questions but there would be time for those later, right then I knew what I wanted. I wanted to see the surgeon as soon as possible. I'd have gone that evening if I could have.

And I knew who I was, who I am, maybe more clearly than I ever have before.

I am too strong to let this stop me.

I am too healthy to be defeated by anything or anyone.

I am too resolved to be afraid.

And I am alive. I will never take that for granted again.

I don't care about my breasts, and I don't need any man who does. Any man I ultimately lose because of this will not have been worthy of me to begin with.

I am going to have this surgery and then I am going to resume my life with no hesitation. The key to life is having a plan, having a destination and then charting a course to reach it, and so I have. I can see the path and I can already see the end of it, I can see *me* at the end of it, and I love where I am and who I am when I get there.

I would consider it a privilege to have any of you who read this accompany me on my journey, and in turn I will walk with you as well, any of you, all of you, on yours. I await your reply. In the meantime, I am going to be absolutely fine. I have never been more certain of anything in my life.

Brooke B.
BreastCancerForum.org
Greenwich, Conn
Date joined: 9/30/2011

I remember the sweet sixteens so well.

It's a stage you go through as a girl, at least where I come from. Some of the girls use their sixteenth birthdays as coming-out parties, debutante balls. I started to be invited to those parties around the time I was twelve. They were so glamorous, it was like being invited to the Oscars every weekend. I had to have a different dress for each event, which meant there were times when I needed two or three in a month, and that lasted about four years.

The next stage was when all my friends started to marry. That was another regular cycle, beginning when I was twenty-two. Scott and I must have attended thirty weddings and I was a bridesmaid in at least half of them. It became a ritual, choosing the bridesmaids' dresses, complaining about the colors behind the bride's back, organizing showers in strip clubs and tea salons. Hair and makeup and hosiery and tears; that lasted three years.

The next stage came very quickly after that. That one was babies. Jill Armel was the first of my group to become a mom. We were so young at the time, and clueless; four of us went to visit her in the hospital just hours after she gave birth. I'll never forget what she looked like, exhausted and pale. She had been in labor for eleven hours. I asked her cheerfully: "How are you, sweetheart?" And she grumpily replied: "I haven't peed in two days." That woke me up a little.

It got easier from there for us, my group of girls, who, one by one, took turns trading in our horrible bridesmaid dresses for equally horrible maternity jumpers and overalls. I think I spent $4,000 in one year at Liz Lange Maternity and I wasn't even pregnant. They were gifts. It was, once again, the stage of life I was in.

The stage that came next was awful. It began in a steady flow when we reached our thirties, all of us young moms, when one by one our parents started to die. I remember it was David Michel's dad who went first, only sixty-one, cancer of the liver. He was an oncologist himself, very prominent in our town. I recall Mother could not bring herself to attend the funeral. "He was such a kind man," she said, "I feel I knew him my entire life." I certainly had. All the mothers and fathers of my group were like family to me, and, one by one, they started to go. A heart attack here, a kidney failure there, they came in a wave. They've slowed some since, they still come now and again, but not as often as they did back then.

And so, as I sit here tonight, introducing myself to you in a state of horror, shock, denial, fear, sadness, and guilt, what I cannot help thinking is that I hope I am not the beginning of the next stage for everyone else. I have this terrible image of my friends gathering for drinks ten years from now, reflecting on this stage of their lives, the stage when their friends started to die. And it's *me* they'll be talking about, the way I talk about Jill in the hospital. I can almost hear them now. "Brooke went first, breast cancer," they'll say, dabbing their eyes with tissue. "Poor thing, she was only forty."

I don't have any idea what the etiquette is here. I have prided myself all my life on knowing the proper thing to do. That was Mother's favorite word when I was a girl, "proper," she could use it in almost any context.

At a proper dinner party, we would never be seated together.

A proper response would be, "Yes, thank you, Daddy."

Please hold your fork properly, a girl without table manners is like spring without sunshine.

Table manners were a big deal. Starting when I was six, I attended lessons in etiquette where I was taught the proper way to behave at a social function. I was there while most of my friends were receiving religious instruction. For my mother, proper behavior *was* a religion.

I know some girls would have rebelled against a childhood like that but I did not. Quite the opposite: I liked it. I liked using the proper fork for the first course at dinner. I liked knowing the proper way to respond to an invitation. I liked all of it and I still do: life is much easier when you know the proper way to behave. That's one of the things that make this so tough right now. I haven't the faintest idea what the proper response is to being told I have triple-negative breast cancer. It's happened so quickly I feel as though I've been watching it happen to someone else, like a character in a book, a character I feel really sorry for right now.

I'm a woman who has two doctors in my life, a gynecologist and a pediatrician, and of the two I see the pediatrician, Dr. Marks, by far more often. He's young and handsome and funny and sweet; I've often thought he was the sort of man I would have an affair with if I ever had an affair. (Which I would not, by the way, not ever.) I happened to mention to Dr. Marks about a month ago, when we casually bumped into each other at the drugstore, that my husband had just turned forty and that I would be forty in a few weeks. And he, because he is this way, asked if I had scheduled my first mammogram. I said I'd thought of it, and he made me promise I'd call my gynecologist that same day. And perhaps because he was just so cute, I did as I was told. A week later I was in the office of Greenwich Radiology, with my shirt off.

"Can you tell they're real?" I asked the technician, looking for a laugh as he maneuvered my chest in the least sexual way I could ever imagine.

"Yes, I can."

"I've been thinking of getting implants," I said. "Would that make this more difficult?"

"Not really, no."

"I guess I just tend to talk a lot when I'm nervous," I said.

"Nothing to be nervous about," he said, as he squashed my breast into the machine, which was shiny and cold and smelled of the spray I used to use to clean the dust off record albums. "Nothing at all."

Turned out he was wrong about that.

If I really was a character in a book, then at the start of the next chapter the radiologist would be telling me he sees a shadow, something really small, too small for me to feel, he would be surprised if I could feel it. It's a solid area on the ultrasound, which needs to be biopsied. He is asking me if I want to call my husband first. I say no. I'm not really listening. Or, I am listening but not hearing, it's not registering. It is as though it is happening to someone else. There is nothing very real about being told you have cancer, even if you are a character in a book.

Then the radiologist is cleaning an area at the outside of my breast with a cotton pad, soft and wet and cold, and there is a needle in my breast, and I am having a sonogram-directed biopsy. It hurts, but not enough to make me cry. I'm not sure I *could* cry anyway. I am having trouble just breathing. And then, just like that, I am in my car, on my way home. There will be no results for forty-eight hours. Blessedly, my husband is away. He'll likely call late tonight. I'll deal with that when it happens. First I need to get through dinner.

The kids are home when I arrive. One of them needs help with homework, the other is upset because "Connor called me stupid." These are real issues for them. They need me, and as always I am there for them. I help with the math, and have a talk about what are and are not appropriate words to use with our friends. "We don't use the word 'stupid,'" I am saying. "It isn't proper behavior at school." In my own head, I hear my mother's voice.

I had planned to make salmon for dinner, but now I am in no mood for all the fuss, so instead I put a pot to boil on the stove. Pasta with olive oil, a little butter, parmesan cheese. I know both kids will eat it happily. I don't even make a vegetable, which I normally insist they eat if they want dessert. Aside from that, I feel as though I am behaving perfectly normally until my daughter bursts that bubble.

"Mommy, you seem sad," she says.

I am seated at the dinner table. The children are on either side of me, eating. I realize I don't even remember setting the table, straining the pasta, mixing in the butter, sprinkling the cheese, pouring the milk.

"I'm sorry, baby," I say, with a smile that comes more easily than I would have expected. "I guess I just miss Daddy, that's all."

"Why aren't you having any wine?" my son asks.

"I don't know, sweetie, I thought I might not drink any wine for a little while."

My two children exchanged looks. "Mommy," Jared says, after a moment, "I'm not sure that's such a good idea."

That makes me laugh and it makes me cry, both at the same time, and I ask the kids to excuse me and I run to the powder room and turn the faucet on full blast. I am pretty sure it drowns out the sounds of my crying.

I don't even remember going back to the table, or what I said, or how

I explained my tears to the children. The next thing I know they are fast asleep in their beds, and I am in the small hallway that separates their rooms. I can see them both resting peacefully in the shadows. There is no sight on earth more beautiful than my sleeping children. They are perfect and they are all mine.

"What more could a woman want?" I ask, aloud.

Then the phone rings. I am ready for the call. It will be Scott and I know what he'll want. And I will give it to him. It doesn't sound like such a bad idea, actually, quite the opposite. It sounds like something very normal, and right now normal sounds really good.

"Hey, big fella," I say as seductively as I can manage, sinking between the sheets of the bed we share. "What can I do for you?"

The conversation doesn't last long, it almost never does. Then I am alone in my room in the dark, staring at the ceiling, waiting for my eyes to adjust to the darkness. And I am thinking of a book I love, with a heroine I love. The book is called *The Hotel New Hampshire,* and the girl is named Franny. And one time when Franny is sad and someone asks if they can do anything for her, she says: "Just bring me yesterday, and most of today." And I realize now that is exactly what I want. Yesterday, and most of today.

THE NEXT CHAPTER BEGINS two days later, when the phone rings again. The voice on the other end is one I do not recognize.

"Hi, Brooke, this is Dr. Downey calling."

For a moment I cannot recall any Dr. Downey. Then I remember the throat infection I had two years before. He is a primary care physician, and when my husband's company switched insurance companies, I had to choose one, so I listed Dr. Downey. Even though I haven't seen him since then, his name is on all my insurance papers. And so it is that the call I have been waiting so impatiently for comes from, essentially, a total stranger.

"Hello, doctor," I say, my throat barely open.

"I was hoping you could come into the office this morning," he says. "I have the results of the test you took the other day and I think we should talk about them."

Then I am in his completely unfamiliar office, staring at his completely unfamiliar face, listening to his completely unfamiliar voice. "We see breast cancer," he is saying, "and we do see an invasive cancer. That means it is the kind of cancer that could involve your lymph nodes. We think it is localized but we'll need some more tests to know for sure. I have the name of an excellent breast surgeon here in Greenwich and I recommend you visit him. Of course, if you have another surgeon you would prefer to see, by all means you should see him or her. But seeing a breast surgeon is the next step in this process."

If I were you, this is the part where I would put the book down. I hate it when things like this happen to characters I like. I can't count the number of books I haven't finished because I didn't like where they appeared to be heading. So if this was a book I was reading, I wouldn't want to read any more. But when you're the lead character, you don't have that choice.

If you're still reading, you're braver than I am.

The next scene takes place six days later, first in the operating room, where the breast surgeon is performing a lumpectomy and a sentinel node, which is where they take out the lump in your breast and, while they are in there, inject a dye that makes its way into a specific lymph node beneath the arm. And then they take me to the recovery room and I wait. And wait. And the seconds feel like hours, much as they did when the twins were small and I was home alone with them, and there were days when they were crabby and uninterested and those were the days when time felt as though it stood still. The difference is now oftentimes I feel nostalgic for *those* days, but I am pretty sure I'll never feel nostalgic for this one.

Then, finally, the doctor comes back, and the news is good.

"Brooke, we got the lump out, it looks to be about a sonometer and a half—"

"How big is that in English?" I ask.

"About an inch."

I like the look of this doctor's face. Which is not to say he is hand-some, but rather that he doesn't look troubled. I am pretty sure his face would look different if he were here to tell me I was going to die.

"The important thing is all the lymph nodes appear to be negative," he continues.

"That's good?"

"Very good, yes," he says. "You are probably only going to need radi-ation to prevent the cancer from coming back in your breast, which means we probably won't need to do a mastectomy. What you will need to do is see a specialist to determine what other treatments may be options for you."

"You say that as though I have some choice in the matter."

"Of course you do," he says, "you're the patient. It's your body and your life, so you're the one who should make the decisions. Don't ever forget that."

I would not forget. In fact, those would prove to be the most memo-rable words I heard through this entire ordeal.

The next chapter takes place in a different office. Now I am listening to an oncologist who specializes in breast cancer explain what he means when he says "the breast, and the rest."

"Your tumor is triple-negative," the doctor says. "That means it does not respond to hormones, or a number of other drugs we commonly use, treatments you may have read about in the newspapers."

I nod my head to affirm, even though I have never read about any cancer treatments in the newspapers. I avoid stories about cancer in the newspapers, and everywhere else as well.

"We are going to use chemotherapy," he continues, "because that gives us the best modality to prevent this cancer from coming back somewhere besides your breast."

"Wait, I think I don't understand," I say. "I had a small tumor in my breast. They removed that. It didn't spread to my lymph nodes. Why do I have to have chemo?"

The doctor's face changed, a little. He looked more professorial now, and I was his student. "Well, we know based on the pathology, based on the tumor's size and other factors, that there is still the potential for the cancer to come back somewhere else. So we do the radiation for the *breast*, and the chemo for the *rest*. That's why we call this approach 'the breast and the rest.'"

I think about it for a minute, as clearly as I am capable of. I'm still not sure I understand. "But why do we have to do this now?" I ask.

"If we wait for the cancer to come back somewhere else, we have lost our window of opportunity. We can *treat* it if it comes back in your liver or your brain or your bones, but right now our goal is to *cure* it."

"But . . ."

I can't really think of what to say after "but." Or maybe I just have so many things to say after "but" that I can't choose one. So I ask questions, lots of them. And the doctor is patient and supportive, but he never tells me what I want to hear. He never offers to give me back yesterday and most of today.

Finally, he says to me: "Brooke, I'll say this to you as directly as I can and I hope you'll excuse my language but this is the best way I can think of to explain this: the time to shit or get off the pot is now. Not in a few years or even a few months. The best way to affect the behavior of this disease, to minimize the chance of it coming back, is to have what we call adjuvant radiation for the breast and adjuvant chemo for the rest of you. The chemo will be directed at any microscopic cells we currently cannot see, with the goal of preventing them from ever becoming an issue."

It is at that point that I tell him I need to go home. It is just too much right now. I understand what he is saying and I will come back soon, as soon as he wants, but right now I cannot talk about it anymore. And, to my surprise, he is not judgmental, he does not scold or browbeat me. There is understanding in his face, in his tone, and he calls in a nurse and instructs her to make time for tomorrow, regardless of what else needs to be postponed.

So that was today.

Tomorrow I go back. Tonight I have a babysitter downstairs with the kids. I called and asked her to spend the night, told her I think I have the flu. I wish I did. I never thought I'd wish that, but right now the flu sounds so good, so normal. I feel so far away from normal. I have no idea when I can expect to feel normal again. I want so badly to feel normal. I've never wanted anything more. I want yesterday, and most of today.

Can anyone here tell me how to get that?

Person2Person
From: Samantha R.
To: Brooke B.
BreastCancerForum.org

Hello Brooke, my name is Samantha.

I'm from Greenwich too. I graduated from Greenwich Academy in 2001, did you go to GA? (Could this be a more awkward introduction? I'm sorry, this is my first person-to-person.)

My situation is a little different from yours. Actually, my whole life is different from yours—I don't have a husband or children, and I guess it's no guarantee that I will ever have either one. What I will be having is a double mastectomy next week. My doctor says I can still have kids; the only tangible effect of my surgery will be that I won't be able to breast-feed, and that seems like a small thing to me now. I imagine it might not seem so small if I ever get there, but right now I'm really not thinking that far ahead. I'm just focused on today, for the time being, maybe tomorrow, not much past that.

I'm not writing to you because of our shared hometown. That may be the reason I was first drawn to your entry yesterday, among the hundreds of others, but it is not the reason I read it over and over, so many times I think I could recite it from memory. It is not the reason I feel I know you, even though we've never met. It is not the reason I am reaching out to you now. I am actually writing to say thank you, because you made me realize the refrigerator had stopped humming. And, as it turns out, that was the single most important thing that has happened to me through this whole ordeal.

You see, I am a crier. I mean, *pathetic.* The way most people behave at the end of the movie *Old Yeller* is the way I often react to television commercials. I have been known to weep after seeing a Subaru ad. I know it's pathetic, but I can't help it.

Which is why it is so interesting that I didn't even notice that I never cried over my diagnosis. I mean, I bawl over a mom choosing her breakfast cereal, but I did not shed a tear when a doctor said to me: "Samantha, you have cancer." I didn't cry that day, and I hadn't cried since. Not a single, solitary time.

Until last night.

As I said, I first opened your entry because of the hometown. It was probably the fiftieth post I have read since I joined the discussion last week. All of them have moved me, inspired me, made me feel less alone. They have done what I believe we are all here to do. But none of them did for me what yours did. You made me cry, and I thank you for that.

I read John Irving too. I have just about every one of his books, and when you quoted Franny saying she wanted yesterday and most of today, I remembered it. And I remembered her. And I realized that she was exactly right, and so were you. That's what I want, too. It's what we all want, to wake up and have it be yesterday, before all the tests and doctors and decisions. I want to remember what I worried about yesterday. Whatever it was, I would so welcome it today.

I got into bed with my laptop and read your words over and over, and I started to cry. And suddenly it was like that moment when the refrigerator stops humming, and you realize you didn't even know the sound was there until it was gone. That's how it felt. I hadn't even realized I hadn't cried until you made me. So I sat there, acutely aware of the silence that replaced the hum, and I cried really hard, by myself, sitting upright on my bed with your letter on the screen in front of me. I didn't have tissues or anything but I didn't even care, I just let the tears fall wherever they wanted.

I feel much more myself now than I did before. It isn't quite like yesterday or most of today, but it's better than it was, and I feel like it's going to get even better still, maybe as soon as tomorrow. I feel I have you to thank for that, at least partly, because I needed to realize the refrigerator was humming and it took your letter to point it out.

Please do not feel an obligation to write me back. I know how much you have on your mind right now, you may not have time or need for a pen pal. I just wanted you to know, even if it's just a voice deep in the wilderness, that your words were read and they made a difference.

I will be following however much of your story you choose to share in the weeks ahead, and please know that I am rooting for the heroine in your story from the bottom of my heart.

Love,
Samantha from Greenwich

Brooke B.
BreastCancerForum.org
Greenwich, Conn
Date joined: 9/30/2011

The following morning I was lounging in a hot bath.

The water was super hot, as hot as I could stand it. I love baths, have since I was a girl, but I seldom indulge anymore; showers are so much more efficient. But this was not a morning for worrying about things like that. This was a time to reflect, and to *feel*, though I wasn't quite sure I could. I'd been numb for days, increasingly so, worst of all in the last few hours. I awoke today devoid of any emotion, any feeling. I wanted to see if I could feel the hot water, and I could, but only a little. Not the way it is meant to be felt. More like the way orange juice tastes right after you brush your teeth: you can tell it's there, but everything that makes it special is missing.

I surprised myself by sleeping soundly. I hadn't expected to sleep at all, but last night I slept hard and long, waking with drool on my pillow.

The babysitter spent the night and she'd handle the kids this morning and get them off to school. There was a part of me that wanted desperately to be downstairs with them, pouring milk over cereal, packing snacks into backpacks, giving goofy hugs and smiles and kisses. Mornings are the best time of day for children, before they have had their energy sapped by the rigors of their day. Mornings are the time when they have the most time and love for their mom. But the first wrinkled nose I saw at the bottom of the stairs was liable to send me into a fit of hysterics I could never control. Right now, perhaps it was better to be numb. Better to sample the hot water, see if I could feel that, and do it alone. There will be other mornings in the kitchen. There may never be another morning quite like this one.

As I dipped my toe in the bath, I realized that not only did I sleep last night but I dreamed as well, which is also unusual. I hardly ever dream anymore; as I say to Scott sometimes, I don't have to dream. I already have everything I want when I'm awake.

But now, as I settled into the scalding water, pausing here and there as my body grew accustomed to the heat—feeling it, but only a little—I was thinking of the dream I had. And, when I finally submerged myself completely, holding my breath, clasping my fingers over my nose, I could see it all behind my closed eyes.

It began at the foot of my stairs, in the entryway from the garage. I was myself but as a young girl, thirteen years old, and I was with my grandmother, after whom I was named and who died when I was that age. I loved my Grammy desperately, and still sometimes feel sad that she never saw the house I live in today. Grammy would have loved it. It is decorated, to the most painstaking detail, the way Grammy would have done had she been alive. I realized now, in a way I never consciously had before, that in nearly every decision I make I consider how Grammy would have reacted. I realized this in the tub, with my head underwater. But not in the dream. In the dream I was thirteen years old, taking Grammy on a tour of a house she did not live long enough to see.

We stopped every two or three steps. There was no detail we ignored, no square inch that was not explained. The mirrors hanging on the walls at the landing of the back staircase, the sequential photos of the children in the rear hallway, the painting Scott bought from a street artist in Paris for less than a dollar. The cabinetry and the cookware and the wine-glasses and the breakfast stools, the rug in the main entry, the furniture in the living room, the desk with the inkwell in the office. The runner on the main stairs, the chandelier above the great room, the painted colors of the children's walls, the linens in the master bedroom. In my dream I proudly explained it all, as a docent might when giving a tour in a museum. And in the tub, I was realizing that every one of the choices had been made with Grammy's silent approval. And it made my eyes fill with tears, just for a moment, even with my head beneath the water, because I realized it meant Grammy was still with me in a way I hadn't been aware of.

The best part of the dream was showing Grammy all the pictures on the wall that separates the kids' bedrooms: my courtship with Scott, my wedding, where the "something old" was Grammy's diamond brooch, and then all the photos of the children, both of them named in her honor: Grammy's middle name was Megan, her last name was Jarret, hence Jared. Had I done that on purpose? Megan I had, I knew that, but I couldn't remember about Jared. All I could recall was saying to Scott: "All my life I have loved the name Jared." And so it was. In the dream I had told Grammy the boy was named for her. And now, in the bath, for the very first time, I realized it was true.

The dream ended with Grammy smiling warmly, exactly as I most love to remember her, with the smell of her cookies somehow wafting in the air, and her saying: "I am so pleased that your life has turned out this way."

And me, at thirteen, replying: "Me too. If I had seen all these pictures when I was this age I would have thought that I was going to have the best life of anyone in the world."

"You do, darling," Grammy said, in the last of the dream I could remember. "You have all you could ask for."

I sit up in the tub and let the water rush through my hair, and I scrub my face hard with my palms. I am more awake now, though I still don't feel very much. And I still think that's probably for the best. I glance at the clock on the face of the radio my husband listens to while he shaves. The kids had gone to school by now. It is almost time to go see the doctor, but I desperately want to stay in the tub a few more minutes. I couldn't possibly bring myself to rush. And so I lie back and let my head drift beneath the water again, and that is when I realize that it hasn't once occurred to me through this entire ordeal that Grammy, my mother's mother, died young from cancer.

I am going to be late for my appointment. I am writing now when I should already be there, and I am the sort of person who is never late for anything. But somehow today that doesn't much seem to matter. It isn't the proper thing to do to make them wait, but today that doesn't feel as though it makes as much difference as it should.

Person2Person
From: Samantha R.
To: Brooke B.
BreastCancerForum.org

Hi, Brooke, I am writing to you from room 324A at Greenwich Hospital, the same building where I was born and where you may have been as well. I've been thinking a lot about that this week, sort of a circle of life, which sounds cheesy but in my mind is a good deal more profound than that.

I spent a lot of time in this hospital as a girl. Not for any horrible reasons; my father was president of the board of trustees. I must have gone to a hundred fund-raising events with him. I remember some of them really well, mostly the Christmases. They always had wonderful events around the holidays, with tinsel and reindeer and visits from Santa. When I got older I was allowed to go to the grown-up functions, dinner dances in fancy dresses, with floral arrangements on the tables and live bands playing standards like "It Had to Be You." The first time I ever slow-danced with a boy was in this hospital, at one of those parties. I was sort of a tomboy then, an athlete, I didn't pay a lot of attention to clothes or my hair, and I didn't pay a lot of attention to boys, either, maybe because I thought they wouldn't pay a lot of attention to me. And then, when I was fourteen, I was here, at a dinner dance, and my father was away from the table, drinking scotch and talking business, and I was peeling the frosting off a piece of chocolate cake, when Andrew Marks came to the table. He was two years ahead of me in school and handsome and athletic and smart, captain of the basketball team *and* the debate team, which is a dream combination if you ask me. His father was the chief of pediatrics, so I had seen Andrew at many hospital functions over the years but had never really spoken to him. I didn't think he even knew who I was.

Then, suddenly, he was standing over me. I don't know how long he was there. People were always milling around at those things, and I was fixated on getting as much of the frosting as I could off the cake. But finally I realized someone was standing over my shoulder, and when I turned I could tell Andrew didn't recognize me.

"Hello, my name is Andrew Marks," he said stiffly and formally, as though he had taken classes in the proper etiquette for asking a young lady to dance and this was his first stab at it. "Would you like to dance?"

Like all girls, I had had crushes before, but that was the first *moment* for me, the first time I learned what it is like when your heart beats a little faster and your breath catches at the back of your throat. I wanted to tell him that he knew me, even if he didn't realize it. I was the same girl he'd seen at these dances a dozen times before, only this time I was wearing a more grown-up dress and mascara and had gotten my hair blown out at a salon. But then I also *didn't* want to tell him. There was something about being the mysterious, pretty girl that appealed to me. It was right there, in that chair, as I said the words "I would love to," that I first realized it was all right to be a girl and also a jock. Maybe that's why I remember the night so well.

Or maybe it's because of the way Andrew held me.

At first, the band was playing "Stayin' Alive" by the Bee Gees and everyone was out of their chairs in full boogie mode, even my dad was dancing with one of the divorcées in town who had been after him since the day my mother died. But I wasn't thinking about that. I was thinking about how well Andrew could dance, how handsome he looked in his suit. He was really tall. I've always liked tall men, beginning with that night.

When they finished the song, the next one they played was "How Deep Is Your Love," also by the Bee Gees. You know that song, don't you? I love that song, and had even before that night. I think it is the most perfectly romantic song I know. When the band began to play it that night, in the ballroom in this very hospital, I felt myself sweat a little beneath my arms. People started leaving the dance floor all around us; lots of people who were willing to boogie were not going to stay out there together for a slow song. Were we? I didn't know. And when I looked up at him I could tell he didn't know either. And I could see that he wanted to, and I knew I did, so I knew ultimately we would but I would leave it to him to make the decision for himself. I just stood there, sweating, trying to smile away the awkwardness until he mustered up the nerve, and when he did it wasn't really much, just an embarrassed shrug of the shoulders, and a look that seemed to say "I'm up for this if you are," but that was enough for me. I took a very deliberate step toward him, and then he opened his arms and I stepped between them and he pulled me in. And then it was as though there was no one else at that party, no one else in the room, no one else in the world, just Andrew Marks and that song and me.

So that was the night I learned that I like being pretty. It didn't matter to me at all before and it has ever since. It still does, now, even as I lie here in this bed, wearing a stained cotton gown that ties in the back, thinking about the dress I wore the night I danced with Andrew Marks. It matters to me, even as I contemplate what life is going to be like for me from now on.

They removed my breasts today.

There's no doubt it was the right thing to do, it was an easy decision to make, but somehow typing out the words isn't quite so easy. Just looking at them now is hard, reading them in the dim backlight of my laptop. *They removed my breasts.* I have a gene that dictates I am at a disproportionately high risk of breast cancer. If not for the gene, the doctor said he would have considered just a lumpectomy, but I think I still might have asked to have the surgery. I want this out of me and I don't want it back.

Still, it was strange to hear.

"I strongly recommend we take your breasts off."

Like they were ski boots.

Next up is reconstructive surgery. And then, for all intents and purposes, I am cured. So, my emotions are in a peculiar state this evening. Because of my breasts, but also probably because of the drugs. And what I find most interesting is that when I woke up from the surgery, my first thought was of you. I needed to go to the forum and find out what has happened to the heroine in your story.

You don't know me at all, and I understand that I have absolutely no right to intrude on your experience, but I can't help myself. You didn't respond to my person-to-person and I fully understand that, but if you can please update your story, I can't explain why, but I need to know.

Person2Person
From: Brooke B.
To: Samantha R.
BreastCancerForum.org

Andrew Marks is my family's pediatrician, and he is super cute. He looks like he'd be an excellent kisser. Is he?

Person2Person
From: Samantha R.
To: Brooke B.
BreastCancerForum.org

I cannot tell you the excitement that raced through me when I logged on this morning and found my icon flashing. No one has ever written to me on the forum before and I just knew it was going to be you. (And, by the way, I don't have very good past associations with surprises in my e-mail. I'll tell you that story someday. *Major* drama.)

It hasn't been the easiest day. The good news is my reconstructive surgery was a complete success, and the surgeon does not foresee any complications. Everything is as good as it can be under the circumstances. Still, I feel tired and sad, and a little worried about ever feeling as good as I did just three weeks ago. I was a serious athlete. Now I am a patient. I know I should feel grateful, I know how much worse this could have been, but I'm sorry, I'm just having a hard time feeling lucky right now.

Your note cheered me. I cannot believe Andrew is your doctor. I knew he had followed in his father's footsteps but I had not heard he was still in Greenwich. I lost track of him while he was at Yale. He's not on Facebook—one of the very few people I grew up with who is not. I think the last time I saw him was at his father's funeral, maybe ten years ago. The whole town was there. I saw Andrew from a distance but I never got the chance to talk to him.

I'm not at all surprised to hear that he is good-looking. He always was, and never more than that night with the Bee Gees in our ears and me in his arms. We danced for a while, through three or four more songs, and when the next slow dance began ("Can You Feel the Love Tonight," by Elton John), my father came barging over and announced loudly that it was his turn to dance with his daughter. I could see a funny look on Andrew's face. He knew my dad (everybody knew my dad), and I think it was at that moment that he realized who I was. And I looked up into his eyes, afraid I'd find regret or embarrassment, but there was neither of those. Andrew just looked very content, and very handsome.

He bowed formally and raised my hand, offering it to my father with an overdone flourish. It was very corny and funny, the sort of thing that could have come off cheesy but I had such a crush on him he could have gotten away with anything. So I danced with my father and then I went back and sat down and continued to pick at the frosting on my chocolate cake. And Andrew never came back to ask me to dance again, or to say good night, or anything. I went home and ran a hot bath and lay in it for a long time.

At school that Monday I found a note in my locker, handwritten in red ink on a sheet of loose-leaf paper with holes on the side where it had been ripped from a binder.

Thank you for a splendid night.
I'll be seeing you.
A. M.

I still have it. I love everything about it. I love that he took the time to find out which was my locker, and I love that he used the word "splendid," which I'm not sure I have ever seen used in any context since. I still remember it as one of the sweetest encounters of my life, even if nothing ever came of it. There is something endlessly romantic about my memory of the whole thing; in fact, if you told me you had it all on videotape I would refuse to watch, because I'd be afraid it wasn't quite as perfect as I remember. And I still think of Andrew as my first boyfriend, even though I'm afraid I can't tell you for sure if he's an excellent kisser.

Please write me back.

Person2Person
From: Brooke B.
To: Samantha R.
BreastCancerForum.org

Pity, he's a hunk.

Person2Person
From: Samantha R.
To: Brooke B.
BreastCancerForum.org

I'm not at all surprised. His father was the only man in town more handsome than mine. Is he married? Does he have a family? Does he seem happy?

You may or may not know the answers to any of those. I realize he is your children's doctor, not necessarily a family friend. Frankly, it's *you* I want to know about. I apologize for prying when it is so clear you don't want to share, but I'll ask one more time and then I promise to leave it alone.

How is your heroine doing?

Person2Person
From: Brooke B.
To: Samantha R.
BreastCancerForum.org

What was the major drama you found by surprise in your e-mail?

Person2Person
From: Samantha R.
To: Brooke B.
BreastCancerForum.org

I found a naked photo of another woman in my husband's inbox. And it happened on my honeymoon. So I was married for two days.

Person2Person
From: Brooke B.
To: Samantha R.
BreastCancerForum.org

Wow, I'm sorry.

I didn't mean to be so glib about something so serious.

I'll tell you, though, maybe in a way you could look at it as though you *are* lucky. You say you're having a hard time feeling lucky, and I understand that, but in a way you are, because you found out more quickly than most that you married the wrong man. Some women don't have the good fortune of discovering that in two days. For some it takes two years, or two decades. And it isn't always so obvious. A nude photo of a woman seems less like a sad surprise than a sign from above, like a flashing light with a megaphone attached, blaring: "You married an asshole, run away before he ruins a lot more than two days of your life!"

I have been married a long time. People often ask me about my marriage, and I always tell them the same thing: being married to the right man is hard work but it is the most wonderful thing in the world. Being married to the wrong man is the worst mistake a woman can make. I know that to be true, not from personal experience but because I have seen it. I have practically lived it with some of my closest friends. I won't get into any names or specifics, but just understand any number of men in the swanky suburbs turn gay when you least expect it, or become addicted to prescription drugs, or develop a sudden longing to travel the world with a backpack. Or, worse, sometimes they just become distant, because they are disappointed in themselves or envious of the husband across the street who just put a six-figure addition on his house, so they drift away emotionally, blaming the women closest to them for their own shortcomings, projecting onto their wives feelings of inadequacy that most times the women don't even feel.

Men are complicated, Samantha, but they are also very simple. If yours was such an asshole that he was cheating on you within two days of your wedding and clumsy enough about it that you caught him, the best thing that ever happened to you is that you found out when you did. Because the alternative would be finding out *after* you had twins and a joint mortgage and reservations to go on safari in Africa. That would be much worse.

What I'm saying is I understand that you are struggling to grasp how lucky you are right now, but if you were able to read it instead of live it, you might decide that where you are is actually a fairly wonderful place. Even if you are wearing a hospital gown instead of a pretty dress.

Person2Person
From: Samantha R.
To: Brooke B.
BreastCancerForum.org

You know, I have had a lot of people say a lot of things designed to make me feel better these last few weeks: my father told me there isn't a medical procedure known to man that will not be considered if I desire it, a nurse told me the nice thing about reconstructed breasts is I can choose the size and they will always be perky, and my best friend from college said, "Dude, you've always been hot and you always will be." I appreciated all their support, but none of them made me feel lucky. You just did. Thank you.

Person2Person
From: Brooke B.
To: Samantha R.
BreastCancerForum.org

You're welcome. Good night.

Person2Person
From: Samantha R.
To: Brooke B.
BreastCancerForum.org

Good morning!!!!

I hope you can sense the energy in my exclamation points. I slept more, and better, than I have since all this began. I awoke feeling strong and optimistic. I am going home either today or tomorrow. The end of this is in sight for me.

I also want to tell you I totally respect that you don't want to share what is going on with you right now. I know how hard and how personal this is for me, and I understand that unlike me you have a husband to share your feelings with, to cry with, to laugh with, to hold you, to make you feel lucky.

You don't need me. I understand that, and I won't ask you again. But I do want you to know that I will help in any way I can if you ever do.

Person2Person
From: Brooke B.
To: Samantha R.
BreastCancerForum.org

Let me tell you about me. When I was first out of college, I worked in marketing for Donna Karan, and I enjoyed the work and the people and mostly the clothes, but to me it was not a career, it was nothing more than a job. I have never had any interest in a career; I never saw the point. What would I do? Sell something? Market something? To what end? Nothing I would be selling or marketing would be really important to me, certainly not in the way my family is.

So that is who I am. And I don't mind at all telling you what is going on with me. What is going on is I am living my life, nothing more, nothing less. And by the way, you are right that I have a lot of people in my life to care for me and I have a wonderful husband to share my feelings with, and he often holds me, and he always makes me feel lucky, and in all the years we have been together I have never kept a secret from him. But I haven't told him about this and I'm not sure I ever will. And if you try to tell me I have to, you will never hear a word from me again.

Person2Person
From: Samantha R.
To: Brooke B.
BreastCancerForum.org

What are you talking about? Why haven't you told him?

Person2Person
From: Brooke B.
To: Samantha R.
BreastCancerForum.org

I said not to ask me that.

Person2Person
From: Samantha R.
To: Brooke B.
BreastCancerForum.org

No you didn't, you told me not to tell you what to do, and that's fine. All I'm doing is asking a question because I am totally confused.

Person2Person
From: Brooke B.
To: Samantha R.
BreastCancerForum.org

You wouldn't understand.

Person2Person
From: Samantha R.
To: Brooke B.
BreastCancerForum.org

Listen, I'm not easily insulted.

I've had a lot of people say things that could have hurt my feelings. A friend of my father's once told me my ass was too small. A soccer coach once told me I was a pretty good player "for a rich girl." When I worked in TV, a news director once said he was sending me on a story because I "wasn't as likely to get hit on" as another field producer we had. I once made out with a boy all night at a fraternity party and then he called me by the wrong name. And, of course, how can we forget: I caught my husband cheating on me during my honeymoon.

The point is that I can ignore or laugh off almost any insult, but for you to tell me I couldn't understand your situation hurts my feelings. Tell me what happened. Help me understand it. I want to be there for you but I can't if you won't let me.

Person2Person
From: Brooke B.
To: Samantha R.
BreastCancerForum.org

I've already told you everything.

I was turning forty, so I went for my first mammogram upon the advice of a handsome young pediatrician who once slow-danced with you and made your insides turn to Cream of Wheat. I did not expect to hear bad news, so I was completely unprepared for what I was told.

Breast cancer.

The sort that does not respond to certain treatment options, triple-negative they call it, invasive cancer, the kind that can spread. The kind that can end your life. None of it made sense. It was like a dream, a bad dream. Life was no longer in color, it was black-and-white. I could listen to my kids but couldn't hear them. I could watch them but couldn't see. For the first time in my life I could not *feel* my own children. I couldn't feel anything.

My husband was not aware of any of this. He is a Wall Street executive and was in China for three weeks, departing the day before the mammogram. I scheduled it that way, figured I'd have nothing much to do that day. I had that wrong.

So he was in China while all of this was going on, and would be for several more days. He called twice each day, without fail, and I told him nothing of this. When he is away he takes great comfort in knowing we are safe and comfortable. He calls once in the morning and once at night, and there is simply no room for bad news.

Then I was back in the doctor's office, and he was explaining why I would still require radiation and chemotherapy even after the lumpectomy, and the good news that the disease was confined to the breast.

"This is very simple, Brooke," he said. "We can minimize the chances of this disease coming back. The statistics are very clear, I can show you the numbers if you like. You substantially reduce the chances of recurrence if you have the adjuvant therapy, radiation and chemo. If the disease comes back, I cannot cure it. I can manage it, but I cannot make it go away forever. So we need for it *not* to return, and this is the way we maximize our chances of that."

I had only one question, but I was embarrassed to ask it, so I found something else to say instead.

"Doctor, I made a mistake when we talked before, when I told you I had no family history. That was wrong. I forgot about my grandmother. She had cancer. She died from it when she was in her late fifties."

The doctor nodded. "What form of cancer did she have?" he asked.

I shook my head.

"I mean, was it breast cancer? Ovarian cancer?"

"I don't know," I said. "No one ever told me." Because no one ever did.

"Were you not born yet when she died?" he asks.

"I was a teenager."

"You were a teenager when she died," the doctor said, with a quizzical look, "and no one ever told you what she died from?"

It sounded strange, but it was the truth.

"Do you have any questions about the treatment?" he asked.

I did. Only one, and it was time to ask it. "Am I going to lose my hair?"

"The best therapy options would likely cause you to lose your hair, yes."

That's when I began to cry. I said I would go home to think about it, even though the doctor was telling me there was nothing to think about.

"It's a hard thing to do," I said.

"It may be a hard thing to do," he responded, "but it should be an easy decision to make."

But he's wrong. It's not easy at all.

So I sat in the tub again that day. I find myself spending an increasing amount of time there lately. Maybe because I feel a constant chill, and the hot water warms my insides. Or maybe because I feel unclean, as though something is all over me, or inside me, and nothing makes me feel more clean than a hot bath.

Then Scott came home.

He was *so* happy to see me. He told me he felt he'd been gone for years, that he felt he'd missed so much, and I said I felt the same way. He was desperate to squeeze his children and then his wife, in that order and in very different ways, so he did and it felt wonderful to be wanted. We snuck upstairs while the kids were busy with homework and did it in the closet, with me bent across a dresser and him fighting to stifle his moans. He squeezed me tightly the entire time, and I felt it all in a way I hadn't been able to feel anything while he was gone. And then ten minutes later I was washed up and back downstairs helping with math problems. And it was just like it was supposed to be. It was my perfect life back again. I just *couldn't* spoil it, not that night. Sometime soon, perhaps, but not that night. It was a night for perfect, and there is no room for cancer in that. So that was ten days ago. And everything is pretty well back to normal. My husband wants me first thing every morning before he dashes to the train, my children need lunches fixed and hair braided and arguments settled, my dog needs walking and tenderness, and offers unwavering affection in return, and when I have time to myself you will find me in the tub, soaking in the hot water, able to feel it now, perhaps not in all of its intensity but certainly more than I could a week ago. I had a lumpectomy and it left behind a scar, nothing huge, nothing my husband has noticed yet. If he does and asks, I will tell him I had a cyst removed. But there is no space for cancer in my life and I don't want to create any, because it would change the way things are and I don't want them changed. I have worked my whole life to make everything perfect, and I'm not at all prepared to have cancer come in and screw the whole thing up.

And when I am alone, when I am in the tub, I alternate between crying uncontrollably and feelings of intense joy, because I have what I begged for when this all began. I have yesterday, and most of today. What more could any woman possibly ask for?

Person2Person
From: Samantha R.
To: Brooke B.
BreastCancerForum.org

Well, you were right, I don't understand.

You're an intelligent woman, Brooke, no one could construct a life as perfectly in tune with her own wishes as you have without being very smart, but maybe in the same way that I could not see how lucky I was to quickly discover my husband was a scumbag, I don't think you can grasp how deeply in denial you are. You *cannot* just pretend you don't have cancer. Life doesn't work that way. A specialist has told you that you need chemotherapy and radiation; you can't just overlook that because you wish it were not true. You need to get fully well, you need to do that for your husband and your kids and, most important, yourself.

Do you worry that your husband will not be able to handle this? Do you worry that it will strain your marriage? Do you worry that he won't love you anymore? Because it almost sounds to me like you do, and if that is the case I can answer your question about what more a woman could want. A woman could want a husband who can handle this.

You have to do this, Brooke. What can I do to help?

Person2Person
From: Brooke B.
To: Samantha R.
BreastCancerForum.org

Help me?

What on earth has given you the impression you can help me? And, while I'm at it, where on earth do you get the nerve to judge me and judge my marriage? I don't want to remind you that one of us in this conversation has been married a little longer than the other, so it seems if there is marital advice to be given, *I'm* the one who should be giving it.

You don't know me, and you don't know anything about my life. The fact that we were born in the same town does not make us alike. I thought perhaps it gave us the ability to understand each other, but it is clear to me you don't understand me at all.

When I was in middle school, we went on a survival trip in the woods and I sliced my hand on a tree branch. The counselors tried but could not get the bleeding to stop, and so they told me I was going to have to come out of the woods to get it stitched up. But even though I have hardly any tolerance for physical pain, I was not going to be the one who let my team down. I gritted my teeth and doused the cut with alcohol to prevent infection, refused to scream, despite a sting that would have stopped an elephant in its tracks, and stitched it up with a needle and blue thread I found in my backpack. It was not until after we had won the competition that I went to the hospital, where the doctor looked at my hand, laughed, and told me to come back in a week to have the stitches removed.

As for my husband, what you are really asking is: How wonderful can this man be if he can't handle what is happening to me? And my answer is that I never said he couldn't handle it. It is *me* who cannot handle it. There is a big difference.

So, I ask you not to reply to this message. If you do, I am not going to read it. I need some time to make up my mind how to proceed and I already know where you stand. I am not telling you I never want to hear from you again, but I am going to have to first get past the way your last message made me feel. When I have done that, I will let you know, and I will tell you then what I have decided to do, and you can think of it whatever you wish. I don't know how long this will take, all of it is just as new to me as it is to you, so I'll just be in touch when I'm ready. Until then, be healthy, be strong, and please leave me alone.

Katherine E.
BreastCancerForum.org
Greenwich, Conn
Date joined: 9/30/2011

Hello? Is there anybody out there?

I am in such desperate need of someone to tell me I am all right, that the last three weeks of my life aren't the beginning of the end of me. I am looking for someone to talk to, to understand. Do they have that here?

My name is Katherine. I just turned forty. And I just finally met the man who was going to change my life, to give me exactly what I am telling you I need now, a partner and a lover and a friend. Someone to take care of me in a way I've never been taken care of before. I waited all my life for him, and then a week after he showed up my life imploded. I suppose this is what they mean when they say it wasn't meant to happen. I hate to think of it that way.

I have worked on Wall Street for twenty years, and without getting into detail I'll simply say I've done very well. Money is not going to be an issue for me, even now. I suppose I should take some comfort from that, but right now *comfortable* just isn't in my vocabulary. I have never been less comfortable. Never.

In the dog-eat-dog world in which I've lived my whole life, I have never allowed myself either of two things that I now regret. The first is weakness. I have not allowed myself any weakness at all. I have always felt that showing any sign of vulnerability would destroy me completely, and as a result I have lived in a rather solitary world. The other is that I've never allowed myself to get over the one man who broke my heart. Perhaps the two are related. Perhaps allowing myself to get past him would have opened the door to a new man, a real relationship, and you can't have one of those without allowing yourself to be vulnerable, and so there we are, back at the beginning again. You can't have love in your life if you aren't willing to suffer for it, and so rather than take that risk I have chosen instead to suffer for a man who hasn't loved me in two decades. It sounds so stupid, which is infuriating, because I am so far from stupid, but this is the way I have lived and that is why in addition to being afraid I am also regretful and angry. There is nothing more debilitating than regret, and no anger worse than that which is directed at yourself. And I have all of that going on now, in addition to cancer.

I guess what I'm saying is I'm a complete mess.

What happened is I turned forty and decided I needed a vacation. That may not sound like much, but I never take a vacation. I have worked practically 365 days a year every year since I got out of business school, because I never want the assholes I work with to feel like they are out-working me.

But this year I turned forty, and I went on a blind date, and I won't bore you with the details of that except to say it was bad enough that I decided I needed a vacation. I went to the mountains in Colorado and fell in love, first with the mountains and then with a man named Stephen. I met him on a hike and then he took me to dinner. He took me not to a restaurant but to a joint, one where they served burgers rather than filet mignon, and the silverware came wrapped in a paper napkin and you ordered your drinks from a bartender, not a sommelier. Oh, and his dog came with us and waited outside. I loved every second of it. I ate burgers and french fries and coleslaw and pickles, I drank three beers and three Cokes and we played darts and watched baseball on television. When we were done, he said he wanted to show me his favorite place in Aspen and he gave me the leash and we walked, the three of us, down a huge hill toward a park just as the sun was setting over the mountain. We walked through a huge grass field where some kids were kicking a soccer ball and a group of teenagers rode skateboards. We kept going, through the soft grass, talking so easily, without awkwardness or long pauses. It was all so easy, in a way it rarely is when you are with a man you hardly know but are aching to sleep with.

We crossed a small bridge with a stream rushing past and then turned into a park, and our feet began to crunch on a gravel path that split into four directions. He pointed to the path on the left and told me to lead the way, he'd be right behind. He wanted me to see it quietly and by myself. He unleashed the dog and she ran ahead, and Stephen pointed and said, "Just follow her, she knows the way." But I was much too conscious of how my ass would look if I walked before him, so instead I put my arm through his and said, "Let's go together," and we did, right into the John Denver sanctuary.

And that was when I entered the most stunningly peaceful, gorgeous, spiritual place I have ever been. There is gentle, rushing water, a trickle from the mountain stream, with large stones that you can sit on spaced deftly about a grassy field, and much larger stones standing proudly, engraved with the words to his songs. And the lyrics, if you do not know them, are beautiful, more like poetry than music.

We sat on the ground in the middle of it all and I closed my eyes and breathed deeply in the mountain air, and then I opened them and Stephen's face was an inch from mine and he kissed me without asking permission. And I grabbed the back of his head and kissed him back, as hard as I could. We made out right there on the grass, with just enough sunlight left to see and the sound of the stream in our ears. And I thought to myself that I'd never had sex in a public place, but if that's where this was headed I was in. I absolutely would have done it right there. I would have done anything he wanted, with no concern at all for what anyone might see.

But that wasn't what he wanted. He kept kissing me for a while and then he scooted closer and wrapped a big arm around my shoulders and squeezed me. He felt so strong, so very good. His hands smelled a little of ketchup and his breath smelled a little of beer, and his shirt smelled as though he had sat in front of a whole lot of campfires in it, and he just held me that way until it was too dark to see the lyrics carved into the stones anymore, and then he kissed me again and popped up to his feet.

"What do you think of it?" he asked, looking around, and I knew he meant the sanctuary but I was referring to absolutely everything when I responded.

I said, "I think it is perfect."

He smiled. "Shall I take you home?"

I surprised even myself with my answer: "You can take me anywhere you want."

He took me all right.

He lives in a stunning house on Red Mountain, with startling views, immaculate décor, and a fully lived-in vibe. When we entered, he excused himself to go to the bathroom and as I waited I decided I wanted to marry him. I ran at him the instant he came back. There was never any chance we would make it to a bed.

I was still floating when I left in the morning. Veritably floating. It was almost ten when we piled into his jeep and went back into town, and he dropped me off with a long kiss and said he'd call me late in the afternoon and I knew he would.

I picked up a warm chocolate croissant and café latte from the Main Street Bakery and savored them as I floated back to my room, where the moment I had most been looking forward to was waiting for me. My girlfriend, who was traveling and staying with me, had not heard from me since I'd texted her the previous afternoon that I had a date.

She'd replied: *IF U DON'T CUM BACK 2NITE I'LL KNOW U'RE EITHER GETTING YOUR HEAD CUT OFF OR YOUR BRAINS FUCKED OUT!!!*

My apologies for the language, but she texts that way.

Well, I threw open the door as loudly as I could, hoping she'd be exactly where I found her, seated in the living room, reading a trashy magazine.

"I'm back, sweetheart," I said, loud and sassy, "and my head is still on!"

I told her the entire story, and I think she was even happier for me than I was for me. And, really, is there anything better than that? If there is, I can't think of it. I can't think of a single time in my life that I was happier than I was right then, telling my friend Marie every detail of the fabulous sex I had just enjoyed, while drinking the last of my latte and tasting the butter and chocolate on my lips. What more could you ask for?

May I be filled with loving-kindness
May I be well
May I be peaceful and at ease
May I be happy

That is a meditation I have taken great comfort in over the years. I have strived to live by those words, used them as a beacon during my dark moments, but I had never really felt I had *achieved* them until that day. That was the day everything would change, because finally I *was* filled with loving-kindness, I *was* peaceful and at ease, I *was* happy. The only trouble was I wasn't well. I just didn't know that yet.

I went back to New York to quit my job, tidy up my affairs, and move back to Aspen for good. Maybe I would marry Stephen, maybe not, but either way I would hike and ski and ride horses and meet other men if this turned out not to be the right one. I was ready. I was expecting to be back in Colorado within two weeks.

When I arrived home, my first appointment was with my therapist, who applauded loudly when I told her my plan. I think she had a tear in her eye; I know I did.

"This is the best decision I have ever known you to make," she said, "regardless of how it turns out. I will miss you very much, but I hope we will never see each other again."

Before I left her office, I mentioned, almost off-handedly, that my back had been bothering me, more and more of late, enough that it was beginning to interfere with my exercise. I told her I'd been putting off seeing a doctor because I feared it was some sort of nerve issue or degenerative disc, which might require surgery, which would keep me off my treadmill for longer than I thought I could bear, but now the pain had risen to a level where I felt it was going to limit me sooner rather than later.

"Go see your doctor before you leave New York," she told me. "Start your new life without anything like that hanging over you."

Seemed like a good idea.

I saw my doctor the following day. She said I needed to see a physical therapist, that I could probably get an appointment before the end of the month.

"No, Sheila," I told her, "I'm leaving town much sooner than that, and I don't plan to be back for a while. We need to figure this out right now."

She told me she didn't think there was any way to figure anything out so quickly, but in the interest of skipping a step or two, she would take X-rays and send me for an MRI. She also wrote me a prescription for a painkiller, which she described as "Aleve on steroids," and told me to take one if the pain got in my way. I took two that night, with a glass of white wine, and fell asleep looking forward to quitting my job.

I woke up feeling great. The painkillers were magical; I hadn't felt so loose in months. I ran effortlessly and without pain on my treadmill for forty minutes before breakfast. I had a noon appointment with the radiologist, which left just enough time to summon my CEO and offer my resignation. (I should tell you that I was more eager for the opportunity to tell him to his face that I was finished than I was anything else. That's a long story. A good one, by the way, filled with sex and betrayal, but I don't have time for it right now.)

I went straight to his office.

"I need to see Phil immediately," I announced to his troglodytic assistant, loudly enough that anyone in the hall might hear.

"Oh, um, well," she said, along with a lot of other meaningless words people use when they are startled and helpless.

"That's insightful," I said bitchily. "Just push the button and tell him I'm on my way in."

What happened next was like a scene from a bad sitcom. The assistant, Danielle, rose from behind the desk and started to run to the door that separated her small office from the huge one she was there to protect. I was closer to the door than she was but she had a fairly good angle of pursuit and she wasn't fooling around. In fact, she would have beaten me there had it not been for the five-inch heels on her Jimmy Choo Lizzy Leather pumps. (I've worn those and trust me they are not meant for running.) The woman took three quick steps toward me and then went sprawling face-first into the carpet, landing with a thump directly between me and the door. All I had to do was step over her, which I did with great relish.

But before I did, I knelt beside her. "Everything you may have heard about Phil and me is true," I hissed, with a smile, "and if you already knew that but insisted on torturing me all these years anyway, all I can say is *fuck you*."

Then I went inside and told the man who almost ruined my life that I wasn't working for him anymore. Now, you tell me, can a day possibly start any better than that?

I AM FEELING A little tired and a little sad at the thought of writing about what happened next. If there is anybody out there who wants to know, I will tell you. Write to me. I see there is a Person2Person feature here. If you use it, I will, too. I could use someone to talk to, someone who understands, someone who knows a little bit about days that start really well but don't remain that way. Because right now I feel like I'm the only one.

Person2Person
From: Samantha R.
To: Katherine E.
BreastCancerForum.org

I'm here.

I'm here to listen. I'm here to cry with you or laugh with you, whichever you need. I'll be here on the lousy days and on the better days, and I promise you there will be those. And I will be here on the day you come out the other side of this, as I have, and I can promise you it is an even more glorious feeling than you imagine it to be.

My name is Samantha. I was first drawn to your profile because we are from the same town. I grew up in Greenwich, though I haven't actually lived there since high school; I'm twenty-eight now. My life story isn't so interesting, not nearly as much as yours. I don't have a dreamy man waiting for me in Aspen, or anywhere else for that matter. I was married once, but that was brief and ended badly. I was diagnosed a few months after my marriage dissolved, and at the time I was feeling healthier, both physically and spiritually, than I ever had before and I am headed back to that now. In fact, I am going to be better for this. I actually believe this is going to wind up being a wonderful blessing in my life.

You see, nothing I have done has ever felt especially significant. I have been supported by my father all my life, and for a short time by my husband, and nothing I have done ever felt as though it really *mattered*.

Until now.

I was diagnosed with noninvasive cancer in my left breast. I was given a few options but immediately chose to have a double mastectomy and reconstruction. I wanted every shred of the disease out of me, and I was perfectly comfortable going to those lengths to assure it. When I woke up from the surgery, the first face I saw belonged to a nurse I had grown to like, named Jenny, a cute young woman, no older than me, maybe a year or two younger. She was kind and reassuring and made me feel like everything would be all right. I told her so before they wheeled me into the operating room and she smiled and promised me she'd be sitting by the bed when I woke up and sure enough she was. And she smiled at me, and as soon as I saw her dimples I knew it had gone well. And her first words to me were: "Congratulations. You no longer have cancer."

I can't repeat those words without crying and I don't think I ever will. I'm choking up now as I type them. But what I decided that night, in that bed with those words still in my ears and the tears still on my cheeks, was that somewhere in the midst of this I had found my calling. I want to dedicate myself, however I can, to making other women feel the way I felt then. I don't know all the ways that is possible yet, this is all new for me, but this is my start. I read the message you posted and here I am. What I am offering you is whatever I have that you need. An ear, a shoulder, a ride to the doctor's office, or the hospital, or the airport, or a Broadway show. If I am able to make one moment of this suck a little bit less for you, I will feel I did my job.

It's a modest plan, I know. I think of it as a support group without the group. Right now there is only me. I reached out to one other woman here, also from Greenwich, and we had a nice exchange for a while and I'm hopeful that we will go forward together, but for right now I am a group of one inviting you to make it two. How to do that is fully up to you.

Just say the word.

Person2Person
From: Katherine E.
To: Samantha R.
BreastCancerForum.org

I am moved by your compassion and the generosity of your spirit. As a rule, I don't have a whole lot of faith in the intrinsic decency of mankind, but you have taken a step toward changing that tonight. It may have been a small step for you, but it was giant for me.

I spend almost no time in Greenwich these days. My mother is still there, rattling about the halls of the house in which I grew up. Honestly, it feels more as though she haunts the place than lives in it. My mother has become the sort of person you can sometimes forget is in a room. It's not the most cheerful time when I see her, and thus I hardly ever do.

I live in Manhattan and quite nicely, though I was—and am—ready to chuck all of it and dash to the mountains. I was about to do it. I was so excited.

Then I went for the MRI.

The first thing I discovered is that I am a tad claustrophobic. I don't know how better to discover that than lying still in a tube like a sausage with the walls closing in while a horrific clanging deafens you. So that was pretty terrible. I just kept telling myself it was temporary, that I just needed to breathe and keep my eyes closed.

I went home after forty minutes of cylindrical torture and treated myself to a really fine bottle of wine, and waited to hear why my back was hurting me so. I was prepared for nerve damage, disc trouble, stress-related muscle fatigue, arthritis, even a tiny broken bone in a place I couldn't find with my fingers. In fact, now that I think of it, I believe that is what I was expecting, a broken bone. An arduous rehabilitation. An admonishment to back off significantly from all my exercise. I drank a toast to my treadmill and how little I was going to miss it. So long as I could climb the occasional mountain, I was sure I would be fine.

Then the phone rang, and a voice on the other end said, "Katherine, I need to see you tomorrow."

What's funny now is that I didn't recognize the voice at first. I thought it was Phil, my CEO, to whom I had resigned earlier in the day. I cackled into the phone at the very thought. I thought he was calling to say he needed me back, the firm could not survive without me, to remind me of the tens of millions of dollars in stock options I was leaving on the table, and oh by the way his wife just left him (which she did) and he realized it was, in fact, me he'd loved all these years and he was begging me to marry him.

Then the voice continued, "There are some things on your MRI that concern me and we're going to need to get you to see an oncologist."

That was when I realized it wasn't Phil on the phone.

But the gravity of the moment did not strike me so quickly. I hardly ever get sick, so I really don't *speak* doctor. I suppose I was aware that an "oncologist" meant "cancer," but I didn't put it together quite so quickly.

"What are we looking at, doc?" I asked, still thinking it was back trouble. "Something serious?"

"We should talk in person," he said. "Tomorrow in the office."

That was when I knew we weren't talking about a herniated disc. I sat down and watched my knees begin to shake. I was gripping the phone really tightly. I didn't want to let go, and I didn't want to stop talking, either. I would be alone the moment he hung up and I really didn't want to be alone.

"We need to talk now," I said, trying to keep my voice steady. "You're scaring me."

"We should sit down and talk in person."

"Okay," I said. "My driver will pick you up in ten minutes."

There was a moment of silence.

"Katherine, I don't know if I can make that work," he said hesitantly.

"Okay, that's fine," I told him. "Then all you need to do is tell me right now this isn't something very serious and I don't need to be that worried about it. Because, frankly, calling me at six o'clock in the evening and scaring the living shit out of me and then going on about your day isn't my idea of bedside manner. If this is serious, doctor, I want to know and I want to talk about it right now."

He paused again.

"What kind of car is it?" he asked.

"Holy shit," I said. "I'm dying, aren't I?"

"I have concerns, Katherine. No one is saying you are dying," he said. "I'll be outside the Madison Avenue entrance in ten minutes."

A half-hour later, Dr. Armitage walked into my apartment with my driver behind him. My eyes went right to Maurice. I wanted to see his face, the way I always look at a flight attendant if there is trouble on an airplane. If the attendant looks calm, all must be well, right? But Maurice never looked at me, never lifted his eyes off the ground. He just shuffled to a chair and sat quietly, staring at his feet.

"I asked Maurice who your closest friend is," the doctor said. "He said it was him."

"He's right," I said, though the words caught in my chest. "Why does he need to be here?"

"We need to talk about what we found on the MRI, and some of it might get a little complicated," he said. "Having another set of ears is always helpful."

"Just tell me," I said. "This drama has gone on too long. I can't wait anymore."

Dr. Armitage took off his glasses. "We see some things that concern me," he said, "some abnormalities. It appears to be some kind of tumor on your spine."

"I have cancer?"

"That is very likely, yes," he said.

There was a lovely gentleness in the way he told me. Even though his expression was stoic and I was aware that he was making a speech he probably makes every day, there was still kindness in his voice.

"It is quite unusual for a tumor to arise in the spine," he continued. "These things typically come from other places, most frequently breast cancer. Either way, I think you need to see an oncologist right away. I've spoken to my friend Dr. Richard Zimmerman, he's the best in the city. He will be able to see you tomorrow. In the meantime, I'm going to give you something for the pain and something for your anxiety, and the best thing you can do is try to relax tonight as best you can. And call me if you have any questions at all."

I didn't have any questions.

Or maybe I had too many to think of one.

Either way, I didn't say anything.

Maurice did. "Doctor, she has a prescription for Ambien. More than anything I think it would be best for her to sleep tonight. Would it be all right if I gave her one of those?"

"Absolutely," I heard the doctor say, but I was already fading away. I would have slept without the pills. And I did, right there on my sofa, with all my clothes and jewelry and makeup on. Maurice didn't move me, though when I woke up I found myself tucked beneath a soft blanket with a pillow from the bedroom beneath my head.

The next afternoon I met Dr. Z, the kindest man in the world. He explained to me, in his heavy Brooklyn accent, that he became a doctor because his beloved mother died of breast cancer and he decided, at her funeral, to dedicate his life to helping other women fight the disease. And I thought to myself that sometimes you meet the best people in the worst of circumstances. I wish I'd known that a long time ago. It doesn't make any of it better, really, but in some ways it does.

After Dr. Z's introductory speech, he brought out the MRI results and laid them on a table. Then he asked me to remove my shirt and bra and gave me a breast exam.

"Did you notice this lump?" he asked, as he kneaded an area just to the side of my right nipple.

"Not really," I said.

I was too ashamed to tell the real answer, which was that I hadn't noticed it at all. I know I'm supposed to give myself breast exams, but I do not, never have. I know that is stupid, but if you think about it it's no more stupid than wasting twenty years of my life pining for a man. We do a lot of stupid things. That's what I was thinking as he continued to manipulate my boob between his thumb and forefinger. For a really intelligent woman, I do a lot of stupid things.

Dr. Z leaned back when he was done and pulled off his eyeglasses. "Okay," he said, his tone unchanged, nothing to read into at all, "here's what we need to do. We need to get some blood work, we need to do some more tests, we should biopsy your breast lump, and we may need to do some other biopsies as well."

"I'm sorry, doctor, but I thought we were worried about my spine and my bones."

"Most cancers start somewhere else and they travel," he said. "For example, it's very uncommon to have liver cancer. Usually, cancer of the liver starts somewhere else, like in the breast."

"So in this case, what you're telling me is I have breast cancer that has spread to my bones?"

I thought I saw just a little bit of emotion then. He seemed to swallow especially hard before he answered. "That's what we need to find out. We're going to send you for a biopsy, we're going to get a CAT scan of your chest and belly, and we're going to do a bone scan. You'll be back by the end of the week and we'll go over the results."

I could go on and on about the subsequent tests I took and the chalky fluid I drank and the Ambien-fueled nights that passed, but there isn't really much point in any of that. By Friday I was back with Dr. Z and he was telling me, in a matter-of-fact tone, that I have breast cancer that has probably spread to my spine.

What was amazing about that moment was that I had no reaction whatsoever. You know how when you see someone in a courtroom be pronounced guilty and sentenced to life in prison, they don't ever seem to scream or cry or even flinch? I've always wondered how they manage to remain so stoic, but now I understand. It is because they already know. Just as I did. I knew what Dr. Z was going to tell me before I set foot in the office.

"Are you saying I have a terminal disease?" I asked.

"What I'm saying is that you have a disease we cannot cure," he said. I could tell he'd made this speech many times. "That does not mean we can't treat it, we can often treat it for years, but based on what we know now this is not a disease that we can cure."

I wanted to ask him how long I had but the words got stuck inside.

"You should know, Katherine," he went on, "that miraculous progress is being made in research every year, every day, every hour. We will treat this, we will make this as comfortable as we can for you, we will see to it that you will live your life however you choose to, and we will be comforted by the fact that five years ago there was a lot less we could do for you than we can today. And by that, I mean that there is every reason to believe that next year there will be more we can do, and even more the following year. So that is the game we are playing."

I closed my eyes and asked, "How much time do you think we have to play it?"

He smiled. "How's your sense of humor?"

"Some people say it's my best quality."

"Okay, then I'll tell you that if you are asking me when you are going to die, I will tell you that if I knew I would arrange right now to take that day off, because there's a lot of paperwork involved. And then you'd smile—just as you are right now—and I'd tell you I'm not giving any thought to when you are going to die. The only thing either of us needs to be thinking about is how you're going to live."

So, Samantha, that is my story. I haven't been back to see him yet. I will go, probably tomorrow or the next day. I just haven't been able to manage it yet. I haven't been able to do anything. I haven't left my apartment, have hardly eaten, barely slept. I can't really describe the way I feel. But I *can* tell you that I'm afraid I can't do what the doctor is asking. Because I am so alone. I don't have a husband, a boyfriend, a sister, or a priest. I can't involve Maurice in this. He's a wonderful man but he's my driver, and I can't put all of this on him. You can't ask people who work for you to do things like this, because the truth is you don't know how they really feel about you and it's probably better that way.

And while I don't know if I can face this alone, I know I would rather try that than involve my mother. I haven't told her a word of this and I don't plan to. If I die, she'll find out when someone invites her to the funeral.

So, what I'm saying is that I just don't know that I am ready to go back to the doctor and hear all of it and ask the questions and get the answers and begin the treatment all by myself. I'm sure I will change my mind tomorrow or the next day. I'll go back because I have to. But it would be a lot easier if there was someone with me. To take notes. And ask questions I don't think of. And maybe hold my hand. No one has held my hand in a long time. I know we have never met, and so I am a little embarrassed to say this, but right now I think you may be the best chance I have. Probably because you're the only chance I have. So if you want to meet in the city tomorrow, maybe I could buy you lunch and we could talk, and who knows what might happen next.

You just might save my life.

Person2Person
From: Samantha R.
To: Katherine E.
BreastCancerForum.org

What time and where?

SAMANTHA □ □ □

I HOPE I DIDN'T do too blatant of a double-take when the maître d' led me to the table. It's just that if you had given me the choice of any of the women in the restaurant—Michael's on the East Side—I think Katherine would have been the last one I'd have guessed. She looked so healthy, so well put together, she didn't look at all unwell or uncertain, or un-anything. She isn't a beautiful woman but she is striking, and younger than I expected.

"I'm Katherine Emerson," she said, rising, as I approached. She had a deep voice, not masculine, more like she might sing opera in her spare time.

"Hi," I said, because I couldn't think of anything else.

She extended her hand and I shook it. Her grip was firm, the way my father shakes hands, but when it was time to let go she didn't. She held my hand a beat longer than I know she normally would have. That's what having cancer does. It makes you hold someone's hand a beat longer than usual, no matter how fabulous you look.

"It's good of you to meet me," Katherine said.

"It's funny," I said, as I sat opposite her at a sunny two-top with a gorgeous centerpiece of white lilies, "I feel as though I should be saying that to you. I know that makes no sense, but somehow I feel like I'm the one who should be grateful."

I laughed a little. Katherine did not, she didn't even smile. Actually, she didn't look like she smiled much, even before she had cancer.

"Here's my story," she said. "I'm a single woman. I quit my job the day I was diagnosed, literally the same day. The timing of that didn't work out so well for me, but there isn't much I can do about it now. I had plans to go out West to be with a man I just met, and that doesn't seem to be in the cards now either. In a nutshell, I am all alone and I have to deal with this, and something inside of me is saying that if I don't have someone to encourage me, then at some point I'll just decide it isn't worth it. So, I guess that's what I'm looking for, someone to tell me it's worth it on days when I'm not so sure."

I heard a clinking sound and thought for a moment someone had dropped some change on the ground, then I realized it was Katherine's silverware. Her demeanor was placid, her voice calm, her facial expression stoic, but her fingers were in a frenzy. She was puttering with the left side of her place setting, the forks rolling frantically in her hand, and I don't think she even realized it, or heard the clinking, or anything. It made me think of when I was a little girl in the country and my father and I saw ducks swimming on the pond, and my father told me ducks were his role models.

"Their feet are paddling like crazy beneath the surface," he said, "but you'd never know it."

I reached out and put my hand over hers, and I heard her breath catch. She let her hand go limp beneath mine, and when she looked up again into my eyes, she was entirely different.

I hadn't realized it at first but she is a small woman. I suppose I didn't notice because her appearance is so striking, her presence so magnified, but everything about her is small. Her hands are tiny, her fingers as narrow as tightly rolled dollar bills. Her facial features are small, her eyes, her teeth. And, looking closely, I had a sense her shoulders ended a long way before her blouse began. She was what my mother would have called "petite," and with my hand on hers, her face told me she didn't mind that I knew it, even if few other people did.

"Let's talk about something else," I said cheerily, giving her hand a squeeze and then taking mine back. "There'll be plenty of time to figure all the rest of this out."

"I like that idea," Katherine said. "Do you want a glass of wine?"

"Can you drink wine?"

"You bet your ass I can drink wine, and right now it sounds awfully good."

"All right, I'll have a glass."

"Perfect," she said, "and I'll have the rest of the bottle."

This time, she smiled.

Two glasses later, she began telling me how bored she is.

"You know, I always wondered what I was missing by working all the time," she said, slurring only slightly. "I realize now I wasn't missing anything. Trips to Paris, London, Aspen, maybe, but you can't do that all the time. This week I have been sitting in my apartment watching television. I have over eight hundred channels and there isn't a single thing worth watching."

"I love game shows," I said.

Katherine almost did a spit take. "Oh my god, those are the worst of all!"

I laughed. "I love them. I love the people."

"The people?" she exclaimed. "They are the worst part! I have to believe the stupidest people in the world are the contestants on these game shows. Because if there are actually stupider people out there, we are doomed as a civilization." She refilled her glass.

"Oh, but they're so earnest," I said, "they try so hard."

"Please." She took a gulp of wine. "I was watching *Family Feud* this morning, the old version, when Richard Dawson used to kiss all the women—which is so gross, and could be a whole *other* reason I hate game shows—but anyway, after this woman gets finished kissing Richard Dawson he asks her to name a country in South America, and she says 'Spain.' And I'm thinking, 'All right, she's not Magellan, but it's not the end of the world.' Then her idiot brother is next in line and Richard asks him to name a country in South America and he looks up, totally cross-eyed, with an expression like a dog going to the bathroom, and he says: 'You know what Richard? I really thought she was right, I'm going to have to say Spain too.'"

I burst out laughing.

"I couldn't believe it," she said, shaking her head, though I could see my laughter was contagious, it was spreading toward her, and then she started to chuckle too. "I guess it *is* funny, if you think about it."

"It's hilarious," I said, "and it's so sad. I feel sorry for the people on those shows, they try so hard. It makes me cry sometimes."

She looked me square in the eyes. "You cry watching game shows?"

"All the time."

"I see," she said, shaking her head. "Well, we're going to get along just great."

"That's right," I said, using the linen napkin to wipe the tears of laughter from my eyes. "We're going to be BFFs."

"I like that," Katherine said. "Breast Friends Forever."

KATHERINE

I LIKED HER IMMEDIATELY.

What is there not to like? She's a sensitive, sweet, intelligent person. If she were a man, I would have fallen in love with her before the cork was out of the second bottle. Maybe I did anyway. Maybe you can fall in love with someone without wanting to make love with them. If you can, then I did. I fell in love with Samantha the first time I met her.

The only thing I told myself before she arrived was that I would have to be fully honest with her. It seems the time for playing games in my life is over, and even if it isn't, there certainly isn't anything to be gained by playing them with her. So I would answer her questions with truthfulness, whatever they might be, rather than the defensive posturing that has characterized pretty much every relationship of my adult life.

When finally we had stopped laughing over the tragic game-show contestants, I sighed deeply and tried to steer the conversation back to what I really needed to talk about with her. "I have been doing a little research on the Internet about the disease. There is so much out there that I feel somewhat overwhelmed. I don't know what's credible and what's not."

"I did the same thing," Samantha said. "I felt the same way. I was all over the place. The truth is I got the most out of the social sites, like message boards and Facebook."

"I'm not even on Facebook. I think that's why I'm always behind on all the gossip," I said. "I don't know why I haven't signed up. I guess I just figured if I haven't heard from you in twenty years it's probably for a reason."

Samantha laughed at that, but I didn't. That wasn't honesty. That wasn't what I promised myself I would bring to this lunch. That was my typical use of humor as a defense mechanism, and what good was that doing me here?

"Actually," I said, glancing away, "that isn't the reason. In all honesty, I think I never signed up because I was afraid no one would friend me. Even now I don't want to go on and talk about my diagnosis. I guess I'm afraid there'd be no one who cared."

I kept my gaze away, waiting for her reply, but she didn't say a word. It was quiet for so long I finally had to look at her. She is a very pretty girl. Her eyes are deep blue and she has the sort of cheekbones people would pay anything to have surgically implanted. But her best feature is her compassion, her humanity. You can see it in her face. It oozes from her.

"My god, Samantha," I said, "I am so alone."

She put her hand back on mine. "Not anymore."

I cleared my throat a time or two. I was afraid I might begin to cry. I wanted to keep talking but I couldn't think of anything to say.

"Do you need a minute?" she asked.

"Not at all," I said. "Just talk to me. Tell me about yourself. All I really know is that you weep during game shows, and, frankly, if I'm going to put my life in your hands I'm going to need to know more than that."

She seemed to get my sense of humor, which is nice, because I happen to think it is my best quality. Not when it is being used to deflect or to compete, in those cases my humor probably does me more harm than good, but in the right moments saying something funny is the best thing you can do for a conversation. I could tell Samantha could appreciate that.

Then, to my shock, she told me the story of her ill-fated marriage. I hope my genuine reaction wasn't evident in my face, meaning I hope my jaw didn't actually hit the table. It all just seemed so unlikely, so unlike the woman Samantha is. She seems so stable, so together. I don't know what type of person you expect to have her marriage annulled after three days, but whoever that is she is the opposite of the woman who was sitting across from me.

"All I can say," I told her, when she finished her story, "is that this guy has got to be one of the most irretrievably stupid people on the planet to let you get away. And while I realize I barely know you, I mean that from the bottom of my heart."

"That's very nice of you."

"What an asshole," I said, for emphasis, and she laughed.

"What about you, Katherine? Have you ever been married?"

"I've never been married," I told her. "I was close one time. At least I thought I was, maybe I wasn't as close as I thought. Actually, my history with men is something of a horror show. You're either going to laugh or punch me when I tell you some of the crap I have put up with."

"Try me."

I took a deep breath. "Well, I once was dumped in the midst of a session with a couples therapist. I suppose being in couples therapy before we were married should have been a sign, but somehow I missed it.

Another time, I cooked dinner for a guy, he arrived, we had sex, then he broke up with me, *then* he asked if he could still stay for dinner because if he left he would hit traffic, and I let him."

Samantha started to respond but I cut her off.

"Then there was the time I tried to break up with a guy and he talked me out of it, and we went home and had sex and *then*, while he was smoking a cigarette in my bed, he told me I was probably right and we should break up."

She was laughing again. Not the contagious, hysterical way she had earlier, but the knowing laugh of a woman who understands what complete scumbags men can be.

"But I didn't almost marry any of those. They were like buses or trains, always another coming along if you miss one," I said. "Phillip was different. We went to business school together. We studied together, traveled together, never actually lived together but may as well have. I don't know that he was ever in his own apartment in the two years we were together. When we were close to finishing school, he told me about another woman he had met in Cambridge, a townie. She was stunning and she was easy. Not just in a sexual sense. She was easy on *him*. She thought everything he said was brilliant and funny, she thought every idea he had was genius. I did too, of course, but I was his equal and she wasn't, and he acknowledged that there was something he liked about that. She worshipped him, and it was fun to be worshipped."

Samantha was leaning forward now, perfectly still.

"I remember where we were sitting when he told me. In a diner, in a booth in the rear. He was drinking a vanilla milkshake and I was having coffee. I listened to every word, and then I said to him: 'Listen, I love you as much as you will ever be loved and I will marry you this minute if you ask me to, but I am a Harvard-educated woman with plans to do exactly what you're planning to do when we get out of here, so play me or trade me, Phillip, but don't ask me not to be your equal.'"

I poured myself a bit more wine before I finished the story.

"I went home and waited. Three days went by, four days, five. I didn't hear a word. Then he called. It was a Saturday. And he said, 'I miss you so much it aches. Can I come see you? I have something important to say.' And I cried with joy, because I knew what it was going to be. He was at my door twenty minutes later, and he carried me into the bedroom and made love to me before either of us said a word, and in the afterglow I could see tears in his eyes and so I started to cry again and I almost told him he didn't have to ask me, because I knew, and I loved him, and I wanted to get dressed right then and run to City Hall and get married that night and decide what to tell our families about it afterward. Then he lit a cigarette and sat up, and his first words were: 'Christ, Kat, I am going to miss you so fuckin' much,' and all the blood just drained out of me. I didn't even get angry, not immediately, or even sad. I just got small. I felt so small it was as though you wouldn't even be able to see me, as though I practically disappeared. And in some ways I guess I've stayed that way for almost twenty years."

A tiny tear rolled down Samantha's cheek.

"He married the townie?" she asked.

"He did indeed. Less than a year later."

"Oh no."

"Wait," I said, "you haven't even heard the worst part yet."

SAMANTHA 🔲 🔲 🔲

I CAN'T BELIEVE SHE worked for him all these years.

I can't imagine going into an office every Monday and asking Robert how his weekend was. I don't care how much money was involved, there isn't any amount that would make that worth it.

What I admire most about Katherine is how aware of herself she is.

She has an excellent understanding of herself, and she is acutely aware of how unhealthy her life has been since Phillip and even more aware of the crisis she is facing now. She understands what she is up against, and she is strong. I could feel her strength that afternoon and I grew to admire it more and more in the weeks that followed.

Perhaps the hardest thing for a strong person to do is admit to needing help, and what I think Katherine learned during our time together was that it was not a sign of weakness but rather of great courage to accept me, to lean on me, to allow me to be her health advocate, which is exactly what I became, right there over a second bottle of Burgundy.

Three days later, we were perfectly sober as we approached the entrance to the massive complex of Memorial Sloan-Kettering, where Katherine would spend two days on the nineteenth floor to have special biopsies performed, receive second and third opinions on all her diagnoses, and then begin her chemotherapy treatment program. Katherine had told me about the nineteenth floor at our first lunch. Apparently, it is an open secret among the rich and famous, like the island David Copperfield owns. It is a special floor for the world's premier cancer patients. There isn't anything different or superior about the treatment, the difference is in the way you are treated. Katherine told me to expect the Four Seasons, but when we arrived it felt more like a motel you'd find on a deserted stretch of road off a highway in a bad neighborhood. Even having money and knowing we would be going to nineteen didn't save us from being caught waiting in the general area on the first floor, which was overrun with people trying to be admitted.

I had a meltdown.

Katherine was anxious enough without having to wait three hours because of a paperwork snafu and a nurses' shift change. She kept trying to quiet me down, and then I thought to myself: *If* she *is comforting* me *then what exactly am I accomplishing? Why am I even here?* And so I took matters into my own hands. I ducked into a supply area when no one was looking and stole a gurney. I beckoned Katherine and before she could balk I said: "Lie down."

Then I was wheeling Katherine past the nurses' station and past security directly to the only bank of elevators I could see from where we'd been waiting. I pressed the button and held my breath. And, to my great relief, the first thing I saw upon entering the elevator was a placard on the rear wall.

SERVICING FLOORS 10 THRU 19

"We're in business," I whispered to Katherine, who seemed to be quite comfortable, stretched out on the gurney, her head resting on two pillowcases I had rolled together. "Going up!"

But then the button didn't light up. Not when I touched it with my thumb, my forefinger, tapped it with a nail, or stuffed my entire palm inside the circle. Nothing. The doors just shut and then we sat there. It's actually quite amazing how jarring it is to feel an elevator not move. It's another of those things, like a refrigerator humming, that you don't notice until it stops.

"I don't think we're moving," Katherine said.

I looked down. Her eyes were shut. Her voice was muted, relaxed.

"I know," I said.

"Why aren't we moving?" she asked.

"All part of the plan," I said, with a confidence I didn't quite feel.

She didn't open her eyes but she broke into a wide smile. "You're funny, you know that," she said. "Wake me up if we ever get to nineteen."

We stayed in the elevator long enough for me to arrive at an idea. I unzipped my purse and dumped the entire contents on the floor. Then I kneeled down and waited, and as soon as I heard the bell chime and the doors open, I shouted, "Oh, shit!"

Two women in lab coats entered the elevator. "Everything all right?" one of them asked.

"Oh, I just dropped everything on the floor," I said, frantically gathering my things. "Would you mind hitting nineteen for me?"

From where I was kneeling, my head was right by Katherine's. And as I heard someone slide a card through a slot and felt the elevator begin to move, I could hear her laugh.

When we got off the elevator, a security guard had to buzz us in, which he did with only a mildly suspicious glare, and then the nurse spent ten minutes scolding me because we hadn't followed protocol. I just kept apologizing and played dumb, happy because Katherine seemed to have fallen asleep, and also because no matter how browbeaten I was I was relieved no one asked anything about the gurney.

Ultimately, we were led into a suite that, in my wildest dreams, I would never have imagined could be found in a hospital. It was every bit as fancy as my honeymoon suite in Hawaii, with marble in the bathroom and two flat-screen televisions, comfortable leather chairs, lush carpeting, and a menu that read as though it was taken from a Fifth Avenue bistro. *Cornish game hen, rosemary potatoes, sautéed broccoli, apple tart with crème anglaise, raspberry sorbet.*

"Pretty swanky," I said, as the door shut behind the attendant who'd led us in.

Katherine popped up off the gurney and strode confidently to the window. "Thanks for getting me here."

"I thought you were asleep," I said.

"Meditating."

She was in a small wooden chair, looking out over the skyline. The day was cloudy and dramatically gray above the sea of skyscrapers.

"If you don't mind, what does this cost?" I asked.

"Three grand a day," she replied, her back to me, staring out the window. "Insurance doesn't cover it."

"It's worth it."

"I wouldn't have gotten here without you," she said, still not looking back at me.

I went over and rested a hand on her shoulder. "Pretty comfortable place to spend a couple nights," I said.

"Aside from *that*," Katherine said, and motioned behind me.

I turned and immediately saw it, the one thing in the room you wouldn't find in a luxury hotel. The bed. It looked like one you might find in any hospital room. I felt a lump in my throat.

"I'm going to Barneys," I said, "and buying out the bedding department."

"No," she said, and put her hand on mine, held me there. "Just stay with me."

KATHERINE

SAMANTHA SLEPT IN THE room with me that night. They made up a sofa for her with fluffy pillows and a down comforter. It looked more comfortable than the bed by the time they were through. That made me feel good. I didn't want her to be uncomfortable.

The following morning, Dr. Z was in my room early. I asked Samantha to stay and hear what he would say, partly because my head hasn't been right since this all began, and also because I just didn't want to be alone.

Dr. Z reiterated the program we would begin that day, told me I would only be in the hospital a few days, and explained that I would then begin my treatments at the chemotherapy center near my apartment. Samantha, bless her, took notes the whole time. I listened with my eyes closed.

Then Dr. Z asked something that stirred me. "Katherine, is there anything you are excited to do?"

I opened my eyes. "What do you mean?"

"I mean *excited* to do."

"What kind of thing?"

"Well, some people want to go on a safari, others want to learn to play the piano. It could be either of those or anything in between."

A bit of panic spread through me. "Are you telling me if there is something I haven't done I'd better hurry up and do it?"

"Not at all," he said, and placed his hand on my foot gently, reassuringly. "I'm sorry if I gave you that impression. I mean I like to work with a goal in mind. The next few weeks aren't going to be a lot of fun, so if we can say, 'Nine more days until I see a giraffe in the wild,' it usually makes it a little easier."

I lay back again and looked over at Samantha. She was staring at the doctor, her hair matted down where she'd slept on it, a pencil between her fingers.

"Can I think about it?" I asked.

"Of course. It isn't mandatory," Dr. Z said. "Sometimes it just helps."

He really did have a lovely smile.

When he was gone, Samantha came and flopped down beside me on the bed. At that moment I felt as though I had known her all my life.

"Did that scare the shit out of you?" I asked. "Because it scared the shit out of me."

"Yes, that scared the shit out of me," she said. "But when he explained it I felt a lot better, and I believe he was telling the truth."

"I do too," I said.

"It makes sense," Samantha said, "at least it does to me."

She went into the bathroom and brushed her teeth and her hair. It took her all of two minutes to get herself together. When she emerged she looked terrific, healthy and pretty and radiant.

"You are very naturally beautiful," I told her, as the sun shining into the windows illuminated her from behind. "I am *very* envious."

Samantha laughed. "Are you kidding? You're twelve years older than I am and I bet people think we're twins. You're the one who looks fabulous."

"Sweetheart, it takes me an hour to look like your sister. You were in and out of that bathroom in a minute. If you only gave me that much time, people would think I was your grandmother."

"That's not true and you know it," she said, and rubbed her chin as though she was thinking it over. "Or maybe you don't know it. That's why I'm here, to make sure you do."

"That's why you're my BFF."

"That's right," Samantha said. "That's why I'm your BFF."

I BEGGED HER TO go out and do something that morning but she wouldn't budge. She kept saying she wasn't going anywhere until we were going together, and after a bit of arguing she admonished me to quit talking about it.

"*This* is what I'm doing," she said. "I don't have anything more important to do."

So, like the girls we are, we started talking about boys.

"Aside from the asshole you married," I asked, "you ever get involved with any good ones?"

"One or two. The most romantic encounter of my life happened when I was fourteen, with a boy who never even kissed me. I still think about it all the time; I was just telling someone about it recently. Is that sad?"

"Seriously?" I asked. "You're asking *me* if that's sad? I've wasted my entire life pining for a jerk who left me for a chick who makes Kim Kardashian look like a Nobel laureate. I hardly think I'm qualified to call you sad."

"What the hell is wrong with us, anyway?" Samantha said. "We're two sensational women. How did we pick such losers?"

"It's an interesting question." I sighed, and gave it a moment's thought. "I think I'm a good rationalizer. I rationalize around almost any deal-breaker if a guy is cute or funny or shows interest in me at all."

"Give me an example," Samantha said.

I sat up in bed. "Let's make it a game," I said. "I'll tell you something about a man and you tell me if it should have been an absolute deal-breaker."

She pulled a chair beside the bed and fell into it, lifting her feet so they were resting on mine, like two girls having a sleepover.

"I'm ready," she said.

"Okay," I said, "let's start with an easy one. He speaks to his mother on the phone every single day."

"Is his mother ill?"

"Perfectly healthy."

"And he's how old?"

"Mid-thirties."

"Absolute deal-breaker!" Samantha exclaimed, and we burst into hysterics.

"I think my problem is that every person in my life is male," I said, when we caught our breath. "If I had girlfriends like in *Sex and the City*, they would have warned me about that."

Samantha rustled about in her seat, wrapped her lower legs around my feet and squeezed. "Give me another one," she said.

I thought for a moment. "Okay, how about if he has a little dog and he refuses to have her fixed because he's afraid it will hurt her, so the dog gets her period and he is constantly putting her into these little shorts and changing her maxi pad."

"You're making that one up," Samantha said.

I laughed. "I swear I'm not."

She jumped out of the chair and put her face by mine. "Are you kidding me? You dated a man who changed his dog's maxi pads?"

"I did. The first time I slept with him he said he needed to stop at a pharmacy on our way back to his apartment. I assumed he was buying condoms."

"But he was buying maxi pads?"

"That's correct."

Samantha was pacing the floor. "Let me get this straight," she said. "You were on your way to his place and he stopped at a drugstore to buy maxi pads for his dog, and that's the night you slept with him for the first time?"

"Yes."

"That is such an absolute deal-breaker I don't think I can take any more. Nothing could top that."

I smiled. "Sweetie, get back in that chair. I'm just getting warmed up."

SAMANTHA 回 回 回

ABSOLUTE DEAL-BREAKER BECAME ONE of our favorites immediately. We laughed for hours that day—and so many others, too—over outrageous scenarios, some of which we'd lived, some we made up, the crazier the better. Through those weeks, seeing Katherine laugh was the most rewarding thing in my life.

We have expressions like "laughter is the best medicine" that we use over and over, but we don't realize they are actually true until we need them. That one is true, for sure. When Katherine was laughing, she was healthy, she was whole. It didn't happen enough because it isn't always easy to find space to laugh when you are fighting for your life, but on the occasions you do, it makes all the difference in the world.

She was only in the hospital for three days. I was excited when we moved her back home; in fact, I think I was more excited than she was. We had wonderful, deep, far-ranging talks in her apartment in those days, we talked about her life and mine. We talked about men and work, about fashion and about family. And we talked about cancer, in a way that only those of us who know it can talk about it. Because until you know it, there is no good way to explain it so anyone else can understand it. It's sort of like trying to recount to someone who wasn't there the details of an event where you *almost* got killed, like the time the engine caught fire and your flight had to make an emergency landing, or the time you were camping in the woods and you came across a bear and you had to lie down and play dead and pray the bear sniffed you and strolled away rather than mauling and eating you. Any experience you are recounting to anyone can never be as scary as it was when it happened, because the very fact that you are the one doing the talking means you survived, when what made the whole thing scary in the first place is that you didn't know for sure you would. So no situation can ever be as scary in the retelling as it was in the moment.

Except for cancer.

Cancer doesn't just land like a plane, or walk away like a bear. Even for me it didn't, and for Katherine it wasn't ever going to. Knowing that makes every moment a little like the one on the plane before the landing when you are crossing yourself and holding the armrest so tightly you emerge with bruised fingers, or when you are lying silent on the ground while the bear sniffs your hair. Not that every moment I had with Katherine was like that, but those feelings are always there, no matter how hard you try to pretend they aren't.

When she talked about cancer, she seemed more sad than scared; I think because she was so filled with regret. It's one thing to fear illness, to fear dying, and another entirely to wonder why you did the things you did and didn't do the ones you could have. I think when Katherine thought about the end of her life, she thought about how differently she would have lived it if she could have done it over, practically every minute of it since Phillip, and that made her sad.

But not nearly as sad as when she talked about Stephen.

"All my life," she told me, "I never believed in love at first sight."

"But you were wrong," I said.

"I was." She smiled. "The instant I saw him I knew. It was like being struck by lightning, except the feeling was warm and gooey and wonderful, like my insides turned to hot fudge. In one day I realized nothing in my life was what I wanted it to be. And, more important, I acted on it. I told him I'd be back in two weeks and I was really going to do it. I left my job, I was going to put my apartment up for sale, I was *all in* on this man. And then . . ."

Her voice trailed off there. Cancer does that sometimes, too. It makes it hard to finish your sentences.

"I'm going to go to Aspen and find him," I said. "If you won't tell me his last name I am just getting on a plane."

Katherine got deadly serious then. "Listen to me," she said. "I know you are saying that for all the right reasons and you'd be doing it for the right reasons, too, and if I were sitting where you are I might do the same thing. But I'm not, and you aren't lying where I am. I need to know you aren't going to go to Aspen, or try to find Stephen on the Internet or anything. I need you to promise me that. Because if every time you walk in the door I have to worry that he'll walk in behind you, I won't be able to go on with this."

I exhaled deeply. "I won't go," I said.

"I need you to promise me."

"I promise," I said. "But if I can't then *you* need to. You have to tell him what happened."

"I can't," Katherine said. "I instructed my assistant to tell him I was no longer employed and she had no further information. I just . . ."

She didn't finish that sentence, either. She didn't really need to. It was pretty obvious that she was *just* too many things to list them all.

The assistant she was talking about was a hilarious and charming woman from Brooklyn named Marie, a year younger than I am and quite possibly the most provocatively dressed person who was not a prostitute that I have ever seen. She was Katherine's most frequent visitor aside from me, and she often accompanied us, or just Katherine, to the chemo center. Marie was cheerful and noisy in just the right way; it wasn't impossible to be sad around her but it was hard. She maintained a stunningly upbeat attitude through even the worst days. I loved her immediately, and it was clear Katherine loved her too. And Marie loved her back, in the most self-less way. She was no longer indebted to Katherine for anything, she just cared, and I think that made all the difference.

Then came a Wednesday when I caught a cold. It was just a little cold, barely more than a sniffle, but I knew they wouldn't let me stay with Katherine at chemotherapy. When you are undergoing treatments, your immune system is practically defenseless; if anyone so much as coughs in the center, he or she is politely escorted to the exit.

So I air-kissed Katherine good-bye, assured that Marie would keep her company, and then I was outside, by myself. It was a hot, sunny afternoon and I needed some air. I felt like I hadn't been outdoors in a month. The fresh air did away with my cold immediately, so I jumped on my bike, rode to Central Park, and spent three hours cycling as hard as I could. Every twenty minutes I took a water break and did calisthenics, right there in the Sheep Meadow, dropping to the grass and doing push-ups and sit-ups and jumping jacks, with who knows how many college kids sunning themselves and sneaking sips and hits of various drinks and drugs all around. It felt great. It reminded me that I must not forget how important my body is to my mind. There was more than enough time to take care of my body while I cared for Katherine. I could be someone else's health advocate and my own at the same time.

I cycled home as it was turning dark, and switched on my laptop. As it warmed up, I dropped to the hardwood floor and did twenty more push-ups. I wanted a good dinner, lean protein, with a hearty grain on the side, and fruit and water. And maybe one glass of wine, too, because life is short.

Then the screen on my laptop sizzled to life and I saw my message icon blinking, and for just one moment it made me think of Robert's inbox, and my fingers trembled as they hovered over the keyboard.

"Stop it, Samantha," I said aloud, as a bead of sweat dripped off my nose. "You can't go through life thinking every e-mail you receive is going to change your life."

Person2Person
From: Brooke B.
To: Samantha R.
BreastCancerForum.org

So, I saw Dr. Marks at Starbucks and I mentioned you.

(Don't worry, I didn't tell him you told me about the dance and the Bee Gees song and how he didn't kiss you or any of that. I was very subtle.)

He's single and totally interested in seeing you.

Let me know what you want to do.

KATHERINE

I'VE NEVER GIVEN THIS much thought to shopping.

Marie is finally getting married. She wants a fabulous, black-tie celebration, she wants it immediately, and she says she won't do it if I don't agree to be her maid of honor. I suspect the rush is because she is secretly pregnant, which she will neither confirm nor deny.

"I don't want this party to be about me," I told her. "If the whole bank is there and I show up, it becomes the 'Katherine is still alive' extravaganza, which is not what the most special night of your life is supposed to be."

"If it's the most special night of my life," she said, "then I can't have it without my best friend."

"You're not doing this for me," I warned her. "I don't need a party."

"I'm not doing it for you," she replied. "I'm asking you to do it for me."

So, I'm going. Samantha and I are going shopping later this week, since none of my couture is going to fit properly right now. I have lost eleven pounds since I began the chemotherapy, and while my hair has hung in better than I expected, I have taken to wearing a flowing brunette wig anyway, a shade darker than my usual, at my colorist's recommendation. He said the shade works better with my pallid complexion.

Marie buzzed my ear off about the arrangements all through my chemo, and then she walked me home and we sat and chatted for a bit, and she hadn't been gone for more than ten minutes when the doorman's station buzzed my phone. That made me smile nostalgically. In all the time she worked for me, Marie never managed to leave the office without forgetting something: a pair of sunglasses, a set of keys, the book she was reading. It was nice to know some things never changed.

I pressed down the intercom button. "Ask her what she left behind, I'll send it down in the elevator."

There was a brief pause before my doorman spoke. "No, ma'am, actually, your visitor is a gentleman. He says to tell you his name is Phillip, and that you'd remember him from school."

BROOKE

I SENT SAMANTHA AN e-mail because I wanted to meet her.

Running into a man I know she once loved gave me the perfect opportunity, but I would have found another reason anyway. I wanted to talk to her. I wanted to see her. I wanted to see what she looked like, hear how she sounded. It's a strange world we live in now where we can have relationships with people without ever seeing their faces and hearing their voices: it's as though they aren't real, just characters in a book and you can envision them any way you like. But Samantha was real and I knew that and I always knew I would reach out to her. It would have been unfair not to.

Besides, Dr. Marks is a total babe and he's smart and seems to be sensitive. He's a pediatrician, for crying out loud; how can you be *that* without being sensitive? He is exactly the sort of man I might have fallen in love with, even though he is so different from the man I married. Scott is all swagger, Dr. Marks is all sweet. And I *love* the swagger, but every now and again I think we could all use a little bit of the sweet, too.

He was loading up a latte with sugar and cinnamon when I saw him.

"Is everything all right with you?" he asked.

It took me a moment to realize what he was referring to. I had forgotten it was he who had initially made me promise to get my first mammogram, who had unwittingly begun what amounted to the worst experience of my life. I had forgotten, but apparently he had not, and as much as I didn't like to be reminded, his remembering made me crush on him just a little bit more.

"I am *fine*," I said, "thank you."

"I'm glad," he said, and he smiled. "You can't be too careful."

"I totally agree," I said, and then I changed the subject.

I could see from the look on his face at the mention of her name that he had feelings for Samantha. I told him I'd come into contact ("a friend of a friend of a friend") with a girl who mentioned she had known him growing up. His right eye narrowed when I said her name, and he smiled using half his face. That's the way some memories work, I think. Some make you laugh, others make you cry, and the really good ones make half your face smile.

Now, after a handful of disasters, I have mostly given up on fix-ups, but this was too easy and it gave me the entrée I needed to invite Samantha to lunch, which I'd wanted to do for some time.

I'll meet you in the city, I wrote to her. *You name the spot.*

I couldn't have her to Greenwich. There isn't anyone in this town I don't know, and I wasn't interested in answering questions about how Samantha and I had come to meet.

You see, I haven't told anyone about my problem. Not my husband or my children, and certainly not all the women in town who live to mind one another's business. I don't really want to talk about *why* I haven't said anything; in fact, I don't want to talk about any of it at all. I have managed to hardly even think about it, to be honest. In all these weeks there was only one time that I broke down, at a dinner party at the home of our friends, the Robertsons; he's a pompous hedge-fund guy and she's an unapologetic trophy wife, but they throw lovely parties and I was having a good time until one of the guests, a tipsy blonde named Emily, suggested a topic over dinner.

"For all the husbands at the table," she said aloud, "and then we'll do the wives after, here's the question . . ."

She paused, with an evil twinkle in her eye, as though she was about to say something so provocative the room would explode before she was through.

"If your wife were to die tomorrow," she said, glass raised as though she were making a toast, "would you get remarried?"

To my horror, there was a murmur in the room as though everyone found the question to be suitable dinner conversation.

"I heard them talking about it on one of the *Housewives* shows," Emily went on, "and I just thought it was so damned interesting!"

I didn't.

I didn't find it interesting. I wasn't interested in answering, I wasn't interested in hearing anyone else's answer, and I *certainly* didn't want to hear what my husband had to say.

I waited an appropriate amount of time before excusing myself to the bathroom, where I waited for what felt like an hour for someone to become concerned. It was Scott who finally tapped on the door.

"Baby, everything all right?" he asked.

"I'm sick," I whispered, hoarsely and fast. "I need to go home."

Through all of this, that was the only time I ever told Scott I was sick. He took me home and helped me up the stairs, and I assured him I would be all right, that I just needed a bit of privacy, and he went downstairs to make a sandwich and open a beer, and soon I heard the sound of a baseball game from the television in the family room, and everything was normal again, just the way I like it.

So, I've said nothing. And I plan to keep it that way.

Samantha chose to meet me at a restaurant called Michael's. She said it was a place she has had good luck in the past.

I'm all for good luck, I wrote her, and we met at noon on a Thursday.

She looked exactly as I pictured her: Ivory-girl skin and athletic, pretty in a natural, effortless way. You can never guess exactly what a person is going to look like, but you can predict a few things about their appearance, and in this case I got all of them right.

I had practiced the speech during the ride down from Connecticut. "I just want to start by saying thank you," I said, when we first sat down after an awkward hug. "It was very sweet of you to show such concern for me. The least I can do is buy you lunch, so I insist you allow me to pay, and then if you end up marrying Dr. Marks you have to invite me to the wedding."

Samantha had an adorable little smile that just curled the corners of her lips. It seemed to me that her memory of him struck her in exactly the same way his memory of her struck him. All these years later and they're still a little bit in love with each other.

"I'll allow you to pay for lunch," she said, "and we'll see about Andrew Marks later, but first I need to know how you are doing."

"I am doing great," I said. "I'm wonderful. I feel healthy and happy and strong. I have my life back exactly as I want it and I'm not allowing myself to worry about things I can't control, so let's talk about other things."

I didn't expect her to be satisfied with that response. I just needed to put it out there so that when I *really* couldn't talk about it anymore I could repeat it.

"Okay," she said breezily, "I'm fine with that. You know I want to know and I want to help you any way I can. But I'm not going to beg you. If you want to talk about other things, that's fine with me."

"Perfect," I said. "Let's talk about your old boyfriend."

"Let's have a drink before we do that."

So we did. We had each finished a glass of wine and ordered seconds before we dug in.

"How in the world is it that this terrific man, whom every girl had a crush on in school, can be single after all these years?" Samantha asked. "One of two things must be going on. Either he is a total womanizer or he's insane."

I stifled a hiccup. "He could be gay."

"That isn't better," she said.

"Well, I'm not saying he is. Maybe he's sexually confused."

"Are you trying to make a match or to make me run in the opposite direction?"

I laughed. "I've seen the way you look when I mention his name," I said. "You aren't running anywhere and we both know it. Do you want me to give him your number or your e-mail?"

"Can't I call *him*?"

"Oh no," I told her. "I don't advise that at all."

"Why not?"

"You're much too cute for that. Let *him* pursue *you*."

Samantha set her glass down and looked at me seriously. "You have a lot of beliefs that I find very unusual," she told me. "They seem like they would come from a much older woman."

"They do," I said. "From my grandmother, and my mother as well, both of whom always told me the most fun part of being a woman is *being* a woman. My grammy used to say, 'These rules seemed to serve just fine for thousands of years.' Of course, she didn't believe a woman should wear pants, either, so I took some of it with a grain of salt, but for the most part the message was received, and I'm not ashamed of it, no matter how dated it all may seem."

Samantha raised her glass to her lips and just let it sit. "It's funny," she said. "If I had never met you and just saw you, I would guess you were my age. If I had never seen you but just heard you talk, I would guess you were my mother's age. And the truth is you're actually directly in between."

"Forty years old and not the least bit ashamed of it."

Samantha seemed to think a minute. "Forty years old and raised in Greenwich, I'll bet you know someone I just recently met. Her name is Katherine Emerson."

"Absolutely," I said. I remembered her. "She was a year ahead of me in school. We were friendly when we were young but she pulled away as we got older."

Samantha leaned closer, as though what I'd said had triggered something she'd been trying to remember. "You know, she talks about that sometimes. She says something bad happened with her father, but she hasn't told me what it was."

"I know what it was," I said. "The whole town knew."

Samantha just stared. I knew I would tell her, there wasn't any reason to keep it secret, but I wanted to make her ask me. It was clear in her eyes she was desperate to know. I'm not sure why this lunch had become such a power struggle, but it had.

"How well do you know her?" I asked.

"I know her very well and at the same time I hardly know her at all," Samantha said. "I met her the same way I met you."

That, right there, stopped all this from being fun.

"Is she going to be all right?" I asked.

"I don't know," Samantha said. "And I don't want to violate her privacy about her father, but if it's something everyone knew perhaps you could just tell me."

I couldn't see any reason to play games with this. "Her father went to jail when we were about twelve years old. I believe it was business-related, not murder or anything, tax evasion or something. But he went away and then he got sick while he was in prison and never came home and Katherine was never the same after that. She was a really smart girl, as I remember, but I always assumed she hadn't recovered from what happened to her family."

"She hasn't," Samantha said.

"So she hasn't done well?"

Samantha paused. "She's incredibly successful, very wealthy. She lives a very glamorous lifestyle, but she hasn't done well, not in any way that really matters."

Then Samantha raised her hand and asked the waiter to come over, and asked him for a pen and paper. When he brought them, she scribbled something quickly and handed the paper to me.

"Thanks for lunch," she said. "Let's do it again soon. That's my number, ask Andrew to call me."

And she was up and gone, just like that.

 KATHERINE

I HADN'T CALLED HIM Phillip in almost twenty years.

That wasn't an accident, and it wasn't as though he hadn't noticed. Back when he first hired me, when he was a managing director, eighteen months after graduating from HBS, he told me everyone called him "Phil," but that I was welcome to still call him by his full name.

"That's all right," I told him that day, "you feel more like a Phil to me now."

So when his full name came up through the intercom, I froze.

"Ms. Emerson," the doorman said hesitantly, after a moment, "shall I send your visitor up?"

Well, wasn't that an interesting question?

On the one hand, the last thing in the world I wanted was to see him, and on the other, there was nothing I wanted more. Which hand takes precedence in a moment such as this? I swear, they don't prepare you in life to make the decisions that really matter. In school they teach you how to add and how to play nice with other kids, and there are books to help you with everything from meditation to how to dismantle a nuclear device, but no one ever tells you what to do if you're staring your own mortality square in the face and the man who ruined your life shows up at your apartment with a conciliatory opening line.

"Of course," I found myself saying, "send him on up."

Then it was like I was on autopilot, drifting from the living room to the study and glancing into a mirror. Not so bad. He hadn't seen me since I began my treatments, since I quit my job. Could that really have been just a few months ago? It felt like a different lifetime.

I went to the sofa and sat with my legs crossed beneath me, took a deep breath and held it, then slowly let it out. Then in again, and held it, and out. Again and again, as deeply as I could manage.

May I be filled with loving-kindness
May I be well
May I be peaceful and at ease
May I be happy

When the doorbell rang, I pressed the button to allow Phillip entry, keeping my eyes closed, continuing to breathe all the while. I heard the door open, then shut softly. Footsteps on hardwood floors, loud, as only expensive dress shoes on wood can be. Then the footsteps stopped and I could faintly hear his breathing over the sound of my own, but I did not open my eyes until he spoke.

"Hi Kat," he said, in his scratchy baritone. "You are a sight for sore eyes."

I took one last deep breath, let it out, then I opened my eyes. The man before me was one I did not recognize. For the first time in all the years I'd known him, from the boy who was Phillip to the man who was Phil, from the most impressive student at the finest school in the country to the shrewdest chief executive on Wall Street, I couldn't see any of it. It was as though his spirit had vacated his body, leaving only the limbs and flesh behind. He was pale and wan, and his lips were severely chapped. He also looked heavier than I had ever seen him.

"My lord, Phil, you look like shit," I said. "I'm supposed to be the one who's dying, what the hell is the matter with you?"

I stopped him dead in his tracks with that. People don't talk like that to him, not even me, not back then or any time since.

To his everlasting credit, he started to laugh. Not just a giggle, but a hearty, chesty laugh, the sort I hadn't heard much from him since Harvard. Wall Street is not an especially funny place. It was good to see him laugh, he looked healthier, but he sounded awful. I could hear it in his chest, in the deep breaths he took between chuckles, in the wheeze of his inhale.

"You're smoking again, aren't you?" I said.

He threw up his hands. "Guilty as charged."

I sighed and patted the sofa beside me. "Come sit down," I said. "You look like you need to talk."

And talk he did, though he didn't sit down. The first thing he did was pull a cigarette from the breast pocket of his sport coat and fiddle it about nervously between his fingers. I watched silently until he fished a silver lighter out of his pants.

"In case you hadn't noticed," I said, "I'm having a few minor health problems."

"I'm sorry," he said, and stubbed the cigarette out with the heel of his shoe, despite the fact he hadn't lit it. "I guess that's sort of just like me." He paused. "I'm sort of an asshole, aren't I, Kat?"

I didn't say anything. He waited, maybe because he wanted me to excuse him, maybe because he wanted me to yell, but I wasn't going to make this easier for him. Whatever he had come to say he was going to have to say it without any help from me.

"When I heard you were sick it made me feel very bad, for a lot of reasons, and I wanted to do something to make it right. Maybe I'm just a scumbag, I don't know, but I feel like if I do right by you then maybe I'll sleep a little better at night."

I stayed quiet. I had waited a really long time to hear whatever this was; I owed it to myself to listen to it all before I threw him out.

"So," he continued, "the first thing I want to tell you is that I never accepted your resignation. I kept it a secret from the board, at first because I thought I would give you some time to change your mind, and then when I heard you were sick I went to the board and told them the rumors they had heard about your departure were untrue, that you were still one hundred percent a part of us and that we would support you in any way possible. That was unanimously approved, of course. So, I bring the warmest wishes of the board. Everyone is concerned about you, and if there is anything they can do they will act immediately."

"That's nice," I said, but I knew the wishes of the board weren't the important part.

"Of course, as a senior executive, all of your medical expenses will be handled, not a cent will come from your pocket, no matter how long it takes or how expensive it becomes. You have my word on that and full agreement of the board."

"That's very nice," I said, though that still wasn't the important part.

"And, because I did not accept your resignation, your profit participation remains intact, which means full compensation at your current levels indefinitely. And you and I both know that's just a small piece of the puzzle."

Now I got it, and I teared up even before he said it.

"With the unanimous approval of the board I have accelerated the maturation of all of your corporate options and bonuses. Effective the first day of next month, every penny you ever had coming to you will be fully vested at current market levels and will be transferred to your personal accounts with no conditions attached."

All the money I walked away from. All of it. I left tens of millions of dollars in options on the table when I quit and didn't care. But now I had it all back. Phillip gave it to me.

"You didn't have to do that," I said.

"I know," he said, and now he sat down beside me. "But it seemed like the right thing."

"Well," I said, and patted him on the thigh, "that's very nice."

"It sort of feels like the least I could do. Like I said, maybe I'll sleep better tonight."

We sat beside each other in a comfortable silence, the distant sound of ticking from my antique grandfather clock clearly audible, echoing through the apartment. After all these years, I realized it was this I had missed most. The comfortable silence. I hadn't thought of it in twenty years, perhaps because I never found it again. But being able to sit like this, two of us on a couch, my hand on his thigh, his hand over mine, listening to a clock ticking, not saying a word. It's very nice.

Then, of course, he ruined it. "Kat," he said, "I have the overwhelming desire to kiss you."

I didn't mean to laugh in his face.

I really didn't. I'm sure it wounded his ego more than I meant to; in fact, I didn't mean to wound him at all. The days when I wanted to see him beaten were gone. When I laughed in his face it was a natural reaction to his clumsy advance, nothing more, nothing less.

"Well, I didn't expect this," he said, the hurt evident in his eyes.

"I'm sorry," I said. "I just didn't see that coming."

He started to stand, but I grabbed his hand.

"Don't," I said. "Don't go. Just sit with me. Don't kiss me or anything, just sit here with me."

He took a deep breath and sat back, crossed his legs, standoffish. He was such a child. An angry little boy not getting what he wants.

"I know what you're thinking," I said, and he perked up a bit and faced me. "You're thinking: If I give a girl fifty million bucks the least I expect is to get in her pants."

That got him.

Suddenly he was laughing harder than I was, and wheezing that smoker's wheeze, and turning a bit red, but it was funny and it was genuine and we were very comfortable sitting together. We laughed for a while, and then I took his hand and put it in my lap and held it with both hands, and we stayed that way quietly until he broke the silence by telling me the second thing he had come to say.

And this one, I really hadn't seen coming.

BROOKE

I WISH I WERE the sort of person who underlined things in books. You know how people do that? They underline, or they dog-ear pages, or the really organized ones have computer files with quotes and paragraphs that touched them, moved them. I have encountered so many of those passages, all my life, but I never write them down. What a mistake that is.

I so envy people who can quote great leaders and writers at the drop of a hat. It happens all the time. At a dinner party someone will say, "You know, it was General Patton who said blah blah blah . . ." I wish I could quote General Patton; that would be so great. Instead, I'm always the one saying: "I can't remember where I read this, but blah blah blah . . ." Let me tell you, the blah blah blahs are always *much* more interesting when they have a name attached to them.

Like right now, for instance, I am thinking about how no two flakes of snow are identical. Isn't that written in a poem somewhere? Didn't someone attach some deeper meaning to it? If they didn't they should have, because it is the most telling and important little fact about science I have ever heard.

No two things are exactly the same. No two people are, either. My twins are a perfect example. They are fraternal, not identical, but if they were identical they would have the same blood, the same DNA, the same fingerprints, but they still wouldn't be the same. My children are different from each other in ways that go well beyond their genetic material, because no two people, no matter how identical, are exactly the same. Just like snowflakes.

That's the part I think Samantha doesn't understand.

She views her life in one way, I view mine in another. She has her values, her concerns, her beliefs, and I respect those. For whatever reason, she cannot seem to do the same for me. She behaves as though I am committing suicide, when I am doing nothing of the kind. As of this moment, I am cancer-free. And I am no fool, nor am I nearly as out of touch with reality as she has made up her mind I am. I talked at great length, *enormous* length, with my doctor about my decision and arrived at a conclusion I am comfortable with. And, not that it matters, but he tells me I am by no means the only patient he has known to make this decision. I could go through all the treatment options available to me, put everything and everyone I know and love on hold, and for what? In the best case, it would alter my chances of the cancer recurring by 10 percent. My chances of recurrence now are what they are. If I sacrifice my entire lifestyle, plus my husband's, plus my children's, they become 10 percent more favorable. Some people will do anything for that 10 percent. I will not.

When I was a girl, I had a friend named Amanda. She got caught up with the wrong crowd as we got a bit older and one night she got in a car with some older boys and there was drinking involved and then they ran into a large truck on the highway at two in the morning. The rumor that went around school was that Amanda was decapitated in the accident. I have always hoped that wasn't the case, but either way she was dead before she turned sixteen. The lesson is that you don't know what happens tomorrow. Would she have chosen differently if she'd known? Of course. But she didn't. We choose based on what we know and we live with the consequences. If you told me undergoing treatments would guarantee that the cancer will never come back but not undergoing them will guarantee that it will, then of course I would do it. But my doctor couldn't tell me that. In fact, he told me he couldn't say with any certainty what would happen in either case. The numbers fluctuate based upon the science, and the genetics, and the advancements in research, and sometimes even socioeconomic status. And a lot of other things I don't fully understand.

So I choose to live for today.

All I have is right now. I have all that I want, and no one can promise me I'll have it forever no matter what I do, so I'm going to live it, love it, treasure it, for every second I can, and whatever comes next I'm prepared for it.

Samantha doesn't understand. "Brooke, if they told me I increased my chance of survival by *one* percent I would go through anything," she says to me every time we talk.

"I know that," I always say, "but you are not me."

"It just doesn't make any sense," she says.

"It does to me," I tell her. "You are living for tomorrow, and there's nothing wrong with that because the best days in your life are in your future. But *this* is the best time in my life. I will never have this back again no matter what I do, so I'm not giving it up for anything."

That's around the time in the conversation I usually tell her we need to change the subject, because I'm not going to be able to be friends with her if we don't.

"You see?" she'll say. "You can't take it because you know I'm right."

But I don't know anything of the kind.

In fact, what she is really doing is proving my point for me.

Samantha is the only person in my life who knows what I have been through, and she is practically incapable of talking to me about anything else. And *that* is exactly what would happen if I battled this publicly. It's all anyone would talk to me about. It's all they would see when they looked at me. It's all they would think of when they see my kids, my husband. It would become my entire life, and that isn't what I want. I want the life I have right now.

She's also wrong because, beneath it all, she thinks this is about Scott. She thinks I worry that if he knew I was sick he wouldn't love me anymore, or he wouldn't want me sexually or he just wouldn't be able to deal with the whole thing. She's so wrong about that. My husband is a good man. He's not perfect, none of them are, but if he knew what the doctors had told me he would absolutely force me to go through *all* the treatment and he would never take no for an answer. And that's precisely why I don't want him to know. I'm choosing today. I'm choosing to have and to cherish every precious moment of this life Scott and I have built for as long as I can have it. I hope it is for a really long time and I know it isn't going to be forever, so I'll just take whatever is given to me and be grateful for it. It doesn't seem to make sense to Samantha and it may not make sense to you, but it makes sense to me and I think that's all that really matters.

Anyway, tonight I am calling Samantha because it is an hour before her date with Dr. Marks and I am so excited I could burst. It's been a long time since I've successfully fixed anyone up. And, as you know, I have a little crush on him, too, which makes this all the more thrilling in a different way.

"*Yes*, I'm getting a blow-out," she said upon answering.

That was it. No greeting, just her complaint that I'd been nagging her about this date for a week. But, come on, the poor girl doesn't have a mother to talk her through these things. Dr. Marks is a handsome, charming, single man; those don't grow on trees. She cannot meet him in a nice restaurant with her hair up and nothing but lip gloss on her face. He is a man worth a little effort.

"You don't have to be so cranky," I said, though I didn't really mind.

"Sorry," she said, sounding frazzled. "I'm just running a little late. What's up?"

"I just wanted to wish you a wonderful evening and good luck," I told her. "I hope that the magic is still there, and I have a funny feeling it is."

"Thank you very much," she said, more quietly. "I'm looking forward to it."

"Are you nervous?" I asked.

"I am *not* nervous." She hesitated. "I'm excited. There's a difference."

"I'll accept that," I told her. "Now remember, don't drink too much, don't even consider offering to pay for anything, and don't forget not to say anything about my situation."

Samantha huffed an exasperated sigh, loudly. "You know," she said, "the best thing I could ever do for you would be to tell him."

"I know you wouldn't do that," I said calmly. "I know you wouldn't violate the trust I have placed in you. I was just reminding you because he's the only person you know who also knows me."

"How about Katherine?"

"Yes, okay, she would remember me, too," I said. "Don't tell her either. Now, you need to get going. Have a wonderful, romantic, memorable night. Don't sleep with him on the first date, under any circumstances. And if you don't call me first thing tomorrow morning with all the details I shall never forgive you."

 KATHERINE

"TELL ME, WHAT HAVE you heard about my marriage?"

The words hung in the air like the echo of a firecracker. Phil was beside me, our hands intertwined, his knee touching mine. It was the closest we had been in a long time. I wasn't going to kiss him. That was out of the question, though it didn't mean there wasn't a part of me that wanted to. Despite myself, despite everything that happened, I had to admit that even now he was just my type. He is strong and smart, decisive and dynamic. Perhaps he is everything my father turned out not to be. I never really thought of it that way but suddenly now I did. Suddenly now, sitting on the couch, near enough to smell the cigarette smoke in his hair and see the tiny spot beneath his jaw he missed when he shaved, I figured it out. He's everything I wish my father had been. Oh, the money I could have saved on therapy if I had seen that before.

Anyway, Phil didn't look so good but he still looked *good*. He still has those huge, strong hands, muscled from a childhood spent helping his father carry milk crates in Brooklyn. You can file the nails and cut the cuticles, but the muscles in a man's hands will always betray him.

And I'm still a woman. Maybe that's the most important thing I figured out sitting here. It's easy to forget sometimes when you're sick, when you become so accustomed to undressing in front of nurses that you stop bothering to close the door, when the attractive male doctor wants only to know how many times you've moved your bowels this week, when you're afraid to fuss with your hair because so much of it remains in the brush when you do, when you take to wearing men's boxer shorts rather than your usual underwear because they are so much easier to manage and more comfortable. I hadn't been in my closet in three months, I realized, but as Phil held my hand I knew I would again, perhaps the moment he left. I wanted to dress like myself. I wanted makeup. I would buy that long, blond wig Samantha has been trying to talk me into. All of a sudden, Marie's black-tie wedding party, which I'd been dreading, sounded pretty good. And, frankly, so did the idea of having sex with Phil.

But then he asked that question about his marriage, and I felt everything inside of me that had begun feeling warm quickly go cold. Gently, I pulled my hand away from his and tugged the collar of my sweater closer to my ears, and I kept my hands to myself the rest of the time we were together.

"I heard that you and Holly separated," I said flatly. "I'm sorry I didn't send a note but I've been a little busy."

"That's not what I mean," he said, shifting a bit uncomfortably. "What did you hear?"

I didn't have any desire to hurt him, I really didn't. Despite all the horrible things I had wished upon him over the years, here was the perfect opportunity to hurt him and I didn't want to do it. Maybe because he looked so vulnerable. Maybe *that* was really all I needed, not to see him suffer, just to see him in a place where he might. I didn't need to tell him what I'd heard just to humiliate him, but the truth is the truth and there didn't seem much point in hiding from it.

"I heard that Holly was having an affair," I said slowly and carefully. "That was the rumor that ran around the office. But I'm aware of how inaccurate the grapevine can be, so I assumed it probably wasn't true."

"It was."

I couldn't quite place the look in his eyes. "Well, I'm sorry to hear that," I said.

"Thank you," he replied, and then paused and took a little breath. "But there's more to the story than that." He pulled another cigarette from the package and held it, unlit, between his fingers. "I don't have any idea why I'm telling you this, but for some reason I want you to know. Maybe it's because of everything that happened between us. Maybe it's because I think it will make you happy. Or maybe it's just because I need to tell somebody and for some reason I feel like, in spite of everything, I'm still closer to you than anybody else."

I just stared at his face, and started to feel a little angry. After all these years, why the hell was he talking like this *now*?

"You're about to become the only person besides my doctor who knows about this. There are confidentiality laws that dictate he *has* to keep it between us. No such laws govern this conversation, of course, but I trust that you understand I am telling you this in confidence and it will stay between us forever."

"I won't say a word," I said.

"My marriage has been in major trouble for years," he said. "And to tell you the truth the reason why is the same reason I chose her instead of you."

I sat up a little taller. "Well, I can't wait to hear this."

"Holly didn't challenge me so much," he said. "When I took her to restaurants, she thought they were the most special evenings in the world. When I talked about going to Europe, she acted as though it would be like flying to the moon. You were different. You had more than I did coming in and just the same vision for the future as me. I felt like anything I could give you, you already expected. She *appreciated* it all so much more. Somehow that made her much easier for me."

I'd heard those words before. I'd heard myself say them, but coming from him I found they left me feeling disappointed. Twenty years of my life boiled down to nothing more than this: Holly was more impressed to have whatever Phil chose to give her than I would have been.

"At first it was fine," he continued, "because of the kids. When they were small I was always working and she was always with them, so the time we had together was usually reserved for sex. But when Daniel was ten or eleven, and Michael was away at boarding school, then it became just her and me, and there was nothing there. She didn't push me. She didn't challenge me. And where I once thought that made her the perfect wife, suddenly it was the opposite."

I cut him off, sharply. "Phil, nothing about this story interests me so far, and I am having really serious doubts about it getting any better. I thank you for taking care of my money, that was a wonderful gesture on your part and even if you did it solely to assuage your own guilt over all the bullshit you put me through, I still appreciate it. And, frankly, I have come to realize in the last few months that it wasn't *you* that put me through all of it anyway. It was me. All you did was dump me, and worse things than that happen to people every day. The fact I chose to let it define me for so long was my problem, not yours. And in the very same way, the fact that you chose to marry a vapid whore is your problem, not mine. So I hope you don't mind if I don't cry over the fact that she cheated on you. She probably saved you half of everything you own, which she would have gotten in the divorce if you had just told her to hit the road. So, it's been great seeing you again, let's do it again real soon. I think I'm done for the evening."

I stood and started toward my bedroom. I was a step from escaping when he said, "Kat, I don't know why I'm telling you this, but the truth is it wasn't her cheating on me, it was me cheating on her."

I stopped. I didn't turn back toward him but I listened.

"I've been running around for years. Started probably the second year of our marriage, even though I was happy at the time. As crazy as it sounds, I just did it because I could. I kept it away from work, but that still left plenty of other options, on airplanes, in hotel bars, at health clubs. I could get any woman I wanted and I did, and I never gave it a second thought. I didn't view it as a referendum on my marriage or my feelings for my wife or even on my own morality, it was just something I did because there didn't seem to be a compelling reason not to."

"Not if you're a narcissistic sociopath, I can see that," I said. "Go on."

"In recent years, it changed. Not the frequency of it but the meaning. I was completely disillusioned in my marriage. I started looking for more from these other women. It wasn't just a little flattery, a little jewelry, a lot of sex. I wanted to talk. I wanted to have dinner. I wanted it to matter, and that was when I knew it had to change."

He paused. I turned to face him. He was still seated, looking smaller than I could ever remember. Phillip is a big man, in every way. But not on that couch. Not today.

He continued, "The question was, what to do? I wanted out, but *getting* out was going to cost me about a hundred million bucks. And then, before I could figure it out, I noticed this thing on my dick. Just a little thing, you know, like a pimple. It got bigger and bigger in just a couple of days and then—"

"Stop telling me this part," I said.

"I finally went to the doctor and, of course, it was herpes. The doctor asked me how I thought I got it and I told him I had no idea. And he asked what I meant by that and I said it could have been five or six different women, and he asked if one of them was my wife and I said that was probably the least likely."

"This is the worst story I've ever heard," I said.

Phil ignored me and kept going. "I asked the doctor what I should do and he said I had better explain to my wife how it happened because she was about to find out anyway. And I told him she would probably leave me, and he said: 'Phil, unless you can convince her that *she* was the one who gave you this, I'd say you're completely fucked.' And it was like a lightbulb went on over my head. I went straight to the bar at the St. Regis and had three drinks, and then I went home and started screaming at her: 'How could you do this to me? I trusted you and now I'm totally humiliated!' I tried as hard as I could to convince her I had no idea how else I could have gotten this disease and I laid it on *thick*. And after about ten minutes of nonstop cursing, I'll give you one guess what she did."

That was when I got it. "She admitted it."

He smiled. "That's exactly right. She broke down and told me she's been sleeping with her tennis pro for two years, and she's apologizing like crazy and begging my forgiveness, and I'm drunk enough that I sort of forget how we got there in the first place, so I'm yelling, 'You bitch! You betrayed me!' And right there in the living room I told her I wanted out of the marriage, that I would make sure she and the boys were always taken care of but that if she went after any of my money I would let the whole world know what a whore she is."

He was breathing heavily, that smoker's wheeze. I wanted to say something, but I couldn't. I was genuinely speechless. I just walked over and sat next to him again on the sofa.

"So that's exactly how it happened," he said.

"You sound as though you're proud of it."

"Not proud," he said, "that isn't the right word, but I'm happy that it's over, and I'm happy it didn't cost me half of everything I have worked my whole life for."

I nodded.

"That doesn't make sense to you?" he asked.

"I suppose it does."

And there was nothing else to be said. I reached over and touched his cheek, left my hand there for a moment, and then I got up and walked away.

"Thanks again for the money, Phil," I said over my shoulder. "I need to get some rest. You can see yourself out."

SAMANTHA

I WANTED TO MEET him in Greenwich.

He offered to come into the city, couldn't have been nicer about it, said all the right things about not wanting to inconvenience me and how he comes in all the time and how many more options there are, but I wanted to. It had been too long since I'd eaten dinner in Greenwich. And something about eating dinner in Greenwich with Andrew Marks sounded especially good. It sounded like going home again. Which they say you can't do, only they're wrong, you *can* go home again a little, and this night seemed like the right time.

I borrowed a car from my old boss. I realized, as I slid behind the wheel, that I hadn't driven a car since I'd been back from Hawaii—you don't drive much living in New York—then it dawned on me that I hadn't driven a car while I was in Hawaii either. Nor in L.A., where Robert had a driver who delivered us everywhere we needed to be. So, as I eased into the light traffic on the West Side Highway, I figured I hadn't driven a car since the last time I was on some shoot somewhere, a year ago at the very least, maybe more. How very strange.

It felt good to drive.

Greenwich has changed since I was a girl. There's an Apple store where the Gap used to be, and there's a new restaurant in the space that was occupied by that little Italian place I loved with the tables where you sat outside, the name of which I can't remember anymore. The auto dealerships are still in the same place, though I think some of them have changed brands. The little movie theater is gone and there's a multiplex at the other end of town. It's all a little different, but it's also the same. My favorite pizza shop is still where it used to be, with the statue in the window of the man in the white suit flipping the dough over his head. The florist at the beginning of Main Street is still open and, in fact, seems to have grown. And, of course, the hospital is still standing proudly at the end of town. I drove straight there and parked and just walked around for a little while. Of all the places that made my hometown feel like home, this was the most important.

The restaurant Andrew suggested was one I used to go to all the time on my birthday or my parents' anniversary, a special-event sort of place. My mother loved it. I remember the chairs seemed so big I would sit with my feet curled beneath me like I was on a couch. My father took me a few times after Mother died, too, but mostly I remember how sad we were then, and how people would stop at our table and say hello and tell us how sorry they were and wish us well. I guess that was why we stopped coming. But I always liked it anyway. You can't hold it against a restaurant that you spent a few sad nights there. It wasn't the restaurant's fault.

I gave my car to the valet and stood out in front for a moment, taking it all in. The awning outside was new but the place looked just as I remembered. The maître d' was wearing a tuxedo and he looked familiar; I think he was the maître d' the last time I was here. I'm not positive, but I think so. Either way, he greeted me graciously and escorted me to my table, where Andrew was waiting.

Much like the auto dealers and the shops and the town itself, Andrew looked the same but a little different. His hair was still wavy and chestnut brown, but thinner, and his shoulders were still broad but he didn't stand as tall or stiffly as I remembered; he stooped a little, as though being so tall had become an inconvenience over the years. He still had that smile, relaxed and confident, and his teeth were terrific, and his eyes alert and energetic. He was a very handsome man, even if he wasn't the high school basketball star anymore. It would have been silly to expect him to be that anyway; none of us are the high school basketball star anymore.

It would also have been silly to expect the sight of him to make me feel just as it did the night he asked me to dance, not because he wasn't the same but because I wasn't. Your heart doesn't flutter like that of a fourteen-year-old girl's when you aren't fourteen anymore. It was as though I was expecting him to appear before me and suddenly we would be in high school again, and the Bee Gees would start playing and we would dance and it would be exactly as it was. That was an unreasonable expectation—*that's* the part they mean when they say you can't go home again. You can't have the music and the dancing. But that doesn't mean you can't have a perfectly lovely time.

"What made you choose pediatrics?" I asked. We were drinking a very crisp white wine, which he'd ordered in French.

"I always knew I'd be a doctor," he said. "I spent so much time in the hospital as a kid, it felt like home. I'm sure it was the same for you."

I nodded.

"As for the specialty, I originally considered surgery. I spent two years in the ER and I hated it. The hours are ridiculous and the drama is off the charts. The work is fulfilling but I was emotionally spent every day. I think I would have had a nervous breakdown before my thirtieth birthday. With pediatrics the hours are reasonable and the calamities are few and far between. Plus, I like the kids. Some of them I've treated since they were a day old. And you get to know the families. That is probably the best part, you really become a part of the community. I think I know half the moms in town."

I laughed. "Like Brooke."

"Yeah, she's something else, isn't she?"

I took a long sip of wine. "Yes, she is."

Our entrées came and we ate quickly, and we laughed some more, it was relaxed and easy and fun. It was as though we had been the best of friends, which was strange, because in truth we had not. We hadn't really known each other that well in high school, or afterward, but we were from the same place. That can go a long way sometimes.

Our plates had been cleared and Andrew was sloshing red wine in his glass when a different look came over his face, as though he wanted to say something but wasn't sure about it. It was the same look he had that night, forever ago, when he stood before me and wanted to dance to a slow song but struggled to ask.

"So, Samantha, I thought I heard you got married."

It wasn't really a question, not technically. It was a statement, but there was a question connected to it even if he didn't ask it.

"Did you hear that from Brooke?"

"No, just around. Not from Brooke."

Life is funny sometimes. It throws you curveballs at the most unusual times. One minute you're rekindling romantic feelings with a boy you adored in high school and the next you're forced to explain why you were married for three days to a man who will very likely someday be the governor of California.

"I didn't mean to bring up an uncomfortable subject," Andrew said, looking concerned he had ruined the mood. "I just wondered if I had heard that wrong. You know how the grapevine can be. You don't have to go there if you don't want to. I'm sorry if it's a bad subject."

"It isn't," I said, "there's no big secret or anything. I was married, briefly, to the wrong man. In retrospect, it was a good thing that it happened the way it did. I could have wasted years of my life with him; instead I only wasted a couple of days."

"I'm sorry," he said.

"There's nothing to be sorry about."

I meant that. I wasn't sorry and I didn't want him to be either. He looked very concerned that he had spoiled the evening, while I was only concerned that there wasn't anything I could say to ease his mind. And then I thought of something.

"I have a much bigger regret than that in my life," I said. "Do you want to know what it is?"

"Only if you want to tell me."

I leaned closer to him. "I *really* regret that I never got to find out if you are as good a kisser as you seemed like you would be."

BROOKE

THE FIRST WORDS OUT of Samantha's mouth when I answered the phone in the morning, ahead of any greeting, with a whirring sound I could not immediately place in the background, brought a huge smile to my face.

"The answer," she said, with great excitement, "is YES!"

"I *love* it," I replied. "I don't even care what the question was, I just love when the answer is yes."

"The question was, is Andrew Marks as good a kisser as he looks like he'd be. You asked me that once and I couldn't answer it. I can answer it now."

"Oh my goodness, tell me everything."

I dropped onto the sofa and curled up and she started talking. I love stories like these. She said they went from the table to the bar, then to another bar for a nightcap, and then, both too drunk to drive, called a taxi to take them to Samantha's father's house. At that point, a hint of an icy feeling went through me. I cut her off.

"Samantha, what is that noise I hear in the background?"

"I don't know," she said, "what noise?"

"Oh my lord, you're in the car, aren't you?" I asked.

"Yes, I am," she said, very cheerily. Like she was throwing it in my face.

"You're just driving home now," I said, horrified. "You spent the night with him, didn't you?"

I could hear the laughter in her voice. "Yes, I did."

"You slut!"

She laughed and laughed, assuring me that her promise not to have sex with him on their first date had remained intact. I didn't believe her at first, I'm still not sure I do, but I can't very well call her a liar, there isn't much point in that.

"In fact," she went on, "one of the things we talked about was whether or not this could truly be called a first date, considering we had what was sort of a date one time before."

"Yes, darling, but that was how long ago?" I asked.

"Almost fourteen years."

"The statute of limitations on this sort of thing varies from situation to situation but in *no* case is it thirteen years," I told her. "That means if you had sex with him last night he is within his rights to assume you are a slut."

"Brooke, I did *not* have sex with him."

"Whatever you say."

"Brooke," she said, sounding a bit annoyed, "I cannot have this conversation with you if you are going to have this attitude. I have no reason to lie to you about this. I didn't sleep with him and that's the end of it."

"You're right," I said. "I'm sorry."

"Thank you."

We sat in silence for a moment. I listened to the wind whizzing by. It sounded like she was flying down the expressway.

"Are you in a convertible?" I asked her.

"No, but all the windows are down and the sun roof is open."

"Do you feel as good as you sound?" I asked.

"Brooke, I've never felt this good in my entire life."

"Tell me more," I said. "What was the single best moment?"

She didn't have to think about it for even a second. "He remembered the song."

I knew what she meant, but I asked anyway, mostly because I knew she'd love telling it even more than I'd love hearing it.

"We were talking about that night when we danced, and I told him it was the first time I had ever danced with a boy, and he made a joke about hoping he had been gentle, and it was all very comfortable, and then he started talking about the things from the night that he remembered, and when he got to the part about the music slowing down, I thought to myself there was no chance he would remember the song. But he did. He said: 'When "How Deep Is Your Love" came on . . .' and honestly I have no idea what he said after that, I just leaned in close to him and said: 'I wanted so badly for you to kiss me that night.' And we stood up and he held me just the same way, and we made out standing there in my father's living room."

"Could you hear the song in your head?" I asked.

"I think I could."

"Samantha," I told her, "I've heard a lot of stories, but *that* is the most romantic first kiss of all time."

I could only barely hear over the wind whipping past. "I know," she said.

SAMANTHA ▣ ▣ ▣

IN THE RIGHT LIGHT, everything is fabulous.

I forget who said that, but I read it somewhere, and it's true. This morning, the light is just right everywhere, and everything is fabulous. The sunshine reflecting off the Hudson River as I passed the George Washington Bridge, in particular, was gleaming with endless possibilities.

On these sorts of days, even a chemotherapy center seems brighter, cheerier, and it helps when the patient is in good spirits, which Katherine clearly was. I could tell the moment I arrived. There was a twinkle in her eye, almost as bright as the sun on the river. Something had happened, and she was excited to tell me, but first she wanted to know about Andrew.

As I recounted, in intricate detail, every second of my evening and long night, I found myself looking around the room more than I ever have before. I've been in this center with Katherine more times than I can count, but I suppose I have usually been so focused on her that I've blocked out everything around us. I haven't paid much attention to the large, open room with the lounging chairs and intravenous drips positioned behind each one. Or the nurses' station in the center of the room, and the rotation of friendly, supportive nurses, one cheerier than the next. Or the table with food and drink, pastries and finger sandwiches, juices and coffee. The food is for the visitors, but I've never eaten anything. Neither has Katherine; usually her treatments leave her nauseated and sleepy, and cold. She always has a large cashmere blanket draped around her shoulders and a quilt over her legs. Today I helped myself to coffee and glanced around at the other patients. Some were dozing, others reading, some were listening to music; not many of them looked sick. They looked alive, and Katherine did, too.

After I finished the story of my date with Andrew, Katherine lowered her reading glasses to the tip of her nose, like a teacher about to ask a tough question.

"Why on earth didn't you fuck him?" she said, too loudly.

I shushed her and looked around. But no one was staring at us. If any of the patients had heard her, it wasn't obvious.

"Please, Katherine," I said, "have a little class."

"Please, Samantha," she said, mimicking my tone, "I have more important things to worry about right now than maintaining the proper decorum."

"To answer your question," I said, "it wasn't the right time and it wasn't the right place."

"Listen to me," she said. "After all the history, I think doing it in your father's house would have been the perfect place, and if he's as good-looking as you say he is then I'm not sure there could ever be a bad time."

"Well, aren't we all riled up this morning?" I said. "What's gotten into you?"

So she told me about her visit from Phillip, and the money and the herpes and his clumsy, pathetic advances, and when she was finished there was only one conclusion to be reached.

"My goodness, Katherine," I said, "we need to celebrate, and *you* need a little action."

"You bet your ass," she said, and we both laughed.

Then it hit me. "Saturday night!" I said, slapping my forehead. "Marie's wedding! Black tie, fancy-schmancy, perfect occasion for a little flirting. We have to shop for your outfit tomorrow."

"It would be perfect, you're right," she said. I saw the arrival of the wistful look that occasionally came over her and heard it in her tone. It was the "but" in everything. That's what living with cancer means, more than anything. There's always a "but."

"Well," I said, moving it along, "I hope you're ready to shop tomorrow, because you are going to be the hottest thing at that party."

It looked to me like Katherine was holding back tears. "Thanks, Samantha," she said.

That's another way I knew she was sad. Katherine is one of those people who doesn't use your name much when she talks to you. When she does, it usually means she's sad.

So I changed the subject. "Kat," I said cheerily, "I would like to ask you the single most inappropriate question in the world."

That seemed to snap her out of it. She raised her eyebrows and waited.

"All the money that Phil made sure you got . . ."

She leaned forward. "Yes?"

"How much is it?"

Katherine tilted her head a little to the side, the way a dog might if it hears a sound it cannot identify. Then she leaned back in her chair and laughed out loud.

"You're right," she said, "highly inappropriate."

"I know," I said. "But I'm asking anyway."

She smiled. "You'll find out when you need to."

"What does that mean?"

"You'll understand pretty soon," she said.

"Katherine, don't get that way on me."

"That's not what I mean," she said reassuringly. "You'll find out what I mean, and how much money Phil gave me, very soon. Long before anything happens to me."

I shook my head. "I don't understand."

"No, you don't," she said cryptically. "But you will."

 KATHERINE

I DIDN'T WANT TO tell Samantha about my plans yet. There would be time for that soon. If there is one thing I have learned in two decades in the corporate world it is that the best time to announce plans is when they are complete. Anything earlier than that leaves too much room for error. So it wasn't time to announce it yet, or even to tell Samantha. But that wasn't far off.

First, I had to get ready for this wedding party. It was honestly sweet of Marie to make me her maid of honor, and to make such a fuss over my presence, including planning the event for the very weekend when I would be finished with my first round of treatment. Today is my last chemo for the time being—certainly not forever. I don't know that I will ever see a day when I have no more treatments ahead, perhaps until the time when there are no more options and hopefully that won't be any time soon. But for now I have a break, and Dr. Z told me to expect to feel great three or four days after my last round. He told Marie the same thing, and she planned her own wedding around that, and I can't think of a kinder gesture.

But it puts a lot of pressure on me. I am assuming practically everyone I know will be at this event, all the people I worked with all these years, and almost none of them has seen me since I became ill. In that way, there is no getting around the fact that this party will be as much about me as it will about Marie. I told her as much, and I told her no bride should ever sacrifice her night that way, but Marie just smiled. And, while she won't admit it, I think she wants it that way. She wants this night for me, and she knows if she or anyone else tried to throw this party for me I would never allow it, so in my heart I believe she has staged this, for the most part, to force me to attend. And while that is the most beautiful thing, it is also a great deal of stress for me.

I confronted her with it only one time. "Marie, I feel like you're inviting me to my own funeral," I said.

She was very calm. "Boss, this is my wedding night. I'm not thinking of it any other way. So you can see it however you want, but I'm asking you to do this for me."

There was no way to say no to that, so I never tried again.

So now Samantha and I would spend a day at Bergdorf Goodman, putting together the most sensational outfit anyone would see all year.

Hell, if this is the last time a lot of these people are going to see me, you'd better believe they are going to remember me looking fabulous.

Before we could shop, however, we had today to get through, one last afternoon of chemo, and I had been preparing for it.

"Let's change the subject," I said. "I came up with a few new Absolute Deal-breakers."

"Perfect," Samantha said, sliding her chair closer to mine. "We can apply them to some of the men you are going to meet at the party Saturday night."

"Okay," I said. "Is it an Absolute Deal-breaker if he named his dog after Jeffrey Dahmer?"

She burst out laughing. "Yes," she said. "Out, out, out!"

"I agree," I said. "Next, is it an Absolute Deal-breaker if you are seated next to an attractive stranger on an airplane and he makes very pleasant small talk, then pulls out an iPad and watches porn?"

Samantha smiled. She looked awfully pretty today. "How much effort does he make to conceal the porn from you?"

"What difference does that make?"

"I feel like if he wants you to see it then he is a pervert and trying to gauge if you're interested in something quick in the bathroom. But if he's hiding it . . ." She thought about it for a moment. "No, you're right, he's out, porn on an airplane is an Absolute Deal-breaker."

"Does it make any difference what kind of porn it is?" I asked her.

"I don't think so."

"So, soft-core stuff is just as bad as bestiality?"

"It's not as bad," she said, "but he's out just the same."

"Fair enough," I said. "Okay, I've got one more great one for you. I was up all night thinking about this one. How about if you're dating a guy and you're having a discussion about the parameters of the relationship and he asks if you would consider it cheating if he got jerked off by a male massage therapist."

I treasured the look of horror on Samantha's face. "OUT!" she screamed.

"Why is he out?" I asked.

"Because why is he even thinking about that?"

"I don't know. Maybe he's just trying to be prepared for any situation that may arise."

"He's out," Samantha said definitively. "That is an Absolute Deal-breaker."

"I figured you'd say that," I told her, "because you're a pretty tough judge."

I looked at my watch. One hour remaining. The hours pass awfully slowly in this room. The days can sometimes fly by, and every now and again the minutes move quickly, but the hours are eternal. I was trying to think of another deal-breaker when Samantha mentioned a name I hadn't heard in a long time.

"I met someone who knows you," she said. "Brooke Biltmore."

You don't forget Brooke, neither the name nor the girl. Brooke was the most social girl in Greenwich, legendarily so. We didn't have girls like Paris Hilton in my school, but Brooke was the closest thing. She was a year behind me, and she was iconic, fashionable and friendly, and beautiful and sweet. The boys adored her, the faculty worshipped her, the younger girls idolized her, and even the girls who envied her had to grudgingly admit she had it together.

I am ashamed to admit it, but the very idea that after all these years Brooke Biltmore remembered me was a little exciting. I guess we never really do leave high school.

"Where did you meet her?" I asked, nonchalant as I could.

"In Greenwich."

"Details?"

"Her kids are patients of Andrew's. It's a long story, but I met her and she seemed around your age so I dropped your name and she totally remembered you," Samantha said.

I had to work to keep the pride from showing on my face. "How does she look?"

"She's gorgeous," Samantha said, with no hesitation.

"She always was."

"You can tell."

"And obviously she's married with kids and still lives in Greenwich?"

"That's right," Samantha said. "She's married, don't know much about her husband, but she has twins, I'm not sure how old."

I nodded. "Sounds right."

"What was she like in high school?" Samantha asked.

"Exactly the same," I said. "Gorgeous, with a successful husband and perfect-looking twins."

"You strike me as the sort of person who wouldn't care for a girl like that."

"You are correct," I said thoughtfully, "but to be fair, she was all right. There was something decent about Brooke that made it impossible to hate her. She was a good person. She was much more real than the average debutante. I'm glad to hear things have turned out well for her."

Samantha got a strange look when I said that, one that suggested maybe things weren't as good for Brooke as they sounded, but I didn't ask. If she wanted to tell me she would.

"What did she remember about me?" I asked instead.

"She said you were really smart."

That's what I mean. That's what I liked about Brooke. Do you think Paris Hilton could tell you which girls in school were really smart? Even if Brooke had more admirers than anyone else, she still knew I was the smart one.

"That's nice," I said. "Anything else?"

Now the look on Samantha's face was even more uncomfortable, and I couldn't read it at all. Maybe it was connected to Brooke not doing so well. I had to ask.

"What?"

"She said that your father was in jail."

And there it was.

That feeling. The nervous gnawing in the pit of my stomach, the slap in the face, the redness in the cheeks that followed. It had been a really long time but now it was back. Because, like I said, you really never do get out of high school.

"Well," I said, "I guess she really does remember me."

"You never told me about that," Samantha said. She sounded hurt, and I understood. Not because she had the right to know anything she wanted, but because she felt, as I did, that we shared everything. Only I hadn't shared this.

"It just didn't seem relevant anymore," I said. But that wasn't true, not at all. When your father goes to jail it is always relevant, even if you live to be a hundred. "Do you want to know the story?"

"Only if you want to tell me," Samantha said.

"I don't want to tell you at all," I said, "but I will."

Samantha frowned.

"That came out wrong," I said. "I mean it isn't a lot of fun talking about it, so I never do, but it's important to me that you know I'm not keeping anything a secret."

"Katherine, you don't—"

I cut her off. "Sit back and relax," I said. "It's not a quick story."

The story is about my mother's brother—Uncle Edward—who was an enormously rich man and a total cretin. He made his money in real estate, buying decrepit buildings, throwing out the poor people who lived in them, tearing down the buildings, and putting up town houses. It's perfectly legal, and I suppose you could argue he was improving neighborhoods, but I always wondered where all the poor people went. I asked him about it one time, and only one time.

"Who gives a shit?" was his reply.

That's why I never asked again.

My father worked for him, in a management role that left him a lot of free time, so my dad was always around when I was a girl, which was terrific. But it was pretty obvious he didn't love his job, and the summer I turned eleven I found out why. We were at my uncle's house in Southampton. We visited once per summer, not more and not less, and it was clear my parents never enjoyed themselves, but I certainly did. The house was sensational. It had a pool and a trampoline and my cousins had a playroom bigger than our house. I used to love it there, until the day I discovered the air vent.

It wasn't actually me who discovered it. My eldest cousin showed it to me. His name was Richard, and I thought he was cool because he looked a little like John Travolta and because he smoked. Richard showed me an air vent in the downstairs playroom where he could sneak a cigarette, blowing the smoke into the air duct. It was genius, and utterly cool.

That year when I turned eleven, I decided I wanted to try it. I knew where to find cigarettes, my uncle kept his on the kitchen counter, and I knew where to go to smoke them. I can still remember my heart beating as I snuck two cigarettes out of the pack and tucked them into the waistband of my sweatpants, then tiptoed down the stairs. There was no one in the playroom. My father and my uncle were the only ones in the house and they'd locked themselves in my uncle's office, telling me they needed to talk in private and were not to be disturbed.

I slid open the vent that covered the air duct and stuck my head inside, but before I could strike a match I heard voices. They sounded tinny, with a hint of echo, but I recognized them immediately and was easily able to make out what they were saying.

"You've never treated me with respect."

That was my father.

"Don't make a fool of yourself."

That was my uncle.

"After the way you've treated me all these years," my father said, "if you think I'm going to get you off the hook you must be out of your mind."

"Let me tell you something," my uncle said. "You've been riding this gravy train for years. This is the first time I've ever asked you to do anything and you will do exactly as I tell you."

"Or else what? Are you threatening to cut your own sister and her family out of the business?"

"No," my uncle replied. "That is not what I'm threatening."

"Then what?" my father asked.

There was a long silence after that. I never heard them say anything else.

A few months later my father went to prison upstate, sentenced to four years for tax evasion. I never told anyone that I knew what happened, and I never read what was in the newspapers. But I did learn two valuable lessons that day. The first is that money without power is worthless. And the other is that there isn't really anything so cool about smoking. I left the two cigarettes right there in the air duct and shut the vent behind me. For all I know they're still there. And I never did try a cigarette, not in my entire life.

When I finished the story, Samantha was stone-faced. I could tell she didn't know what to say.

"What happened after he went to prison?" she finally asked.

"We visited him."

"And how was that?"

"The jail wasn't so terrible. Visiting him was like going to a mediocre restaurant for lunch, except that you wouldn't normally drive upstate to eat at a mediocre restaurant, nor would you leave your father there after you paid the check. That was the worst part. It wasn't seeing him in there that was so bad, it was getting back into the car without him when we left."

"What did you talk about when you were with him?" she asked.

"I hardly remember. It feels like a different lifetime, like it happened in a dream."

"And how about when he came home?"

That was the hard part. "He never came home. He died of a heart attack less than two years after he went in."

"Oh my god," Samantha said.

"My mother has never been the same, not even close. She'll never get over it. I suppose I won't either. And she and I have always had trouble talking about it, because she says he did it all for me, which seems to make it okay in her mind but always makes it much worse to me."

We sat quietly in the room, listening to the humming of the machines. Every now and again someone would laugh, or a phone would ring. There was soft music in the distance that I couldn't recall hearing before. It was almost time to go.

"Let me tell you something, Samantha," I said. "The lesson in all of it is that money without power is meaningless. So the lesson for you should be to stop apologizing all the time for the way you were raised and all the advantages you had. What you're doing now is wonderful and there isn't any way to put a price tag on it."

Samantha was very still. She didn't say anything.

"Besides," I added, "money isn't everything it's cracked up to be. What makes life worth living is all the wonderful things that could happen to you. Remember that."

"Are you talking about Andrew?" she asked.

"I am if you want me to be."

She was thinking of him now, I could tell.

"Samantha," I said. "Earlier, when I told you Brooke seemed like the sort who'd have the perfect life, I could tell from your face she does not. Right now, I could really use a story about her life that isn't so perfect. Would you tell me?"

She seemed to think very hard. "Her life isn't perfect, Katherine, believe me."

"In what way?"

Samantha put her hand up near her mouth. "I'll just tell you this, because I don't want to betray her trust. Brooke is one of those women who judges herself and every other woman based on the men in their lives."

I nodded. I wasn't particularly surprised to hear that. "Women like that have always treated me like I'm pathetic," I said.

"Maybe they treat you that way because they are intimidated by you."

"Baloney," I said. "They act as though they consider everything I have a substitute for what *they* have."

"Maybe *you're* intimidated by them."

That slowed me down. "I don't know. I guess it doesn't make any difference anyway."

Samantha came closer and fluffed the pillow at the base of my achy back. "I think there's a lesson in that for all of us," she said. "Something about just needing to give each other a break now and then."

That stopped me, completely.

"Well," I sniffed, "when you put it that way it sounds so simple."

Then she sat back down in the chair opposite mine and we waited quietly for the rest of the poison to finish dripping into my veins. It would only be a few more minutes.

BROOKE

SO, I'LL MAKE THESE my final words on the subject.

There isn't any need to continue talking about it all, because that only serves to defeat the purpose, which is to live. Not just to stay alive, to *live*. As I, and only I, define living. I don't tell anyone else how they should define it, and I don't ask for advice, either.

For me, happiness is the only goal I can imagine. I don't really have any others. Some people pursue happiness in boardrooms or on mountaintops, they spend their lives negotiating and climbing, and it seems to me what they are doing is looking for happiness in the profits and the pretty views. But I don't need to look so far away for happiness. I have it here, all around me, every day, nearly every minute. I don't need to accomplish anything in order to feel happy. Happiness is not something I hope to discover along the way to vague, distant goals; happiness is a means to its own end. It *is* the destination, the only one worth striving for, at least that's the way I see it and I tell my kids that all the time. *The only thing I wish for you is happiness*. I don't care if they are ambitious, athletic, or academic. I don't care if they want to be doctors or school-teachers or garbage collectors; I only want them to be happy. Living happily ever after is always the best ending. Any story that ends differently isn't worth telling, as far as I'm concerned.

So, sometimes I think to myself: *How dare she try to tell me how to live my life?*

Cancer, I mean.

Not Samantha. I love *her* for trying to tell me how to live my life. She's young enough not to have learned that there are different ways of thinking, and she's sweet enough to care. I appreciate her for both of those. I don't get angry with her when she pesters me about my decisions, which she does less and less frequently anyway. That's nice. Now we can just be friends. Perhaps someday she'll meet Scott and my kids. I think she'd like that, and I would too. Perhaps we could double-date, if things progress with Dr. Marks, which I have a funny feeling they are going to.

Actually, it's more than a funny feeling, more like a premonition. Or a matter of faith. Something good has to come from what I've been through. Perhaps this is what it is meant to be. Perhaps Dr. Marks and Samantha will marry and they'll have a son or a daughter who becomes a brilliant scientist who discovers the cure for cancer, and it would never have happened if I hadn't become sick and met Samantha and fixed her up with Andrew.

So, it's not Samantha who infuriates me. It is cancer. How dare this disease, this creeping, crawling creature I can neither see nor feel, show up unannounced and uninvited and start dictating all this change. Cancer has a whole list of ways in which my life is going to be different, a list of things I need to do, a list of things I will never do again. Even now, when it is no longer inside me, it wants to tell me how to behave so it will never return.

Well, guess what: I'm not listening. I have my own plans and my own schedule and I will deal with cancer on my own terms, no one else's. If I choose to drive car pools and chaperone class trips and get my hair blown out every Saturday night and talk dirty to my husband on the phone when he is away, then that is exactly what I'm going to do, with apologies to no one and absolutely no second thoughts.

And to anyone who judges me, I simply say: Mind your own business.

And to cancer, I simply say: FUCK YOU.

 KATHERINE

I LOOK BEAUTIFUL.

There really aren't three better words in the English language than those, are there?

Even *I love you* isn't always better. Hell, I've probably had more pain and suffering as a result of *I love you* than I have any three other words, with the exception of *You have cancer*, and even that may be a toss-up.

Right now, I'll take *I look beautiful*, because it's been so long since I've said them, or thought them, or even thought about them.

It starts with the wig, which is fabulous. I can't decide now why I resisted it. It is long and blond and wavy—it's like having Charlize Theron's hair in the blink of an eye. And I love it.

But it isn't only the wig that looks fabulous tonight.

As I stand before the full-length mirror in my dressing area, I am thrilled beyond words at what I see. For the first time I am not looking for the flaws. Usually when I observe myself in the mirror I am trying to find the faults, the blemishes, the crow's-feet, the faint stain on the blazer where the salad dressing never fully came out. Tonight is the opposite. I am looking for the places where I look fabulous, and there are many. Not just the hair, or the wig, but plenty more. My eyes are alive and glowing. My coloring has come back—most of it, anyway—so I don't look pale or gaunt. I am still thin, and there is a pride in my posture I have never seen before, something in the arch of my back, the rise of my chin, the heat of my stare. It says I am here. It says if I was ever gone I am back, and wherever I am going can wait. Tonight I am here, and I am wonderful to behold. And if it took cancer to make me feel this way, to allow me to see myself like this, then so be it. At least something good came of it.

When the intercom sounds, I am ready. I give myself a final glance in the mirror, and a wink, and as I smooth a tiny piece of hair above my eyes I think to myself that I really am filled with loving-kindness, and I am peaceful and at ease, and I am happy. Maybe for the first time since I was a little girl, I am truly happy.

It is Marie who is downstairs. Maurice picked her up and now they are here for me. She is stunningly beautiful in her gown, long and flowing, white in all the right places. By her standards, the dress is conservative; you can hardly see her breasts, which I have become so accustomed to seeing on full display that now I miss them.

"Well, well," I say proudly, as I step off the elevator. "Here comes the bride."

Marie is shivering with excitement. "You look so beautiful, Katherine, I could honestly cry."

"Remember," I tell her, "it is your night. This is not Katherine's Going Away Party, this is your wedding and if you aren't going to act like it I'm going back upstairs."

Marie smiles. I can see tears in her eyes. "I'm perfect, boss," she says. "You told me in Aspen that I needed to figure out what makes life worth living. Well, I figured it out, and that's what tonight is about."

She reaches out her hand and I take it in mine and squeeze it. She is such a sweet girl, and sometimes so much more insightful than I ever gave her credit for. I love her tonight, with all of my heart.

"It makes me very proud . . ." I start to say, but to my own surprise the words stick in my throat. If I finish the sentence I will start to cry, and I don't want to cry, not in the lobby, not on Marie's night.

"I love you, boss," she says, and I squeeze her hand again, and we go out through the revolving door.

Maurice is standing by the car with the door open, smiling broadly, his hat tucked beneath his arm. It is a beautiful, crisp night, the first of the season that has truly felt like fall. That first night when you feel as though it has been a year since last you were cold. I've been cold plenty this year, but not like this. The air is invigorating, and I pause a long moment before I get into the car, just taking it in, looking about at all the twinkling lights of an early New York evening.

"Maurice," I say, "there is so much beauty in this world, so much in this life that is so beautiful. I don't know why I haven't seen it before."

"You've always seen it, boss," he says. "You've just been too busy to pay attention." If I'm not mistaken, it sounds as though there is a lump in his throat as well. "It's wonderful to see you looking like this," he continues. "I've never seen you look better than you do right now."

I smile wickedly. "Well, maybe I'll get lucky tonight."

And with one final glance around, I duck my head and slide into the car beside Marie.

We sit in silence for most of the drive, which doesn't take very long. It's only a few blocks, and traffic is light. As we cross through Central Park, a taxi pulls alongside at a red light, just outside Marie's window, an old-fashioned checker cab, the sort I haven't seen in years. I remember that when I was a girl my parents took me into the city to see the Christmas show once at Radio City Music Hall. We took the train from Connecticut and we had lunch near Grand Central station, egg salad sandwiches and chocolate malts, and then my father hailed a taxi and I was so excited to pull up the reclining bench seat from the floor. That was our last Christmas together, I think.

Then the light changes to green and the taxi pulls away behind Marie's head and I lean over and put my face to her ear. "How do you feel?" I ask.

She doesn't even blink. "I just can't wait to get there."

I smile. That seems right. I think if I were her I wouldn't be able to wait either.

We emerge from the park just as the last natural light of the afternoon fades away, and the street lamps begin to flicker, coming to life for the evening. Before I know it, we pull into a circular driveway and over toward the expansive entrance of an elegant Central Park West skyscraper.

"There's a private elevator for us," Marie says to Maurice, pointing to a secondary entrance near the corner. "Pull up, please."

Then we park and Maurice gets out of the car, holding open the door. The air has turned slightly colder, and I can see his breath wafting from beneath his hat, drifting into the darkening sky as he waits.

"The elevator is directly inside," Marie says to me. "Take it to the penthouse."

"You're not coming in?"

"I'd just like a minute to myself," she says, "I'll meet you upstairs."

I put my hand on her leg and squeeze it, then slide outside and smooth my dress as I stretch my legs. I pat Maurice on the shoulder and motion into the car toward Marie. "If she needs anything please run and get it."

"Of course I will," Maurice says. "Now you go ahead up, it's chilly out here."

We still have an hour before the ceremony is to begin. There isn't any rush.

The electric doors part before me and I feel a rush of warm air, a stark contrast to the crispness of the night. When the elevator arrives I select the top floor and lean back against the handrail in the rear wall. There is a tiny, circular mirror in the upper corner of the elevator, above the buttons and the glass cases displaying the certificates of inspection. I try to see myself in it but it is too far away and distorted, as those mirrors always are, like a funhouse. I hold the rail behind me, tapping my foot, listening to the speedy hum of the floors whooshing past. Then I feel a gentle slowing and a melodious *ding*, and the letters PH illuminate in red.

The music begins just as the doors open directly into the apartment, as they do in mine. There is a band on a stage facing the door, seven or eight pieces, in formal dress, and as I step out of the elevator, they begin to play the song "Isn't It Romantic." I love that song.

The room is glowing, awash in pink and green, with a chandelier sparkling like cut diamonds, casting jagged streaks of silver and gold. The music is rich and loud and fills my ears completely, fills my head, makes me dizzy, enough that I do not notice anything unusual at first. It does not register that there is merely a dance floor and a single table where there should be rows of chairs separated by an aisle for the bridal march. But none of that enters my mind as I walk slowly toward the table, where a man sits facing away, his tuxedo-clad back broad and distantly familiar. And the band continues to play and the lights continue to sparkle and the room continues to glow and my heels make just the faintest tapping sounds on the dance floor as I approach. And I take a moment to look around, and I see there is no one else there. It is just the band and the man at the table and me.

And then, in case there is any question, I hear a clattering off to my right and a door pushes open and out of the darkness appears the golden retriever. She bounds toward me and then veers away, making an acrobatic leap, then stopping and stretching and curling at the foot of the table, just steps away. And the band continues to play, and my heart beats so fast I can feel it in my temples and hear it in my ears. And I open my mouth but no sound comes out, so I simply place my hand on his shoulder, and he looks up and smiles at me, and I realize I have seen his face a thousand times in the past three months. I have seen it every time I closed my eyes to transport myself from where I was to where I wished I could be, and now here it is and it is even better than it had been in my head. And he takes my hand and he stands, and kisses me gently on the cheek, and then he wraps his arms around my waist and we begin to dance as the band plays on and the golden retriever nods approvingly at our feet.

BROOKE

I FINALLY DID IT.

I have been meaning for the longest time to begin memorizing quotes and who said them. I love to read, and I have promised myself I will begin to do what I know other people do, underlining meaningful passages, phrases, posting them as notes on my refrigerator or bathroom mirror, or as reminders on my iPad.

Well, I've begun.

The idea came to me last night, during dinner with my husband and the twins and a dear friend of the family, a darling young girl named Ashley, who grew up on our street and used to babysit for my kids before she went off to college. She is twenty-one now, and home to see her parents, and she always stops for a visit with us, and last night she sat down to a heaping plate of macaroni and cheese with steamed broccoli on the side and laughed about wonderful memories we all share.

She first babysat for us when the twins were just a year old, and she always tells them stories of how cute they were, which we all love, and the kids especially never tire of hearing of the night Megan had projectile diarrhea that grazed Ashley's hair and splattered against the wall four feet behind her. Both kids, even now, at eight, practically fall out of their chairs at that one.

Ashley has blossomed into such a lovely young woman, poised and pretty. I view her with a degree of pride and I know Scott does as well. We both remember her when she was hardly older than the twins are now, walking up our driveway with a tray of brownies she and her mother had baked to welcome us to the neighborhood. It was our first house, and right away she made it feel like a home. When the twins came four years later, Ashley became a fixture; I cried at her high school graduation.

Anyway, we were all having the most wonderful time when Jared began to reminisce about a night none of us had ever heard about, even his sister. He remembered Ashley's high school boyfriend, a shy kid named Eric, who frequently visited while she babysat. Scott and I were perfectly comfortable with that so long as her parents were, and they were; Eric was a sweet boy and he liked to play with our kids and when the twins were in bed he and Ashley would sit on our couch and watch television until Scott and I came home. It was all very innocent and sweet.

Well, last night over dinner Jared told us of a night, back in the days of Eric, when he awoke during the night with an upset stomach and came downstairs and saw Eric and Ashley kissing! Oh, the horror of it, he told us, as he is still of an age where he finds kissing to be repulsive, as does his sister. Scott and I roared with wine-infused laughter, and Megan made a funny face to indicate how gross the kissing must have been, and it was all very funny. Except that Ashley wasn't laughing.

"Jared," she said, turning a bit red, "I don't remember that happening. You must have dreamt it."

"No," he said, shaking his head for emphasis, "I was awake. I remember. You were kissing!"

And then Megan was out of her chair and mimicking a make-out session, her arms wrapped dramatically around her own sides, making smooching sounds loud enough to startle the dog.

Scott, who had managed to get his laughter under control, looked over at Jared. "Was *that* how it looked when Ashley and Eric were kissing?"

"Well, sort of," Jared said, his attention back to his macaroni, "only they weren't wearing clothes."

The words hung in the air for an instant. Scott immediately took an enormous gulp of his Pinot Noir and glanced quickly at Ashley, who was now bright red, her lips parting, no doubt to futilely insist Jared had dreamt or imagined the entire event, but before she could say a word the silence was broken by Megan, who started dancing uncontrollably about the room, smooching and laughing so hard she fell to the ground, where she continued to writhe with laughter and scream, "KISSING NAKED! KISSING NAKED!"

"Jared," Ashley said, because she had to protest even though it was obviously true, "you are making this up. That's not nice."

"No," he said matter-of-factly, "I saw your boobies."

That was more than Megan could take.

"SAW YOUR BOOBIES! SAW YOUR BOOBIES!"

Tears were streaming down her cheeks as she rolled about the kitchen floor, howling in that combination of humor and wonder of which only children are capable. She knew it was funny and she knew it was awkward, and she knew there was something about it all that wasn't right but she didn't really know what, or why. So the most she could do was make noise and she did that for all she was worth until Scott finally stopped it.

"That's enough."

He didn't shout, he almost never does, he just has a certain tone in his voice that makes it clear he is not making a request, he is making a demand. It is a tone I like a lot; I have heard it used in many settings that do not involve macaroni and cheese. Megan quickly got back in her seat and resumed eating, and Jared drank his milk, and I poured more wine into my glass and Ashley's and I took a long sip. And it was all quiet, aside from the clanking of the silverware, and I couldn't bring myself to look at Ashley's face for fear of how horrified she must have been.

And then Scott started to laugh. It was a quiet laugh at first, under his breath, as though he knew it was something he shouldn't find funny, but he did. And so did I. And as Scott began to allow himself to laugh, I did too, and soon we were both laughing hard, and the kids were too, even though they had no idea why, they will just laugh pretty much any time they can find a good excuse to. And I got up and walked around the table to stand behind Ashley and put my arms around her and squeezed tight, and to my great joy she began to laugh as well, and so we sat there, enjoying a bottle of wine, or a glass of milk, and most of all enjoying each other, my husband and my son and my daughter and their former babysitter and me, and there was so much love in the room it hung in the air like mist on a spring morning.

And so today, after I kissed my husband good-bye and got my kids off to school, I sat down at my computer and found the quote I remembered from college. It is from the play *Faust*, by Goethe, which I didn't enjoy at all when I read it back then, but I've always remembered the concept: a man makes a deal with the devil; he offers his soul in exchange for a single moment of perfection, one moment where he feels whole and complete happiness.

The quote didn't take long to find.

> *If ever I to the moment shall say:*
> *Beautiful moment, do not pass away!*
> *Then you may forge your chains to bind me,*
> *Then I will put my life behind me.*

I printed it out and I am going to laminate the words and keep them with me. Maybe I'll hang them on the fridge. And they won't be the only ones. This is just the beginning. There will be other quotes, other ideas, other people who have understood me without ever meeting me, other words and phrases I will be able to summon when I need them, perhaps in church, or at a dinner party, or to impart a lesson to my kids. I can use them when I argue with Samantha about the decisions I have made, or when I am alone in the bath and questioning them myself. It just feels good to know that there are people out there who can use words better than I can to explain my life. Not that it needs to be explained, if you ask me. But it still feels good.

SAMANTHA ▣ ▣ ▣

Seven months later

SEVEN O'CLOCK IS SUCH a lively time of the morning out here.

Up early on this Sunday to check e-mail and I hardly even mind it, didn't need to set an alarm, even as hard as I've been working since we started. Something in the salty fresh air of the ocean feels so familiar, so invigorating, it makes my mind feel sharp. In the bustle of the city, I tend to wake with a foggy brain no matter how much I've slept. But here at the beach I feel focused and rested, even after all the wine last night, and the midnight skinny-dipping.

The house is just sensational, everything Katherine told me and more. Drinking coffee now in the kitchen I can feel the warmth of the sun as it slips between the vanishing clouds and climbs above the ocean. I can hear gulls squawking in the surf as they dive after whatever washed ashore during the night. Up the way the surfers are arriving en masse. I see three of them on the water but there must be twenty more on the beach, pulling on wetsuits; the morning is chilly, probably no more than sixty degrees out there now, going to seventy after breakfast.

Katherine left filled closets behind; I am in a silver dressing robe of soft flannel, which is hers, over silk pajamas, which are my own. I don't like to wear her clothes, here or in the city, but now and again I make an exception. This morning it felt just right, luxurious and decadent, like a fudge sundae.

There are more than seventy e-mails waiting for me when I log in. I need to hire more staff. This endeavor has become bigger than Katherine or I dreamt it might, which is remarkable, considering how ambitious we both were from the outset. But it has become clear to me now that I need more help. Seventy is too many messages for a Sunday morning, especially one as pretty and serene as this. I would love to hire Marie, but she is due any day and the sense I get when I speak with her is that her working days are behind her. We'll see after the baby comes and she settles in, perhaps she'll change her mind, but I'm not going to count on it. She seems quite content. I won't push her, but I will ask again.

I've never been more impressed by any person in all my life than I am by Marie. What she did, and the way she did it, constitutes the single most dynamic act of courage and love that I have ever witnessed. I told Katherine that I had nothing to do with it and that I knew nothing of it, and both of those were true, whether Katherine believed it or not. I made her a promise that I would not interfere when it came to Stephen and there is no way I would ever have disregarded my word to her.

I found out about it the same time Katherine did, the night of the wedding, when Maurice pulled the car into the driveway in front of my building and I found, to my surprise, that Marie was inside and Katherine was not. When Maurice came around to open the door for me, I gave him a questioning look.

"Hop in," he said. "I'm sure she'll explain."

The *she* he meant was Marie, not Katherine, and she did explain, right then and there, sitting in her wedding gown while the car idled in the driveway and the last of the sunlight peeked through the open window.

"I've done something really big," she said. She was trembling with excitement, her hands shaking so hard she could hardly take a sip from the bottle of water she held. "I think it might be the best thing I've ever done. I hope so. I really, really hope so."

She just kept saying that, over and over, staring into the distance. The sounds of a New York City Saturday night were all around us.

"Marie," I said, "where is Katherine?"

She broke into a smile at that, so wide it spread to us all. There was such electricity in her face it made me tingle, and while I hadn't yet heard exactly what it was, I knew right then she was right, it was the biggest thing she'd ever done.

And so she took a deep breath and she told us.

She told us about the first time Stephen called the office looking for Katherine. Marie did as she was told, explained that Katherine had resigned and left no forwarding information. The second time he called, the following day, she did the same. The third time, when he tried to disguise his voice and used a phony name, clumsy and nervous, Marie had tears in her eyes as she sent him away.

The following day, he didn't call, nor the day after that. And as the days passed, and Marie didn't have to turn away his calls, the ache in the pit of her stomach grew. It grew and grew until it grew into a memory, began to feel as though it had been in a dream, or another life. Which, in a way, she said, it sort of had.

And then a month passed and she had given up that dream and settled into the rhythm of caring for Katherine, and tending to her job, and contemplating her future, when on the third Thursday after her period nothing happened. This was unprecedented; Marie was as regular as you could be, she had never been even a day late since she was seventeen. And she knew immediately she was pregnant, knew for sure, even before the drugstore and the powder-blue tip and the week that passed before she said a word to her doctor or her fiancé. When she finally told Adam, they agreed they would be married as quickly as was feasible. They wouldn't have a big, glamorous wedding, they both knew that, because his family thought she was a gold-digger and her family thought his family was pretentious, and there was just no need to deal with any of that. So they got into bed and made love more passionately than Marie could ever remember, and then they lay in the dark and drank sparkling apple cider out of champagne flutes and fantasized about what they would do for a wedding if their options were unlimited.

"I would have Bruce Springsteen walk you down the aisle, shake my hand, and then play 'Born to Run' on a harmonica," he said.

"I would have us go up in a hot-air balloon and we could recite our vows as we watch the sun rise," she said.

"I actually like that," Adam said, and then he paused to think a minute. "You know, we could do that if we wanted to. Where would we do it?"

"Aspen," she said, without hesitation, "and we'd bring an iPod and speakers and have 'Annie's Song' by John Denver playing."

And then, just like that, it all came flooding back, and she told Adam right there, that night, nude and newly pregnant in their bed, that she needed to go to Aspen to look for Stephen. She couldn't Google him, because she didn't know his last name, and even if she could she didn't want to talk to him on the phone—or, even worse, over e-mail—she needed to see his face when she told him. She needed to know, for herself, if he felt as Katherine did, that they were perfect for each other. She needed to know if he was willing to fight for her, and to be there when it got hard, which there was little doubt it eventually would. And so she went, on a wing and a prayer, and Adam went too, and they took a room in the Grand Hyatt at the base of Aspen Mountain, and on the first day they hiked up Smuggler's Mountain and waited in vain on the observation deck for a ruggedly handsome man and a gorgeous golden retriever. That night they went to Jimmy's and sat at the bar and ate burgers, and Adam drank beer, and they looked carefully at every man that entered. Marie was certain she would know Stephen if she saw him. There was no reason she should but she was sure she would.

Around nine they gave up and walked to Main Street for ice cream, and along the way they heard music and found a jazz concert in the grassy field across from the skateboard park, so they sat and listened and enjoyed the clean air and gentle breeze. And just when it was time for bed she remembered what was on the other side of the park, and she took Adam by the hand.

"Follow me," she said, "I need to show you something."

"What is it?"

"I just thought of where I want to get married."

The sound of the water rushing across the stones became louder as they walked farther from the music, and as they reached the gravel path and passed the sign that said JOHN DENVER SANCTUARY, the jazz behind them faded away and all that was left was the rumble of the stream and the crunching of their footsteps. And she held his hand the entire way, and was thinking of how perfect it would be to make all the most important promises of her life in this place, when she saw the dog.

She cried when she told us about her meeting with Stephen, about how she cried that night, too, and how he was exactly as she had imagined, and how he remembered every detail of his time with Katherine, including Marie's own explicit texts. They spent a long time sitting on stones that night, and Stephen listened closely as she explained it all, including the details of Katherine's diagnosis, her treatment, what she was facing, how she was feeling. And when she was finished, she said, Stephen never budged, didn't hesitate, and had only five words to say.

"I want to see her."

It was over breakfast the following morning that they devised the plan and began to make the arrangements.

"And the rest," Marie said to Maurice and me in the car that night, "is history."

And she took another deep breath and there was silence, and then we were all overcome at exactly the same time. I reached out for Marie and kissed her repeatedly, and I held her until I felt her tears mingling with my own on my cheeks. And I heard a car door slam shut and then another open, and then Maurice slid in beside us.

"I don't know if this is appropriate," he said, "but I need a hug too."

The three of us embraced for a long time, thinking of Katherine and Stephen, wondering what they were doing at just that moment. What were they saying to each other? Were they holding hands, were they dancing?

Then Maurice adjusted his chauffeur's cap. "Ladies," he said, "what do we do now?"

"We go to my apartment," Marie said. "Adam is waiting with a justice of the peace to marry me."

So that's where we went. Maurice and I were the only witnesses. And now they are having a little girl, any minute, and they are naming her Katherine.

So I would love to hire Marie; she is a miracle worker. And there is no doubt Katherine always intended for her to be involved in what we are doing now. Maybe at some point I will be able to talk her into it.

I miss Katherine.

I am joyous to know that she is in a better place, but that doesn't change the fact that I miss her terribly. The energy in her stare, the length of her stride, even when the pain in her back was the worst and the chemo left her nauseous and dry-mouthed, it was still an effort to keep up with her when she walked. She had an amazing presence, always, on her best days and her worst. I miss every bit of it.

It was the morning after her reunion with Stephen that she first told me of her idea. I had hardly slept at all, rolling about in bed with my phone beside me on the pillow to be sure it would wake me up when Katherine called, which she finally did just after nine.

"Good morning, sunshine," she said. "How much do you know about my evening?"

"I know everything and nothing," I said. "You know I had nothing to do with it."

"I know," she said. "You did exactly what you should have. And so did Marie. I'm blessed to have both of you in my life."

"Don't forget Maurice," I said. "He cried like a baby when he found out what was going on."

That made her laugh.

"Where are you?" I asked.

"I'm home. I need to talk to you about something. I've been meaning to for a while, and this finally seems like the perfect time."

"Katherine, whatever it is can wait," I said. "If you don't tell me every single thing about last night in the next thirty seconds I am going to jump out of my own skin."

She laughed again. "I will, I promise. But I need you to come over here. I'll tell you all about it over breakfast."

"Will I meet any special someone who might have spent the night?"

"You just might."

I was in a taxi within five minutes.

I didn't meet Stephen right away; he was in the bedroom, asleep. Katherine told me about their evening, about the way they danced and drank champagne until midnight and then went back to her apartment where they made love and then realized neither of them had eaten any dinner so they raided her refrigerator and sat at the kitchen table and watched the sun come up. And now he was sleeping and she was not, because she had something even more important she wanted to tell me and it couldn't wait any longer.

"Do you remember the time you asked me how much money I was worth and I said you would find out when the time was right?" she began.

"I do."

"Well, the time is right."

And so, seated there at her kitchen table, while I drank coffee and ate a bagel with cream cheese, she told me everything. I say it that way because it is remarkable how detailed her vision was. I learned that morning that Katherine really was a genius, which I suppose should have been obvious from all her professional accomplishments, but sometimes you have to witness a genius in action to truly appreciate her.

She told me that during all the hours she had spent alone, watching chemicals drip into her veins, she had kept her mind occupied by arranging these plans in her head. In that way, she said, she spent more time and mental energy on this deal than she had on any of those she had put together on Wall Street.

"Some of those were worth a hundred billion dollars," she said, "but in the end, that's only money. And if Wall Street and my father taught me anything, it's that money is meaningless. And someone else taught me that it's what you do with money that matters." She looked straight into my eyes. "*You* did."

Katherine pulled a beautiful leather binder out of a briefcase she had by her feet and opened it to the first page. "I wrote this out because I wanted to say it exactly right," she said. "I've never been very good at telling people how I feel, so it seemed much safer to me to do it this way. I hope it doesn't seem impersonal. I promise you, whatever this piece of paper lacks in emotion, it makes up for in sincerity." Then Katherine cleared her throat and began to read. "In the very first written connection we ever made with each other, Samantha, I told you that you had given me faith in the intrinsic decency of mankind. And, every day since then, you have exceeded that. I don't believe it is possible for me to ever express in words what your friendship and commitment have meant to me the last three months. But I do believe I can say, without question, that I could not have made it to here without you. That sounds like a cliché, but it is actually the truth. So, I think if I were to say that you saved my life, it would be mostly accurate. And it's very hard to find a way to say thank you for that."

Katherine took a sip of coffee. Both our hands were shaking a little.

When she read on, it was in a different tone, it was her professional voice, like she was making a presentation in a boardroom.

"I have spent a great deal of time thinking, over the past few weeks, about what to do with my money. I hope to be around for a long time, but you never know what may happen, and I want all of this to be very clear. The only people I need to take care of are my mother and Maurice, so I will see they are both always secure. I plan to leave Marie all my clothes and jewelry, lord knows she needs them. And I am going to leave my apartment to you. I think you'd like it uptown, closer to the park."

I started to speak but she held up her hand.

"Let me get to the part of this that matters," she said. "The really big idea I have been working on has nothing to do with any of those. And it has everything to do with you. In another conversation we had online before we met, you told me that you considered yourself a support group without the group. Today, I am proposing that we give you the group. Inside this envelope are the founding documents of the charitable endeavor that will be my legacy, and a job offer. I would like you to be the chief executive of the foundation, with total authority to shape its vision and its mission. We are going to provide thousands of women the sort of support you have given me, and we are going to do it however you see fit."

She closed the binder and slid it across the table. When I saw the letters emblazoned upon the front, my lips began to quiver.

"Almost all of the legal work to get us started has been done. We have a meeting this afternoon with the lawyers. You'll need to get to know them quickly. We'll meet with Dr. Z tomorrow. I have asked him to be our first medical consultant. And then, after that, it's pretty much going to be up to you to figure it out. I have the utmost confidence in you, Samantha, to take this and make a real difference. To make thousands of women feel the way you did when the cute nurse with the dimples told you that you no longer had cancer. That's your mission."

I ran my fingers over the smooth leather cover silently. I had no idea what to say.

"It's a little overwhelming, I know," Katherine said, more softly now. "If you want to take a little time to think it over, I'll understand."

I didn't need any time to think about anything. I stood and walked around the table and put my arms around her shoulders, and just like that my life was changed.

So that was how it began.

And what it begat has been the most fulfilling experience of my life. I am exhausted and frazzled and fully consumed by this job, and I love every second of it. I have never known what it is like to feel this committed to anything. It is rewarding beyond words, and in its own way it is freeing as well. I wouldn't change a moment of my life the last few months, and I don't have any other plans for the immediate future. My goal is to run this foundation until it is no longer necessary, until the day when a woman like Katherine or Brooke or me will be diagnosed with cancer and say: "Shoot, I'm going to be out of work for a week." Or: "I hope the medication doesn't upset my stomach." I honestly believe I will live to see that day.

Katherine gave me the authority to decide exactly how best to utilize the enormous endowment she designated to the Breast Friends Foundation. My first idea was to provide counseling and support for patients immediately after diagnosis, so we began with that, and that is an ever-expanding goal. We also provide grants for women who have to leave their jobs, or substantially reduce their hours, during their treatment cycles. That is a complicated process but it is wonderfully rewarding. We have made a real difference; there are at least two women I am convinced would have lost their homes were it not for our assistance. So that is a big part of what we do. But I quickly realized there wasn't any way we could justify all the dollars Katherine gave us in those endeavors alone. So, about a month into the process, I decided our primary function would be to fund cutting-edge medical research. We have already donated more than $15 million toward breast cancer research in Katherine's name, and in the next year we should double that. Phillip Rogers, the Wall Street powerhouse who once broke Katherine's heart, is in charge of our investments and has done brilliantly well, even in a challenging economy. His passion for this cause, and his devotion to honoring Katherine's wishes, have been invaluable and, in their own way, heartwarming.

As for Katherine, she and Stephen were in Aspen by the end of the first week. When she said she was entrusting it all to me she wasn't exaggerating. She said she had spent enough time working in her life, and not enough climbing mountains. She also said she thought I had climbed my share of mountains and needed to try the work.

"And," she said, "don't count on hearing a lot from me. My philosophy has always been to put the right people in the right jobs and then get out of their way. You are the right person for this job. I'm getting out of your way."

She stayed true to that as well. For the first month or so, I think I heard from her twice a day. Soon enough that shrunk to once. Then, less than that. These days I hear from her about once a week, usually via e-mails, and while I miss the sound of her voice, nothing makes me happier than knowing she is in a place that brings her such joy and peace. It is a miracle to me how happy she sounds and how well she feels. She begins her next round of chemotherapy next week, and, as she has in the past, she will fly Dr. Z out to Colorado to meet with her doctors. To date,

I know all of them are very satisfied with her treatment. I speak with Dr. Z quite often about foundation matters and he updates me about Katherine as much as is appropriate; I speak with him far more often than I do with her.

The last time I heard from her was three days ago. She has taken to sending me notes from the tops of mountains, mostly in the Maroon Bells, which is part of the Elk Range, where there are six peaks known as "Fourteeners," which means fourteen thousand feet of elevation. After she told me about making the first hike of that sort, I asked Dr. Z if it was all right for her to be in such elevation.

"Have you ever heard her happier than she is up there?" he asked me. I had not.

"Then there is no better place in the world she could be," he said.

That made sense to me, and so I am always thrilled when an e-mail comes in from her and the message says it was sent nineteen hours ago. That means she was in a place too close to the sky for cellular service. And Stephen, bless him, is always by her side. They always attach a photo, and each time their choice in hats seems to have become more and more outrageous. And, always, there is the dog at their feet.

So that's where she is now, and I'm here in her home in the Hamptons. She has ceaselessly encouraged me to spend my weekends out here but this is the first time I have taken her up on it; there has just been too much to do in the city. But when I awoke this morning and smelled the salt in the air, it took me back, in a way that only the sense of smell is able, to Hawaii, and I thought to myself: I need to be here more. I need to ride my bicycle out here in this air, and run on the beach, and swim, when the ocean gets a little warmer. Maybe I'll do another triathlon next year. I could set aside some time to train. That would feel great. I feel good now, but I could feel even better and that would be the way.

Maurice drove us out. He continues working for Katherine, at full salary, and I suspect he always will. They love each other, those two, and there is no doubt he misses her more than I do and he hears from her more often as well. In the meantime, he drives me around the city when

I need him, which isn't often, and looks after the house. It is easy to understand why Katherine leaned on him over the years as she did: he has an air of serenity that is soothing on even the longest days.

And so that is pretty much the story up to now. It is difficult to say for sure where it will go from here. Right now I need to go. I hear Andrew rustling upstairs. He sleeps a lot later than I do. I think I'll run upstairs and jump into bed with him before he wakes up too much. This is our first weekend together in a while and I've missed him. Usually he sneaks into the city for dinner with me or I race up to Connecticut to see him. It isn't ideal but such is life; he's busy, I'm busy, you know how it can be. We're having a good time. Brooke is apoplectic we aren't talking about getting married. Actually, her disapproval is one of my favorite things; it adds an air of danger and naughtiness to the relationship, which it really doesn't deserve. I like him a lot. I think I might even love him, but for the moment liking him is working just fine.

From: Katherine Emerson
To: Dr. Gray
Sent: Tuesday, April 11, 2012
6:02:07 A.M.

Greetings from the top of the world!

Get a load of this picture Stephen just took of me as the sun first peeked over the horizon. It is about the most beautiful thing I have ever seen. That lump behind me is Florence. Cute, isn't she?

I had to write immediately to tell you, even though I have no idea when this will actually make it to you, that I have finally figured it out and I wanted you to be the first to know. You challenged me, before I came here the first time, to discover what makes life worth living. And I thought I did. I thought what makes life worth living is all the wonderful things that might happen. I could tell you weren't crazy about that answer when I came home, and now I know why. I realize I was wrong. I realized it just now as I felt the sun brush my cheek.

So here it is.

What makes life worth living is not anything that might happen. It is what is happening right now. It is *this* moment, which I own every bit as much as anyone else. It doesn't matter how many moments I have left; all that matters is right now I am as alive as I have ever been and as alive as anyone else, and this moment belongs to me as much as it does to anyone. And that's what it's about, whether you have cancer or not. What makes life worth living is what is happening right now.

Not yesterday, not tomorrow, right now.

I hope you're proud of me, and I hope you'll come soon for a visit. Right now I need to go. Stephen just finished cooking breakfast and we have a tight schedule if we're going to make it down in time for our massage appointments. Give my love to New York, and if anyone should ask how I'm doing, tell them I'm having the best day of my entire life.

HEIDI

NIKKI WAS A MONTH shy of two when we met and she's twelve now, so the math is easy to do. It was the first day of nursery school and Stacy and I were there with Nikki, and Heidi and Adam were there with Walker. Stacy and Heidi were both hugely pregnant, and as hugely pregnant women often tend to do in crowded places, they found each other. A few months later Heidi had Georgia and Stacy had Stevie, and after that what we had was a whole lot of fun together.

No one was more fun than Heidi was. Especially on skis. Heidi was as beautiful a skier as I have ever seen. And she was delightfully patient with me, even though I could barely keep up with her. My favorite memory of Heidi on skis was the time she implored me to ski faster by suggesting I chase her down the mountain as though I were James Bond and she a beautiful villain. I went after her as best I could, and any time I got close I could hear she was humming the James Bond theme as loudly as she could. It was so much fun.

I told that story at her memorial service.

If you, like I, believe there must be some justice in the universe, then you would have struggled as much as I did with what happened to Heidi.

One day she was a wonderfully healthy, happy, sexy, outdoorsy, soccer-coaching mom and wife, the next day she had a pain in her back. By the time they figured out it was cancer that began in her breast and spread to her bones there was almost nothing they could do. When it spread to her brain, it was over. She died September 30th, 2009.

At the service held to celebrate her memory, before I told the James Bond story, I was sitting two rows behind Walker and Georgia and Adam and I was the angriest I can ever remember being. I had never witnessed anything that felt like more of an injustice. And then I sat and listened to the reading of what sounded like letters but I later found out were internet posts written by women whose names I did not know. They were some of the most emotional passages I had ever heard; they spoke of Heidi as though she had been their sister. But Heidi didn't have a sister. By the end of the night, I wasn't as angry anymore.

We were in the kitchen, Stacy and I, a few days later when I remembered those words and I asked who had written them. That was when Stacy told me that Heidi, during her illness, had developed these incredibly intense relationships with a group of women from a cancer support website, women she called her "breast friends." She died without ever actually meeting any of them, but they loved her and cried for her and wrote of her, again, like she was their sister. Which, in a way, I suppose she was.

So that is where this book came from, and that is who it is for. It is for Adam and Walker and Georgia, and Bobby and Natalie and Bob Sr. and Carole, and all the rest of Heidi's family. And it is for all the other husbands and sons and daughters and brothers and sisters and mothers and fathers living with holes in their lives that will never be filled. And, most of all, it is for Heidi. If there is any justice in the universe, we will ski with her again someday.

ACKNOWLEDGMENTS

There are always people without whom a book *would* not have been written. In this case, however, there are several without whom the book *could* not have been written, beginning with Jacques de Spoelberch, my literary agent, golf companion, and friend. A month or so after I began to write, I awoke one morning in a cold sweat, convinced I was wasting my time. I sent what I had written to Jacques, with instructions not to spare my feelings. I asked him to tell this sportscaster he had no business trying to write a novel in three distinct female voices. To my astonishment, he called the next day and said: "Mike, I think you have it, keep going." That was the beginning. And every day, from that one until this, he has been a tireless champion of this project and of Heidi's Angels. Jacques is the best friend and agent you could ever ask for, and Lou Oppenheim of Headline Media Management and Peter Benedek from United Talent Agency are exactly the sort of agents you dream of having, the kind who care more about your happiness than anything else. I am very lucky to have Jacques, Lou, and Peter on my side.

This book could also not have been written without Dr. Richard Zelkowitz from the Whittingham Cancer Center in Norwalk, Connecticut; he was Heidi's doctor. The last months of Heidi's life were difficult, but Dr. Z made them better, as much better as they could possibly be. He is a doctor in the way we all imagine we want our doctors to be; he treats his patients the way he would treat his family. When I began to write I knew I needed Dr. Z to help me get the medical parts right. Anything I did get right is thanks to him.

This book next found its way to the hands of a yoga instructor named Sarah McGrath and an artist named Elaine de Spoelberch, who, along with my wife, Stacy, read it when I was halfway through and showed me all the parts I had gotten wrong. Elaine told me: "Forget the men; I want to read about the women." And Sarah, quite bluntly, told me that no twenty-eight-year-old woman would use the word "blouse." They also wrote the ending for me with their ideas, even if they didn't mean to. I adore them both; thank you, ladies.

As for Kate Nintzel from William Morrow, there aren't words. Or, if there are, I don't know them. From the instant we met she understood what this book meant to me and she knew how to make it the best it could be. You can't do a job any better than Kate edited this novel, and you can't do it with a cheerier disposition, either. Thank you, Kate, you are the reason this happened.

Thanks, too, to Richard Koenigsberg of Spielman Koenigsberg & Parker, Mark and Jason Bradburn of Morgan Stanley Smith Barney, and Michael Prevett of the Gotham Group for their valued counsel, assistance, and friendship.

I would like to thank my colleagues at ESPN, all of whom work so hard to support the V Foundation, and especially my partner of fourteen years, Mike Golic, who has taught me more than he'll ever know. I am very proud to have had the seat next to Mike's for all these years, and forever proud to have the letters ESPN attached to my name.

Finally, I should explain that I invented the phrase "Heidi's Angels" with no celestial connotation in mind. The nickname was derived from the show Charlie's Angels and Heidi loved it. I used it to describe the three friends who came together for her in a way I had never seen before and would never have believed possible had I not seen it for myself. The unconditional love these women demonstrated was worth writing a book about. This is not that book, I couldn't write that book. All I can say is that I will live the rest of my life in awe of the way three women rallied around their friend and never wavered, no matter how hard it became. And so, again, this book is dedicated to them, and to all the other angels everywhere.

About the author

About the book

Insights,
Interviews
& More . . .

Meet Mike Greenberg

Pamela Einarsen

MIKE GREENBERG is cohost of ESPN's *Mike & Mike in the Morning* and the author of two previous *New York Times* bestsellers. He is a graduate of the Medill School of Journalism at Northwestern University and a native of New York City. He lives with his wife, Stacy, and their two children in Connecticut. In conjunction with the release of this book, Mike and Stacy have created a foundation called Heidi's Angels, through which all of the author's profits from the sale of this book will be donated to the V Foundation for Cancer Research to combat breast cancer. ᔧ

Meet the Ladies

These three women are brought together during challenging circumstances, but through supporting one another, they learn how alike they are. The truth is we are all alike in the ways that really matter.

BROOKE is the woman who still has inside her a little bit of the prom queen she used to be. She is madly in love with her husband and has two beautiful children and a white picket fence to boot. She's always felt she leads a charmed life.

Favorite Song: "Free Fallin'," by Tom Petty.
Favorite Band: Cheap Trick.
Favorite Movie: *The Big Chill*.
Favorite Food: root beer float.
Can't live without: bubble baths, blowouts,
    my Louis Vuitton Neverfull bag, and
    my husband.
On Friday night I'm: probably watching *Wizards
    of Waverly Place* and eating chicken tenders
    with the twins.
I'm thankful for: my health.

    Stacy says, "Brooke is my least favorite of the three women. I have a hard time relating to the way she lives her life and the choice she makes at the end of the book."
    Greeny says, "Stacy has disliked Brooke from the moment I began writing, but she is my favorite of the three; she has a purity of purpose that I admire."

SAMANTHA is young and idealistic with a huge heart. She is strong and adventurous, and a bit of a nomad. Her impulsive streak can sometimes lead to bad decisions, but she always has the best intentions in mind.

Favorite Song: "Stronger," by Kelly Clarkson
Favorite Band: Fun.
Favorite Movie: *The Notebook*.
Favorite Food: quinoa. ▶

3

Meet the Ladies *(continued)*

Can't live without: my friends, yoga, my running
shoes, fresh flowers, kombucha, and
chocolate.
On Friday night I'm: ideally, sharing good food
and good wine with a great man.
I'm thankful for: my health.

*Stacy says, "She's my favorite, and the star of
the book as far as I'm concerned. I find her the most
real, and the one that I would be most interested in
knowing."*

*Greeny says, "There's no doubt, Samantha is the
moral center of the book. She is much younger than
the other two main characters and still has a more
idealistic view of life."*

KATHERINE is a powerhouse Wall Street
executive who places a premium on structure,
discipline, and success. One terrible heartbreak
has followed her around, into adulthood. She is
learning to balance her tough-cookie "one of the
boys" attitude with a healthy dose of
vulnerability.

Favorite Song: "Hold On," by Wilson Phillips.
Favorite Band: N.W.A.
Favorite Movie: *North by Northwest.*
Favorite food: banana pudding from Magnolia
Bakery.
Can't live without: La Mer, vodka martinis,
Louboutins, therapy, and my incredible
assistant.
On Friday night I'm: eating pancakes for dinner
in front of a fire.
I'm thankful for: my health.

*Stacy says, "I love her. I know a ton of women
like her. Everybody does."*

*Greeny says, "I think Katherine is the most
relatable of the women. We all know highly
successful people who are tragically flawed."* ∼

Just for fun

Casting *All You Could Ask For*

Samantha: Olivia Wilde
Katherine: Sandra Bullock
Brooke: Leslie Mann
Maurice: Joe Pantoliano
Marie: Amanda Setton
Phillip: Dermot Mulroney
Eduardo: Chris Diamantopoulos
Adam: Jeffrey Dean Morgan
Scott: Aaron Eckhart
Andrew: Zach Gilford
Pamela: Susan Sarandon

Remembering Heidi:
"You would have loved her, too."

This piece originally appeared on the espnW website.

Sometimes in life we have out-of-body experiences. All of this has been one for me. My name is Stacy Steponate Greenberg. Many of you know my husband, the smaller of the two Mikes from Mike & Mike in the Morning *and the author of this book. I have worked all my adult life in marketing, mostly for luxury hotels. Mike and I have two kids and a happy life. This is the story of one of the unhappiest times we have shared. And of how our friend Heidi, for whom this book was written, has brought us together in a way we never imagined, even though she has been gone for more than three years.*

"SOMETHING'S WRONG."

I'm not clairvoyant. I don't know whether I believe anyone is, but even if they are, I am certainly not. So I can't really explain how I knew, with such certainty, before Heidi told me.

Maybe it's because she loved Aspen so much that she would never have missed a moment, much less a day or a week, of her ski vacation. So when we had been there for a couple of days and I had not heard from her, I developed a sinking feeling in my stomach. This was our special time together and she was supposed to have arrived the day after we did. I had left her two messages.

We were in the car, driving home from a day of skiing at Buttermilk. The kids were in the back, exhausted. Mike was driving. I was worried.

"Something's wrong," I said, again.

"What?" he asked.

"With Heidi," I said, with no idea how right I was.

Heidi and I met on the first day we took our

kids to school. Her son and my daughter were two, and she and I were pregnant. And, as Mike wrote in the book, two hugely pregnant women tend to seek each other out. Although, in truth, Heidi wasn't huge. Not at all. Heidi looked like a skinny woman who swallowed a basketball. I, meanwhile, looked like I belonged in Willy Wonka's Chocolate Factory. But the point was well-taken aside from that—we did seek each other out and quickly became the best of friends.

I want to tell you so much about Heidi, but I have no idea where to begin. She was the truest friend you could have—she never judged, she listened, she laughed, she supported. Her husband worked late nights; mine went to sleep hours before I did. So many, many nights we would be on the phone for hours, just chatting. It's impossible to quantify the value of chatting late at night on the phone. To me, it is invaluable. I could tell her anything, she could tell me anything. She was my confidante, my good friend. I loved her.

Our best times together were in Aspen. Heidi was a beautiful skier and she loved it, and as good as she was, she also was patient enough to ski with me. I am not on her level. In fact, my own family refuses to ski with me because I am so slow. And none of them are on Heidi's level, either. But she was always happy to hang back with me. Mostly so we could gab on the chairlift.

Late in 2008, Heidi began to complain about pain in her back. She was concerned but not scared. Mostly she was worried that whatever it was (disk problem? pulled muscle?) would interfere with her ski season. She visited doctors, chiropractors, physical therapists, all to no avail. Then the chiropractor recommended she get an MRI. So she did.

I wasn't with her when she received the news. I can't imagine what it would be like to be told you have stage 4 breast cancer that has spread to your bones. I hope I never know. I wish no one ever had to know. But that's what she was told, early in 2009.

So then it was a few weeks later, and I hadn't heard from her, and I knew something was wrong. When I got the email from her I was devastated, but I wasn't surprised. We were in Aspen, Heidi wasn't. And she never would be again.

I left my job in the corporate world right after Heidi was diagnosed. Those two were not connected to each other; I left because the demands on my time and Mike's were becoming impossible to manage and neither of us wanted our kids to be raised by babysitters. So I made the difficult decision to leave a job I loved for something more important. Or, as it turned out, two things.

Because I had the time, I became Heidi's health advocate. Along with two other dear friends, Jane Green and Wendy Gardiner, I was with her every day. Literally, every single day. We took her to doctor's appointments, made her laugh during chemotherapy treatments. When she needed a spinal tap, I held her hands. When she needed another, I did it again. It wasn't just me. Jane and Wendy were there too, just as much. Mike called us "Heidi's Angels," after the TV show *Charlie's Angels*. Heidi loved the name. She started to call us that, too.

During that summer, she was determined to live. And for Heidi, living meant being outside, doing sports. She was a great athlete. She probably ▶

couldn't have named a single player in the NBA or NFL, but she participated in sports every chance she had. In the winter, that meant skiing. In the summer, at her beloved cottage in her native Canada, that meant canoeing and hiking and swimming. She went to Canada with her kids that summer. Nothing was going to keep her from doing that.

It was in Canada that the headaches began, so severe she had to be hospitalized. The pain cut her summer in Canada short—she had to come home to be examined by the doctors at Memorial Sloan-Kettering. The news was horrifying. The cancer had spread to her brain. The treatments became more intense, the days harder, the chances lesser. But, through it all, Heidi never lost her sparkle.

The day I will always remember best was when they told us she needed to remain at MSK. She begged me to run out and shop for her. She needed sleeping clothes.

"Stace," she said to me, "I should still look hot, even in a hospital bed."

She had lost her hair by then and much of her strength, but she never lost her sense of humor. She never stopped being Heidi.

Her courageous battle ended quietly on September 30, 2009, at home, with her family around her. I had been saying goodbye every day that week, because we knew it was close. She was not responsive, but I knew she could hear me. She could hear me promise to make sure Adam didn't forget the kids' coats at soccer practice, promise to keep pushing myself to ski better, promise to always remember her and love her. The phone rang that day and it was Adam. "It happened," was all he said. As much as I thought I would have been prepared, I wasn't.

None of the women in Mike's book are Heidi, but in some ways all of them are. They are strong women, facing their mortality in their own individual ways. I may not agree with all of them—you may not, either, if you read it. But I respect that they are strong women, and they make their own decisions. Heidi was that way. She lived on her terms, and she died that way, too.

In conjunction with the release of *All You Could Ask For*, Mike and I have created a foundation called Heidi's Angels, through which 100 percent of our proceeds will be donated to the V Foundation for Cancer Research in memory of an athlete, a mother, a wife, and the kind of friend who knows your secrets and your fears and makes you feel better about them and about yourself. It is the least I can do to repay Heidi for all she taught me, in sickness and in health. The journey we took together was among the most meaningful experiences of my life. I only wish you could have known her. You would have loved her, too. ∾

All I Could Ask For

Mike Greenberg recounts inspirational experiences from his book tour. This piece originally appeared on espn.com.

YOU MAY KNOW I released a book this month called *All You Could Ask For*, a novel, which was inspired by the death of a dear friend named Heidi, and the way her closest friends rallied around her, rose up for her, cared for her, and loved her during the seven months she bravely battled the breast cancer that took her life on September 30, 2009. You may also know that my wife, Stacy, and I are proudly donating 100 percent of our proceeds from the book to the V Foundation for Cancer Research, in Heidi's honor. What you do not know is that the time I spent promoting the book was the most surprising, inspiring, educational experience of my life. You couldn't have known about that because the most surprised person in any of it was me. I would never have imagined I would learn so much from this. The following is that story, of how I gained much more than I could ever give from thousands of people I met during seventeen book signings in fourteen days.

I put everything I had into writing the book. It took me eighteen months from start to finish, and then another ten months from the day ▶

I handed in the finished manuscript until it was released on April 2. So, perhaps in retrospect it isn't a surprise that the first time I saw it on a shelf in a bookstore, I felt as though I had reached the finish line.

You see, writing a book is a lonely business, certainly as compared to my day job, where I trade insults and occasional insight with Mike Golic on *Mike & Mike*. Writing is something I made time for at night alone in my bedroom, or tucked away in a back corner of a library, or in an airplane or the backseat of a car. For me, writing is very hard work; rewarding, for sure, but solitary and difficult. And then, once I had finished the writing, that was when the really hard part began. Because the next piece of business was to sell it. And what I quickly discovered was, no matter how popular your radio show is, when you walk into a publisher's office and say, "I'm a sportscaster and I've written a novel narrated in three female voices and I'm going to give all the money to breast cancer research," they look at you funny. Real funny. This was a long shot from the very beginning.

So, when the day finally came that it was in stores and online and in people's tablets and Nooks and Kindles, I was thrilled. I breathed the longest, loudest, proudest sigh of relief of my entire career. "I did it. It's over." But what I didn't realize at the time was that the really important part hadn't yet begun.

I went on tour with the book, as I had my previous two, fully ready to tell stories, shake hands, take pictures, sign copies. I looked forward to seeing a lot of sports fans, answering questions about their favorite teams and players, and laughing over all the ridiculous things Golic and I have said and done during our fourteen years together. But what I found, in New York, Connecticut, Dallas, Pittsburgh, Cleveland, Columbus, Indianapolis, Chicago, New Jersey, Raleigh, Charleston, Charlotte, and Myrtle Beach, was a world I didn't know existed. And a community of people I will forever be proud to call my friends.

They are a community that comes in all shapes and sizes and colors. They speak in an endless variety of tones: some in conspiratorial whispers, others in bold proclamations, a few in clichés, three or four on the verge of tears. They are people for whom cancer has entered their lives and set up shop, taken over, started making all the rules. The image I have in my mind is of cancer as a horrible houseguest that will not leave; it plops itself down in the middle of your life, puts its feet on the coffee table, and defies you to ignore it. "Go ahead, try to live your life as though I'm not here."

But most of the ones I met are fighting back. They may not be able to throw the unwanted houseguest out the door, but that doesn't mean they aren't protecting what's theirs. I met a man in Pittsburgh who told me his wife had a double mastectomy in January; she's training for a marathon in the fall. A woman in Columbus told me her sister died a year ago; she organized a charity dinner in her honor that raised six thousand dollars. I've seen people raise a lot more money than that, but I've never seen anyone prouder of it than she was. I had a man in Charlotte break down when he told me how badly his wife wanted to come to the signing but she just wasn't strong enough; he gave me a check that she signed for fifty dollars and asked me to give it to the

V Foundation. In Dallas, a girl who couldn't have been more than six years old told me her mom died but that doesn't mean she can't talk to her anymore. There are a lot of brave people in the world. None of them braver than people staring down cancer.

I live most of my life in the world of sports, where we can tell which team someone plays for by the uniform. What I learned on my book tour is that the breast cancer community has uniforms, too. They're pink, they're usually T-shirts, and they're all a little different from each other. But the one thing they have in common is they are all strong. I never saw a single T-shirt that said: "I have cancer, pity me." Or: "My life will never be the same again." To the contrary, the shirts were all wonderful. I asked some of them to send me photos and those are what you see displayed in the photo at the top. One of my favorites, which unfortunately I did not get a picture of, was worn by a woman who had to be six feet tall, long curly hair, beautiful, and no more than thirty years old. Her shirt said: "Sure they're fake. The real ones tried to kill me." It took me a minute to understand the message. Once I did, that was when I decided I would write about this.

So, these are my words of thanks, to everyone, for your support of my project and for much more than that as well. It was a privilege to meet all of you, to be invited for a few moments at a time into the very personal world each of you inhabits. And I assure you, no matter how much money I eventually donate on your behalf, I will have received far more from this experience than I have given. ∽

Reading Group Guide

1. Would Samantha have become friends with Katherine and Brooke under different circumstances? What do the three women have in common besides the event that brings them together?

2. Samantha is horrified when she finds those pictures on Robert's laptop, but is she partially to blame for invading his privacy?

3. Why do you think Katherine chose to stay at the company for as long as she did? With her education and experience, she could have found a comparable position elsewhere. Is there a part of her that wants to suffer by witnessing Phillip's success? Is there a small part of her that believes she can win him back if she sticks around? Or is it something else entirely?

4. Brooke stakes much of her own happiness on her husband's satisfaction and his perception of her. Is this problematic?

5. Brooke says you need three core girlfriends: one who's like a sister, one who knows everything, and one a generation ahead of you. Do you agree? Who occupies these roles in your own life?

6. Robert seemed genuinely contrite when he went to see Samantha. Would you have taken him back? Why or why not?

7. Samantha is always trying to help people, and she wants to extend her generosity of spirit to Brooke. Do you think she was wrong in forcing Brooke to share her story? Was she at all motivated by guilt?

8. Why do you think Brooke decides to do what she does? Do you agree with her choice? Do her loved ones deserve to be included in her decisions?

9. Brooke sees her life as divided into stages— her sweet sixteen, her wedding. What are the stages of your life?

10. Samantha reflects on her evening with Andrew Marks as "the night [she] learned that [she likes] being pretty." Despite confronting a serious life hurdle, she does not abandon her vanity. Is this something many women can relate to? What does being pretty mean to you?

11. When Katherine meets Stephen, she knows she has "met the man who [is] going to change [her] life." Do you believe in love at first sight? Are her strong, serendipitous feelings for Adam in any way related to this phase of her life?

12. Katherine and Samantha have a few "absolute deal-breakers": a grown-up who calls his mother every day, a man who buys maxi pads for his dog. What are your absolute deal-breakers?

13. In her last person-to-person to Samantha, Brooke writes, "Please leave me alone." She tells her she'll be in touch when she's ready. What do you think ultimately moved her to reach out? What changed?

14. Brooke is the only one with a husband by her side, and yet she does not share her secret with him. Is she motivated by fear? Do you think that has more to do with her or with Scott?

15. In the last chapter, Katherine has run off to Aspen to be with her dream guy, Samantha is dating a pediatrician, and Brooke is laminating meaningful quotes for her fridge. Where do you see them each in five years?

Don't miss the next book by your favorite author. Sign up now for AuthorTracker by visiting www.AuthorTracker.com.